HOW LONG A SHADOW

A Novel

To Shaun — Thanks — Hope you enjoy!

Dan Powers

Dan Powers

outskirts press

How Long A Shadow
A Novel

v4.0

This is a work of fiction. Names, characters, businesses, places, events, locales, and incidents are either the products of the author's imagination or used in a fictitious manner. Any resemblance to actual persons, living or dead, or actual events is purely coincidental.

The opinions expressed in this manuscript are solely the opinions of the author and do not represent the opinions or thoughts of the publisher. The author has represented and warranted full ownership and/or legal right to publish all the materials in this book.

Outskirts Press, Inc.
http://www.outskirtspress.com

Paperback ISBN: 978-1-9772-2889-5

PRINTED IN THE UNITED STATES OF AMERICA

Author's Note:

Some references to real and historic people, events, and places are used to provide a sense of authenticity and background and are altered to fit the author's needs. Some names of living people are used fictitiously and with permission.

Parts of this book incorporate characters and events loosely based on family history. Such use is meant to honor and show respect for them and their lives. All scenes and dialogue in which such characters appear are fictional.

For Shamus and his family, my wife Joan, and all my nephews, cousins, and relatives past, present, and future.

Life is a handful of short stories, pretending to be a novel.
Anonymous

November 1, 2015

Dear Kevin,

It's been a long long time, hasn't it? Maybe too long but that can't be changed. You'll have to be the judge. I found your address on Mom's old Xmas list. I'm glad I kept that. I hope it is current and this gets to you. Otherwise I'll be very disappointed. When you read this, I'll already have been dead for awhile. How strange that is to say about yourself. Can you feel disappointment after you're dead? I've mostly come to grips with that and besides I'm very tired and always feel like crap and my cancer (ovarian) has spread all over. My body isn't what I hope you remember it to be, though it was pretty dark that night wasn't it?

1959, July

Flipped on its back, it looked skeletal. Tires and pedals pointed to the blue summer sky, seat and handlebars resting in the grass. But to Kevin, who considered his bicycle a living extension of himself, it was his alter-ego turned patient – *flat out on the operating table.* But the thought faded into frustration and helplessness. His father had already shown him twice how to get the chain back on the sprocket, but still he lacked confidence and feared making it worse. This time the chain was solidly wedged between the rear wheel gear and the hub. It wouldn't budge. If he yanked too hard he might break it.

He'd been out of commission all afternoon, like a cowboy whose horse had come up lame or had been shot out from beneath him. He sat, crossed-legged in anxious contemplation. He let out his breath slowly, thinking how lucky he'd been not to go over the handlebars and land on his head when the chain suddenly jammed. He gently turned the pedals by hand, not wanting to cause further injury. They produced only a scraping sound, but no resistance. They moved easily but uselessly since they were disconnected from any functionality. *That's how I feel,* Kevin thought. He didn't really understand "functionality", but viscerally felt the emotional repercussion. To soothe himself and the patient – for by now he was thoroughly invested in the idea of his bike as his faithful but injured steed – he said, "That's OK, boy. Dad's home now and will be out in a minute to help us."

When he heard the back door, he jumped up and began talking even before he had completely turned around. "Dad, I'm sorry. I know you showed me how to do this before, but the stupid chain is jammed again and I didn't want to accidentally break it."

"That's OK. We'll get it fixed." Mr. Cullerton's assuring words seemed almost visible and a bit magical as they came wrapped in the exhaled smoke of his cigarette. He had changed into his household chore trousers, marked by the paint on his right thigh that matched the color of the living room. They were held up by a black belt with a buckle bearing the silver plated initial C for Cullerton. It had been a gift from Mrs. Cullerton so long ago that as far as Kevin knew it was the only belt his dad had ever owned. His buttoned-down shirt, pocket-protector and tie were gone and his v-necked white tee shirt, tucked into his waistband, hung loose against his chest and the afternoon air. He gave the back of Kevin's neck a light squeeze as he knelt next to the injured red Schwinn. "I see you started off on the right foot. You have the back wheel nuts loosened up."

Kevin felt a tiny flash of pride. He took a knee in imitation of his dad's position. "They were tight, but I got them. I even remember you told me they were 9/16 inch and to use the box wrench instead of the open-ended so it wouldn't slip off and smush my knuckles."

"That's always a good thing to remember. I had to learn that the hard way. I think we're going to need a flat head screw driver here."

Kevin was off toward the tiny garage before his dad finished. "There's one on your bench in here. I'll get it." He was back in seconds. "Here, Dad." He handed it to him and took a knee again, this time on the other side so he could better see and also to be out of the haze from the cigarette now dangling from his dad's lips. Mr. Cullerton squinted through the smoke as he worked the driver blade beneath the chain and braced it against the hub.

"I tried pulling it out, but it was too tight. See?" Kevin held up his hands to show his father the grease marks from where he'd grasped the chain. He wanted his dad to know he'd tried and not just waited for him to come home.

"You can usually pry it out as long as you're careful not to bend the links." His dad wiggled the blade and dislodged the stuck chain with a flick of his wrist. "There we go," he said, as he handed the screwdriver back. "Well, since you already have your hands oily, why don't you put the chain back on while I slacken the back wheel?"

Again a surge of pride ran up Kevin's neck. "OK." He stood and re-fit the loosened chain onto the teeth of the pedal gear. As he did so he noticed something odd. One of the links looked different than the others. "What's this, Dad? This link looks strange."

His father leaned forward as Kevin held the chain towards him, managing again to show off his oil-stained fingers.

"That's called the master link," his dad said. He coughed twice then crushed out his cigarette on the grass.

"Huh?" Kevin said. "What the heck is that?"

"Here, let me show you." His dad slipped his hand between Kevin's without the slightest hesitation about getting oil on it. His left palm supported the chain, so the link was facing up and Kevin could see what he was pointing at with his little finger. "You see these two pins? And how this side has a double slot. It slides onto the pins and then the tension holds the link tight. This small clip then makes sure they don't come apart. It's called a master link because you can pop the clip off and take the link apart and open up the chain."

"Why would you ever want to do that?" Kevin asked.

"Well, sometimes there can be a problem, like you need to thread it through a tight spot, or you need to add more links to make it larger." He looked up from his hands to make sure Kevin was following his explanation.

Kevin found himself eyeball to eyeball. Dad's eyes were blue, the same shade as his own. Surely he must have stared into his dad's eyes sometime before, back when he was little and didn't know it was rude to stare. But this felt different, like he was looking inside and seeing back to when he was just a kid his own age. Maintaining eye contact, he asked, "Dad? Who taught you all of this stuff?"

Kevin would always remember the moment, or at least how it felt. Tiny and quick as it was, it etched itself deep into him. In later years, sometimes it would float to the surface as one of those precious moments of deep connection between father and son. At other times it seemed, in retrospect, a moment of sadness. The visual memory, though, when it drifted into his mind's eye, was always the same. His father's eyes seemed in that moment to slide from blue to a grey drizzly color, washed out like faded jeans. He'd also remember the words, even long after the sound of his father's voice had faded from memory.

"I guess…" his dad started, and slipped his palm from beneath the chain, leaving it in Kevin's hands. "That was a long time ago."

Part 1

Jimmy
1918-1945

Shamus

1918, November 23

"Shamus, hurry now son. Eddie is ready to go."

Jimmy liked when Ma called him Shamus. It felt good, special. What he hated was wrestling the two old hens for their eggs. *Thank God*, he thought, the job of cleaning the coop had passed on to his next younger brother Tom. It was frosty back in this corner of the yard where the November sun never reached, stuck between the ruin of the old carriage shed and the neighbor's back building. Rising and brushing off the knees of his cold weather school trousers, Jimmy stuck out his tongue at Amen who had twice pecked his cold hands, leaving two red marks. His thin legs hurried up the wooden back steps, into the warmth of the kitchen. Today, especially today, no chicken, not even the devil-spirited Amen, was going to dent his excitement. He handed the two eggs to his ma.

"They look grand. Now you boys hurry along and Shamus, I'll have your cake ready and cooled on the sill by the time you get back." She set his brown snap-cap on his head and pulled it over his brown thatch, pulled his muffler up over his nose, and turned up his coat collar. "It's chilly and breezy, so you keep your new hat tight. And don't let anyone be sneezing on you."

Turning to her oldest boy, she added, "Now remember what I

told you and don't go falling for any of that man's sass or rubbish. Keep your mind to your brother, especially when you're there."

"Shake a leg there, Jimmy," his brother prompted as he started briskly up Albany Street to catch the Elevated Ravenswood line to the Loop. Jimmy hurried and caught up. His excitement pushed him along, what with it being his tenth birthday and all, plus this would be the first time he'd be taking the trip. His mother didn't ever let his two older sisters go, even when they volunteered. Usually Richard, who at thirteen was the second eldest boy, accompanied Ed. But Richard had picked up some work sweeping and stocking at the corner grocery, and money was too tight to turn any offer down. When Ma told him to go, it had taken him by surprise, and although he would never admit it, he felt more than a little apprehension. After all, he couldn't remember the last time he'd seen the man.

Jimmy had ridden the streetcars before, but never the Elevated train and certainly not all the way downtown and beyond. There was just no need and often no money. According to Ma, everything he required was right there in the parish, safely in the confines of Our Lady of Mercy. Church, school, groceries – and that was his ma's priority order – all were within walking or biking distance. While walking was the family's default mode of transportation, the Cullerton kids did share two bicycles they had managed to obtain. Jimmy, though just in the middle of the pack age-wise, proved to have a talent with his hands and figuring things out and had become the family mechanic: fixing flats and broken chains, raising and lowering the seats and handlebars. He took pride in his skills, though at times, being on the skinny side, he needed help from Ed or Richard to loosen a rusted or over-tightened nut.

At the corner Jimmy paused to give a quick hello and pet to Dobbins, the local milk-horse, who patiently waited in harness for Mr. Stone to return with the empties and click-click him on to their next stop. A small American flag was tucked into his harness. They were everywhere, hung on doors, in windows, stuck in the ground. Each was an individual celebration of the eleventh hour of the eleventh day of the eleventh month that had just ended the war. At

Montrose, Ed waited out several automobiles and a streetcar before jaywalking across in the middle of the block. Jimmy scampered to keep up, adjusting his gait to avoid stepping on a memento left by one of Dobbin's dwindling brethren that still hauled commercial wagons on Chicago's streets. They headed east, deftly moving around slower pedestrian traffic, slacking only briefly to take in the warm aromas as they passed the bakery. Along the sidewalk, on the storefronts and light poles, more flags draped and hung, creating a flapping corridor of red, white, and blue.

Anticipation helped Jimmy keep up with his brother's longer strides. Nearing the Kedzie Street station, the chill in the air no longer registered. When they entered the dimness, Ed handed him a dime to pay his own fare. Jimmy tried to imitate his brother's nonchalance as he handed the coin up to the man in the booth and echoed, "Transfer to the South Side line, please," as if he did this every day. The boys hurried up the open-back cast-iron steps to the loop-bound platform. Trying to match Ed's two-step stride, Jimmy tripped. He was grateful to Ed for not turning around or teasing him. They emerged onto the dark-stained decking. The smell of creosote scented the frost in the air.

The platform felt awfully narrow to Jimmy. He unconsciously backed away from the painted edge that dropped off to the tracks. Again imitating his brother, he stuffed his hands in his too large coat pockets and leaned back against the advertisement boards, which displayed route maps, service times, ads for war bonds, and a few color posters touting the many places and experiences around the city to which the El could carry you. With a slight elbow and side nod of his head, Ed indicated a vandalized poster left over from the Cubs – Red Sox World Series played back in early September. The games had been moved up a month due to the war's "Work or Fight" order. The Cullertons, one and all, were serious baseball fans and none was yet over the four games to two loss to Boston. In fact, Ma still spoke ill of "that Babe Ruth fellow", the young Red Sox pitcher, who had whipped the Cubs twice.

The two boys stood silently in the open air, side by side. Despite the six-year difference in their ages, any casual observer would take them to be brothers. Besides thick brown hair, blue eyes and narrow noses, they shared a natural leanness and a visible sense of being content and comfortable in each other's company. Ed kept his stare in the direction from which the train would come. Jimmy's eyes moved constantly, surveying everything. He spied several posters across the tracks on the opposite platform urging women BECOME a NURSE - LEARN at HOME. Earn $15-$25 per week. It was another sad reminder of the Spanish influenza epidemic that was just starting to ease up around the city. Ma had even kept them home from school for a week after a classmate, who Jimmy had liked, died when her flu turned to pneumonia. On the second day of their absence, a health official had visited the house to make sure they weren't sick and contagious.

Jimmy's sad reverie exploded when his ears were suddenly assaulted by the scream of steel scraping steel. His spine stiffened and he turned toward the sound. A flat-faced line of train cars negotiated the curved track, hurtling toward the platform, growing each second in size and volume. Since Ed hadn't, he forced himself not to cover his ears, but his heartbeat crescendoed with the roar which came to a sudden halt just feet in front of him.

The doors opened like huge gaping eyes, daring him to step forward. A few passengers disembarked. Ed placed his hand on his brother's capped head and stepped forward, "Come on." Jimmy knew he'd have taken his brother's hand if it had been offered.

They sat facing forward, Jimmy closest to the window. The car gave a jerk and gathered speed. Sure in the route and familiar with the sounds and sights, Ed relaxed against the back of the seat and closed his eyes. Jimmy tried to keep his body still so as not to disturb his brother, while his head swiveled, not wanting to miss a thing. The rhythmic clacking of the rails and the regular stops and starts lulled him at first. Gradually, as buildings began to huddle closer and closer together and appear to move in closer and closer along side the rails, he became more and more uneasy. The tracks elevated, living up to their moniker. He was startled by the whir and blur of the flats that now seemed keen to take his arm off if he was foolish enough to stick it out the window. He was being inhaled into the depths of the city. Stained brick walls and mullioned windows, back staircases with peeling paint and flat tarred roofs leaned in on the passing train. Wall, window, window, roof, wall, broken window, child's face, stairs, wall, window flew by in such a blur Jimmy needed to turn his gaze forward to keep from going dizzy. The bright autumnal sky disappeared, replaced by flashes of light flung at them through the tight, narrow slits between buildings. Reprieve only came when they crossed over an arterial street or slowed into the next station.

Jimmy's slight frame pressed against the window when the train cars began their counterclockwise swing around the loop like blood platelets pumped through a heart before coursing back on their return trip. The wheel on rail screeching became constant and so unbearable that he finally did cover his ears. Embarrassed, he glanced to Ed who kept his gaze ahead, apparently gauging their location, though a half grin mingled with the tension in his jaw. The train began to slow. "Come on, Jimmy. This is where we transfer." They exited.

The downtown throngs moved in both directions. With the close proximity, many held coat collars, mufflers, or handkerchiefs over their noses ready to flee any cough or sneeze. The sheer noise engulfed Jimmy like the cold air itself. Sounds, which in the past he'd heard only one at a time or in small clusters, scrummed together in massed chaos. It bounced and amplified off the tall surrounding concrete and steel. Ed's hands kept Jimmy in front of him as he steered him by his shoulders through the cross-currents of people and noise. He guided him down one flight of shadowy stairs and then back up another toward an approaching rumbling which plowed its way through the ambient cacophony. It was like ascending into a thunder cloud. They emerged onto the opposite platform. Half guided, half pushed, Jimmy was propelled into the just arrived southbound train seconds before the doors closed behind them. "Luck of the Irish," Ed said. He lightened his grip on Jimmy's shoulders and guided him to two open seats, one on either side of the aisle.

When the train jerked them into motion, Ed leaned across and said to him as softly as he could while still being audible, "When we get there, just let me do the talking – and don't be asking no questions."

Jimmy turned to his brother, also keeping his response low, instinctively wanting to keep family matters private. "What's he like? I mean, I know I've seen him, but I don't remember – except he seemed tall and looked kind of old."

"Well, you'll see soon enough, won't you?" Ed considered a moment and added, "He's mostly angry and all stiff-like, at least around me. I guess being the oldest he figures I remember the most and hold the biggest grudge. Or maybe I'm like some kind of mirror for him, and I bet sure, he can't like his own reflection much. Sometimes I think he's just a big showoff, you know…trying to be manly and acting all put out like we're stealing his money. I think he must feel guilty about being so…you know being our pa, but not a real one." Ed's face tightened. "Heck, most times I just hate the selfish old bastard and wish I didn't have to come for Ma's money."

The last sentence stiffened Jimmy into his seat. His brother's sudden anger and hurt startled him. He'd not seen it before. It was something new and raw, and he didn't want to hear, or feel it, not now…not just before meeting his own father… not today on his birthday. He closed his eyes against the words which had landed in his stomach like a gut punch.

"Let's go. It's our stop coming."

"May I use the bathroom, sir?" Jimmy asked. *Sir?* He had meant to say Dad or even Pa, but his tongue refused to shape either word. He raised his glance high enough to take in the tall man's mouth but not enough to risk eye contact. The distinct chin and lips sparked a shadow of familiarity. The white stubble revealed he hadn't bothered to shave.

"Down the hall there. And make sure you flush."

Two steps out of the dimly lit room, he paused to listen. The man asked his brother, "That's…" he hesitated, "Tom, Jimmy? I get them mixed up. Your ma got a baby every time I but looked at her. And now she can't hardly feed…" His voice trailed off. "No wonder why I don't come 'round no more."

"It's Jimmy. How can you not even know your own?" Jimmy heard the barely restrained anger in his brother's voice. "It's not like you didn't have anything to do with Ma's babies."

"Now don't you be sassing me!"

Jimmy hurried along the darkened hallway towards the back of the house, trying not to hear anymore than he already had. The old man's question was another gut-punch; he hadn't even tried to hush his voice. Before a forming tear could blur his eye, he wiped it away. He saw a single frame hung on the long wall between two of the door jambs. He recognized Jesus pointing to his valentine-shaped Sacred Heart. Jimmy's own heart felt a stab – his own father didn't even remember his name.

It was then he realized he couldn't remember the old man's Christian name either. The thought caused panic, like he'd dropped his house key and had no idea where. How could he forget? *I'm as bad as he is.* He tried to force the name into his consciousness.

He pulled the light chain in the bathroom and began to rationalize the memory lapse. After all, Ma only refers to him as "that man." But mostly, his father was simply never mentioned. Until a few moments ago, Jimmy had just accepted this as normal. Now it didn't feel so right. He closed the bathroom door behind him, trying to shut out the hurt and confusion. He unbuttoned his fly and raised the toilet seat the way his sisters had drummed into him. As he tried to relax to pee, the name "Edward" drifted into his consciousness. *That's it!* Of course, the same as Eddie. *How could I forget that? No wonder they butt heads.* Jimmy imagined his brother's face on a coin opposite his father's, each face flashing and fighting as they flipped through the air. He couldn't pinpoint how he'd learned the name originally, but now he put it carefully back in his head so he wouldn't forget again, all the while thinking, *I don't want to be like him.*

He finished his business, flushed and rinsed his hands (his sisters' nagging again), but decided not to disturb the piece of soap lying there on the wash basin. He didn't want to chance soiling the towel hanging on the back of the door, so he shook his hands and wiped them on his trouser legs. He stepped back into the dim hall.

From the front room to his left he heard "that man's" voice excitedly punctuate some point and then the room went silent. He hoped his brother was holding his own. To his right, the hall opened into the kitchen area, which was bright from the sunlight passing through the window over the sink. Green curtains were hooked back to the side trim. Curiosity turned him in that direction. Stepping lightly, he hoped the floor boards wouldn't betray his clandestine exploration. He entered the room, nervously taking a quick glance back up the narrow passage. When his head came back into the kitchen, he froze under the unblinking gaze of the old woman.

She sat behind the small table facing him, as if expecting his arrival. Her face was ancient, worn, and lacking any signs of attractiveness that it might have once held before life and time had taken their due. Her whitish grey hair was loosely pulled back, and a dark blue large knit sweater hung half buttoned across her full chest. Her countenance was divided, the left side washed out by the window light, while the right dissolved into her shadow upon the wall. The effect enlarged and distorted the contour of her jaw. Her expression registered neither pleasure nor displeasure, just acceptance of his sudden appearance. Her gaze remained firm, but not at all hostile.

Jimmy, by contrast, felt naked standing there as she studied him matter-of-factly. He was transfixed, too surprised to move under the inspection. Finally he stammered, "Sorry, ma'am. I turned the wrong way."

"I'd rather you say you was curious, lad. Curiosity can be good in small doses. But, lying is always, an sure, the devil's work." Her voice reminded Jimmy of dust while the thick brogue lent a lyrical quality to her statement. The words carried no judgment but rather some warmth, even a faint sense of home. He thought he saw interest in her old eyes, a softening of her gaze. "You'd be Mary and Edward's James, if I'm not addled?"

"Pardon, ma'am?" He'd understood the question, but was startled when she knew his name when his own dad was confused. She made no response, so he answered, "Yes ma'am. I'm Jimmy."

Her eyes moved across the ceiling as if looking back through time and space. She spoke in short broken phrases. "I remember – sure as the saints – St. Viator Church – January cold, but Mary had you swaddled proper. I was there, you know. When the good Father…" She paused to retrieve a face and name. "Father McCormick 'twas poured the baptism water. You didn't cry, you know, just looked a wee gob-smacked. We all chuckled, we did." Another pause. "Tell me, Jimmy, does your ma still call you by Shamus?"

That the old lady would know this swelled his puzzlement like a quickly inflated balloon. But it also pleased him. "Yes ma'am, she does. It's Irish for Jimmy." He immediately felt dumb in light of the old woman's brogue and comments.

"How old are you now, lad?"

"I'm ten, ma'am. Just today actually. It's my birthday."

"Ah, that's grand, an sure!" She looked at the cup and saucer in front of her, then pulled a crumpled white handkerchief from the sleeve of her sweater and coughed into it. Carefully replacing it, she looked back to him and almost sang, "Lá Breithe Shona dhuit, Shamus. Now, you best be back to your brother." She winked at him.

He simply stammered, "Thank you, ma'am."

He wasn't sure why he was thanking her. Maybe because unlike his own father, she knew who he was and seemed pleased to see him. Maybe it was for the words she'd just said but he hadn't understood. Or maybe, just maybe, it was for the wink.

He turned to go. At the last second he looked back, but her concentration was focused on raising her cup of tea toward her mouth. He couldn't think of anything to say, so he retraced his way back through the hallway. His slight shadow, cast from the sunny window, scouted ahead of him but retreated as he moved toward the dimness of the living room.

Twenty minutes later, as their train click-clacked back to the North Side, his brother gave him a light poke on the arm. "What took you so long in the bathroom? I wanted to get out of there. That man's not the easiest, you know, to talk to. He kept going on about how work and money was going to get harder to come by with the war in Europe ended and all."

Jimmy jumped at the chance to tell his brother. "There was an old lady. I talked to her. She was in the kitchen."

For a moment Ed peered over Jimmy's head and smiled. "You eejit." He playfully tousled Jimmy's cap. "That old lady is your Granny, you know."

"My Granny?" The phrase she'd used sprang from his mouth. "I'll be gob-smacked." He tried to reconcile the old lady's face with his concept of a granny. "Dad's ma? For real?" he squeaked.

"She is. When I come down to get Ma's money and the old man ain't around, we'll sit and talk some. She asks about everyone. I don't think she and the old man get on so good. When he's there, he's always telling her to go back to the kitchen. That's another thing that makes me hate him."

"Who takes care of her then?" Jimmy asked remembering how she had winked at him. "She looks really old."

"Uncle James." Ed's face scrunched up in thought. "I think maybe you were named for him. Anyhow, it's actually his place, you know. He and Maggie, his wife, live upstairs. He part-owns a grocery store nearby. I like him. He's not like Pa at all near as I can tell. He's got a proper job and cares for his mother. Much more a proper person and son than the old man."

Jimmy fair sputtered. "I have an uncle with my name?" He tried not to yell the words, but the volume and pitch of his voice rose, only partially drowned out by another screech as the train went into still another curve. "I have a granny and an uncle and aunty, and nobody tells me? Does anyone else know about them?"

"Calm down. Ma won't even talk about the old man. You know that. If she didn't need the money to make ends meet, I think she'd just leave them all to the grave. Richard knows, 'cause he comes with me most times. Maybe the older girls do, and somehow Mary always seems to know more than she should for her age. But the younger boys don't know, because Ma doesn't want them to. I was knocked over when she sent you with me today. So don't be telling them, or talking with anyone else because it would hurt Ma and get her mad like you don't want to see."

They went quiet. It wasn't until they had transferred back to the Ravenswood line that Jimmy again broke their silence. "Eddie, doesn't Ma like Granny Cullerton?" She seemed real nice."

"I've never figured that out. I remember when I was younger than you even, she'd still come around a little. She was old even then. That was back when the old man was home most nights. I never thought to ask after that. Things were tough enough, what with one thing or the next."

Ed stopped and seemed to draw on a distant memory. "I shouldn't tell you this 'cause you're just a kid. I don't think anyone else knows, not even the older girls, so you have to swear to keep it to yourself." Jimmy nodded.

"A few years back, Ma was sending me to the store. She was busy and told me to get the house money box from her room. I get it, but it's not locked like usual so I take a look figuring to just see some cash, but I see some papers too. I shouldn't have, but I take a peek and see our certificates from when we were baptized. Baby Bud's is on top so I guess mine is on the bottom, since I'm the oldest. But the bottom one is Ma's. And below her name is her God-mother: Jane Cullerton."

Ed ran his hand slowly through his hair as if he still could not believe it. "So, bold as can be, I ask Ma if Jane Cullerton was Granny Cullerton. If looks could kill, I wouldn't be here today. She grabs it out of my hand in a way like she's never done before and locks it back in the box and tells me to 'never-mind.' I could see she was upset bad. So was I. You know, for making her feel that way. Then last year one time when I was down for Ma's money and Richard wasn't with me, I asked the old man about it. He says flat out, 'Yeah, I was there too. She fussed and cried when I tried to hold her.' That part hits me real queer-like. I couldn't picture that man holding Ma as a baby. It seemed, I don't know, kind of wrong somehow."

Jimmy couldn't picture it either. Ed was right; he was just a kid and couldn't really process all of this. At ten his focus was locked on the here and now, so he filed it away and instead asked his brother, "So why doesn't anyone visit?" he asked. His friends were always having relatives over. Some had their grandmas living right there with them. That's what regular families did. Why not his?

Ed shook his head. "I don't really know. I guess when Pa left for good, or Ma threw him out, I don't know which, she just decided his whole family had to go too. Maybe she blamed the whole kit and caboodle of them." Suddenly he stopped, thinking maybe he'd said too much. His blue eyes looked directly into Jimmy's face and he warned, "Now, don't you go asking Ma about any of this either, you hear? Or, I swear I'll lay you out. She'd skin me. It would kill her if she thought we were taking his side, or talking behind her. It would kill all of us." They both retreated back into their own thoughts.

Jimmy stared blankly ahead, lost in the roll and roar of the train and of his thoughts, not noticing the city again flying past the window, this time in reverse order as if they were going back in time. He realized he couldn't ever go back, couldn't ever unknow what he now knew, and he knew he would never question his mother about such things. He dug a hole deep inside into which he placed his questions and confusion. *Best to bury it and just go on.*

The train was slowing back into the Kedzie Street station when Jimmy remembered the other thing on his mind. "Ed, Granny Cullerton knows Ma calls me Shamus. She even asked me if she still does. And she said something to me in another language; it was Irish I think, when I told her it was my birthday."

Ed smiled a real smile. Jimmy realized it was a sight becoming more rare each passing year. "Let me guess. Lá Breithe Shona dhuit," he said with an exaggerated brogue.

Jimmy's eyes popped wide. "That's it. That's it! How did you know that?"

"It means Happy Birthday in Irish, you eejit. Ma use to say it too you know, long ago. But she never speaks any Irish anymore… Except, of course, when she calls you Shamus."

When they were finally back on their street, Ed wrapped an arm around his little brother. "Come on, Jimmy. Let's go get some of that birthday cake Ma's got waiting for you."

Christmas Break

1918, December

By 9:00 AM the time had come. It was now or never. He pounded his baseball one last time into the almost new mitt he'd gotten for Christmas from his sisters. All of the Cullerton boys old enough to not put the ball in their mouth were crazy for the game. His sisters too had inherited the family fervor. No beau stood a chance if he didn't show a healthy interest and knowledge of the game and of the Cubs' prospects that year. It would have been like dating a non-Catholic. Ma wouldn't abide. But in the family, Jimmy showed the most passion and potential.

After two days of this regimen, the glove began to feel like his. He ground his prized stained and scuffed baseball deep into the pocket, coaxing the leather into the size and shape he wanted. He rewound the twine tightly several times around the glove to hold the ball in place. Tying the ends off with a double knot, he slid the mitt back under his pillow, which helped hold the mitt closed and imprinted the smell of the leather which, he hoped, would produce dreams of summer and being on the field.

With a house full of kids, try as she might, Mrs. Cullerton couldn't keep tabs on all of their comings and goings. Her focus was naturally on the youngest boys. Except for the before school inspection to make sure each was properly cleaned, dressed and had their homework, the older ones sooner or later discovered they could sometimes – if they moved quickly enough – escape without close questioning. Jimmy buttoned up his winter coat and wrapped a wool scarf around his neck. Cap in hand and swallowing back a large dose of guilt, he took advantage of the maneuver. "I'm going out, Ma," he hollered while she was at the other end of the house and quickly closed the door against any possible query.

On Christmas Day the city had awoke to four inches of fresh snow. Last night had brought more snow, but Richard had already shoveled the porch and sidewalk clear, adding the new inches to the previous storm remnants covering the frozen lawns. There'd be no tracks to give away his direction. Time was short. He had three, maybe four hours at best. The limited time and single-digit cold quickened his steps. He retraced the route he and his brother Ed had taken five weeks earlier. He'd been thinking about this since they'd returned home that day, even as his family was singing Happy Birthday to him and making short work of his birthday cake.

Lying in bed each night since then, he'd replayed that trip in his mind. He found he just couldn't think of that man as his dad. So for now he was filed away in Jimmy's head under the generic category of "father" – in small case letters. After years of not knowing him, Jimmy could only muster a grudging interest in knowing about the man, rather than any drive to actually get to know him. Still he had to admit he did have questions. Lots of them actually.

What mostly spurred his desire to go back was the old lady. She was the one who remembered. Besides that, she knew things about him and possibly interesting stuff about his father and Ma. When she had asked about Ma calling him Shamus and had winked at him, somewhere down deep in his brain a need to return took root, though it took a while before he consciously began to hatch a plan.

He knew his brother Ed had been right in warning him not to tell Ma about talking with the old lady – his Granny? He didn't like it, but nonetheless realized there were things you didn't talk about or share, even with your mother. Especially with your mother. He'd have to learn to live with that. *But why had she sent me along? Was that a mistake, like letting Ed see her baptismal certificate?* He tried, but was only partially successful at using the "secret family mystery" to assuage his guilt about sneaking behind Ma's back. He knew it would hurt her – what? ...sense of loyalty, pride, love for him? He didn't have the vocabulary or experience to dig deeper into the first two, and didn't dare explore the last. Still, he couldn't understand how and why he could have family, and no one ever talked about them. Even if you didn't like them, it didn't seem right to pretend they didn't exist. Was she trying to protect us...or herself from something? Not knowing what others already knew made Jimmy feel stupid, and that feeling, along with feeling betrayed, were the motivations pushing him on.

At the Kedzie Station for the second time in just a month, he boarded the El. This time a train was waiting, as if it knew his time was precious. He got in the front car. Post rush-hour and Christmas rush, the car was mostly empty. He took the very front seat. When they pulled out of the station, he stood resting his forehead against the window inches in front of him. He tried to stand without using his hands for balance or support. He pretended to be flying. The sensation was almost overwhelming with only the pane of glass separating him from the oncoming emptiness of air and space, tracks and curves, railings and buildings, all of which began racing directly at him. When the train slowed for the next station, he strained his neck to keep his face from flattening against the cold glass. Starting back up, he had to adjust so as not to fall back into his seat. For a few stations he rode this way to keep himself from thinking. By the time they reached the station at Damen, he became self-conscious and sat down before some adult said something or asked questions.

He began to focus on the route. He had played it out in his head several times and was confident he'd remember. Young as he was, he had a natural sense of direction in the city. He already knew Chicago's grid numbering system, so he didn't fear getting lost. When he bought his ticket, he'd confirmed where he'd have to transfer. In the Loop, he had no trouble following their previous path down and back up the stairs to the tracks heading south. At Indiana Avenue, he alighted and exited the station. He didn't know the exact house number, but in spite of the line of ubiquitous Chicago two-and-three-flats, he was sure he'd recognize the building. His heart began to pound. *What if I run into... that man?* He was hoping he'd be working or gone somewhere. Besides, he figured chances were good his father wouldn't even recognize him if he answered the door and Jimmy avoided eye contact. The thought hurt.

A frigid mid-morning work day meant there was no foot traffic on the block. Jimmy walked past the brownish brick building the first time without looking directly up at the covered porch and door. At the end of the block, he turned, checked his courage, and walked back. He hesitated on the shoveled sidewalk and looked up at the front windows for any sign of life. Just like before, the drapes were closed, holding in their secrets. It was then he noticed there were actually two doors, side by side. He was confident this was the right place, and assumed his anxiety on that first trip caused him to miss that detail the first time. Taking a deep breath, he released a steamy exhale as he climbed the wooden steps. They'd been shoveled. He held his breath, willing himself not to run. He knocked, and then stared at the door in the cold and silence. He pushed his hands deep into his coat pockets both to shield them from the bitter air and to keep them from betraying his anxiety. As the silence and stress stretched out, he wished he could stuff his whole self into his pockets. He stood absolutely still for a full two minutes. It seemed like two years. The doorknob began to turn.

Just like last time, her eyes held no sense of surprise. Her head made three small nods as if to affirm something. Jimmy couldn't decide if he should say, "It's me, Granny", or run. Instead he just stood silent hunched in his coat and scarf.

"Come in, Shamus, and close the door. Way too cold it 'tis for these old bones to stand about waiting to freeze." She turned and shuffled back through the front parlor, heading towards the kitchen. He closed the door, making sure it clicked tight against the outside world and weather, and followed her stooped figure.

Jimmy again glanced at Jesus still hanging in his spot in the hallway. He checked to make sure The Sacred Heart eyes weren't following him as he passed. Just beyond the iconic image, a door opposite the toilet was open. He slowed and glanced into the room. A single bed and night stand. He instantly knew it must be her room. A blue quilted coverlet with laced edges on the bed. A crucifix centered above the headboard. He thought the room looked and smelled like a granny's room and actually quite similar to his Ma's small bedroom. A picture of the Virgin was framed on the sidewall. Jimmy could picture the old lady struggling up from her knees after saying her prayers, beseeching the Virgin to bless…who? He wondered who or what she might pray for. Was he, or his brothers or sisters ever mentioned? Was Ma? Did she pray for her sons – his father? If so, Jesus must sometimes turn a deaf ear to His mother, just like he and his brothers did sometimes with Ma.

On the nightstand lay a brush and a rosary with its small crucified Jesus dangling off the edge of the stand. Two photos stood in their frames separated by a small red votive candle. They were angled off, so all Jimmy could make out was that each showed a young man's torso apparently wearing his Sunday best.

When they finally reached the kitchen his supposed Granny lowered herself onto her same chair. Her breathing seemed hard. Once settled, she looked up and asked straight off, "Now, would your ma be knowing you came all this way down here by yourself?"

It never occurred to Jimmy to cover with a lie this time. He knew it wouldn't have done any good. "No ma'am. I snuck here and I feel bad about it." He tried to stand still, watching as she leaned forward, setting her wrinkled elbows and age-spotted hands akimbo style on the wooden table surface.

"An sure, I would think you would be. But, I am glad you found telling the truth straight off. What brought you, son?" Her voice held no rebuke, freeing Jimmy to grab onto the "son" and the warmth it was wrapped in. After all, it was a word his own dad didn't go near during his last visit.

However, he really didn't know how to answer the question, so instead he asked one of his own. "Eddie, my brother Ed, not my father, told me you're my Granny Cullerton, my dad's ma. Is that true?"

She removed her wire-rimmed spectacles one ear at a time and set them on the table. "Well… since you thought yourself big enough to come all this way alone, and the good Lord got you here safe and sound, I guess He'd want me to answer you right and proper. I'm your Granny. Now be a good lad; take off your coat and light a match under the kettle there on the stove so we can have a wee gab and tea."

The confirmation and the invitation buoyed Jimmy's confidence. He took a wooden match from the box on the side of the stove and carefully lit the burner. Adjusting the gas flame, he filled and set the kettle. He took the chair across from her, draping his coat across its back. For a moment they quietly, but comfortably, looked at each other, each trying to see something in the other's face, perhaps a bit of themselves – perhaps a glimpse of the past or even the future.

After several seconds Jimmy broke the quiet. "I was worried my father would be here and give me 'the what for' for coming. Is he at work?"

"He is. It's Friday – pay day, you know. He'll be off then spending it on the cards or the dice with his…" She paused, and looked over Jimmy's head and out the window. He wondered what she could see without her glasses.

A few moments passed before she started again, with a new direction. "You being a curious lad and all, Shamus, I'd be guessing you have more questions you might want to be knowing." She said it gentle-like; more statement than question. She returned her gaze back into the room and replaced her spectacles on her face. "Can I be calling you Shamus, or 'tis that just between your ma and you? Being a good American boy, you probably prefer Jimmy?"

"Yes ma'am. I mean…no ma'am. I mean I do have some questions and all." As he spoke, another part of him explored the Shamus question and finding he liked how it sounded coming off her tongue. It seemed natural, like being at home. "And, no ma'am. Shamus is fine, especially you being so Irish and all."

"Sure an, I'm Irish… 'and all.' For a body 'tis never just one thing you know. They always have the 'and all' part tucked away inside them."

Jimmy didn't know exactly what that meant, but it felt and sounded right, so he nodded. She moved her forearm to her lips to cover a cough. Her lungs worked hard for half a minute. Like last visit, she pulled a handkerchief from her sleeve and held it to her mouth. Jimmy wasn't sure, but thought maybe she spit into it. "Do you want some water, Granny?" he asked.

"Water would be grand," she wheezed. Jimmy filled a glass that was sitting upside down on the drain board. When he returned, the handkerchief was gone. She gave a small smile as he handed the water to her. She took a few sips. "Go raibh maith agat, thank you, Shamus. The chill and cold gets inside me chest sometimes." She set the half-full glass on the table, keeping her hands around it. "So, just what might you be wanting to be knowing, Shamus? I'll tell you straight out though, I'll not be telling you anything bad between your da and ma. That's their pot to stir." She cleared her throat and then took another small sip from the glass as if to wash down her last words, or maybe some more phlegm.

"My brother thought maybe I was named for your other son, James. Is that true? Does he live here too?"

"James and his Maggie live upstairs, sure. He goes down to the store everyday and Margaret helps out at the church on Fridays. Getting it ready, you know, for the Sunday masses. I can't be telling you though if Edward named you for his brother or because his own grand-da was called James. That's how they do back in the old county, you know."

Jimmy asked, "Why do you call him James and not Shamus?"

"Ah, that be me Patrick's doing. After we got to America in 1800 and 52 it was, we came straight for Chicago, being where other family and friends were. Three years later James was born. So natural sure, Patrick wanted his first son to be called for his da – like in Ireland. But, being born here in our new home he took to mind to call him the American way, James, not Shamus.

"Maybe your brother is right about the naming though. Sure, me boys never got on so good with each other, what with James being years older than Ed. Still, maybe 'twas Ed's way of telling his big brother he loved him. Sure he didn't know no other way to say it. So maybe? God knows I never much knew what that man thinks. Not since he was quite wee."

"How old is Da?" Jimmy caught himself and quickly added, "My father, I mean." With no thought of possible impropriety he continued. "He looks pretty old."

The old woman showed no offense. "April, it was. My Edward got born early April, 1800 and 63. It was right in the middle of that terrible bloody war and when my Patrick, your grand-da, was so busy down at the rail yard."

This news completely confused the ten year old. All he knew was the Great War was only finally over weeks ago, not years. Old Glory still hung everywhere proclaiming it so. How could his father have been born in the war? His puzzlement showed clear, and he was scrambling to formulate a question when the whistle from the kettle rose, calling for a pause in the tale.

"Ah, will you wet the tea there, Shamus?" Her request and the steady whistle of steam took awhile to work its way though a skull gone to mush.

Finally, he got up and turned off the burner. The steam dropped in pitch and disappeared. He carefully poured the hot water into the pot to let the tea steep. Turning, he set the pot on the table between them along with two cups, saucers, and teaspoons she'd pointed to on the open shelves. She pointed at the icebox, which Jimmy took to mean he should fetch the cream.

When all was settled, he sat back down and said with point blank honesty as only a child can, "Granny? The war just ended! I don't understand."

"Not this war," she chuckled, "long ago before that, the States War. Back when Mr. Lincoln – bless his soul – was President and then got shot. An sure, you know, I seen the great man's coffin. The funeral train stopped here on its way to Springfield. Two hours we waited in the line down by the old Court House to pay our respects. My little Eddie was cradled in me own arms and James holding tight on to me skirts."

Her arms folded – an unconscious imitation of the memory. Jimmy picked up on the gesture and use of the diminutive "Eddie."

He knew she had gone back in her head to that long ago day when his dad was an Eddie, not Edward or "That Man." Try as best he could, Jimmy's young imagination couldn't paint the picture, and so he was glad when she continued – still from somewhere deep in her own thoughts. "Bad times it 'twas for us back then, that being the spring after when we lost Patrick. Eddie, just being a babe, never got to know his da. Maybe 'twas what made him not know 'tis more to children then just having them." She offered Jimmy a weak smile then reached for the pot.

Jimmy gave her time while she poured the tea and added sugar and cream to both cups without asking. He wasn't surprised that she somehow knew that was how he liked it. When he thought she was ready, he pressed on. "Was Patrick killed in a battle?"

"He was not, thank God. With two little ones and him almost two score years, he wasn't about to sign on to soldiering. Figured, he did, there was plenty enough Irish already fighting. And when they started drafting men, Patrick wasn't called because he drove dray down at the rail yard. The war goods came and went you know, day and night. The city and the yards 'twas always a bustle. New folks were coming every day, and there were more horses than folks back then. They'd come in on one train and off to the battles on another.

"I remember it clear. Some horses broke out, and Patrick's load got turned over and wrecked. They brought his dead self home to me with his wages stuffed into his shirt pocket and not so much as a 'Sorry for your troubles, Mrs. Cullerton.' The boss men never even came for a drink to the wake. There I sit with a dead husband to bury, your da a wee babe, and James not even your age yet. Lucky it 'twas Issy, your own ma's ma, was gold, like me own little sister to me she was in those weeks after we put poor Patrick in the ground up in the old Catholic cemetery – what they then made to Lincoln Park. Later, 'twas a hard cry I had when they come tell me I have to move poor Patrick. Issy's husband helped me some to pay for a new grave and to move Patrick way up north to the new Calvary Cemetery. That was all long before even your ma was born."

Jimmy knew Issy was his Granny Isabelle. To a ten year old, she too was old, but not so much as the woman across the table. Granny

Isabelle still came round, sitting and chatting over her tea, while Ma ironed or washed dishes or in general did chores. Jimmy saw this was a new link for him, an unexpected connection between the two old women. Just as his new mystery family was getting bigger, it was also closing circle. He was beginning to feel filled up to overflowing with what he had just heard. He had no idea what he should say to all the tragedy so he echoed what he always heard the adults say, "I'm sorry for your bad troubles, Gram-ma." Mixed in with his genuine sadness for her hard times, Jimmy took note of the warm way the word "Gram-ma" felt on his tongue. He liked it a lot. Then and there he changed her from a Granny to Gram-ma.

Gram-ma Cullerton stopped talking, poured more tea and added sugar and cream to each cup. She was spent, which brought on another coughing spell. They just sat, sipping at their tea, lost in the silence of the moment, each seeing these long ago events in their own way, according to their age, according to their own experiences; neither seemed in a hurry to move on.

The quiet stretched. If asked, neither could have said how long. After awhile, Jimmy started to talk, sharing more at one time that he'd ever done in his life and perhaps would ever do again. He began slow at first, and then poured out words like he'd sprung a leak. The old lady drank them up like it was filling some dry place inside her, a rain breaking a long drought. He told her about his brothers and sisters, about school and about his baseball mitt which his sisters gave him for Christmas. He told about the fear he'd never told anyone else about when the influenza was killing people – even a girl in his grade. It had scared him more than the war over there, which everyone knew we would win, because "America always wins – right, Gram-ma?"

By the time he finally ran dry, they had finished off the pot of tea. Jimmy still had one more question banging around inside his head about why her name was on Ma's baptism papers and if his dad was really there and holding Ma on that day. But he knew he couldn't ask it. Not now. Not today. Maybe next time. Instead, he ended by worrying out loud to her about the sin he'd committed by sneaking here and not telling his mother. Gram-ma was quite sure it was venial. That made him feel better, and he promised to go to confession tomorrow, it being Saturday.

With all the tea, he needed to pee before the long trip home. This time he used both the soap and the towel without thinking about it. He exited the bathroom and found her standing in her room straight across, getting something from her top dresser drawer. Jimmy took one step in, just enough so he could see the photos he'd noticed earlier. Without turning, but with a motion of a wrinkled very white hand she said, "Those be your da and James long ago. They were handsome boys. Just like you."

Jimmy took a couple steps further into her room to look more closely. The photos looked quite old, but the faces were of young men. The younger, his father's face, looked to be eighteen or nineteen. Jimmy was aware this would have been about when he made Ma cry at her baptism. The figures were dressed up, so it might have even been that very day. He decided not to ask. He did see some resemblance around the nose and eyes to his older brothers and maybe even himself. The older boy, Uncle James, looked to be in his mid-twenties and, unlike his father, was smiling full on.

"Thanks, Gram-ma, and for telling me about your family, like I was grown. Maybe next time you can tell me about my father and Uncle James when they were young? What did they like to do? Did they like baseball like we all do?"

"Remember, Shamus, 'tis your family too. And remember my Patrick, your gram-pa is in heaven, an sure he's watching and praying for you. And when I join him, I'll be asking Jesus and His Mother to be good to you too." She hugged him. He let himself be swallowed into her bounty.

"This is for you." She slid a two-bit coin into his palm. "For the fare… and maybe a bit o' sweets. My treat, for coming to visit your Gram-ma. But, Shamus… maybe 'tis best we keep our gab to just us. Your ma may not take too kind to you coming here to visit. I'll confess my part of the sin too before Sunday mass. Now, Slán abhaile. Be off home, and God love you. And don't be talking with strangers on your way, or let anybody be sneezing or coughing on you. For me, 'tis a wee nap I need after all our grown-up talk."

He hugged her a last time, leaving her sitting on the bed. At the front door he buttoned up his coat all the way over his muffler, turned up the frayed collar and pulled his cap tight on his head, lowering the ear flaps. At the bottom of the steps he looked back up, wondering about the other door and James and Maggie who lived there. *Next time I'll ask to meet them.*

He hurried toward the intersection, crossing the street and walking close to the brick wall of an apartment building to block the north wind. To brace against an arctic blast when he'd turn straight into it, he pulled his scarf up on his face and again stuffed his hands into his coat pockets. At the end of the building he plunged round the corner, running smack into a man coming his way. He almost tumbled over.

The man steadied Jimmy's shoulders so as not to let him fall. "Sorry, son, I should be looking where I'm going." Jimmy knew the man couldn't see his face because of the scarf. But he could see the man plain. His white hair and warm smile and something about his narrow nose and blue eyes looked familiar. He released Jimmy's shoulders and stepped around him saying, "Have a grand day, son." There was that word again, "son", sounding much like the way his Gram-ma had said it.

Head down into the wind, Jimmy pushed on another half dozen steps before curiosity made him retrace them in spite of the cold. He glanced back around the corner. The man had crossed the street and headed up the steps of the house he'd just left. He disappeared behind the second door. Jimmy considered heading back, but knew time was short and he needed to get home quick.

Lost in his thoughts, he almost missed his transfer. He kept trying to make sense of all he'd heard. Even without the promise to Gram-ma Cullerton, Jimmy again knew he could never share the conversation, or even the visit, with anyone. Just as before, he didn't like it, but the lesson seemed clear. The past was something to be locked away inside. Ma and the older brothers and sisters obviously felt that way. He could do it too. Living in such a crowded, busy house, he was used to keeping his deepest thoughts and feelings tucked away. It avoided conflict. It avoided confrontation and bad times, even if it meant keeping the past and part of yourself in the shadows. Besides, for sure Ma would feel betrayed by his trip, and he would never risk hurting her. He couldn't tell his brother Ed, even if he went with him again to get Ma's money. Maybe hardest of all was he couldn't tell his sister Mary, the one he always went to when he really needed to think out loud. She was the only one who knew he was already considering Quigley Seminary in a few years after eighth grade if he could find a way to raise the tuition.

He felt alone. He stared through the reflection of himself on the El window, looking for something but not knowing what.

The O'bits

1919, January 27

Half-hidden under the table on a kitchen chair, *The Daily News* lay open, folded in quarters. It caught Jimmy's eye when he flipped on the light and headed to the sink for a glass of water. *Ma doesn't usually splurge on a paper.* As he drank, he glanced at the columns of print that stared back at him, as if beckoning. *The Obits.* The word made him cringe, remembering how dumb he'd felt when he first heard it. He'd been maybe five then, just a kid, and had thought O'Bits was the family who had just moved in down the block in the house next to the O'Malleys. He knew it was 'O' something or other. When he asked, his brother Richard told him, "Don't be an eejit. The Obits is the obituaries, a list of people who died." This only further confused him, wondering how so many people in one family could have died at one time.

His eyes ran down the folded page as he drank. They suddenly stopped at a pencil circled notice and two names leapt out at him, making him sputter. He grabbed the paper, wiping off the water spots he'd sprayed. Fully awake now, he read as if his life depended on it.

O'Rourke – Mrs. Jane, January 24, 1919, beloved mother of James and Edward Cullerton, Mrs. John Carroll, Mrs. Michael Smith, and Mrs. Adam Franenholtz, and the late Mrs. John F. Owens at residence 1612 Indiana to St. John's Church where a requiem high mass will be celebrated, then by carriage to Calvary.

Jimmy's second reading made it clear that neither Edward nor James had died, but their mother. *MOTHER? But, Gram-ma Cullerton is their mother. Who the heck is O'Rourke, Mrs. Jane?* Two more readings teased out the facts from his confusion. *Dad and Uncle James and Gram-ma live on Indiana...I've been there...but was that 1612? They can't have two mothers...did Gram-ma have two names? And who the heck are all these other women? Could I have even more aunts?* His head buzzed with combined confusion and a creeping sadness.

He tried to puzzle it out. Knowing now what he did about his ma's lack of relationship with "that man" and his secret family, he quickly decided that Ma surely didn't mean to leave the paper lying about to be discovered. He grabbed the dishtowel, wiped up the remaining water spots, and replaced the paper the way he'd found it. He grabbed his coat from the peg by the back door and put it on over his pajamas. He quietly stepped out onto the back porch. He sat on the top step, pulling his coat about him and trying to sort out what exactly was going on. Below him in the yard in the dim early light he could barely make out the hens scratching around in the pre-dawn. Amen and her sister looked up as they pecked along the frozen ground scrounging for any missed chicken feed from yesterday. They began clucking, demanding breakfast. Jimmy took a handful of feed from the porch container and tossed it at them to shut them up while he thought.

He knew in his gut that Jane O'Rourke must be Gram-ma Cullerton. She hadn't been in his life long enough for the obituary to produce true grief, but his sadness and disbelief swelled, along with a sense of loss that felt like a pinching inside his chest and gut. He'd just talked with her a month ago. How could she have died so quickly?

As if to cling to the hope that he was wrong, he again considered the puzzling different last name. His life experience to date had not yet presented him with second marriages, or step parents. He could ask one of his older brothers later, but they'd call him daft, so he'd check with Mary. She was younger, but girls knew more about families, and he could trust her not to tell Ma or anyone – and she wouldn't call him dumb. He loved her for both those things. One thing for sure, he couldn't ask Ma. He didn't like that part at all. In fact he hated it. It was confusing and maddening that the truth was such a secret, and getting answers had already caused him to lie and sneak around.

He retreated from the cold, back into the kitchen. Checking to make sure Ma wasn't up yet, he quickly flipped the paper over to check the date – yesterday, Monday, January 26, 1919. He assumed that meant that the funeral was today. It was early, so maybe there was time. When he turned around, his brother was standing in the door.

"Oh, shit." Ed's face looked worried. "Did you read that?"

"No," Jimmy tried to lie, but couldn't. "Maybe, a little."

"Ma will wear me out if she knows you seen that." He had a look of genuine concern on his face. "Remember, Jimmy, you promised not to let Ma know you know anything. Give me that." Jimmy handed over the folded *Daily News*. "Now not a word of this to Ma. You promised… or, I'll chop you up and feed you to Amen."

Jimmy knew he was kidding about the chopping part, but the chicken still scared him some. He now knew for sure that, in spite of a different last name, Gram-ma Cullerton, the sweet old lady who knew Ma called him Shamus, was dead. "OK. Is Ma still asleep?" he asked in a hushed tone.

"Ma went out early. She told me to get you guys up and off to school. Go wake up the others and get ready."

"Where did Ma go?"

"Not your business. Now go!" Edward said in a loud whisper.

He moved quickly. His first stop was his own room where he quietly scribbled a note at the desk he shared with his sleeping brother, Tom. Then he made the rounds, starting with the older boy's room, making sure Richard acknowledged being awake before moving on. In the girls' rooms, he found Mary's eyes already opened while the other three still had their heads buried under the covers. Jimmy stuck the note in her hand while holding a finger to his lips and turned to wake the others before she could ask a question. Last of all, he went back to his room. He quickly dressed, grabbing two quarters from the jar on his book shelf where he kept his savings, before waking his younger brother.

Returning to the kitchen, he found Ed setting out breakfast dishes for the crew. "I gotta leave early to see Sister about an assignment. Bye." He was out the door before Ed could ask about his lack of books or make him repeat his promise again.

For the third time, Jimmy retraced his journey back to the house where Gram-ma lived, or at least she used to live. On the train he sat crowded in by half-asleep adults on their way to work. Most wore winter coats and hats, some brandishing mufflers or handkerchiefs to cover their faces against any remaining flu bugs. The cut and styles marked most as the clerks and office workers needed to keep Chicago's mercantile economy humming. A few, meaner dressed laborers were evident. No one paid him any attention. He sat quietly staring straight ahead. This time there was no feeling of exhilaration, only a few minutes of guilt about sneaking off again, lying to his brother and cutting school – something he'd never even considered doing before. He could only hope that Mary would cover for him.

Two overriding issues pressed down on his slender shoulders: If caught, how would he explain cutting school without divulging what he knew? And, of course, the more immediate problem was he had no idea where St. John's Church was. *Jesus, Mary, Joseph, I need some help.* He silently evoked the mantra over and over until it revealed the obvious to him. He'd simply ask someone when he got in the neighborhood and hope St. John's was nearby.

A lady waiting for the streetcar outside the station, wrapped tight in a long cloth coat and headscarf, directed him, "Two blocks down, Dearie, to 18th Street. Turn right a couple blocks to Clark." There was no missing it; the old church, a Gothic limestone edifice, dominated the northeast corner.

As he approached, his heart skipped a beat, stopping him in his tracks. One of the new motorized hearses was parked at the corner, engine running to keep the driver warm. A deep sadness overtook all his other thoughts. He didn't want to think of Gram-ma never being warm again.

From behind the hearse the exhaust, made visible in the frozen January air, rose and swirled like ghosts playing tag. Jimmy brushed his eyes clear and continued. Except for the driver, there was no one out front. He looked up at the over-sized double wood doors encased in a massive stone archway.

It took a mighty tug on Jimmy's part to open the large doors far enough to slip into the barely warmer vestibule. He carefully ascended the marble steps to the opened doors that led into the church proper. There he stood behind the doorframe to make himself invisible while his eyes adjusted to the dimness and vast high emptiness of the interior space.

Except it wasn't empty. Way up at the altar rail rested a rectangle, covered by a white cloth with a golden cross embroidered. He felt relief not to see the actual casket. An elderly priest, chanting in Latin as he shook the aspergillum, was sprinkling droplets of holy water over the pall-covered coffin. Jimmy loved the sound of Latin. He'd be old enough to become an altar boy this spring, and already had half of the common mass service responses memorized. But now, he was too far away to hear distinct words.

The sun broke into colors as it passed through the stained glass window scenes. It provided enough light so he could see the dozen mourners standing in the first couple of pews. It was a full minute later before he noticed a solitary figure hunched in prayer a number of rows behind the others. Jimmy wondered if she – for the black veil indicated it was a woman – was one of those pious old parish women who cared for and haunted every church. There were always two or three at Our Lady of Mercy Church no matter when or why he was there. He admired their devotion but also felt sad for them. They never seemed able to soak up enough grace and comfort to live outside the church walls. When he became an altar boy, maybe he'd ask the monsignor about them.

With everyone's eyes on the priest, Jimmy slipped into a back side pew and slid all the way over into a shadow near the wall. Out of respect he knelt, also knowing it made him harder to see. The last thing he wanted was to be spotted and called out by his father. His sense of loss gathered more weight as he realized that his dad would probably not even recognize him if he tripped him going down the aisle. *"Is that Tom or Jimmy?"* The words from his visit last November echoed in his ears. *Forget him.* For Gram-ma's and his own sake, he tried to pray the bitter taste out of his mouth.

As he became calmer, his eyes wandered over the backs of the distant mourners and he wondered how many were part of his secret family. From the six male figures scattered across the pews Jimmy picked out his dad, even though he couldn't see their faces. It didn't occur to him to wonder how or why he recognized him. He guessed the taller of the two men flanking his father was his uncle James with his wife Maggie at his side. Probably the other people were those aunts and uncles listed in the obituary.

His eyes stayed glued on all these unknown relatives, but he occupied his mind by pulling out and beginning his rosary which resided in the pocket of his school pants. Every student, from fifth grade up to eighth, was required to carry a rosary on them at all times. (Below fifth, Jimmy assumed, they were afraid one of the little kids might swallow some of the beads and enter the Kingdom of God prematurely.) At least once a week some rule-breaker was discovered to not have his. It was almost always a guy and easily recognizable because he'd be kneeling in the hallway outside his classroom, reflecting on sins of omission or mumbling cusses under his breath.

Jimmy's thoughts were brought back to the service when everyone, including his "not really a dad" father, sat as the priest headed to the pulpit. Wishing to stay concealed, Jimmy remained kneeling, but leaned forward with his chin on the back of the next pew and cupping his hands behind his ears. Maybe, he grinned, if the priest should see him at all, he'd look like a leftover Halloween Jack-o-lantern.

The priest began, "We are gathered here today in the name of Jesus to..." Jimmy paid attention, but only distantly. His eyes wandered along the high roof beams until he heard: "His servant Jane

O'Rourke, the former Jane Cullerton, has now joined in the glory of God with her late husband Nicholas O'Rourke and also with her first husband, Patrick Cullerton – the man she journeyed here with all the way from Ireland those many years ago. Both good men surely were waiting with St. Peter at the gates to welcome Jane to her eternal rest…"

Jimmy thought that sounded like a fight about to happen but was glad he now knew why Jane had two names. Nicholas was another new unknown. He wondered if getting a new dad had been hard for his father. He assumed it could go either way.

But Patrick, his grandfather, became even more real to him. He recalled Gram-ma's stories. *Was that only a month ago?* The priest's words moved Patrick from a minor character in a story to a real person, his Gram-pa. The more you heard about the dead, the more alive they became. That thought swirled around his young head until it collided with another reality. About ninety feet ahead of him, the distance from home plate to first base on a major league baseball field, sat an entire branch of his family tree that had until recently been unknown – so basically dead to him. Yet there they were, very much alive – except, of course, for Gram-ma. He blinked to make sure his family wouldn't disappear like the exhaust tendrils from the waiting hearse. One minute there, the next whisked away.

The homily ended. The priest remounted the steps to the altar and began the most holy and dramatic part of the mass, the part that captured Jimmy's imagination, the Consecration of the Eucharist. He watched with interest to see how the altar boys handled their part. He wanted it to be done right for Gram-ma. With a final genuflection towards the tabernacle, the priest descended with a chalice of Communion hosts. He was followed by the shorter of the altar boys who carried the gold-covered plate used to catch any bit of wafer which, now transubstantiated into the body of Christ, might drop from the out-stretched tongue of each believer.

All stood, except Jimmy, and filed towards the center aisle to approach the rail and receive Communion. He looked about for a way to sneak up and participate in the sacrament but quickly decided it would be pressing his luck, maybe even with God, since he shouldn't be here in the first place.

He again noticed the veiled woman who had been keeping her distance from the others. She too rose and went up to receive. Jimmy's eyes followed her as she knelt at the rail. She maintained some distance from the next person, the figure he'd decided was his father, who was glaring down at her.

When the host was placed on her tongue, she returned to her pew, circling down the side aisle at the end of which Jimmy hid. His father's eyes follow her even as he turned into the front pew. The distance was too great to read anything into his gaze. She continued on, passing into a beam of sunlight turned red by some saint's stained glass cloak. Even with her eyes appropriately cast down, her face was unmistakable.

Jee-sus, Mary and Joseph! *It's Ma!* Jimmy's thought exploded so hard he was afraid he had yelled it out loud.

His entire body flooded with panic and guilt. He tried to will himself still and slammed his eyelids shut, trying to become invisible, hoping the distance and dim light made him part of the shadow. Opening one eye, he saw Ma's back turn toward him as she reentered her pew and knelt back in the same spot. His panic drained to a tolerable level. He braved opening the other eye and stared at her solitary figure, hunched in prayer in the space between him and his unknown relatives. All of his life she had been the center, the rock around which all things family flowed. She was the source of gravity that held their lives, his life, together. It was through her eyes, through her words, he had learned to see himself and how to interact with the world. He watched her kneeling figure dressed in black like a small shadow between him and this unknown family. She seemed a lonely distant solitary planet. If the tabernacle was the sun, the center of her world, she was Pluto.

But she's supposed to be the link between me and those people up there, Jimmy thought. Unexpected anger rose. His thoughts careened crazily like a car on ice. Sure, *I lied when I snuck off… but I only did it because she never told me about them. Wasn't it a kind of lie if she never told me about those people, about my other family?* Yet hadn't she just last month on his birthday, sent him with Ed to see his father? *Why did she do that?*

It was way too confusing. He'd have to think about it later. For now, he had to decide what to do. The Requiem was coming to its close, and they'd be bringing Gram-ma back down the aisle. That would put him in full view if anyone glanced over his way. Checking to make sure all eyes were still forward, he slid out of the pew. Praying himself to be invisible, he quickly retreated.

Jimmy was back on the street before he'd finished buttoning up his coat. He knew he should move on quickly. He needed to beat Ma home. But his confused state of mind, mixed with knowing he'd never again see or talk to Gram-ma, kept him anchored to the sidewalk. He scanned the intersection. He scampered across the street to the southeast corner where he could stand in the partially shadowed entrance under the portico of the corner store. From there, a few minutes later, he watched Gram-ma's casket carried down the steps. The sight pushed Jimmy even further back into the shadow of the overhang. The pall was gone now. In the sunlight he made out the wood grain of the box as his father, uncle and four other men carried it. Gram-ma disappeared into the hearse and the driver closed the door.

Suddenly, his father turned away from the others and walked a few steps toward Jimmy, who couldn't back up any further without falling backwards into the store. He pulled his cap lower and held his breath. The way his father stared into the shadow where he stood, Jimmy was sure he'd been spotted. He simply looked back; there was nothing else to do. Other than the shadow, nothing but cold clear air and ten years of neglect lay between the boy and the father who wasn't sure of his own son's name.

For ten seconds, or maybe ten minutes or ten years, both stood still, just looking. Finally the world intervened in the form of a South Shore Motor Express truck followed by a string of autos. When the last vehicle passed, Jimmy saw his father take a couple of backward steps as he returned a handkerchief to his hip pocket. Then he turned and retreated to the waiting group of mourners. Jimmy finally let his breath out. *He didn't see me!*

Jimmy grabbed the opportunity and high-tailed it east on 18th. He circled the block at a trot and headed back towards Gram-ma's and the El station. After a bit, he slowed to a purposeful walk. He would need time to process what he'd seen and, more importantly, what he was feeling. He was thankful he'd not been brave, or stupid, enough to march up the aisle when he first got there and sit with his dad and his family. The thought of the look on Ma's face when she saw him was both scary and comical. Even scarier would have been the look on his own face when she called him out. There was nothing funny in that at all. His sense of panic eased by the time he walked one last time past the two-flat on Indiana. Knowing time was of the essence, he didn't break his stride and only gave a quick glance up at the doors behind which so much of his past had been secreted away until only a couple of months ago. A black mourning wreath hung on Uncle James' door.

He'd probably never be back here, unless Ma sent him for her money. He wondered if Ma regretted sending him last November with Ed. *Did she do it without thinking, like when Ed found her Baptism certificate, or was it a lapse in judgment? Did she really want me to meet him... or Gram-ma?* He'd been careful not to say anything about that first trip, and she had never asked. *Was that lucky...or on purpose?* Now that he knew a lot more, he felt the burden of knowledge increase. These silent secrets may be Ma's way, but they weighed heavy on Jimmy's young mind and shoulders. He pulled his coat tighter and increased his pace again.

He remembered Ed's warning not to mention any of this to Ma, but he had to sort his thoughts and questions out with someone. Of all his siblings, the only candidate was Mary. *I don't want to put any more troubles on her,* he said to himself as he pulled his cap down further against the chill. *I already asked her to cover for me today. She'll do it, but she'll be off to confession as soon as possible.* Mary was a good listener, but too young to know all this. Maybe he'd just have to risk bringing it up with Ed. *But for now, I need to get back to school.* The note he'd forged only excused him for the morning.

As the train jumped to life, Jimmy knew much had changed, he had changed, but he had no idea what any of it meant. The tumbling thoughts and images, sights and sounds felt too much. He was grateful the El car was mostly empty but for two women on the other end of the car. They couldn't see him because they were seated facing forward, happily chatting, while his seat faced backwards toward the past he'd just discovered and now lost behind a wall of silence. He squeezed his eyes as a tear trickled, one from each lid. He couldn't have said if they were from sadness or anger, frustration or loss. *No matter what, I won't blame Ma, or turn against her. Even if I never see "that man" again. He's not worth Ma's little finger to us. He should have died instead of Gram-ma.* Jimmy squeezed his eyes tighter, trying to hold everything in. He worked on burying his anger and confusion as deep as a coffin. Only a few more tears escaped. Not near enough to help.

Quigley

1922-24

Jimmy stood at the rectory door. The swaying leafy canopy of the two large elms standing sentry dappled the porch with dancing brushstrokes of sun and shadow. He tilted his ball cap back and wiped his brow with the back of his hand. The heat of the day exacerbated his edgy nerves. He wasn't sure why the monsignor had sent for him. He already knew he was serving 9:00 AM Mass on Sunday; he'd checked the schedule in the sacristy at the beginning of the month. Besides, he had never missed an assignment in the almost three years he'd been an altar boy. He'd even showed up that Sunday in seventh grade when a stomach virus attacked him late Saturday afternoon. The following week he got bawled out good when the visiting priest he'd poured wine for came down with the same bug.

The door opened and he was surprised when the bulk of Monsignor Cahill himself loomed above him. "Jimmy Cullerton, you're right on time as usual, lad. Come in. Come in."

Jimmy removed his cap and followed the priest to his office just off the foyer, where the priest settled behind a mahogany desk and pointed Jimmy to one of two matching upholstered chairs in front of the desk. "How are you, son?"

Cullerton knew the Monsignor's usual greeting was meant

rhetorically and not as an actual query. But he nodded to signify he'd heard the question and not appear rude.

The priest leaned forward and tee-peed his hands prayer fashion. He rested his chin on the tips of his index finger. His lips were pursed. Jimmy wasn't sure if he was thinking or sizing him up before delivering a dressing down. His stress level ticked up a notch. He sat up a little straighter and folded his hands around his cap so as not to fidget. After a few uncomfortable seconds, Father Cahill looked him square in the eye and said, "Now, Jimmy, I want to ask you something important. I know you'll think hard on this and tell me God's truth." Another pause caused a small trickle of sweat on Jimmy's neck. The priest lifted his head off his fingertips and asked, "What are you planning, Jimmy Cullerton...you know now you've graduated the eighth grade?"

Father Cahill had been Our Lady of Mercy's pastor for years, as long as Jimmy could recall. Like most priests in Jimmy's experience he could, on occasion, get his Irish up when provoked, but mostly he was even-keeled, a decent listener, and even told an occasional joke. He displayed just enough fire and brimstone on occasion so that his older parishioners were reassured that he carried sterner stuff in his spine should the need arise. All in all, adults accepted and appreciated him and his work. The parish church and school hummed along in the work of the Lord.

Most of Jimmy's friends, like kids everywhere, appreciated an authority figure that was good natured and friendly. They spent not a thought on the managerial duties a pastor might have. If asked, they'd have said the parish probably ran itself, like a lawn grew of its own accord, needing only occasional water and a cutting. They – again like kids everywhere – assumed everything outside their personal lives ran by some master plan requiring no cognition on their part. The older students, being wiser and more experienced, assumed things ran efficiently because the nuns wouldn't tolerate any fly in the ointment of Catholic education or worship. For the upper grade kids like Jimmy, there was another attribute that cemented Father Cahill into the "good guy" category. Every once in a while he pitched batting practice for the boys. He was pretty darn good too; Jimmy knew because pitching was his own claim to fame. It had earned him a place this summer on Alderman Buckley's city team where he got to pitch against all star teams from other wards around the North Side. *Maybe, that's it – he just wants to know how our team's doing?*

Although most would not be able to articulate it, Father Cahill was mostly appreciated by the older boys because he didn't pry into their private lives or put their faults or insecurities on public display, unless one was called on the carpet for behavior that went beyond what the good Sisters of Mercy felt comfortable dealing with.

While the question eased Jimmy's apprehension of having done something grievously wrong, it still put him off balance, like a batter facing an unexpected curveball rather than a straight fastball. "I'm doing good, Father. Sorry, I mean I'm doing well. But…I'm not so sure about next year yet. Money's pretty tight at home right now."

"Times are tough for sure, Jimmy. Your ma's doing a wonderful job, what with all of you, and her all on her own, and then the tragic loss of your…" the priest's voice trailed off. Jimmy heard his heart beat three times before Father Cahill picked up the thread by jumping to his main point. "But, Jimmy, this is what I'm really wondering. You've been one of the most faithful and serious altar boys I've known in my years here. Your ma's talked with me a few times, and got me wondering." He took a long inhale through his thick nose and put his finger tips back under his double chin as he exhaled and continued. "Have you ever thought God might have put The Calling in you, son?" Another curveball, this time over the heart of the plate. The monsignor continued, "I've been praying on this awhile, Jimmy. You may or may not know lad, but each pastor can nominate one of his boys for a high school scholarship to attend Quigley Seminary."

Jimmy's fingers edged his cap round and round between his knees while he processed the information. It took a few moments, but then without looking up he began to talk, or as his sister Mary said that evening when he told her about the interview, "You spilled your guts, didn't you?"

The cornerstone for Quigley Memorial Preparatory Seminary was laid in November of 1916 on Chestnut Street and Rush. The buildings were early French Gothic, anchored by St. James Chapel and its dazzling stained glass windows. Its first classes began in September 1918, but by 1922 when Jimmy enrolled, it had already crowded 600 students into a space built for 500.

Classes started promptly at 8:00 AM and the Rev. Francis Andrew "Doc" Purcell, the seminary's first rector, did not abide tardiness. When one was preparing to follow in the footsteps of such luminaries as Jesus, or the seminary's namesake, mere earthly discomforts such as snow, ice, cold, rain were not acceptable excuses. Quigley required students to attend daily early morning Mass in their respective parishes before school. Jimmy was up by 5:15 each morning to attend Our Lady of Mercy before catching the Irving Park streetcar at 7:00 AM for the ride to the lakefront campus. Throughout his freshmen year, this longest leg of his morning odyssey offered him some time to indulge his love of reading.

However, now in the spring of sophomore year, more and more frequently he found himself merely staring out the window, and even more alarmingly, falling asleep. At least twice in the last few weeks he would have missed his transfer, and faced the shame of having to hand over his demerit card to record the infraction, if one of the other regular passengers hadn't nudged him awake in time to disembark.

For awhile, he told himself he had just been lost in thought and prayer about his vocation. But the drain on him was evident. Always of slight build at five foot seven, he'd yet to reach 120 pounds. Ma and Mary thought he'd actually gone down a couple of pounds lately.

He valiantly tried to stay in harness, relying on his faith and desire to learn to face each day and all that needed to be done. After all, Quigley's motto was "Ora et Labora" – Pray and Work. But each day was becoming more grueling. Daily Mass offered solace, but the long days, crowded jostling hallways, demanding instructors and school work seemed to be catching up to him. He'd get home around 5:00 PM, help with chores, and go off to his bedroom to start his homework and study. After dinner it was straight back to his books, often until midnight or later.

Last spring, on warm evenings his younger brothers begged for him to come out and toss the ball around or pitch to them – something their father had never done with him or any of the boys. The temptation and regret on his face was unmistakable, but his purpose and work ethic were resolute. Only on rare occasions did he allow himself the escape of a Sunday pick-up game after mass. For Jimmy, his scholarship was a commitment, a solemn pledge to develop his "calling" and eventually make the lifetime commitment to service through the priesthood. Increasingly tired but resolute, Jimmy limped into summer break. He'd have some time to get his stamina back and evaluate his commitment.

Summer break at Quigley was a shorter respite than most high schools, and soon the start of his junior year loomed. The days waned, and so too did Jimmy's health. He fell into an unnatural listlessness attended by a hacking cough. Despite his protests, his decline culminated with a visit to Dr. Koonis. The diagnosis of early stage pneumonia in the days before penicillin was a sentence not to be trifled with – as the family had found in January of 1920 when they lost Richard to pneumonia brought on by the flu. The problem, of course, was that the required rest and quiet conflicted with the restart of classes. Monsignor Cahill again stepped in. After a long private talk with Jimmy and then with his mother, he suggested that a semester hiatus might be a wise move. His last pronouncement before leaving the house on Berteau Street was, "Jimmy Cullerton, you're to use the time to regain your health, lad. Pray for Divine Guidance and then abide by *HIS* decision."

It was the lowest and hardest point in Jimmy's life since Richard's death. He felt the burden of responsibility and commitment to the Monsignor and the seminary. But he also thought of the time he'd just been handed, time to think and to read, to let his body and mind rest, and to determine what both he and God thought best going forward. He caught only muffled snippets of conversation between Father Cahill and his mother as she saw him out. He felt himself fading off.

Mary took the opportunity to check on him, to see if he had anything to say outside of earshot of the adults. She stepped onto the back porch where Jimmy was resting, a wool blanket pulled up to his chin, on the summer lounger. He was already napping.

Birmingham, England

1944, September

"Private," the familiar voice came from a table at the far end of the bar. "Two more Guinness and scotch for the Major here?" The familiar voice penetrated his reverie. The night was slow. He'd been drying and stacking glasses while, for some unknown reason, thinking back to his two years at Quigley seminary. Surely he'd have been of more use as a chaplain rather than working in the postal unit and bartending in the officers' club?

Private Jimmy Cullerton acknowledged the order with a raised pointing hand. They outranked him, but at nearly age thirty-six he had several years on them and was not easily impressed or intimidated. Besides, the trio was well on their way to feeling as lousy as he had last Monday when he and a couple buddies spent too long at their favorite hangout, Queens Pub. He grabbed two clean pint glasses. He set his cigarette aside, exhaling into the already smoke-filled air, and tapped their beers, slowly giving each a proper pour, and letting them settle while he poured the scotch.

Private Cullerton set the liquor and then the draughts on a tray and walked them to the table, placing them in front of each. Captain Kivi was from Virginia, not far from Camp Lee where Jimmy had taken his basic training. Lieutenant Willard Leline was, like himself, from Chicago, though from the South Side. He and Jimmy enjoyed sparring back and forth over the Cubs and White Sox cross-town rivalry. He liked both men and knew they liked him. They often included him in their bar-talk and occasionally asked about the enlisted man's point of view on a variety of subjects, including the ubiquitous war rumors that swirled around the base and local bars.

Along side the two Americans was a UK Major, one Randolph Stewart. From the look of him, he'd apparently spent some time at his own Officers' Club before joining the Americans. "Here you go, Sirs. And may the road rise up to meet you."

As Jimmy turned to leave, Major Stewart spoke up, rather too loudly, "Cullerton, that's Irish if I'm not mistaken." A few heads turned at the bar, knowing where this might be heading.

"You're not mistaken, Major."

"Damn good people the Irish; that is, when they're not trying to foment revolt against the Crown, or killing each other. My father was there in Dublin you know, back in '16 during the laughable Easter Uprising. What a joke. Those Mick bastards got what they deserved, by God, if you ask me."

Jimmy knew something of the Uprising. He'd been just a kid, not yet eight years old and a third of the globe away in third grade. But the Chicago newspapers covered the story and he remembered hearing his mother and some parishioners vent about the murderous manners of England toward Catholic Ireland. He recalled hearing the principal participants had been shot, thereby – according to the Irish adults in his neighborhood – assuring the unrest would continue. Even back then, he knew first hand that the Irish were not big on turning the other cheek.

However, Private Jimmy Cullerton was not a fighter. As a middle child, he'd learned the value of diplomacy. His two years at Quigley Seminary, before deciding the priesthood was not something to which he could give his life, had solidified his nature as a reflective rather than reactionary man. Also, he'd done some part-time bartending before the war and he knew better than to get mad at comments by loud mouth drunks – especially when they outranked you. The extra pay helped, making life a little easier for his wife Julia and his mother back home in the small apartment they shared on Montrose. His tips let him get around a bit, take in some concerts and the historical sites that surrounded him here at every turn. So, it never crossed his mind to jeopardize the job over a random slur from a guy he'd never see again. On top of that, all the troops, especially those of Irish heritage, had been warned during transport to England not to rehash old scores with the Brits. "We're on the same side now."

Jimmy had no dog in this fight and let the remarks pass. "Yes, sir. I'm sure you'd know best."

Lt. Leline jumped in before Major Stewart could figure out if he'd been insulted. "Come on now, Major, don't we have enough to do yet with the Krauts? Besides, your job here, if you remember, is to explain why you Limeys think cricket holds a candle to baseball." Jimmy took the opportunity to move away, sensing more potential danger in getting involved arguing about the game he loved.

He lit another smoke and resumed cleaning and stacking glasses. To keep time moving, he thought of the sites he'd seen since landing here. He conjured up his trip to Staffordshire to tour the three-spired medieval Lichfield Cathedral and the day he spent at Warwick Castle. He sent Julia a postcard from each landmark, though he could never come up with more than a simple line, "Spent Wednesday here", or "Quite the place". He hoped the old adage "a picture is worth a thousand words" would suffice. He always just signed them "Jim."

He loved visiting historic places. He'd seen some of them in books. They gave him real pleasure and broadened his perspective on time. But the National Symphony concert at Birmingham Town Hall just two Fridays ago remained the highlight of his tour of duty here. He still had the ticket stub tucked away with his papers. It had been a first. He'd never heard a live performance by a symphony orchestra, only on the wireless or a few scratchy recordings. And what a concert. He'd sat on the ground floor, row K, seat twelve. He still remembered that. The power and drive of Beethoven had swept him up in rhythmic waves of melodic grandeur, moving him in a way he couldn't find words to express. In spite of the cigarette dangling from the corner of his mouth, he hummed the opening theme of the *Emperor Piano Concerto.*

Just before closing, after Major Stewart had drifted off into the night, Leline and Kivi moved to the bar for a nightcap and a proposal. "Jimmy, listen. The CO says we're heading over the Channel in a few weeks, to the Seine Section. He'd like some steady reliable types to manage the bar at the Officers' Club. You interested?"

"Paris? Sure! Notre Dame, The Louvre, I'd love that. But I'm in 1st Base Postal. How'd I swing a transfer like that?"

"They get mail in Paris too, you know. Actually, now that we got that Hitler son-of-a-bitch on the run most of it will start going directly through the mainland to keep up with the boys as they cake-walk into Berlin. We'll talk to the CO and see what we can do."

The Brandon Victory

1945, October 20

From the steel deck of the USS Brandon Victory, thirty-five feet above the ocean surface, the horizon lay just over seven miles ahead. As dusk morphed into night, the illusionary line in the west between sky and water quivered and then vanished in a wash of yellows and reds. The lingering sun, scissored in half mere minutes ago, slid into a kaleidoscope of its own creation, mixing and remixing its palette until it finally slipped the sky completely to fly ahead and announce their imminent arrival.

Standing at the rail, Private Jimmy Cullerton marveled at the spectacle. As a Midwest city boy, sunsets at sea were a treasure to be held forever. After a final moment of silent appreciation, he took a last drag and then flicked the butt of his cigarette into the Atlantic's darkness. He and his companion at the rail watched the glowing ash twist in the air and quickly disappear. Private Cullerton clung to the pleasure of the smoke in his lungs for an extra few moments before exhaling it slowly into the salt air. "You know, Lieutenant, a smoke up here on deck in the open air somehow tastes so much better than below deck." Such a thing had been impossible two years ago when they were heading in the opposite direction. Then the fear of German submarines had been very real. At night, ships ran without lights and smoking on deck was banned.

Lieutenant Leline had joined Jimmy at the rail to watch the sun's evening swan song. The remains of his Lucky Strike now followed Cullerton's overboard as he said, "In a week we're both civilians again, Private." Jimmy just nodded.

When the sun disappeared, most of the men retreated below deck to escape the cold and dark, to join the others and break out the cards or dice, to talk, to laugh, to argue away their last night at sea before again standing on home soil. "I'm going to stay up here awhile," Jimmy said.

"Mind company, Private?"

The two men found a spot to sit out of the breeze against the housing of the Brandon Victory's three-inch bow gun. Shortly after embarking in France, Jimmy's interest in all things mechanical had sparked a conversation with an off-duty engine mate and he'd learned the ship's short history. Its keel had only been laid in February 1945 in Baltimore and launched on the tenth of April. It was one of 534 newly built cargo vessels dubbed Victory Ships. Its name honored Brandon, Vermont making it one of 218 such ships named for American cities and towns.

At the moment the Brandon and her sister ship, the SS Robin Sherwood, were just eighteen hours out from making port in New York. Being in no great hurry, they cruised along at a comfortable twelve knots to save fuel and make for smoother passage – to the gratitude of the fifteen hundred troops crammed aboard. The steam turbine engines propelled the 455 foot length along, caressed and cradled by long slow waves. Between the two ships, 101 Chicago GIs would soon be back in civilian life, a mere fraction of the 24,000 troops reaching the home ports of New York, Newport News, and San Francisco that day.

For most, as they drew near to home, their theater of war and personal hells slowly retreated. Each nautical mile was a shovelful of present gratitude and enthusiasm tossed upon the graves of the war and of their recent personal pasts. But for many, being so long and far from home and love ones and fearing they may never again experience the simple pleasures of home life had led to some incident or indiscretion which meant they were carrying at least one regret, one shadow, hidden among their meager belongings. Private Cullerton was one of these.

Both men buttoned and pulled up the collars of their wool great-coats and pulled caps low against the night cold. They sat, quietly at first. Each pulled his mind inside to take measure.

For several minutes Jimmy's thoughts raced backwards in circles, bumping along like the steel ball on a roulette wheel. Each strike gave off a momentary spark of memory. The roulette ball froze in midair when a particularly bright spark illuminated the memory he'd just as soon forget. He'd been standing in The Louvre, first floor, beneath a large painting, *Liberty Leading the People*. As if she'd stepped out of the crowded painting, a woman stood hip to hip with him. He again smelled a scent of perfume and seduction and heard her whispered offer. *"Ah, the two things men love most, no? To fight for the noble cause… and a woman with large bare breasts. Which do you prefer, Private?"* He could almost feel her arm as she hooked it through his.

Lieutenant Leline spoke, "Looking forward to getting home, Cullerton?"

"Yes, sir. How about you?"

"I think we all are," Leline said. "But I can't shake the feeling we're all going to find the war changed us. For better or worse, we're all going to find we're not who we once were."

The statement made Jimmy probe, "So, Lieutenant, any regrets?"

"Maybe a couple, but none big enough to hang onto. How about you?"

For a moment Jimmy wished he hadn't asked the question, but immediately knew why he had. "Just one that sent me to confession."

"Ah, that's right, you Catholics can always confess and forget. Smart."

"Confess yes, but forget…not always."

"Is it something you want to talk about, Jimmy? After all, back in Chicago chances are we'll never see each other again."

Jimmy considered for a moment, "No, but thanks. I think I just wanted to say it out loud. By the way, Will, thanks again for getting me the Officers' Club job in Paris. The extra pay helped at home."

They both fell quiet again as the darkness settled around them.

The steel ball in Jimmy's head started up again, jumping now back several months to the sights, sounds, smells, and tastes of England. Eventually, however, the wheel lost inertia, slowing until it fell quiet. And there in the quiet was his wife, Julia.

He'd mailed her the official postcard before departure, letting her know he'd be arriving in New York on the twenty-first. He still didn't know exactly when he'd be discharged. *How many more days would it be?* He took a long breath and settled deeper into the memories – their wedding on a late November fall day, the eve, in fact, of his twenty-ninth birthday, and Julia but nineteen. They'd expected children to follow, but none did. Julia was disappointed. She blamed herself. He said he was disappointed too but knew he wasn't being completely honest. For five years they tried to start a family. Then came the war. Truth be told, he didn't mind trying something different and seeing some of the world, maybe jump-start things, maybe become a mechanic in the carpool.

But at age thirty-five and his post-office experience, he'd been tapped for similar work in the Army. Now, having seen some of southern England and the Seine Sector of France, he knew he was ready to settle back into married life and the city he knew. The future looked good. Julia and his job were waiting. Even his beloved Cubs had done well. Sure, they had just lost game seven of the 1945 Series to Detroit. But many of the best players were still in uniform and had not been on the field. "Hey Lieutenant, you think, since the Cubs were in the Series again, you might want to drop the White Sox and convert?"

Lieutenant Leline laughed into the dark. "Didn't you read what that Chicago sports writer said? They asked him to predict a winner before the series started. He said, 'I don't think either one of them can win.' Thanks for the offer, Cullerton, but I think I'll stick with the Sox. Their day is coming."

The Lieutenant continued, "Besides, didn't you see that *Chicago Sun* story a while back? Seems a guy named Billy Sianis – he owns the Billy Goat Tavern. I've actually had a few beers there. Anyhow, he tried to bring the tavern's name-sake goat, Murphy, to game four of the last Series. When they wouldn't let Murphy into Wrigley Field,

Sianis had to leave the goat tied to a stake outside. Made him plenty mad it seems. There's talk about Sianis and the goat having put a curse on your Cubbies."

It was Jimmy's turn to laugh. "Well, curse or no, I have no doubt that Wrigley Field will fly plenty more World Championship pennants in my lifetime."

Cupping the flame behind his left hand, as had become his habit, he lit another cigarette for himself and for the Lieutenant. They fell quiet again. Jimmy's thoughts looked ahead, to the near future, to Julia and the prospect, or at this point, the odds of having a family. This led to a mortifying recollection of the limited correspondence he'd sent her while away. Specifically the card he'd sent last November for their seventh anniversary came to mind. For a guy who liked words and read everything he got his hands on, he should have been able to add something more inspiring, more romantic to the pre-printed verse. What the heck, once upon a time he'd even dabbled with poetry.

Thinking back, he felt embarrassed. He knew Julia loved him, and two years of separation by ocean and war had reaffirmed that she was what he wanted. She knew and accepted, or at least put up with his quiet nature. He remembered – because she'd told him – how his sisters had warned her. "When it comes to Jimmy talking, you're lucky if you ever get more than a few sentences." His oldest sister had added, "But it's what you don't hear, honey, that keeps him steady and will keep you safe." But it was Mary's words to Julia that made him want to jump overboard in shame now, considering his lapse at the Louvre. Mary had said, "Jimmy's first instinct will always be to do the right thing."

His exhaled smoke quickly disappear into the night, his mind meandered back through their courtship, landing on the wedding, which, of course, was at Our Lady of Mercy. Julia's family consisted only of two aunts, a half brother and his wife, Ann, who was Julia's best friend and instrumental in her conversion to the Catholic faith. Everyone was there … *except my old man, and more importantly, my two older brothers.*

At that thought, Cullerton stared deep into the darkness and allowed his brothers' faces to rise-up. *Richard,* born Christmas Day,

1905. Ma used to call him God's Christmas present to her. *Dead in the eighth grade from pneumonia. Ma still wears black on December 25th. And Ed,* the oldest. He'd taken a promotion in '36, a year prior to the wedding, and was working for the Santa Fe line near Los Angeles. Ed was part of so many memories growing up. He'd been "the dad" in the family for the most part. He still remembered the day when they'd taken the El together and he met his father...and an unknown grandmother.

Huddled next to the lieutenant in the dark against the gun turret, Jimmy was surprised to find Ed's words from that day long ago still hiding in the way-back of his brain. The gentle roll of the sea lulled him into thinking he was safe, hunched there inside his warm coat. He foolishly replayed them inside his head "*trying to be manly... guilty... but not being a real dad... I hate him...*"

The phrases stumbled out in slow broken fragments. He felt the resentment that Ed must have felt. It still felt like a jagged knife in his belly. The anger dug deeper than he thought possible after all these years. His teeth and fists clenched. The taste of his father's betrayal rose like bile in his throat, amplifying his own betrayal. He scrambled to his feet and used the sounds and movement of the ship and ocean to steady himself.

Concerned by the suddenness of his friend's action, Lieutenant Leline asked, "Are you okay, Jimmy?"

Once he was sure of his balance, Cullerton answered as he anxiously reached into his coat pocket. "Yeah, sure. I'm okay. I must have dozed off and startled myself." He pulled out a cigarette and lit it. The familiar clicking when he opened and closed the lighter helped ground him. The sound had become as much of the ritual pleasure as the first drag. He repeated the motion using the sound as a mantra: open click...close – click... click...click...click... until the frantic pace of his mind slowed.

His nerves relaxed and he stood there, feet apart for balance and cupping the embers against a freshening wind coming off the starboard bow. The anger and nausea dissipated with the smoke as he exhaled into the night. He felt drained, like he'd vomited up something that had been eating at his gut. Relief replaced the rot, and then began to radiate slowly up, suturing the metaphoric wound in his gut. When it reached his brain, he felt steadier.

Lieutenant Leline stood. His eyes now adapted to the dark, he reached out and put a hand on Cullerton's shoulder. "Private...Jimmy, you're a good man. I'm sure you'll be good at whatever you do. I'm going to head below deck and finish packing my stuff for tomorrow. I'll tell you what, if there is ever a cross-town World Series, I'll look for you and we can go together." The two men shook hands instead of saluting.

When the lieutenant was gone, Jimmy took another drag and slowly blew the smoke toward the bow light, the direction of home and of his past and future. Now that the thoughts and feelings about his father had been opened, he wanted closure before getting home. He took in more smoke and stared at the lit end of his cigarette. It helped focus his thoughts. *I'm not Ed, and I'm not Ma. And that man is no more than a shadow.* One, as far as he could recall, had crossed his path but a handful of times. He'd let the man become a wizard behind the curtain like in that Judy Garland movie he and Julia had seen back before Pearl Harbor changed everything. But the curtain was pulled back now. He saw that "that man", the one who had affected so much of his life, so much of Ma's and his siblings' lives, was really only a humbug. Jimmy made a vow to himself. He'd refuse to keep shadow boxing with the past. He declared the battle and war he hadn't even known he'd been waging was over. He'd not speak of *that man* again.

The cold finally reached beneath his coat. It was time to go below deck and hope his bunk was unoccupied. He stretched and looked to the incredible sky where universes of stars had quietly revealed their existence while he had been engaged along that thin elusive battle line where past meets future. He cleared a loose piece of tobacco from his lower lip and flipped the butt overboard. He exhaled long and slow into the cold of the October night sky, blowing his thoughts ahead to Julia, and thinking of kissing her, maybe having children, and ignoring, at least for now, how he had no idea at all of how to be a father.

November 1, 2015

Dear Kevin . . .
It's been a long long time...

. . . It's hard dying, but the hardest part has been watching Tommi (she prefers Tomina, but I always call her Tommi, just like I did with Thomas). She is trying to put on a positive face. We've cried together and laughed and talked a lot. I told her stories from before she was born, about the early days and about Tommy and what was he like. I still have several of his drawings. Last month I was telling her that funny story about Tommy and you getting busted by a cop in sixth grade for smoking on the roof of the ice skating hut at Norwood Park (I was always thankful to you guys for not ratting me out and telling Mom that I was the one who gave you the cigarettes).

Anyhow Tomina's daughter, Samantha (Sam) -Yes, I'm a grandmother - noticed that whenever I told stories about my brother you were always in them. I was always jealous of the bond you two had – I didn't even have that with Tim – by the way we divorced when Tomina was seven. You should know that Tim was / is a good guy. We just weren't meant for each other. He was all work and I guess I wanted something else – something like you and Thomas had. Tim remarried a long time ago and moved to Texas. I'm very glad that Tommi and Sam have a relationship with him though they don't get to see each other much.

I'm going to lay down and rest for awhile. I'll finish this later.

January 18, 2016
(9:35 AM...)

Long ago consigned to the most out-of-the-way corner of his basement and life, the battered green metal file cabinet stood shrouded beneath an old discarded sheet. Perched on four house bricks, it appeared to levitate a couple of inches above the short-napped indoor-outdoor carpeting that covered the concrete floor. If noticed at all, placed there under the staircase as if to minimize casual interaction or scrutiny, one might think it a shadow, shod in old fashioned square-toed hobnailed boots.

A mere fifteen feet away and only minutes into his thrice-weekly workout on the elliptical, Kevin Cullerton was already reduced to mouth-breathing, having abandoned efforts to force air through his infected sinuses, while simultaneously attempting to ignore the clicking in his left knee. He hoped the joint would hold out another four or five years before discussing a replacement with his doctor. Maybe as a seventieth birthday gift to himself.

Since his retirement, it was disconcerting how often aches, pains and the contemplation of mortality impinged on his day. In an effort to fight back, Kevin – partially at his wife Nelson's insistence – finally decided he needed to "get a life", or at least fill this one with more activity if not substance. Hence, his current battle to coordinate breathing with flailing arms and legs, all the while feeling like a bludgeoned boxer, beaten and near collapse. Seeking a distraction, his eyes scurried about the basement, eventually alighting on the ghost-like relic exiled under the stairs.

Mausoleum, was his first thought. Then, in order to keep his mind occupied, Kevin conjured scenes of the multiple times he and his buddies had hauled the cabinet from apartment to apartment, then house to house. In each successive tableau the group appeared a little older and the cabinet a little heavier to bear. Each time, one or another of his friends would grunt, "This damn thing is heavy as hell! What you got, a body in it?" And each time Kevin only half-kiddingly replied, "In a way. It holds the story of my life, BN – Before Nelson. You know, for posterity."

The thing was, prior to marrying Nelson, Cullerton was obsessed with documents. He was constantly frustrated by his inability to remember the wheres and whens of his life and sometimes not recalling some things at all. If asked the years Beethoven published his nine symphonies, he could rattle them off – in order. But ask him when he had worked at the local paint store, or the year he graduated from college, or how much the cable bill was a year ago, he came up blank. So keeping records became his strategy. He had considered keeping a diary or just a notebook a couple of times but found it too big a commitment. A file cabinet was faster and easier. Not that he used the stored information very often; still he felt better knowing he could access it. At a deeper level he knew that the documents may well be the only proof that he had existed at all.

As he labored to breathe while keeping his arms and legs moving, he recalled acquiring the file. It had been partial payment for giving music lessons in the church basement of a tiny parochial school back in Chicago. Even then it was dented and scratched, already retired and forgotten. They had probably been glad to get rid of the thing. Ever since, it had sat in one corner or another of Kevin's life throughout his almost forty-year teaching career. Originally, it was a functional file. However, for many years now, it was just a buried archive, supporting newer forgotten miscellanea piled on top. He wondered how old it might actually be. What stories, beyond his own, did it hold?

Kevin looked down and checked the timer – *three minutes! Shit.*

His thoughts went back to the file and he tried to recall the contents but could only picture what was in the top drawers. He hadn't opened it since he and Nelson had bought the house a dozen years ago. *Time flies – he* thought, then glanced down again – *four minutes! Except when you're FUCKING exercising.*

Although it was probably not related – Kevin tried not to believe in direct divine interventions of any kind – his expletive was followed by a sudden sharp twinge in his knee, then by a rattling wheeze and a combination sneeze-cough shooting a painful flash through his upper sinus cavities. *That's all, damn it.*

He dismounted, rubbed his knee and gimped towards the corner. Stepping around the couch and ducking his head to avoid the stair risers, he folded back the sheet and pulled the top drawer open. Stuffed up as he was, he still noted a slight moldy smell from the tightly packed paper trail of his previous life. When they'd moved into this place, Nelson convinced him to banish the overfed old thing down here, and bought him a new smaller file for his office upstairs. Since the online world pushed to go paperless and most of his files were now stored on his hard drive anyway, he considered it a workable compromise, as long as the new file had three drawers. He needed the security of paper and refused to rely solely on electronic storage. After all, losing a part of his existence to a miss-hit "delete" button or hackers was a real (and growing) concern, at least in Kevin's head. For him, the threat of digitally induced Alzheimer's was scarier than the real thing.

Pushing the top drawer closed, he hooked a nearby plastic storage container with his foot and dragged it over so he could sit. Rummaging through the next two drawers, he found materials and paperwork reaching back decades to college, miscellaneous yellowed notebooks from miscellaneous old classes: *Music of the Baroque to the Romantic Era; Teaching Beginning Strings, Woodwinds, Brass and Percussion Instruments in the Elementary School; K-8 General Music;* and even grad-class texts on *Acoustics,* and *Composition: Form and Structure.* They shared the cramped space with hanging files of transcripts, resumes, paid bills, pay stubs, and other various scraps of his life and career. *Why did I keep all this crap?* But his mumbling was disingenuous. Kevin knew exactly why he saved much of it. What he used to tell his friends as they lugged the thing about carried a fair amount of truth. And even now, coming around the final turn of his life, he still harbored a small bit of his fantasy that some diligent biographer would someday scrutinize his flotsam to reconstruct his life because his existence had somehow mattered; because he'd done something worth remembering. This, however, was a part of his ego he preferred to keep secret, even from Nelson.

He moved on.

The cabinet's bottom drawer – nearest the floor and thus in greatest danger of oblivion due to a backed-up sewer or a hot-water tank malfunction – beckoned. It slid open easily, but somehow the action felt substantial, perhaps even consequential, like weighing anchor before setting sail. The musty smell of age had collected even stronger here in the cabinet's bilges. He felt like an archeologist breaking into a long sealed tomb.

Kevin began to excavate. The top layer consisted of a half-dozen musical scores: some original flute duets and wind quintets and an attempt at a Bartok-like string quartet, all written back in the late 1970s when he was studying composition. He tried recalling where and when he'd written each of them but came up blank. What he did remember was the feeling of joy and sense of accomplishment that came with the act of creation. He picked up a couple and scanned through the opening pages. From his current perspective, he recognized them for what they actually were: youthful imitations, unfulfilled fantasias. Music had actually been his second attempt at learning and mastering an artistic craft; the second time a creative passion had kindled, flared and been extinguished in his life; the second time he'd desperately tried to give birth to something beautiful, something that could live on its own. *Where had that youthful desire and hubris come from?* He had no answer. He did know fully well, however, where, when, and why each had died.

With music, the passion arose suddenly and late. It had propelled him in a completely unanticipated and unprepared for direction. Such *carpe diem* leaps were not Kevinesque, not generally in his nature – not then, and certainly not now. Life as a Cullerton was pretty much a straight line. Sure, curves and occasional detours were to be expected, but spontaneous trajectory changes were not in his character or experience. Nonetheless, after two years of liberal arts at nearby Wright Junior College, he'd abruptly enrolled to study and major in music at the North Side Northeastern Illinois campus. Since his musical background was minimal, consisting of a few guitar chords and a group keyboard class he had taken at Wright, his mom and dad naturally asked about this sudden educational digression. Kevin explained, that having no idea what he wanted to do, maybe he'd "check music out for a semester or two, while I decide. Besides," he added, "music is a lot like art and remember how I wanted to be an artist when I was a kid?"

His parents had kept their doubts unspoken. Probably preferring their son try out music rather than soldiering in Vietnam.

Now, looking back as an old retired music teacher, sitting on a crate in his basement, Kevin felt gratitude for his folks. They had been practical people who'd lived through The Great Depression and a World War. Yet somehow, a spark for the impractical must have survived in them, for they never tried to discourage him.

Luckily, the university's legacy as a former teacher college held pedagogy and general musical knowledge, not performance, as the school's mission. His lack of musical background and substantive talent was frequently discouraging and frustrating. But in the end, hard work, perseverance, and a piano teacher who nurtured his desire to understand the language of music and had patiently overlooked his technical limitations, got him through. And after three years, the school certified him as a teacher of music – if not a musician. Kevin thought that more than fair. At graduation, he walked across the stage thinking himself the poster child for the derogatory cliché, "Those who can, do – those who can't, teach". But walking off stage, diploma in hand, he thought, *"Hells bells,"* as his mother used to say. *Graduate, I did… and cum laude at that.*

Once he overcame the reality shock that teacher prep bore little resemblance to actual day-to-day teaching, Kevin found his stride.

He'd gone on and manufactured a successful and moderately fulfilling career as a middle-grades music teacher. He liked the kids (though often they'd remind him why he'd never wanted any of his own); he interacted well with colleagues and parents, and took pride in becoming a teacher, not just dispenser of directions and information. A friend had once said, "Having TEACHER carved on your gravestone is something to be proud of." He liked that thought.

However, along the way there had been casualties. Early on, his desire to create and compose music capable of evoking tears and joy had needed to be faced realistically – just as when he was a kid trying to draw pictures like his best friend Thomas. Each dream in turn had been euthanized and buried, but not forgotten. In fact, he still mourned both.

A sudden sneeze brought him back to the present. He set the musical scores aside and looked back into the bottom drawer. He saw a shirt box; the brand name was spelled out in cursive: Wieboldt's. The name sparked more rusty neurons, these tethered to his childhood. When he was a kid, Wieboldt's had been a large Chicago-land general merchandise retail chain. Its unpretentious stores – including one just a short bus ride away from Kevin's childhood house – were popular for their promotional S&H Green Stamps and in-store redemption centers. Their clientele were mostly middle and lower-middle-class women, like his own mother, who couldn't easily access nor afford the fancier downtown big-name retailers.

The box was tied shut with rough straw-colored twine. He stared blankly with pursed lips and furrowed achy brow, until his mind snagged a memory, one in which his mother was handing him this very box. It was the day he moved into his first apartment, about a year after his dad died. He couldn't recall opening it, but surprisingly thought he knew what it held. And although long ago his parents' voices had evaporated into the past, he fancied he could almost hear his mother ticking off its contents: "Some things you might need or want some day...report cards, your baptismal rosary, immunization records…"

Back then, none of the items held much tangible meaning to him. He was a young man with his eyes fixed forward and, at the time, with no interest or experience in looking backwards. So the box remained unopened. Now, a lifetime later, the urge to look back felt visceral and insistent.

The box, indeed this whole excavation, buoyed his spirits. He dismissed any residual thought about getting back on the damn elliptical. Instead, he lifted the old box from the drawer. The cardboard felt uncomfortably similar to his own skin in the cold dry winter air. He stood and coughed – undoubtedly from the mold spores he'd dislodged over the last half hour. Getting up required several seconds of willing his knee and back to return to vertical. He stepped around the couch and eased himself down onto it, the leather murmuring its comforting moan. He placed the box on his lap. The twine scratched at his fingers as he undid the knot. Reflexively he thought of his mother, feeling belated gratefulness for her meticulous ways and attention to detail, ironically the same traits which caused him regular frustration growing up. He lifted the top with anticipation.

He found eight report cards, one from each year at Holy Gospel Elementary. They were clipped together and, of course – bless his mother – in chronological order.

He glanced at each teacher's signature, trying to put a face and memory to each. All he could remember of his first grade nun was she had pulled his ears for whispering during reading group while they were sitting on the little chairs at the front of the room. He was quite sure he was in the B*luebird* group and not an *Eagle* or *Buzzard.*

Mrs. Ryan, his second grade teacher, still brought a kindly face to mind. He felt, more than remembered, he'd been "in love" with her. He remembered, for the first time in decades, that it was in her second grade he'd met Thomas. They'd become as inseparable as two seven-year-olds who lived a mile and a half from each other could be. The thought stopped him. He waited to see if the pain would come. After a full minute, he decided it wasn't.

He shuffled his third and fourth grade cards to the bottom of the stack, and then stared at his fifth grade report card. He opened it slowly and looked at his grade for art class, C+. The only grade not at least a B or an A. His art teacher had written "Tries hard."

Part 2

Kevin
1960-1969

June 15, 1960

As of that very Wednesday, the day before the last day of fifth grade, Kevin knew only two other dead people. One was his mother's ancient aunt. Her wake was the first, and to date only, he had ever attended. He had actually touched her cold rubbery hands on a dare from a distant cousin. The second was Jesus. Of course, he had never really met Jesus, but due to the hundreds of hours of religion classes and masses he'd sat through he certainly knew a lot more about Him than he did about his great-aunt. And besides, Jesus had been murdered dead. That made him a lot more interesting than an old lady he'd only met a few times when he was little.

Kevin was pretty sure that Mr. Thom hadn't been murdered. But now, three years after first hearing about him, he still didn't dare ask Thomas any questions about his dad, just in case. He was protective of his friend's feelings. Even with people he didn't like, Kevin was careful with what he said. He'd learned feelings got bruised and confused real easily. He knew he didn't really have a good grasp on being dead. Any time he thought about Thomas' dad, or Jesus, or even Great-Aunt Ida, it was like trying to stand on water. It was unsettling, like he'd lost something but couldn't remember exactly what.

Kevin was holding the Father's Day card he'd made so Thomas, who was in line just behind him, wouldn't see it. The cards were the ritualistic last art project of the school year because Fathers'

Day was the Sunday right after school got out. Except Thomas didn't have a father. He seemed content to make a Father's Day card for his mother. Still, since second grade the project had bothered and embarrassed Kevin.

The class was snaking its way back up the stairs from their late morning art class held in the dimly fluorescent lit basement beneath the old church. Peter and Marty, who'd been goofing around and causing a ruckus in class, were left under the supervision of the sole lunch-mom to wash down the brown utilitarian folding tables on which they'd just been working. No surprise there. Kevin didn't much care for either boy, or anyone who tried to get attention by acting out or being snotty or mean.

The tables doubled as the lunch tables for those students, like Thomas, who lived more than a mile away and ate their bag lunch at school. Living only three blocks away, Kevin had to walk home for lunch. Walking was the only option because a mile was the magical distance required before students were allowed to ride their bikes to school. There was no sneaking either. The nuns had an unfailing eye and memory for matching bikes to faces of kids on the "Bike List." Any mismatch was quickly apprehended and parents were summoned.

Kevin's section of the line made the turn in the stairwell. He pretended to be straightening his uniform tie while whispering back over his shoulder to Thomas, "We still okay for Friday night?"

"Mr. Cullerton!" Sister Ellisa's hawkish voice fell upon him from her perch at the top of the stairwell. It hit like a cold bucket of water. Sometimes, if she was really mad, it could feel like the water was still in the bucket when it hit you. "I would think an aspiring altar boy like yourself would possess enough discipline to walk back to the room in silence."

"Yes, Sister. Sorry." He knew Thomas behind him was struggling to keep a straight face. From the back of the line, which had not yet made the turn onto the stairs, he heard a soft but not unkind giggle. It was Dory, Dolores, the girl whose olive skin, brown eyes, and developing breasts he sometimes found himself staring at in class; and her friend Arlene, who he definitely could do without. Kevin's usual blush crept up from his collar. God, he hated that.

"Got'cha," Thomas whispered when they topped the steps, and he could see Sister Ellisa's back now safely up at the front of the line. "And yep, we're still on. Mom's going to get a pizza for us."

June 17, 1960 (AM...)

At first, he thought it was the sun tugging him into consciousness. Being the very first day of summer vacation, he fluffed his pillow and rolled over. But the distant rumbling and metallic squealing reached into his knotty pine bedroom at the back of the small frame house and into his dreams. It came in irregular intervals on the breeze like distant waves. There it was again.

Curiosity piqued, he got up and sleepily padded barefoot across the kitchen linoleum and living room carpet to the front door. Opening it, the mildness of the morning and the curious noises rushed in together through the screened storm door. He clearly detected a crunching and chewing underneath the rumbling and scraping sound which funneled like a bowling ball straight down the street which terminated directly at the Cullerton's front door, where it formed a T- intersection with his street. Standing in his summer pajamas in the tiny entry hall, his senses finally fully wakened, the source became very apparent. Trucks – big ones – and bulldozers. He rushed back to his room and quickly pulled on his jeans, a tee shirt, and tied on his Keds sneakers. He was heading out the back door when his mom, still in pajamas and robe, came out of her bedroom. "Kevin? Hold on. Where do you think you're headed so early?"

"Mom, there's construction going on up the street. I gotta go see what's happening! I'll be careful and stay out of the way," he added preemptively.

"Oh, that. Okay, but walk your bike across Higgins, and look both ways," she said to his back as he half skipped, half jumped down the four wooden steps of the back porch his dad had rebuilt last summer. Five long strides had him across the postage stamp-sized back yard. He undid the clasp and opened the door. The small white shingle-sided enclosure was more shed than garage. A young blue spruce Dad had planted alongside was still too small to even screen the garbage cans. By comparison, it made the building appear larger than it was in reality, but it was clear that eventually the tree would overtake and dwarf it. If they owned a car – and they didn't – it would have to be a Volkswagen Beetle to fit through the low single overhead door facing onto the gravel alleyway.

Inside, his dad's home-made workbench occupied the space below the rough-cut window. A ten-inch vise was attached to the right corner. Two handsaws, a Stanley Shortcut saw and a Metropolitan twenty-five inch cross-cut, lay on the bench, both with sawdust clinging to their teeth from the current remodeling project. His father spent most weekends finishing, reshaping, updating and fixing. Kevin's Flexible Flyer sled hung by its steering bar from two nails pounded into the rough studs of the west wall. His pride and joy, his red Schwinn, and a dented wheel barrow, were the lone occupants of the floor.

Kevin was relieved to see his front tire tube, which his dad had helped him patch, was still holding air. He maneuvered the handlebars carefully through the narrow doorway he'd just entered so as not to smash his fingers against the jamb – a lesson he learned the hard way more than once. Rushing down the gangway, he closed the chain-link gate with a forceful backward push with his foot, only to hear it bang right through the locking mechanism. *Figures,* he thought, as he impatiently leaned his bike against the house and went back. He gave the gate a cursory pull to secure it. *Why bother, what are we trying to lock in…we don't have a dog or anything.* Then he was off.

For two blocks he pedaled the balloon tires up the incline of the street. At Higgins, he dismounted, keeping his promise as he always tried to do, and ran his bike through a gap in the morning traffic. Once across, he remounted and hurried along the sidewalk flanking the tan brick wall of Ted's Pharmacy. The sound and fury were now just ahead, drawing him like a moth to a light. At the end of the block, he jammed his right foot in reverse on the pedal brakes, sliding his bike to a stop. He gaped at the scene unfolding before him.

Fixated on the action, Kevin set the kickstand and eased himself down on the curb overlooking the excavation in progress. Elbows on knees and hands covering ears against the roar, he watched, trying not to blink in spite of the dust in the air and was quickly lost somewhere between the cacophony of chaotic sounds and the silence of his own puzzlement and curiosity.

Kevin had no idea how long he sat and watched. Ten minutes, twenty? At first each sight was its own individual event. Huge machines belching black diesel smoke ripped at the earth. They dropped huge bucket loads into one giant dump truck after another. Tandems of side-by-side bulldozers pushed dirt and gravel. Dust rose and rolled in great quantity and mingled with the sounds and smells of the powerful engines overwhelming the very air as well as Kevin's senses. Luckily, they mostly drifted towards the west, leaving Kevin's position on the south bank of the action tenable.

Across the maw through the haze, smashed and smoldering heaps of several houses were visible. More bulldozers and trucks crushed and carried away the remaining homes standing above the excavation. There was an army of workers next to and inside of the machines. They looked like ants, climbing and pointing and waving at each other.

"Kevin? Kevin Cullerton?" He thought he heard his name somewhere within the other noises. He jumped when he felt a hand on his shoulder and turned to see Ted Sr. "Hi, Kevin. Sorry to startle you," the old man half shouted as it was apparent in the din the boy hadn't seen or heard him approach. With his usual grin in place Ted hollered, "Good morning. Quite a project and racket isn't it? I was just on my way to open up the store when I spotted you sitting here."

Kevin jumped up and questions burst out of him like a ruptured water main. "Do you know what's going on? Why are they knocking down those houses? What's this huge ditch they're digging for?"

The old pharmacist leaned in to catch Kevin's words then, pushing his thick black glasses back up his nose, surveyed the scene which spread out like a battlefield. His head made slight side-to-side movements as if to protest the project. "They're finally out this far," he bellowed against the noise towards Kevin. "They call it the Northwest Expressway. It'll connect downtown," Ted looked and pointed east, "and will reach all the way out to O'Hare Airport." He pointed west out beyond the end of Kevin's known world.

"Expressway?" Even as the word left his mouth, Kevin worried he sounded dumb. Ever since the humiliation last winter when his teacher had announced out loud he'd written "take it for granite", instead of "granted", he'd become particularly sensitive about sounding stupid. But this was too big not to ask. Gratefully Ted Sr. didn't blink an eye or hesitate in responding.

"Express, you know, as in 'fast.' Everybody wants everything to be fast now days. It'll have three lanes in each direction and handle lots of cars at one time with no stoplights. Supposedly, someday the trains will run smack down the middle out to the airport. Then your dad will be able to get downtown a lot faster than now." Ted Sr. paused and looked over the sight, perhaps pondering the effect of the new road on his business, perhaps seeing the world move past him and towards the future. Kevin detected a hint of something in his gaze that looked sad. "Some things get pushed out of the way. Others just get lost and forgotten."

He put his hand back on Kevin's shoulder. "Well, I better go open the store." He gave a gentle squeeze and smile and set off. "Say hello to your mom and dad."

Alone with his thoughts, Kevin remained standing. Armed with this new information he looked back again over the entire scene. What at first had seemed like random chaos, individual tableaus of workers and actions, began to make some sense. He left his bike and carefully stepped around the scattered stakes and small flags pounded into the ground. He got as close as he could to his edge of the dig. The channel extended as far as he could see back into the morning sun while simultaneously, slowly but inexorably, eating its way westward.

A single word flooded his head. *Downtown*! Ted Sr. had said, "Dad will be able to get downtown faster." Kevin knew, of course, his dad worked downtown, at the main branch of the post office. But it just now dawned on him he'd never thought about where downtown actually was, or what it might entail "to go downtown". His entire world consisted of the quiet streets – mostly lined with young trees too small to cast much shade or shadow – surrounding his house and Holy Gospel School and Church. At most, sometimes they took a bus or taxi to one of his uncles' house. They'd never gone on a vacation like some of his friends did every summer.

In his inner ear he heard the mocking sarcastic voice he only used on himself… *Dad gets up every day in the dark and then comes home for supper at 5:00 and I don't even know what he does, where he goes, or how he gets there?* The "dumb kid" feeling he hated flared again. It was quickly extinguished when an even bigger consideration, a personal epiphany took hold – *Dad has a secret life – one I don't know diddly-squat about.*

The realization startled Kevin as much as Ted Sr.'s sudden touch on his shoulder had. And similarly, it had snuck up on him out of the surrounding noise and chaos – both within and outside of his head. It was one of those childhood moments that hit at different times, at different ages and in different ways and eliminates the possibility of ever going back.

Unraveled by the thought, Kevin felt something open up deep inside and out came a long-ago memory. He was holding his mother's hand amidst the loud screeching and clacking of trains coming and going from a station on a hill, beyond a tall chain-link fence. *Were we waiting for Dad to come home from downtown?* His thoughts skipped to his dad's favorite movie in which a young Dorothy had to follow a perilous yellow brick road through Oz on her way to the *Emerald City* to meet with the great Wizard and get back home. He'd try to remember to ask his dad about all of this tonight.

His breakfast-less stomach rumbled and gurgled, breaking the spell. With a mere blink of his eyes, his imagination and memory flipped back into the reality of the construction site. But before leaving, Kevin again scanned the expressway being born right before his eyes. A conflicted tension began to rise inside of him, but faded before it could topple into his consciousness. He retraced his steps, reclaimed his faithful bike and headed home, wondering why neither dad nor mom had told him about all this. *They never tell me anything.* He tried to recall what he was going to ask his dad about, but it was gone just like the scoops of earth and old houses.

His mind shifted forward in anticipation. School was out, it was summer and after lunch, Mom was letting him bike over to Thomas' house. Things were looking pretty darn good. He was going to stay overnight, and tomorrow morning Thomas' uncle was letting them ride along – all the way to Indiana. He was excited. He'd never been in a different state before.

When he got home he saw that even with two tries the gate was not completely closed, the lock not completely set. He tapped it open with his front tire. He could feel his world expanding.

June 17, 1960
(...PM)

Kevin pedaled east. The asphalt offered minimal resistance. The midday sun, unencumbered by clouds, was behind him. Its touch on his thin bare arms and the back of his neck was in perfect balance with the gentle breeze. His focus was on the foreshortened shadow racing in front of him. Leaning left then right, gliding his bike in a lazy, wavy S-shape pattern, he playfully tried to catch the backend of the flat darkened image of himself. It stayed just beyond his reach.

He waved, forcing the shadow to reciprocate and acknowledge his presence. A paper shopping bag from the local A&P hung from the handlebars, creating an awkward shadowy appendage. Inside was his most recent sketch book, a color pencil set from his birthday back in the spring, and his Eddie Mathews' signature baseball mitt, along with some overnight things, including *The Hardy Boys' Detective Handbook*, which he'd just started last night.

Accepting that shadows can only be seen and never caught, he straightened his trajectory. The slow, steady pumping of his legs felt good. He could keep this up all the way to Thomas' house, especially since he'd be coasting down the only significant hill he'd encounter. His eyes swept along both sides of the street. When not pressed by time or the elements, he liked to checkout the houses and consider what secrets lay within. There were a few scattered older wooden or shingle-sided homes like his, but the majority was post-war, dormered, brick houses built in an unostentatious style and common to the extremities of Chicago. For the first block or so, Kevin knew a story, or at least a face, for each dwelling. Beyond that, his route was like a realtor's catalogue – facades without context, houses unconnected to his life with no link to his reality. Only the sporadic home of a schoolmate allowed his imagination to again picture the life within.

What intrigued him most were the few remaining small outdated abodes. His favorite was set well back from the street as if seeking separation from the here and now, from day-to-day goings-on. It was a ramshackle, brown shingled cottage, and it always sparked his imagination. A mailbox jury-rigged to a wood post at the sidewalk identified the owners as Aufenbach. This lonely anachronism had caught Kevin's eye the first time he passed it. All the other houses, including his, had mail slots in or adjacent to the front door. But this aged receptacle seemed a lonely sentinel, an odd portal though which the daily mail passed between the present and past. It stood stoically, separated by the much newer sidewalk from its owners and the weathered, shadowed, stone pathway winding toward the back of the lot through and under ancient-looking pines.

Kevin had never seen an Aufenbach. He pictured them as being as old as their home. Peter Biggert, who lived the next block over, enjoyed telling everyone that the Aufenbachs were probably old Nazis, escaped here after the war. He'd amuse some of the other boys by recounting how he would sometimes sneak up behind the cottage and lob stones at the back door, pretending they were hand grenades. He even bragged that his parents approved, saying, "If two world wars taught us anything, it's you can't trust the Krauts."

Kevin instinctively and specifically disliked Peter, not only because he said and did stupid things, but also because he frequently picked on other kids. Biggert was slightly shorter than Kevin but had ten pounds on him. He was constantly wisecracking in some nasty way about somebody's height, weight, stutter, glasses, or anything else he thought would get him a cheap laugh. Like the time he tried to label Kevin and Thomas as *The Bobbsey Twins*. That got

Biggert a bloody nose and Kevin an afternoon in Sister Jeanette's office followed by three days of house arrest that lasted through the weekend. He had been surprised by his sudden outburst of violence. But the confinement gave him time to reflect and he wondered what else was in him he didn't know about.

For more than a year now, each time he passed Aufenbachs, Kevin promised himself some day he'd stop and collect the sentinel's messages and carry them up the path through the trees. He pictured himself knocking on the door, handing over the mail and saying, "Hi, I'm Kevin Cullerton. I love your neat mailbox and can you tell me about the old days around here?" When he was leaving, he'd remember to say, "Oh, by the way, if you hear stones hitting your back wall, it's Peter Biggert who lives in that red house behind you. He's a creep, so you should probably call the cops." But until he built up the nerve, he'd try (again) to remember to ask Dad and Mom if they knew about the Aufenbachs.

He approached the corner where his street ended and he'd turn south. Kevin braked when he saw two newly poured foundations. The smell of curing concrete was strong. He assumed they must have been poured just this morning. The crew was gone and he knew they would not return for several days until the cement was cured and they could begin to build the walls. New houses popped up every summer. Soon there'd be no lots or open fields to explore or play in. But for now, he and the other guys in the neighborhood would have two more construction sites to themselves in the summer evening. From excavation, until locks were put on the doors, they'd play tag and gather scrap wood and bent nails and explore every nook and cranny. He pictured last summer when "Rip" Repileski's leg had suddenly materialized through the new ceiling plasterboard when he slipped while hiding up in the rafters. Kevin made another mental note to return and check these new foundations later with Thomas.

He started up again and glided around the turn, watching his shadow gradually rearrange itself of its own accord onto his left side. For the second time that day the *Wizard of Oz* came to mind. This time it was the black and white scene in which the nasty Miss Almira Gulch furiously pedals along not knowing Dorothy's dog

Toto has already escaped from the basket on the back of her bike.

Arriving at his friend's gabled red-brick just after 3:00, he glided his faithful Schwinn onto the narrow walkway alongside the house. The side storm-door screen was down and the interior door open to catch the breeze. He raised his voice just enough to be heard. Calling always made him self-conscious. "Yo, Thom-as."

A pleasant female voice responded, "Hi, Kevin. Put your bike in back and come on in. The door's open."

He walked his bike to the yard and stood it next to the garden hose neatly looped around a rack attached to the back wall. Just in case it should fall over, he made sure it was a safe distance from the young tomato plants Thomas' mom had sunning in pots. He retraced his steps and shyly entered, saying, "Hi, Mrs. Thom. How are you?"

Immediately in front of him were stairs leading to the basement. Just to his left two steps led up to the kitchen where Mrs. Thom sat at the table. Her sleeveless light green housedress perfectly fit her smiling face and the warm day. "I'm fine, Kevin. Thank you. How are you?" she asked in return. "Are you as glad as Thomas to be out of school for the summer?"

Kevin thought Mrs. Thom was pretty. He wondered if it was wrong, or just weird, to think that, so he never mentioned it to anyone, not even Thomas. He knew that the dead Mr. Thom must miss her. He felt his face flush. Looking at the floor he hoped that she couldn't read his mind. He said, "It's great to be out, but I hope me and Thomas are in the same room again next year."

"It looks like you've been outside. I can see you've got some sun already." She smiled, lifted her coffee cup and arched her brows toward another set of stairs just off the kitchen. "Thomas is upstairs in his room. Why don't you take your bag on up. Pat went to the store to get pop and chips and later I'll get a pizza for dinner."

Pat was Thomas' older sister by two years. She was popular and usually out with friends. She was always nice to them when she was home and obviously liked her brother. Sometimes she'd pass along messages from Mrs. Thom but always like a friend would, not like a bossy mom the way some older sisters did. Kevin sometimes got the feeling that Pat was observing or studying them. Not like they were bugs under a magnifying glass but like she was trying to figure out or decide something. It never crossed his mind that in a few years her breasts would be the first he'd ever touch when she "accidentally" guided his hand to her chest under the diving raft at the eighth grade picnic at Cedar Lake.

"Thanks," Kevin replied to Mrs. Thom. Paper bag in hand, he headed up the carpeted steps. As he climbed he remembered how he and Thomas had first become friends back in Mrs. Ryan's second grade class. They had bonded over a mutual interest in drawing. More accurately, Thomas was really talented, and Kevin wanted to be. While most kids used circles and rectangles to represent themselves and their family, Thomas was already drawing recognizable faces.

Kevin reached the top of the stairs. He remembered how even way back then, Thomas had – unlike the three Toms in their grade – always used his given formal name and not the diminutive. "Thomas" sounded grown-up, solid. Kevin liked that about his friend, especially since he never felt that way himself. Even Mrs. Thom called him Thomas. Everyone did, that is except for his sister Pat. To her, he was Tommy, and that was that.

"Hey, Mr. Thomas," Kevin announced is arrival and sauntered into his friend's room at the end of the hallway. Perhaps to counter Pat's informality, Kevin had started occasionally adding the honorific of "Mr." to his friend's given name. He couldn't recall if he'd made it up or had gotten the idea from some book or TV show. He was careful to use it sparingly and never when others were around. He didn't want to wear it out – or share it. It was how he showed respect for his one real friend, a respect that he hoped to earn some day for himself.

On the other hand, he also thought it a rather clever play on his friend's name – a private pun between them. Kevin took words and puns seriously and except when with Thomas, he tended to keep them to himself. On the school playground, he'd learned that words could have a decidedly unpleasant use. And at home, his mother used words kindly, but mostly in a functional fashion: "Dinner's ready. Time to come in. Is your homework done?"

His dad though, had a quiet but serious relationship with words. Mr. Cullerton loved to read and work crossword puzzles. Each evening he'd finish his *Daily News* puzzle after the CBS news. His well-thumbed crossword dictionary always sat next to his chair. It had been a birthday gift from Kevin and Mom. However, Dad's love of words was mostly confined to the written word, not the spoken. While his parents were not overly serious people, Kevin couldn't remember either Dad or Mom telling a joke or even a story. Conversations were nonfiction. When the past tense was used, it was pretty much kept to how their day had gone. A true child of his parents, Kevin learned to keep his words and puns, and therefore his thoughts, close to the vest.

Thomas' room was bigger and sunnier than the knotty pine rectangle which Kevin occupied at home. A large dormer and two windows allowed plenty of afternoon light. Beneath the dormer was a dresser which served as a night stand for the twin beds that it separated. A reading lamp stood at each end of the dresser like miniature bookend light houses. Kevin thought it was really cool that even though Thomas was the sole occupant, there were two beds, and he'd come to think of the additional bed as his own.

Thomas sat at his desk under one of the side windows. His left arm danced over the surface, through sunspots and shadows. He glanced up at Kevin. "Rest your bones a bit," he said nodding at "Kevin's" bed. "I just need to finish this part. I'm trying something new. I'll be done in a minute." His glance moved back to a photo tacked to the cork board just above his desk. He seemed to be absorbing it. Then his hand and elbow again skated in smooth fluid motions. Kevin couldn't tell whether the hand or arm was leading. They seemed a single unit with a life separate from the rest of his body. This always looked odd to Kevin who drew with his hand only.

Thomas' eyes flitted between the sporty car in the photo and the paper on the desk. Even though he couldn't see Thomas' face, Kevin knew the tip of his tongue would be just barely protruding from the left corner of his mouth as it always did when he drew. Kevin tossed his bag on "his" bed and then looked over his friend's shoulder to see the magic happen. He immediately spotted the something new going on. Thomas added a few strokes, some new, some darkening previous lines. Then his right hand twisted the sketch completely upside down and he lightly added a shadow, then he twisted the paper again to add to the background, then to the foreground. Kevin was familiar with how Thomas jumped around on the paper, never spending more than a few moments on any section. It was as if he put down the entire image at the same time, coaxing each section to grow into the others. But this was the first time that he'd seen this strange twisting of the paper left then right then upside down, then back again. He wanted to ask about it, but knew better. You don't ask questions in the middle of a magic show; you just watch in awe. In moments like this Thomas was "Mr. Thomas."

Thomas drew everything, but lately he'd become fascinated by cars. Car photos from magazines and his drawings of them had taken over one corner of the room. The current photograph on the cork board was a '57 Thunderbird convertible posed on a polished tiled showroom floor under bright lights. But what was emerging on the paper was an animated thing, coming alive, in motion, speeding along a curved city street to some mysterious location around the next corner and off the paper's surface. The illusion of speed accelerated each time Thomas twisted the paper. Kevin watched in silent appreciation. *It's amazing, he's amazing. Is that how God made things even… when He made his dad die? That would be a big price to pay.*

There was something else too, something Kevin was suddenly aware of but didn't want to feel – a seed of sadness. It fell heavily on a place of doubt deep inside of him. It wasn't exactly jealousy, at least not completely. He was truly happy that his friend had such talent. It was an understanding, a lump, a fat slab of reality he'd not tasted before now.

This is what real talent looks like. Thomas has the ability to make lines and shapes that speak louder and bolder than words, to make images that forced people to look and listen and pay attention. And that was the problem. Kevin could listen; he was a good listener, but he'd never be able to enter the places Thomas could go or to make people pay attention. He'd never be more than a "wanna-be" and a stutterer in the language of images. He'd always be outside, looking in. He felt his ambition being yanked like roots from the soil. He was surprised how much it hurt.

Thomas stopped. He looked at his work and tossed his pencil down on the desk. He turned his full attention toward Kevin and smiled. "There, that's enough. Sorry for that. Did you bring your sketches and pencils? Let me see what you've been up to?"

"No. Um…a…" Kevin lied. "I got in a hurry and forgot them. I brought my mitt, though. Let's play catch. I gotta tell you what I saw this morning." He quickly turned and fumbled around in his bag so Thomas wouldn't see the shame in his face.

The summer solstice was only days away, and daylight hung around well into the evening. Thomas' uncle was picking them up early tomorrow. Mrs. Thom urged them to bed not long after the day lost its fight against the dark. The boys talked for a bit, but Thomas faded quickly and turned off his light. "Good night, Kevin. We're going to have a great summer. Thanks for being the best friend a guy could have."

Kevin picked up his book, but found he was just staring, resisting entering the world of the young detectives Frank and Joe Hardy, and their world of fiction. He felt stuck in this world of unwanted facts and revelations. He told himself he really didn't want to read anyhow. Turning off his light, he rolled onto his side and stared into the darkness for some time before falling asleep.

June 18, 1960 (AM...)

The boys were more than ready when Uncle Bob pulled up to the curb in his boxy green Chevy station wagon, a perfect vehicle for Uncle Bob who also was built like a box, or at least a five-foot-six rectangle. This puzzled Kevin. His dad's brothers all looked somewhat alike and had similar builds. Uncle Bob and Thomas' mother, Mrs. Thom, looked nothing alike, until he smiled – which he did a lot. Their eyes and mouth made it clear they were indeed siblings.

Before the gearshift hit PARK, the boys were halfway into the seats, Thomas shot-gun and Kevin in back. "Hold on," Uncle Bob said, "You guys want to ride in the boot?"

Thomas jumped at the opportunity. "Absolutely! That would be cool." His uncle walked around to the rear and dropped the tailgate, exposing a rear-facing seat. "All aboard," he said, as he walked up to the house to hug and briefly talk with his sister who stood an inch taller. Five minutes later he returned and they were off.

Riding backwards was a new experience for Kevin. Not having a family car, even riding forward wasn't a daily occurrence. Uncle Bob started down the block. It was weird, and a bit disconcerting, facing where they'd come from rather than where they were going, like living in the past rather than the present. The electronic tailgate window hummed up to half way. "That will keep the exhaust out of your face," Uncle Bob said, as he readjusted his rearview mirror.

"We're off, but I have to make a stop before we hit the expressway."

The word "expressway" caught Kevin's attention, bringing back to mind his earlier adventure. He'd told Thomas all about it while playing catch yesterday. They'd agreed to check it out on Monday, along with those two new house foundations Kevin had spotted.

Fifteen minutes later Uncle Bob smoothly parallel parked between a pick-up and a rusty Oldsmobile. "I won't be long," he said as his door thumped closed. He dodged between traffic as he headed across the street.

"Where are we?" Kevin asked. Outside of his own neighborhood his orientation was severely limited by lack of experience. What he knew of Chicago's sites and street scenes was mostly second hand, gathered from local television stations, his dad's *Daily News*, or the few times each summer when he and his mother rode the Foster Avenue buses for a day at the beach.

"We're on Lawrence. Up by the light is Kimball. That's Bob's plumbing supply business over there." Thomas pointed across the traffic in the direction his uncle had headed.

Seated low in the boot, with only their shoulders and heads showing above the tailgate, gave Kevin a sense of clandestine anonymity. Both the sidewalk and street teemed with Saturday morning traffic that Kevin wasn't used to. Their unique perspective added a sense of drama and discovery. Like hunters in a blind, the boys scanned the pedestrians, cars, buses, trucks and the reckless bikes weaving in and out of the melee that streamed past in both directions. Thomas broke their silent surveillance by bringing up the floundering Cubs. The boys tried to sound upbeat about the team's chances of overcoming yet another slow start. Lou Boudreau had recently replaced old Charlie Grimm as manager. "Maybe that'll help," Thomas noted. But his voice lacked conviction.

Kevin started to commiserate with Mr. Cub. "Poor Ernie Banks, he's never going to..." He stopped mid-sentence when he saw three approaching figures. He elbowed Thomas and moved his eyes in the direction of the trio. The man wore a long shaggy beard, black with a few contrasting grey streaks. Each of his arms was draped over the shoulder of a boy. Kevin assumed them to be his sons. They were a single unit, moving quickly with purposeful steps. The man talked non-stop while the boys nodded agreement. The father and the younger boy, not much older than Kevin and Thomas, wore dark framed glasses. All three were neatly dressed in black trousers and shoes with a starched white shirt and thin black tie. The two boys wore buttoned black suit jackets. Their black broad brimmed hats seemed balanced upon their heads, and each carried what appeared to Kevin to be a prayer book much like the missal he carried to Mass each Sunday.

As they neared, the boys pretended not to stare. In the few moments it took for them to pass, Kevin clearly heard the man's deep voice but was startled to realize he didn't understand a word that was said. Thomas read the puzzlement on his face. "It's very Jewish around here. The real religious ones speak Hebrew and are called Orthodontic Jews or something like that. Some of the men dress like that for church."

Kevin's puzzled look stayed in place. "Church? It's Saturday."

"And they're Jewish, not Catholic, you dummy. Saturday is their temple day."

"But why the hats?" was all Kevin could think to ask.

"I guess that's just who they are and what they do. You know, like a tradition."

"Isn't it a bit, I don't know… odd?"

Thomas looked quizzically at Kevin. "And what do you call what nuns and priests wear?"

"Good point," Kevin conceded. Then something a long time coming came out of his mouth. Perhaps it was prompted by the way the man had his arms draped over his sons and how they appeared so together, so in touch.

"Is it hard, Thomas?" he asked. He wanted to stop, take it back, but he couldn't, so he plunged on. "You know, not having a dad?"

Thomas looked over his shoulder after the three figures in black and then shifted to face his friend more squarely. "Wow," he said, "talk about pissing on a guy's shoes."

One day last fall, while the boys had been standing side-by-side at the urinals in the school bathroom, talking about something or other that seemed important at the time, Thomas observed, "You ever notice how guys always do their serious talking while they're standing side by side peeing and staring at a spot on the wall twelve inches in front of their faces."

Kevin almost peed on himself laughing. He pretended as if he were about to turn and face Thomas and said, "If you faced each other, you'd end up pissing on each other's shoes." They laughed until Sister Stella rapped loudly on the washroom door, telling them to hurry and quit goofing around. They laughed about it for days after, finally deciding when needed, they'd broach serious personal conversations with "I need to piss on your shoes."

"I'm sorry. Forget it. I don't know why I asked that."

Thomas glanced down the street. "He died when I was only a baby." He looked back to his friend. "My mom used to tell me stories about him. I have to admit I wonder sometimes. But I can't really miss something I never knew I had. I'm sure it's harder for my sister because she was older and remembers him some. Anyhow, I guess it's easier than being born without a leg or foot or something. You'd miss that all the time because you couldn't keep up with everyone else. But even then, you'd probably be used to it by the time you got old enough to realize everyone else has two of them." Thomas tried to lighten the mood by adding, "But even with one leg I'd still be able to out run our favorite loudmouth, Peter Biggert."

"But what if you were born without your hands and couldn't draw?" Kevin asked.

This cut closer to the bone. Thomas' eyes flashed momentary fear, and then he smiled. "I'd hold the pencil in my mouth, or with my foot, because I'd still have to draw. I was born with that. I couldn't be me if I didn't draw."

Kevin wondered if the same were true for him. He knew for sure he'd never have thought about drawing with his mouth or foot.

Gradually the boys turned back to the passing humanity. Thomas reprised his original theme. "Well, anyway, maybe Boudreau will piss on the Cubs' cleats and they'll start winning." The unexpected non sequitur caught both of them off-guard and they were totally dissolved in laughter when Thomas' uncle returned.

"What's so funny?" he asked as he tossed a length of curved pipe and a couple of fittings in the back seat and started up the ignition. He didn't wait for an answer but glanced over his left shoulder, signaled and pulled out, only to catch a red light at the intersection. "Next stop is Oss Steel and Pipe Design in beautiful Gary, Indiana." He launched into singing, "We're off to see the Wizard, the wonderful Wizard of Oss." Uncle Bob laughed at his own pun. The boys groaned out loud.

Bob continued humming as they waited for the light to change. A sudden loud screech from around the corner grabbed the boys' attention. They twisted to see. A dozen feet above street-level, on an embankment behind tall chain-link fencing, two CTA elevated trains clattered past each other. The roar of the one approaching the station was amplified by the departing cars.

"I've been here before." Kevin's words were meant more for himself than for the others.

"Been where?" asked Uncle Bob.

"Here, at this train station. I remember it was cold and noisy." The trains tugged on an old memory. "I was pretty small. Maybe we were waiting for my dad, or no. I think we'd gone downtown to see the Christmas lights and windows at Marshall Fields and the other big stores."

The light changed and they moved through the intersection. Uncle Bob was saying something about the city's Christmas decorations, but his voice was lost to Kevin, whose thoughts had turned inward, trying to look backwards. The memory was as vague as a face in a steamed-up mirror. Only a shadowy outline, the details murky and hidden.

The station and trains were left behind. Thomas asked Kevin, "Is that where your dad catches the El?"

"I guess," he replied. "Would this be the closet station to our house?" *God, how dumb can I be?* "I'll have to check with Dad. I should know that kind of stuff."

Since he'd opened the front door yesterday morning to the sound of bulldozers, an outside world he'd never considered before had suddenly come rushing in on him. Sights and sounds, thoughts and feelings were bumping into each other, causing cranial chaos and confusion. His neighborhood and life suddenly felt small, just a tiny part of something much bigger, something far beyond himself. It reached in toward him, tugging him from his safe place to some place else.

Some minutes later, the present forcefully grabbed his attention as they suddenly sped up. The unexpected acceleration nudged Kevin towards the rear window as they raced down a ramp and merged onto the expressway. The adrenaline of riding backwards quadrupled as approaching cars and trucks threatened to overtake them. He felt like a target. Uncle Bob maneuvered into the left lane. The vehicles flying in the opposite direction intensified the sensation of speed.

Sounds and smells flew in through the open windows: the swirling, buffeting wind; the accelerating and air-braking of trucks and cars careening around curves and through tunnels and underpasses; the smell of exploding exhaust. All propelled them forward. Staring backwards gave the sense of falling into a funnel. Steeples, warehouses, apartment buildings, billboards, and store signage flashed from behind them to be whisked away like flotsam in a hurricane. Sudden shadows from unseen over-passes plunged and startled the boys as if they were crashing down on them. Try as they might not to duck, they'd reflexively flinch in unison at each flash from light to dark.

Kevin's face mingled excitement with fear. This was by far the most intense exhilaration he'd ever experienced. He shouted to Thomas over the traffic noise, "This is so cool!" He'd feel foolish, only to repeat himself two minutes later. He'd been on rides like the Tilt-a-Whirl – which made him puke – and the Ferris Wheel and roller coaster when traveling carnivals set up in a local parking lot, but he'd never felt such an overpowering sense of speed and surrender to fate.

Walls and pillars of concrete squeezed in closer and tighter. Overpasses now crisscrossed above them every few seconds, blocking out most of the sky. At one point Uncle Bob hollered back at them, "We just went under the Congress Expressway. It goes right underneath the main post office. Once upon a time it was the largest building in the world."

Thomas lightly jabbed Kevin's left shoulder to get his attention, signaling he knew the information would hold special significance for his friend. Kevin smiled back. He strained in vain to see the building where his father worked, but it was impossible. They were flying through concrete chutes like a bobsled. He made a small waving motion even though his father wouldn't be in the building on a Saturday. He was passing at the edge of his father's world, the opaque adult world into which his father disappeared for so many hours each week. The world his dad had inhabited long before Kevin was born.

Looking up, the grill of a huge loaded dump-truck came up so close that the driver's face disappeared above the roofline before abruptly changing lanes and going around them. Kevin's thoughts were swept away with it.

They were back at Thomas' house by late afternoon. Kevin went upstairs to gather his belongings into his bag. He rolled up yesterday's underpants inside yesterday's tee shirt. Envisioning the unthinkable horror of a bike accident and having his skivvies on display scattered about the street, he balled them up and, with an apology to Eddie Mathews, stuffed them into the pocket of his baseball glove in the hope the weight of the glove would keep them from spilling out in such an event. He placed these on top of yesterday's lie – the sketchbook he had told Thomas he'd forgotten. He stepped over and looked at Thomas' unfinished picture on the desk. *He's really good.* He thought about how, more and more lately, there were things he didn't share or didn't know how to talk about, even with Thomas. Maybe especially with Thomas. *What would he think if he knew I was jealous of him, or, what if he knew I thought his mom was... was what? Attractive? Sexy?* He wasn't even sure what that meant.

Picking up his bag he felt empty. *You can't be telling everything you do or feel. Who'd want to be around you? They'd think something was wrong with you.* He wondered if Thomas ever hid things from him. He looked around the room at all the pictures before leaving.

As he passed Thomas' older sister's door he surreptitiously glanced in. Pat sat on the edge of her bed looking directly at him. Caught short and off-guard, he blushed as if she'd caught him peeking in her window. He'd thought he was alone up here. He hadn't seen her when he'd come upstairs. He frantically hoped he hadn't spoken any of his thoughts out loud. He stood frozen, locked in her gaze. Then she smiled at him. He flustered and barely managed an embarrassed grin. *God, she must think I'm dumb.*

He reached the bottom of the stairs. The others still were talking on the front porch. He headed that way to say goodbye and thank Uncle Bob again but hesitated at the open door into Mrs. Thom's bedroom. The door was always closed, probably because it was right off the living room. He'd never glimpsed inside the room before. The front door was pulled so he wasn't visible from the porch. He glanced backwards to make sure Pat hadn't come down behind him.

He didn't dare step in but craned his neck in that direction. A framed picture standing on a bureau of dark wood drew his attention. It was clearly a wedding picture. The man was in a tux and Mrs. Thom in a bridal gown. Mr. Thom's face was only slightly familiar, but this larger version of him in full figure standing next to Mrs. Thom somehow made him more real.

Kevin's eyes drifted from the photo to the dresser. When he realized he was wondering if her underwear was in the top drawer, he blushed so fully the heat engulfed his entire body and made him abandon going out the front door. He knew he'd look guilty. Instead, he quickly headed for the back door to get his bike – and let the blood drain.

Once outside, his embarrassment faded. He walked his bike around to the front, quickly thanked all of them again, and told Thomas he'd call him on Monday. At the corner he turned west and started up the long hill.

June 18, 1960
(...PM)

Turning into the gangway alongside the house, Kevin braked and dismounted. He put his bike in the garage and stiff-legged his way up the back steps and into the house. "I'm home," he hollered to his mother who was vacuuming the living room. "Where's Dad?"

She shut off the machine. "He's in the basement. He just got home from vending and has the clippers out, so go down and get your haircut before he's too tired."

Once a month Mr. Cullerton trimmed Kevin's hair with clippers bought – like many of his tools – from Sears. Kevin preferred longer hair but also looked forward to the contact and one-on-one time with his dad. The smell of tobacco and the gentle grip of his father's hand as he manipulated Kevin's head to get the best angle was a subconscious physical baseline to the rhythm of the ritual and melody of their conversation. However, on the conscious level, both thought the haircut was about saving a few bucks.

His dad never cut off more than what was necessary, and he'd always run the clippers over his son's smooth cheeks and ears as if he were an old man with wild hairs sprouting everywhere. He knew Kevin liked the way it tickled. The routine helped assuage some of Mr. Cullerton's guilt about the lack of time he got to spend with his son. He'd only made it to two of Kevin's Little League games last summer. He wasn't sure this year would be any better. True to the

Cullerton bloodline, neither Kevin nor his dad ever mentioned any of this out loud.

His dad draped a towel around Kevin's shoulders and sprayed a little water on his head to keep the hairs down as he worked. With one hand atop Kevin's head, he tilted it forward. The clippers buzzed to life and he began on the neckline. Having his chin on his chest made talking awkward, but he couldn't wait any longer. "Guess what I saw today?"

Mr. Cullerton gently pushed his head back down. "Keep your noggin down unless you want a baldy-sour." Kevin couldn't see the grin on his dad's face as he remembered how his son had declared last year that, after a particularly short cut, he never wanted to be a baldy again. Mr. Cullerton let Kevin and his mother work out the compromise. They'd agreed on longer hair, as long as it was kept trimmed and never in his eyes or over his ears.

"Thomas' Uncle Bob took us to Indiana on the expressway. We got to sit in the back of his station wagon and ride backwards."

His dad raised Kevin's head back to level and moved in front of him and combed his hair forward. "That sounds like fun."

"But the coolest thing," Kevin paused and closed his eyes and mouth while his dad trimmed his bangs. He stuck out his lower lip and blew upward to dislodge a cut hair from the side of his nose. With eyes still squeezed shut, he continued. "The coolest thing was I saw where you work. I mean, I didn't really see the whole building 'cause we were going so fast. We went under the street that goes right under the post office. That's where you work, right? That must be cool to have an expressway go right under where you work. Can you hear it or feel it?"

Mr. Cullerton used a soft brush to remove more fallen hair from Kevin's face. When he stopped, Kevin opened his eyes to find his dad looking at him. "That was the coolest thing? To go under the Congress Expressway?" he asked.

"No, Dad. Seeing where you work was. I was just thinking the other day how I didn't even know where your post office was. And now I saw it, or almost saw it. That's a long way to go every day. And, you know what else; we stopped at Uncle Bob's store on Lawrence, right by the trains on..." He hesitated because he couldn't remember the name of the cross street.

"Kimball," Mr. Cullerton supplied.

"Yeah, that's it. Is that where you get the train to go to work?"

"It is. I take two buses, then the El."

"No wonder you have to leave so early. Can't you work closer? Then we could play catch or something when you got home." A picture of his dad tossing a ball to him crossed his mind. "Did you play much ball when you were a kid?" Kevin asked. "I'll bet you were good."

Mr. Cullerton tried to keep up with his son's questions. "Yeah, I used to. I guess I was pretty decent when I was young, but I've worked downtown now for a long time. I'm not sure I'd want to start over at one of the smaller branches."

"Was it really once the largest building in the world? Can I go to work with you sometime?"

Mr. Cullerton didn't answer right away. He lowered Kevin's head and trimmed around his left ear while realizing he'd never had the chance to ask his own father that question. He banished the thought and ran the clippers lightly over the top of Kevin's ear and cheek. Kevin didn't connect the word "caress" with his father's touch because his only context for the word was something you did to babies. Mr. Cullerton recognized it for what it was.

His dad stepped behind him to trim the other side. With his hand back on Kevin's noggin, as he often called it, he finally answered the first question. "The post office was the largest building, way back when it was first built, but only for a little while. Now hold still."

Kevin complied, but asked again, "So, can I go with you someday?"

"You'd be bored. Anyhow, they don't allow visitors up on the mail floors. Federal regulations."

"Is what you do there secret?" he asked, wondering how many secrets his dad might actually have.

"No, not secret. But they have to keep the mail secure. It wouldn't be good if mail got lost or disappeared, would it?" The response made Mr. Cullerton feel like he'd put a wedge between them so he added,

"But I'll tell you what. Do you know where I was working today?"

"Mom said you were vending." Then Kevin sheepishly added, "But I've never really been sure what that is."

"It means selling stuff. Sometimes I work for a friend selling stuff, like hot dogs and pop and beer at games when they need extra help." The buzz of the clippers fell silent, and Mr. Cullerton brushed the last of the fallen hair from Kevin's shoulders.

Kevin turned in the chair. "What kind of games?" he asked.

"At Wrigley Field, sometimes at Soldier Field."

Kevin almost shouted. "Wrigley Field? Where the Cubs play?"

"Yep. And, I'll tell you what. When you get to be sixteen, if I'm still doing it, you can come and work and even get paid."

Kevin was stunned. This was by far the most exciting secret he could remember his dad ever telling him.

Mr. Cullerton cleaned out the clippers, blowing out trapped hair onto the floor where, unlike the memory of his son's excitement, he'd sweep it up and discard it.

"Dad, can we go to a game sometime before then? I won't be sixteen for a bunch of years."

"Sure. I'll see what I can do."

That night, still damp from his bath, Kevin sat at his desk barefoot, clad in his pajama bottoms and a clean undershirt. The overhead light was off, leaving little resistance to the darkness as it finally overcame the long June day and poured through the window screen. The summer sound of crickets and cicadas calling to each other entered with it. With no more than an occasional slight breeze from the south, the traffic noise couldn't reach as far as Kevin's back bedroom. Only the yellow beam from the bullet lamp his dad had mounted above the desk he'd built for Kevin illuminated the field of battle.

A fresh blank sheet of paper waited in the middle of the pool of light, staring up at him – daring him to try. His fingers clutched too tightly around a freshly sharpened pencil. Along the edge of the light, like reserves ready to be called upon, were a ruler, a gum eraser, and his colored pencils. Kevin stared back at the paper. Thomas had suggested he visualize what he was going to draw. He closed his eyes and pictured himself alone and standing in the dimly lit aisle of Holy Gospel Church before Stations eleven and twelve: Jesus is Nailed to the Cross and Jesus Dies on the Cross. Paired together, they hung on the wall between two stained glass windows through which the available colored light came broken and scattered, mingling in his mind with a memory of incense from the Good Friday service.

For over a year now, Kevin had tried and tried again to capture and replicate the scene, the blood and pain of Jesus hanging nailed to the wood. But his imagination and skills failed him – again and again. He tightened his eyes harder and tried to remember how Thomas' hand glided around yesterday as if merely tracing over lines that already existed on the page. Opening his eyes, no such lines appeared on the blank adversary. It seemed to taunt him, awaiting his opening move. Intimidation and critical despair crept over the blank page from the shadows outside the circle of light. Nonetheless, bravely, he plunged forward.

When he finally crawled into bed, he didn't look into the corner, toward the half dozen discarded crumpled balls of frustration and self-rejection he'd flung to the floor one by one. If he did, he was sure he'd see Thomas there too, staring at him and shaking his head, reminding Kevin: "These failures, these scribblings, are yours. Not my fault." Kevin covered his ears against the imagined and painfully true recrimination.

He wanted someone to blame, someone to help absorb the awful empty feeling of failure. His stomach hurt and the wet in his eyes made him mad and even more frustrated. Over and over he repeated to himself, "I don't care, I don't care!" He got out of bed and down on his knees. Before he could check the words coming out of his mouth, he mumbled a prayer that he immediately and forever wished he could take back.

November 22, 1963

With only a friendly smile and outstretched hands in white cloth gloves, the crossing guard held back the mid-Friday traffic while Kevin and a few younger kids crossed Foster to the relative safety of the playground. He had made short work of his diagonally cut bologna on Butternut white bread (with a slice of processed American cheese and yellow mustard). He said thanks and good-by to Mom and hurried out the back door, down the alley and back to school. He and Thomas were going to meet up and make plans for after church on Sunday. They were serving together at the 8:00 mass.

His shoes barely touched the blacktop before Marty Natting, 'the Gnat' (so nick-named by Biggert for his size and annoying habit of intruding into conversations), raced up, still chewing on something. His excitement was obvious as he burst out with his news, along with what looked like a chocolate chip that hit one of the younger kids. "He's shot!" he exclaimed, then replaced the lost morsel by stuffing the rest of the cookie into his mouth.

Kevin assumed he was referring to the kid who just took the chip to the head. He looked around Marty, trying to spot Thomas, so his query was half-hearted and dismissive. "Who's shot?"

"Sorry kid," Natting muttered to the kid. He swallowed and then shouted, calling attention to himself and his news. "President Kennedy was just shot. I swear; I'm not kidding!"

Kevin wasn't biting. "Sure, Marty." There simply was no context in his head for such a thing. He replied sarcastically, "I shot him while I was home for lunch." Kevin spotted Thomas coming out of the school's north door which led between the convent and rectory and out to the recently asphalted upper grades playground-parking lot. He moved in that direction. Though he tried to dismiss Natting's news, he felt like he'd just unknowingly stepped in dog shit – that initial dismal sensation of something amiss, something slippery and wrong, just before the smell is recognized and you are forced to accept the unpleasant reality.

As the boys approached each other, Thomas looked up and the metaphorical stink reached Kevin's brain and heart. He saw his friend's tears held temporarily in place by the frosty air. An ugliness the likes of which he'd never known, penetrated and then fell inside him, landing with a sickening thud in his gut. His head buzzed and went empty. There was nothing to think, nothing to say. He stopped in his tracks and held his breath, trying to suspend himself. He felt a visceral fear and knew with his next breath life would, from now on, forever be soiled with the potential of dog shit.

Neither boy spoke. Together, the two friends simply hunkered down in silence on their haunches against the chain-link fence. The bell rang, insisting they move into the building. They watched without seeing their classmates, most of whom had no idea what had happened minutes ago in Dallas, line up and enter the building. They sat together along the fence unable to process or comprehend, sharing their uncomprehending silence and unable to summon any words to break it. Both boys knew that the world had just pissed all over their shoes.

They watched the news unfold on a black and white television in their classroom and then at each other's houses. Kevin's mom, like the nuns, focused on the fact that President Kennedy was the first Catholic president. Thomas' mother mourned for Mrs. Kennedy. That made sense to Kevin. She'd also lost a husband – though not shot – and like Mrs. Kennedy, had two kids to raise on her own. Kevin felt sorrier for Mrs. Thom than for Mrs. Kennedy. After all, she was in his real world.

The national tragedy felt powerfully sad and real. But it couldn't totally penetrate the personal world of eighth grade boys. Thirteen-year-old boys, living in a safe edge-of-Chicago neighborhood, far from Dallas or Washington DC, were not equipped to fully absorb such events or political and historical upheaval. Nonetheless, the shock of the young president, whose picture was in every classroom throughout Holy Gospel School, being shot in the head injected violence and tragedy into their world, making it visible and imaginable for the first time

Over the following days, Kevin saw adults weeping as they stood in line to pay their respects as the President's casket lay in state. The sight was unnerving. Nearer to home he witnessed tears too. They wet Mrs. Thom's cheek as she watched the slain President's little boy step from his mother's side to salute the passing caisson. Kevin knew his mother would be watching at home and wondered if the scene would make her cry. Probably not. He'd never seen her cry. Besides, she was older than Mrs. Thom.

His dad seemed even more quiet than usual. Kevin wasn't sure if the change was in his father, or in himself. Monday after dinner, they watched the news and repeat coverage together without comment. Walter Cronkite's calming vocal timbre, which had become the voice of a stricken nation, hung in the air, along with the smoke from his dad's chain of Camel cigarettes. Having already seen many of the live scenes earlier in the day, Kevin found himself watching his dad watch the news. His hair had changed from silver to white. In the flickering cast from the TV tube, Kevin was struck by how Dad's evening stubble was now also white. Even his once blue eyes reflected a shadowy gray sadness. Kevin shifted on the couch trying to dismiss these discomforting thoughts. He twisted his legs up so he actually faced his dad's chair. *When did Dad get so old?*

Last Saturday, the day after the shots had changed America's world, had been Mr. Cullerton's birthday. It had been a low key celebration – a card he and Mom both signed and a gift of a collared light blue work shirt and tie clip. Mom had lit the solo candle on the Betty Crocker chocolate cake. She had bravely, but softly, sung a verse of "Happy birthday." When she sang the last line, "Happy birthday, dear Jimmy," Kevin realized he'd never heard her call him

Jimmy. He was always, Your Dad, or Jim. "Jimmy" sounded tender but strange to Kevin's ear. Like Mom was trying to make him younger again.

"Jimmy" Cullerton blew the candle out and watched the residual smoke drift toward the ceiling and disappear. Neither Kevin nor his mother could have guessed the smoke reminded Mr. Cullerton of the exhaust from his grandmother's hearse on that cold day so many years ago.

Kevin moved his feet back to the carpet. His dad didn't react to the erratic shifting. From the TV came the same sound of muffled drums that had been tattooed into Kevin's brain earlier that afternoon. On the screen, Kennedy's casket was on the same old-fashioned dray, pulled by the same two white horses. Again, it was followed by the single black horse with tall empty boots locked into its stirrups. The boots faced backwards. As Kevin already knew, Cronkite would soon explain the boots symbolized a fallen leader. Some reporter would again make much of the fact that many of these details were based on Abraham Lincoln's funeral, right down to the bier which had held both men's caskets in the Capitol Rotunda.

Kevin's mind began to tumble and clank like a piece of chain in a dryer. He wished Dad had been home to watch this earlier, when it was "new" news. It wasn't fair Dad had to work so much. It wasn't fair that his whiskers were suddenly white, and he looked so tired and so overwhelmingly sad. He'd never thought about his dad being sad before. The thought hurt.

While his father's tired eyes absorbed the repeat images of the funeral procession to Arlington Cemetery, Kevin tried to picture him as a kid, hanging out with his own dad. But the picture would not come into focus. Kevin wondered about his own father's father for the first time in his life. He realized he didn't know a thing. The man had never been mentioned by Dad, Mom, or even Grandma. He'd never even seen a photograph. The guy must have died a long time ago, probably even before his parents were married. *When did they get married?* He had plenty of questions to ask. But now wasn't the right time.

Kevin got up and said, "Dad, I'll dry the dishes tonight. You catch up with the news." As he passed his dad's chair, he leaned over and kissed the white bristly cheek. He couldn't remember when he'd stopped kissing his dad goodnight, but he wished he hadn't.

Over the next weeks the Chicago City Council renamed the Northwest Expressway for the assassinated president, and the news coverage focused on men named Oswald and Ruby, commissions and conspiracies. Kevin's and Thomas' attention span strained and gradually turned to thoughts of Christmas. As it happened, the winter solstice, the longest night of the year, fell on a Saturday, coinciding with the first day of Christmas break. After an afternoon of sledding at Oriole Park, the boys took refuge from the early dark and cold up in Thomas' room.

"Done any new cars?" Kevin asked, giving a head-nod toward Thomas' desk and art paraphernalia.

"I haven't been drawing cars lately."

"You... not drawing? I don't believe it."

"I've been drawing." Thomas pulled a sketch pad from his desk drawer. "Here, you want to see?" He handed the pad to Kevin who was sitting on his guest bed before flopping down on his own bed.

Kevin opened to the first page, stared for several seconds, and then slowly flipped through a half dozen more. He returned to the first page, a sketch of Kennedy except the top right part of his head was left un-drawn. Thomas hadn't seriously tried portraits before. On occasion he'd sketched his sister's friends for fun, and his caricature of Peter Biggert with Kevin's fist in his mouth still hung in the corner of his room. So too were some drawings he'd made of the Beatles from their album covers. Earlier that year, the group had awakened in both boys an interest in music beyond slow dance songs. Once they'd used a tennis racket and broom as guitars, and wildly pantomimed Paul and John, lip-syncing along to the *Meet the Beatles* album. When they noticed Thomas' sister standing in the door smiling at them, they shook their decidedly not mopped-topped heads all the harder.

But these drawings were something new. Kevin leafed through the pages which depicted various views of the assassination scene in Dealey Plaza a second time. Although none were completed, each captured details and moods that brought the whole event back to life.

Thomas took the sketches back and slowly turned the pages. "It's weird isn't it? Why am I drawing unfinished scenes of someone getting killed?"

Kevin thought of his failed attempts to draw the crucifixion scenes from the Stations of the Cross. "No. I don't think it's weird." He wanted to say more, because there was more to say. But all he came up with was, "Remember when we were kids and used to play army? We'd pretend to get shot and die in slow motion. It was like we wanted to see what death was like. Maybe it's like that?"

"Yeah, I guess," Thomas said. "But Kennedy is really dead. Just like my dad." His voice rose. "They're not coming back, no matter what I draw."

Thomas' vehemence was startling. He had never before spontaneously mentioned his father as being dead. "What good does it do…looking backwards?" He closed the sketchbook and dropped it on the floor between their beds.

Without consciously choosing any specific words, Kevin said, "That time we rode backwards in your uncle's station wagon all the way to Indiana, we thought it was pretty cool to see where we'd been instead of where we were going."

"Yeah," Thomas sighed. "I guess."

They flopped back on their beds, heads cradled in palms. Kevin wasn't sure how long he'd lain there before he became aware of Pat's presence. She was quietly contemplating the two of them. Her brown eyes looked curious. She stood a moment longer before speaking; her gaze lingered on Kevin even as she spoke to her brother. "Mom said she's going to Turnstyle to finish some Christmas shopping and if you guys want something to eat, there's leftover spaghetti in the refrigerator." She left without waiting for an answer and went into her room, closing the door behind her.

Pat's presence had shifted Kevin's mood. Without looking at Thomas, he said, "Would it be weird to say I think your sister has gotten to be kind of… I don't know, pretty?"

"Pretty? Or, do you mean stacked?"
"Well, both, I guess."
"At least that proves you're not dead, which is good because I don't want to start drawing pictures of you too. And, no, it's not weird. It would be weird if you didn't think she was…'pretty'."
After striking Thomas in the head, Kevin's pillow fell to the floor.

1966-1967

When Kevin Cullerton turned sixteen, he bought a vanilla white '59 Ford. He'd been working part time jobs since he was twelve. First, a paper route, then in a local fish store, and for the last couple of years, at the corner paint store. He was a saver by nature.

His Schwinn bicycle was retired to a corner of the garage. When he'd see it there, he'd remember its years of faithful service and companionship as he rode it from childhood into young adulthood. It conjured memories of his dad helping and teaching him how to fix and maintain this or that. He'd miss those times. However, those occasions and memories were fading. His Ford didn't fit in the small garage space.

Truth be told, even before he'd bought the car, Kevin was feeling a bit embarrassed by his bike in much the same way teenagers sometimes feel embarrassed about their parents. It began as his interest in girls rose from the launch pad and solidly locked into the orbit of his life. Riding a bike seemed less and less cool. By high school, most of his friends had abandoned their bikes in favor of their parents shuttling them about. However, his parents didn't own a car, never had as far as he knew.

Now, his Ford was proudly parked out front of the house. Kevin's sole criterion for choosing this particular car was that of the few vehicles he could afford, it looked the least old fashioned. But the sole reason the actual purchase occurred was due to Frank, his boss, who had kicked in a couple hundred bucks towards the price as a birthday bonus, saying he needed Kevin to start making some deliveries and pick-ups.

It had been Frank who had taught Kevin to drive. He treated Kevin more like a kid brother than just a kid who worked for him. He was too young to be an authority figure – he was exactly ten years to the day older – but he was a mentor and major influence. Frank, and the store, became a critical part of Kevin's education. From the stories he heard from Ray, his elderly co-worker who had once headed security at Carson's downtown back in Chicago's gangster days, to the jokes, anecdotes, and bawdy tales he heard from the painters who frequented the back room before and after their work day, Kevin learned a lot. He gained glimpses into people and life, including certain elements he'd never expect to learn from his parents or school.

Kevin had found the advertisement for the used Ford in his dad's Sunday paper. That Monday, Frank drove him down to check it out. Frank knew cars. He'd been a gear-head in his day, back before marriage, babies and mortgages on a house and a store. He also knew business and how to dicker with sales people. His skills had been on full displayed during the negotiations. Kevin wavered between panic and awe when they twice walked out on the salesman before Frank got a price he considered fair.

When Kevin got home, barely brushing the tires on the curb, his parents came out to take a look. His mother inspected it from the front door before, as mothers tend to do, reminding him, "You be careful, and drive safe, or you'll be back on the bus to school." His father slowly walked around the car before pronouncing it, "clean, and sharp looking." He popped the hood. Kevin knew his father was mechanically handy, but had assumed since they didn't have a car, he'd know little about engines. Reaching in, Mr. Cullerton undid a wing-nut and lifted the air filter. He made a short whistle and then immediately replaced it, having Kevin retighten the nut. He lit a Camel, blowing the exhaled smoke in a stream towards the engine block. "That's a big V-8. And it has a four-barrel carburetor on it. You may want to work a few more hours a week. It's going to suck a lot of gas."

Mr. Cullerton closed the hood. He put his hand on Kevin's shoulder and said, "If you want, we can change the oil and filter this weekend. Then you'll know how to do it from now on." Kevin was impressed and proud as his father walked back toward the steps. He remembered an image of his dad, cigarette hanging from his lips and oiled stained hands, quietly and patiently teaching him how to unjam and fix the chain on his bicycle. That seemed like a long time ago.

Two days after the purchase, Frank sent Kevin in his washed and waxed pride and joy on his first errand to pick up some paint at another store. Two hours after starting off on the forty-five minute errand, he returned with the two boxes he'd been sent for, a yellow traffic ticket he'd managed to obtain with an illegal left turn, and an out-sized fear of Chicago streets and traffic.

Over the summer, however, Kevin gained confidence in his driving skills and his ability to navigate the city's streets – at least on the Northwest Side. The Kennedy Expressway no longer terrified him. He was wary but comfortable on it, at least as far as Fullerton, which was as far as he had needed to travel. He never ventured further into the city to experience and explore the downtown and loop area. That felt a reach too far.

With junior year about to begin, Kevin was spending Labor Day at Thomas' house. Over grilled hamburgers, chips, and their favorite RC Cola, they worked out the details of their upcoming morning school commute. They had cruised the route a couple of times and had a good idea of how long it would take. The Ford would let them sleep in an extra thirty minutes. They'd readjust once winter weather set in.

The boys were overjoyed they'd no longer have to negotiate two CTA buses to get to St. Brendan's. For the past couple years they'd timed their separate departures so they'd end up on the same bus in the morning. It usually worked, but it was also often the case that the bus was so packed with working adults and students heading off to various high schools that they couldn't get close enough to talk until they transferred at Austin. Now, that was in the past. They agreed on a morning pick-up time and gas sharing costs.

When Pat joined the conversation, they also agreed to a contingency plan in case she needed a ride when her girlfriend couldn't pick her up. The girls attended morning classes at Wright Junior College, and the boys would be driving right past there anyway. As it turned out, this happened more often than not. Pat's less-than-dependable friend, it seemed, was not really the morning class type.

Neither Thomas nor Kevin minded at all. They enjoyed having Pat ride along. Thomas and Pat had never shown the typical brother sister antipathy for each other. They shared an obvious and genuine affection and appreciation for each other. Pat loved her brother's art – at least after he'd moved on from his preoccupation with cars. She sometimes got her friends to pose for him which they loved. It made them feel like models. She had several of the pictures hanging in her room.

Thomas loved his sister's spontaneous and adventurous nature. Kevin assumed their closeness came from losing their father quite young and having been raised by a single mother. He thought of Thomas and Pat as two sides of a coin. Thomas was "heads" and Pat, "tails." He sometimes considered the Freudian psychology behind the metaphor, especially ever since the summer of '63 and the incident under the raft at Cedar Lake, when Pat had kindled a secret lust in him.

Kevin knew having her in his car could only raise his stature. Besides, she shared her cigarettes and enjoyed offering insider's advice about girls.

April 12, 1968

Kevin filled the coffeemaker with fresh water and grounds. It needed to be ready when he opened the store tomorrow at 7:30 AM. He locked the front door, and refilled a half-dozen gallon cans with benzene from the barrel out back. The professional painters used it for cleaning their brushes, and he wanted plenty ready for morning. Several of the guys tended to stop in on Saturdays to stock up for an early start on Monday. Between mixing their colors and writing invoices, things could back up quickly since retail customers also arrived early. Except for the window signage and display illuminations, all the store lights had been turned off. Kevin stared out through the interior dimness at the homebound traffic on Harlem Avenue clearly visible through the streak-free plate-glass windows he'd washed when he first came in. He hid the daily carry-over cash register money in the usual place and filled out the bank deposit slip. Leaving by the backdoor, he set and double-checked both locks.

He'd started at noon – Catholic schools being closed for Good Friday – and he'd manned the store by himself from 5:00 until closing time at 6:00. The mid-April sun still had plenty of light and some warmth to share. He wanted to enjoy some of it alone before meeting up with Thomas later. A two-minute walk down the alley got him home. Grabbing his car keys and book, he told Mom he'd eat later with Thomas.

"Remember it's Good Friday, so..."

"I know, no meat." He cut her off with a hug. His parents paid his tuition at St. Brendan's and, of course, it was their house, so Kevin felt it only fair to honor most of their traditions, even though they knew he usually skipped mass on Sundays. By unspoken agreement, that was left undiscussed.

Being Catholic had been an identity he'd seriously clung to as a child. But the church's grip had begun slipping as far back as seventh grade. His seepage of faith became an outflow in 1963 after both Pope John XXIII and President Kennedy died. He now entertained more unanswered questions than articles of faith. However, the Good Friday image of the gruesome and public execution remained a deeply set hook in his psyche, at least partially because it brought back to mind his frustrating attempts as a kid to capture the scene on paper.

Back when he was ten or so, he only saw the noble romantic nature of such a selfless sacrificial offering. He had naively believed if he could just draw it well enough, he could understand and absorb the ability to do the same if called upon some day. That would surely prove him worthy, recognized like Thomas, and maybe even deserving of being remembered. Back then, he couldn't fathom it not working that way. But now, eight years later, it was Jesus' acquiescence to being nailed to a cross, especially for a cause he surely knew was unlikely to actually turn out well, that had become the unfathomable part.

Over their high school years, Kevin shared his sacrilegious ruminations with Thomas. "I just can't see it anymore. I can understand dying to save someone's life – though, I admit, for me it would have to happen almost accidentally. After all, remember I was the Cowardly Lion for Halloween back in fourth grade. And you know I plan on skipping the marriage and kid scene. It's just too unpredictable and scares the hell out of me. But Jesus dying? And on purpose? Just so people might quit being assholes and maybe treat each other a little better some day. It seems a pretty iffy proposition, doesn't it?"

"I keep telling you, man," Thomas replied, "Faith is believing in iffy propositions."

"When we were altar boys," Kevin said, "it seemed to make sense. But not anymore. It's like maybe Jesus wasn't using the brains and the commonsense God supposedly gave us. Doesn't that seem odd, especially if God actually was his father, He'd let that happen? I'll bet if we could actually talk to Jesus today, he might be seriously rethinking the whole thing."

Thomas usually ignored Kevin's dubious theological reasoning, and teased his friend. "I don't know, I can just see you with a big fat wife and a dozen kids of your own. I don't know who I'd feel sorrier for: you, the wife, or the kids."

After depositing the day's checks and cash in the after-hours slot at the bank, Kevin headed west on Higgins. Just over the city limits in Des Plaines was Ax Head Lake, one of the many Cook County Forest Preserve areas. Ax Head had become a sanctuary ever since his Ford gave him access to what lay beyond the city. Chicago streets still held some vague stress for Kevin. It was more than just the speed, traffic, and occasional semi-dicey neighborhoods he passed through. Shadowy family mysteries lurked about the city, maybe in its very DNA. Sometimes the shadows gave him a slight tug. Sometimes they yanked at some invisible string he seemed to have attached to him. But mostly they just made him wary and on edge, leery about exploring beneath the city's surface façade.

In contrast, Kevin found independence and a sense of freedom driving the wider, less congested roads out here where you didn't get caught by a traffic light every block or two. The farther out he went, the more towns were still surrounded by open land. It was fun to explore, to escape, to see new vistas and to leave the confusing decisions he'd soon have to make behind – even for just a little while.

He especially liked joy-riding new areas when Thomas, with a road map on his lap, served as navigator. On occasion Pat rode along. She'd show them some suburban teen hangouts and even some of the places she and her new boyfriend, Tim, liked to come for "some privacy." Ax Head Lake fell into this latter category.

As he slogged along now with the heavy traffic, he was thinking maybe later this summer, after graduation when he'd have more time, he'd search even further a field. He'd be eighteen in a few days, and more and more he'd begun to realize how appallingly small his world was. *Maybe I'll head up to Round Lake.* His grandmother lived there, and he couldn't remember the last time he'd seen her. If his recollection of long ago train visits was correct, she lived on a gravel road in a tiny old house. *She must be well into her eighties.* If he was going to do it, he concluded, he'd better not dick around too much longer.

He approached the Ax Head Lake entrance. He flipped on his turn signal which in turn clicked off the thought of how strange it was that he really didn't know anything about his grandmother, except that she lived alone up in Round Lake.

Thankfully, the parking area was empty. It was too near dinner for walkers and too early for teens to begin to gather. No radios blaring or hooting and hollering to annoy him. "Yes!" Kevin muttered to himself as he nosed the Ford into a space with a view facing the tiny lake and giving the rest of the world his back bumper. He killed the engine and stretched his legs out along the front seat, resting his head against the half-opened side window. His eyes sought refuge amidst the emerging greens of spring as they bathed in the late afternoon sun. Closing his eyes, Kevin reveled in the calming olfactory bliss of recently mowed grass from the picnic areas. Eventually, he reached into the back seat and grabbed his book.

To Kill a Mockingbird was the only novel Kevin had reread. He loved how Harper Lee cleverly separated the two main plot lines, only to converge and entangle them later on. Now on his third reading, it was Scout's slow unraveling of her father's nature that found a sympathetic vibration in him. He was still trying to do the same with his father.

Kevin's literary interests had, as far as he remembered, begun around fifth grade. He'd begun to observe that each evening about 7:30, his father took to his chair with a book and his cigarettes. It was obvious this was the best part of Dad's day. Not long afterwards, likely in imitation, Kevin grew to relish propping up his pillows beneath the reading light his father had hung above his bed. He loved how the directed beam relegated the rest of the room to darkness as the illuminated world on the page unfolded before him.

His first literary fare had been *The Hardy Boys* mysteries. He read all the Bookmobile carried. Eventually, he'd ride his bike to the branch library in Jefferson Park. Thomas sometimes rode along to browse books on, or about, art. It was here Kevin ventured into more exotic tales with the likes of *The Adventures of Robinson Crusoe* and *The Three Musketeers,* and later still into the world of fantasy with J.R.R. Tolkien.

During high school, novels appeared on his nightstand. He came to appreciate how a well written story grew line by line – much like a painting – creating an essence, a living thing, akin to what Thomas could do in his drawings and to what he himself had failed to achieve. True, books left him in the passive role of observer rather than creator. However, since he never conceived of himself as a writer, nor coveted an author's ability to create, reading gradually assuaged his abandoned fantasy of becoming a great artist. It brought him pleasure and was enough to help soothe the scar. Kevin finally threw away his old sketch books. He didn't want to look back anymore. The competition was over. He'd stepped out from under Thomas' artistic shadow and realized how much closer he felt to his friend.

Kevin glanced up at the lake, pursed and twisted his lips to clear his mind, and pushed himself up straight. Getting out, he walked over to a nearby picnic bench and table. Taking a seat facing the water, he opened his well worn copy of *Mockingbird* to his bookmark, to where he'd left off last night. He read the next paragraph three times before realizing his mind wasn't going to engage with Scout, and her brother, and the mysterious objects Boo Radley was leaving for them in the hollow of a tree.

Instead, without explanation or an obvious connection, his thoughts wondered off toward another mystery, a real life enigma, to the only person – other than his father – who had turned him into a reader, a person who not only loved fiction, but believed it more evocative of actual human life than reality itself. Kevin had encountered Mr. Jurgenson junior year in English III. He always thought of him as Mister Jurgenson, never just Jurgenson, and never, as some of the more Neanderthal types referred to him, The Jerg.

Mr. Daniel Jurgenson was a new, slender, lay teacher at St. Brendan and had immediately stood out as different. He wasn't much older looking than some of the upperclassmen, and he obviously wasn't a sports enthusiast. Not only did he never reference the football, basketball, or wrestling teams, he didn't show any preference whatsoever to the starting athletes, which, of course, tweaked their egos and noses. But most damaging was that he sported an "r"-less Boston accent, which often got him imitated and, of course, mocked.

Mr. Daniel Jurgenson was an unlikely boundary stretcher, at a time when Kevin was ripe for and in need of stretching. As a teacher, he had the unmitigated cajones to push students to ask questions instead of recite answers. He wanted them to voice and support opinions. This made him rather unpopular with many students and staff, and in particular with Brother Donald T. who administrated St. Brendan.

Kevin's favorite Mr. Jurgenson memory occurred after lunch one day when he asked the thirty slugs slouching before him, most of who saw sixth period as rest and digest time, a question. "So, gentlemen, why do you suppose GI Joe 'action' figures," he said adding air quotation marks around the word 'action', "don't have a penis?" Thirty jaws dropped open, and one kid fell out of his desk.

Just before school let out last June, Mr. Jurgenson suggested Kevin might enjoy reading *Catcher in the Rye*, but he would have to read it on his own since it wasn't approved for St. Brendan's curriculum. By the end of the week, Kevin had bought a copy and read it cover to cover. But he was disappointed. He found Holden Caulfield obnoxious and abrasive. Being a person who had spent life trying to "fit in", Kevin found little in common with the guy. Caulfield was motivated by a sense of disconnection. Kevin felt pretty sure he himself was connected, or at least associated, with life, although lately he wasn't sure how or to what anymore.

He wished he had liked the book more since Mr. Jurgenson had recommended it. Surely he was missing some layer of meaning that had escaped him. Neither Dad nor Thomas had read the book, so Kevin looked forward to talking about it with Mr. Jurgenson, who would surely help him see what he was missing.

However, in late August, he learned his favorite teacher was gone, had moved on, or – as he later surmised – was pushed on to somewhere else, some place Kevin sincerely hoped his "r"-less pedagogic style and gentle soul might be understood and appreciated. The memory of the abuse and loss of the man still made Kevin feel cheated and wanting to piss on Brother Donald T's shoes and those of his hairy-knuckled St. Brendan classmates.

He shifted on the cedar wood bench and stood up. In so doing his anger and sense of loss gave way to a more immediate issue. Here he was, sitting alone at a picnic table, looking at the sun sparkles on the water, trying to shut out the traffic noise infringing from behind him and pondering the past, when there were just six weeks left before graduating high school. Six weeks and he still had no clue about what he wanted to do, let alone become.

He did know what he didn't want. Frank had recently offered him a generous post-graduation deal – promising almost as much as his father was making after thirty-five plus years at the post office. He wanted Kevin to co-manage the store, and eventually, maybe run a branch store. Kevin knew he couldn't do it. In spite of all the things Frank had done for him, the thought of spending his life in a store, waiting for customers to decide on a wallpaper pattern or just the right color to put in their living room and bedroom, made him claustrophobic and panicky. He had hugged his boss. Then graciously declined.

Thomas had his scholarship to the Art Academy already in hand. But all he had was an interim stop-gap measure. He'd enroll at Wright Junior College come September. He hoped a year or two of liberal arts might help him find a path forward. It wasn't exactly the plan of a young man to be reckoned with. But at least he was young and had time as long as he stayed in school and didn't get drafted. Nonetheless, he was disappointed in himself. Thomas' skill and vision would propel him toward new horizons, speeding across the vast and treacherous ocean of post-high school. Meanwhile, his own lack of skill and direction was forcing him to tread water and keep close to the shoreline because no other horizon was in sight.

Kevin walked back to the car and tossed Harper Lee onto the passenger seat. Still unsettled, he started down the cut path, which weaved in and out of the trees as it circumnavigated the lake. However, glancing at his watch, he pulled up after just a hundred yards. Time had become short if he was to meet Thomas by 7:30. He stood there in place as if stuck. Turning to face the lake, he tried to absorb the calmness of the water for a few minutes and shake off his uneasiness about the future.

A couple of mallard ducks glided in from the east over the tree line. They banked and, not very gracefully, splashed down just off shore. The lowering rays of the sun illuminated the male's iridescent green head and white collar as the pair settled and paddled toward the new grasses and attending bugs.

Kevin closed his eyes. He took some long slow deep breaths to clear his mind. It was undoubtedly some grass pollen that caused his sudden sneeze, which in turn caused the ducks to unceremoniously leap together into the air, leaving an explosion of water and aggravated quacking behind. Kevin watched them fly just over his head towards the evening sun. *I hope you guys know where you're heading.*

He was heading back to the car when he saw the pair reverse course and fly back overhead, eastward this time – back from whence they had come.

November 1, 2015

Dear Kevin . . .
It's been a long long time...

Tuesday, November 4, (2015)

. . . It was a tough few days. I better finish this but it's hard and I see I've been rambling. I guess I want you to know that everything is ok with Tommi and Sam and Tim, so when I tell you this you don't have to do anything. AND PLEASE DON"T BE TOO MAD AT ME!

December 1, 1969

Pat appeared as a lighter shadow in the dark hallway. "How's Tommy?" she whispered.

"Out cold, I think. I've never seen him drink like that."

"He knows, doesn't he? Damn it! Kevin, he was number fifteen."

"Yeah, we watched. He knows."

She paused, "Thanks for taking care of him. I'm glad you got a safe number."

"I'm three months older. I should have gotten the shitty number."

She stepped closer. "You've got booze on your breath. It's after midnight. You shouldn't be out there driving."

"I'll take the side streets home and go slow. "It'll be..." Pat leaned in and kissed him.

The alcohol layered a haze over the surreal moment. He was surprised. Pat had never thanked him with a kiss before, but she was obviously worried for her brother. The kiss lingered. Kevin's breathing halted. She pressed up against him, and he was suddenly aware he had an erection. He tried not to sway or move a muscle, not wanting it to stop and fearful it might continue.

There were, of course, several reasons this could not, should not, be happening. Sliding through the bit of his mind still processing rationally was the fact she was recently engaged to her boyfriend Tim, who was home on leave. Even worse, this was Thomas' sister. For God's sake, they had known each other since he was in second grade. They were background in each other's lives, not main characters.

Kevin had never considered flirting with her for fear she, or worse, Thomas or their mother, would have thought him creepy. Sure, after the raft incident at Cedar Lake years ago, she occasionally became the proximate cause for a spontaneous hard-on and, once recently, a disturbingly detailed dream. Until this moment, Kevin could assuage his guilt by reminding himself even the women's underwear section of the Sears or Wards catalogues could have the same effect. Besides, that whole raft event had been so fleeting and unexpected that he was no longer even sure if it had really happened. It could have just been his imagination.

Nevertheless, while his mind argued with itself, his arms closed around her. No bra, thin cotton between his moist hands and her skin. The sudden feel of her exploring tongue uncorked something. It trickled up his spine like champagne bubbles and streamed across his mind's eye even as his tongue responded to hers. He feared that somehow she could read his mind, knew his dream. The thought only further stiffened his erection.

... he watched himself surreptitiously watching Pat pose nude for her brother. He remembered feeling some shame for spying. However, it didn't stop him from inserting himself into the tableau; moving from voyeur to participant, he directed Pat into more and more erotic poses and eventually sex acts with him. They eagerly performed for Thomas who sketched more and more feverishly...

Suddenly, Pat paused, offering a chance for either to reconsider. She took a small step back. Side-lit by the ambient streetlight peeking through the thin curtain on her bedroom window, Kevin recognized her brother's white Cubs tee shirt. It swelled at her breasts and barely covered her panties. Her hand sought and opened his pants. For Kevin, shame was now too far away to be summoned. Every part of him flooded, carrying them into her room while the debris of his concerns washed away. Neither closed the door behind them.

When they lay spent among the covers and shadows, she slowly and softly ran her nails along his back. She began to probe with whispered questions about secret thoughts he might have had over the years about her until she uncovered his dream. There was a moment, while he described the embarrassing details but couldn't see her face or reaction in the dark, when he thought he had said too much, exposed too much. Instead, she straddled his hips, enveloping him like a warm ocean wave, insistently, rhythmically, urging him again towards the inevitable, the brief spectacular moments in which the line between past, present, and future is obliterated.

Kevin woke suddenly. It was almost 3:30 AM. He closed his eyes again, not knowing what to think and hoping no thoughts would come. Eventually, when he could no longer sustain sublime nothingness, what came to mind was a conversation from last September. One he thought he had put out of mind.

He'd come across Pat in the cafeteria of the junior college at which they were both enrolled. It was late afternoon, between the end of the day classes and before the start of evening ones. He was heading for the parking lot and home. She was waiting for her class to begin, a course she had previously dropped. Except for them, the tables were empty. As far as Kevin could recall, it was the only time he and Pat had exchanged personal intimacies.

At first, they had discussed Thomas and how much he was enjoying classes at the Art Institute. After awhile, out of nowhere, Pat asked, "Do you remember that time, years ago, when you were leaving the house? You stopped and looked into my room and I was sitting on my bed. Remember? We just looked at each other like, I don't know... like we were sharing some secret or something. You gave me such a sweet smile."

Kevin wasn't sure if he should admit that he very much remembered the moment, though not the smile. After a few seconds, he simply nodded.

Some silence followed. He watched her, hoping she might say more, explain why she remembered that momentary event from years ago. He wondered why he did. However, when she did speak, she went in a totally different direction. She confided Tim had enlisted in the army as a mechanic. She was furious with him. Then she added, "I think he might ask me to marry him before leaving for basic training." She quickly continued, "No one knows, except Tommy, and now you. So please don't say anything, especially to Mom or, of course, to Tim."

Something about the way she had said all this prompted Kevin not to automatically offer congratulations. Instead, he replied, "He's a lot braver than I am. I mean, about the enlisting part." He cautiously asked, "What will you say?"

"I don't know," she replied. "That's the problem. What do you think I should say?"

The question caught Kevin off balance. While he had expressed his doubts about marriage and kids in her presence many times, he was surprised to hear she too might think that way. However, in his hurry to say something, he did not quite sort out the swirling bits in his head, and he came out with, "What would I know? I'm a virgin."

He froze, instantly embarrassed and appalled by his verbal clumsiness. He quickly looked around to make sure no one else had happened in and heard his blunder. *My God, I can't believe I just blurted that out loud!* He had no idea how or why he had conflated those two things into a sentence. He looked around again, this time searching for some place to hide.

With absolutely no hint of sarcasm or teasing Pat replied, "Hmm, I would have thought you've been with a girl by now. Mom said you quiet types are always the ones that run the deepest or, something like that." With the mention of Mrs. Thom, whom he had always thought was pretty, he felt his blush deepen. He managed to drag his eyes back to hers. They were brown, he noticed for the first time, a deep brown, and they were diving and probing into his as if searching for something, deciding if he was telling the truth.

"Really?" he responded to the reference to her mother as calmly as he could, and then found himself looking about again.

"Can I ask you if my brother is a virgin, or wouldn't that be fair?" The question snapped his attention back toward her. She reached over and pushed back some strands of Kevin's straight brown hair from his brow. She smiled at him. Both the touch and the curious smile made him feel important.

Before he could think of a way to handle the question, she suddenly said, "Anyhow, I'd better be going." She stood. "Class is starting; then Tim is picking me up. Besides, I know he's not."

This latter part confused Kevin. "Tim or Thomas?"

"Bye," she said as she gathered her books and coat. Then she was gone.

Kevin had never mentioned the odd conversation to anyone, not even Thomas. Pat said her brother already knew about Tim, so it was not as if he was holding something back. As for the rest of the conversation, it was just too confusing. Why would Pat remember, let alone bring up, that long ago glance? And, what was with the cryptic question and remark about Thomas' virginity? At that time, Kevin thought Thomas was closing in on his first time with an older girl from one of his art classes who was "interested" in his work. Kevin figured his friend's talent and good looks would soon lead to lots of sex if he chose. However, while Thomas would never brag or share details, he did assume – as he assumed for himself – that each would let his best friend know when the deed had been done.

Could Thomas have told Pat about it, but not him? Telling her would be understandable. They were close, and Pat often offered insights into the female psyche to both of them, so the idea of sex was not a taboo subject among the three of them. But, telling her and not telling him? No way! Kevin had dismissed the whole thing as preposterous. Pat had been undoubtedly just speculating about her brother.

However, now lying naked next to her in the dark Kevin wondered if this would have happened if he had not told Pat that he was a virgin. For several moments he was sure he didn't care. But then, the sobering thought of telling Thomas about this extinguished his warm erotic memories as if he'd stepped naked into the cold December night. On the worst night of his best friend's life, he slept with his sister. He had zero ideas of how to handle or escape the situation, but for now, he needed to get away. Trying not to wake Pat – or God forbid, anyone else – Kevin slowly disentangled himself from her and the covers, slid from the mussed bed, and snuck from the Thom house as quietly as he could in his confused state of mind.

Wanting to hide from any early riser looking out their window, he kept his headlights off until he reached the corner. By the intersection, an undigested kernel of self-incrimination popped up as it always did when he was being less than honest with himself or with Thomas. How and why this seed of guilt still clung to him was a mystery. After all, it had been ages ago when he had childishly cursed his only true friend for having a talent he himself would never possess. In the pain and frustration of being forced to face his own inadequacy and lack of skills, he had momentarily sought revenge. On that June night long ago, after crumpling and throwing his illusion of also being an artist into a shadowy corner of his room, he got onto his knees. "God, I'm glad Thomas doesn't have a dad, so we both have something the other one doesn't," he'd prayed. Immediately, he had tried to take the thought back. It was too late. The guilt had already rooted itself and made his stomach hurt even more. And now he'd betrayed his friend again.

As Kevin drove into the early morning darkness, he felt this newest treason settle in his bowels. Maybe like the raft incident, tonight might have been in his imagination. After all, he had been pretty drunk. Maybe like Thomas, he had passed out, and Pat had simply helped him to the nearest bed – hers. Unfortunately, waking up with the both of them naked and entwined lent little support for this line of defense. *How will I ever tell Thomas? Hey brother, I don't want to piss on your shoes, but guess who just lost his virginity? Oh, and by the way, it was with your sister right after you got your ticket punched for Vietnam.*

He turned onto Newland, realizing he was retracing his old bike path between their houses. Since getting his car three years ago, he'd always taken a more direct route. Turning left onto his own street, a too bright nightlight on a modern brick house caught his eye. Imprudently, considering there was undoubtedly still alcohol on his breath, he stopped in the middle of the street.

What the hell?

Kevin rolled down his window and stared. Where the old

Aufenbach house had discreetly stood well back under the trees, keeping its secrets and distance, was a two story house. It intrusively encroached upon the sidewalk like a pugnacious bully challenging and defiling Kevin's memories.

What the fuck? Why is everything changing? I don't like it; it's ugly and stupid!

Sitting alone in the dark of his car angrily staring at the ostentatious structure, part of his brain tried to discern the difference between loss and regret. Lost, was his opportunity to walk his bicycle up the mysterious pathway beneath the tress and meet the old couple before they disappeared. Regret, was his willingness to take advantage of Pat's impulsive behavior. However, wanting to be honest, at least with himself, he could not completely regret that. He knew the last eight hours held its share of both regret and loss – probably for all three of them.

He let his foot slowly off the brake and allowed the car to move him slowly forward. He stared into the rear view mirror. His gut, having its own visceral sense of right and wrong, reminded him that consequences usually sneak up from behind.

Kevin parked in front of the house. He quietly closed and locked the Ford. He went around to the backdoor, closer to his room. He opened and closed the gate and walked down the gangway in the dimness of morning's first hint of light, feeling the weight of the night heavy on his shoulders. The small garage looked ghostly. It absorbed his gaze for a moment as he thought of his bike and sled, both abandoned within, along with his childhood and the times when his pleasure and pain carried less weight.

His mood descended further as he ascended the back steps. Later this morning, when they all woke, Thomas would still have number fifteen, and Kevin would still have to decide what to say about tonight. Life had just taken a major league piss on Thomas' shoes. He was quite sure it had also splashed onto his. More likely, he had pissed on himself. At least he could be grateful Thomas had been out cold and sleeping while... his mind was too tired to finish the thought.

Once in the house, he peed for what seemed like forever and brushed his teeth. When he exited the bathroom, he smelled tobacco smoke. His dad was sitting at the kitchen table, illuminated only by the night light and the glow of his cigarette.

"Pretty late night. Are you okay?"

It never crossed Kevin's mind his father might be upset at him for coming home so late. Kevin had never seen his dad mad at anyone, a fact that amazed him when he finally realized it years later. "I'm okay," he lied. "But, Dad, Thomas got number fifteen. He's going to get drafted. He doesn't have a fighting bone in his body. He's never even hit anyone. It's not right."

"Your mom said one of those early birthdates was his. I'm sorry. Look, Nixon is desperate to end this thing. It can't go on much longer. Besides, you know, for every soldier fighting, there has to be a dozen guys drafted who don't end up in combat. There were thousands in the Army post office system alone when I was in Europe. So, try not to worry too much. Things usually work out."

"Dad," Kevin said, "I'm scared. This was not a good night. When I was a kid, whatever the problem was – my homework, something in my room wasn't working, my bike broke – I knew when you got home, you'd show me how to fix it. But, tonight… well tonight's stuff… I'm not sure it's fixable."

Mr. Cullerton wondered what Kevin meant by "tonight's stuff", but he didn't want to press his son. Instead, he crushed out his cigarette and stood. "Kevin, it's true some things can't be fixed. That's when you'll find out who you really are. But, with work and effort, most can. And what can't be patched up, you eventually learn to live with or without. That is all you, me, or anyone can do." Then in the dim morning light, for the first time that Kevin could recall, his father initiated a hug. "Just always remember I'm proud of you, son, and I'll always love you. Now you better get to bed before your mother hears us. I've got to get ready for work."

Removing only his shoes, Kevin crawled into his bed, pulling the covers over his head. His world was not a place with a lot of spontaneous hugging. Now within hours, he had received two, each under circumstances he would never have imagined. One had rocked his boat, leading to mindless, confused passion. The other had steadied him, like setting a storm anchor against rough seas to come. However, his last conscious thought, just as sleep overtook him, was that maybe Pat would explain everything to Thomas, handle the whole thing. Maybe potential storms heading his way would miss his boat altogether.

Part 3
2016-2019

I don't know who my grandfather was;
I am much more concerned to know what his grandson will be.

Abraham Lincoln

January 18, 2016 (...10:07 AM)

... **KEVIN RELUCTANTLY** set aside his report cards and his memories of school and Thomas as if they were a long lost looking glass he'd just found cracked and buried – a mirror in which he'd glimpsed fragments of other times and places, other versions of himself. It was surprising how many vivid broken pieces of his life survived in the reflection. Parts of that boy must still remain, buried inside the old man sitting in his basement going through a shirt box of mementoes his mother had left him. Had she hoped for, maybe even envisioned, just such a moment as she tied the rough twine around the box and gave it to him?

He looked back to the opened file cabinet drawer. Two letter-sized envelopes stared up at him. He lifted the first. KEVIN MEDICAL RECORDS, written in his mother's all large case printing. As far back as he could remember his mother had lived with macular degeneration. She compensated by printing in large block letters and using a magnifying glass to read. Belatedly, he now realized how difficult that must have been for her, especially after he'd moved out and she lived alone.

The envelope wasn't sealed, as if wanting to share its news with him. He extracted a dingy sheet of 5x8 inch blue lined note paper and unfolded it carefully, not wanting to accidentally lose part of his past. As promised, it recorded the forgotten childhood illnesses he'd survived, along with dates and immunizations for the diseases he'd avoided. The vaccine list raised a sharp image: a line of children, including himself, being led into the Jefferson Park Field House, each child barely held in check by his or her mother's grip on their sweaty little hands and maternal reassurances that "it won't hurt at all". The line shuffled forward. At some point as they got closer, both tactics failed to distract attention, and could no longer stem the rising panic caused by the smell of alcohol-saturated cotton balls. Even sitting here in his basement with a sinus infection he could smell the fear spreading and hear the wailing coming from the head of the line.

When the imagined odor of rubbing alcohol faded, Kevin turned to the second envelope. It lacked any identifying marking and had been sealed. The flap glue was dried by time and gave way easily. It surrendered two thin packets. Each was folded over on itself, hiding its content from the other. He undid the first.

Across the top of the single sheet, his mother had printed her maiden name followed by the names of her mother (Minnie) and father (Paul). No other information was recorded. Information about his mother's family had never been part of any conversation Kevin could recall. All he knew was that her parents died young by today's standards, first her mother and then her father. *But, why no dates? Surely Mom knew when they'd been born and died?* He wondered why he'd never thought to ask about them or how old she'd been when orphaned.

He paused, curious if he himself was the last leaf hanging on to the last branch of his mother's extinct family tree? An odd memory came to mind: rows of straight-backed chairs and an overwhelming scent from floral arrangements pressed around a tiny wrinkled old body laid out in a high collared black dress with a corsage pinned just above her flattened breasts. He recalled touching the cold hands while studying the closed dead eyes beneath polished glasses. Like a dreamer intuitively knows the identity of a faceless specter, Kevin was sure the woman was his mother's aunt. Why wasn't her name at least included on the paper in his hand?

But it wasn't. There was nothing more. Two names, a body in a casket, and the smell of funeral flowers. Not much. Tidbits and scraps. Not even enough crumbs to follow back...*but, back where?* Frustration mingled with a mixture of other regrets and guilt. Guilt of a son for his lack of patience with his mother simply being a mother, regret for a childish self-centeredness and lack of curiosity about his parents, and of course, regret for his own irretrievable youth. How much longer before his leaf let go? He'd felt these feelings before. He assumed most men did somewhere along the line, especially if they – unlike him – had kids of their own. Although, wasn't it the kids who usually paid back the parents for their own parental neglect?

What *was* new about these feelings for Kevin was their intensity, the increased sense of importance and loss he now attached to them.

He unfolded the other packet, a single sheet wrapped around some smaller and obviously older and more fragile stationery. On the first page, his mother had printed four more names. They didn't register until he read them a second time.

PATRICK CULLERTON & JANE OWENS
EDWARD P. CULLERTON & MARY C. FINNELL

This time, one name, MARY C. FINNELL penetrated his foggy head. *Grandma? This must be Dad's family.* Kevin stared at the name, EDWARD P. CULLERTON. He searched his memory for any stirring. Nothing came.

"Well...Hello, Grandpa," he said aloud. "I don't believe we've met before." The word "grandpa" sounded like static. He'd heard and read the word a thousand times but never in connection to himself or his family. An actual name for an actual Cullerton grandpa scratched at his sense of self. He felt irritated, as if toward the end of a long novel he'd come across a name that lacked any context or antecedent. "Where and why have you been hiding?" Again nothing came to him. He took a deep breath in through his mouth and forced it back out through tightly pursed lips.

He looked to PATRICK and JANE. "I'm guessing these are your folks, my great-grandparents." His voice trailed off into the quiet of the basement. He wondered why his dad had never mentioned any of them. At least his mom had told him her parents' names. Kevin's eyes traced the names again, trying to make them real. *No wonder this old file cabinet seemed so heavy. It was holding a lot more than just my past.*

He leaned back against the wall and tried to think things out. Mary C. Finnell – his white-haired Grandma, always dressed in old-fashion housedresses – was probably the youngest of the grouping. He considered how he never really knew her. He remembered driving out to Round Lake once to talk to her after his father died. He came away knowing a bit more about his dad; she'd even given him a faded photo of him when he was a boy (*where is that now?*), but with no more information or insight into her, or her past, than he'd had when he'd walked in the door of her odd little house. He tried to reach back through the years to that visit, to see if he could remember any possible clue of her shadowy ghost-husband named Edward. Once again, nothing came.

His grandfather, Edward P; and his great-grandparents, Patrick and Jane, were just ink on old paper, less real than characters in the novels he read. That they now existed for him at all was because his mother – not his father – had taken the time to write them down for him. He felt his irritation turn to an itch.

When Kevin's thoughts refocused, he considered taking a break but dismissed the idea. He refolded the page, noticing a name printed on the backside. *Hmm, I wonder if the names came from her?* He placed it back into the envelope and examined the older more delicate pages. They felt brittle. He unfolded them, exposing a flowing cursive every bit as easy to read as his mother's block printing. But, the difference in effect was that of poetry versus recipe. The bolder, wider line indicated the use of a fountain pen, a tool that was all but gone when he started school. *Did mom write this before her eyes went bad?* The flow showed no sign of hesitation or self-doubt between letters or words. The author knew what she was about, and brooked no nonsense. The content was of a similar nature to his mother's minimalist genealogy. However, while the contrast in scripts was evocative, the quantity of family information was astonishingly more so.

Another sneeze shattered his reverie. The suddenness seemed a physical reaction to the mysterious pages he held. He barely caught it in the crook of his elbow – just as he'd always urged his students to do – careful not to let it molest the fragile document in his hands. For the briefest second, Kevin had an urge to wipe his arm across his nose. Predictably, the very thought felt disrespectful, as if names on the list would be appalled. Even now in retirement, Kevin clung to certain old-fashioned civilities that he'd been raised with – though a long career of teaching had taught him the effort to pass them on to the next generation was as useless as trying to fight a sneeze. Wiping his nose with his arm was as anathema to him as, say, wearing a hat at the dinner table. Hats worn inside, along with body piercings, were two of Kevin's major taboos. Both provoked him to snarky remarks about current manners and fashion, which in turn made him feel righteously grounded in his own past and sensibilities. Such comments caused Nelson to roll her eyes at him. He was adamant, though. Holding on to the basics of civility was a matter of respect and humility, a link to the past that allowed him to feel slightly aloof from and afloat in the present.

For the moment, the past and present were inextricably entangled in the elegant lettering and fragility of the document he held. It was a true artifact. Maybe it even lent validation – of a sort – for having lugged this green metal sarcophagus around all these years and for its current squatter's residency here under the stairs.

Feeling another sneeze ascendant, he crossed the room to seek a Kleenex and better lighting. He eased down onto a wing-backed chair inherited from Nelson's parents and examined the text more closely. Almost immediately an intuition stepped up to the plate. This must be his grandmother's writing. Mary C. Cullerton (nee Finnell) herself was providing him with a deeper glance into the Cullerton looking glass. He was sure of it. There was no doubt. After all, it *was* a list of her children he held, including his dad.

Ten first names and ten middle names. After each, the surname

Cullerton was spelled out as if to certify the paternity, followed by birthdates and addresses. The Chicago street names were mostly familiar to Kevin; though he wasn't sure where in the city a couple of the addresses were located. He remembered how his father amazingly seemed to know exactly what hundred block any given street was, as well as its east-west or north-south orientation, including the intersecting diagonal streets like Milwaukee and Lincoln Avenue, which cut through Chicago's grid and always got Kevin disorientated and lost.

After each address came an interesting bit. His grandmother had written: Mother's Age ___ Father's Age___, as if she were recording census data of other people's kids. After so recording the eldest four, she had changed to the abbreviations, MA and FA. Kevin imagined her growing weary from the long chain of births, though he decided it was more likely a matter of saving space – which would surely have been a precious commodity in a house with ten kids.

It had been a very long time since he'd thought about his dad's childhood. Growing up, Kevin seldom saw his uncles and aunts, and as far as he knew, never all together. He had no memory of having ever seen his oldest uncle, Edward. Among those relatives he did see once or twice a year at holiday events, he couldn't recall overhearing any "Remember the time when" conversations which might have left some impression of their past.

His eyes started down Grandma's list: Edward (1902), undoubtedly named for his father, followed at one and two year intervals by two sisters and a brother, Richard. He turned to the next page. There, at the top, he saw his father's nativity recorded: James Anthony Cullerton, 1908. *One hundred and eight years ago. Incredible.* He noticed the MA and FA differential was eighteen. *Eighteen years! Did Grandma record their ages simply as a matter of fact, or to emphasize the gap for some reason?* Considering this eighteen-year age difference between his grandparents, along with the seventeen year span of listed birth dates (1902 - 1919), Kevin found himself a bit awed. In 1919, when Grandma gave birth to her last child, his grandfather was fifty-six. *Only ten years less than I am now!*

Then he was struck by an over-riding question: *How do you father ten kids and yet not a word about you comes down to your grandkids?* Until this moment, he had never considered the matter. *But was he forgotten or ignored? Either way, why?*

Kevin shook his head which had re-congested. A tinge of shame and ignorance at never having considered his lineage contributed to the physical discomfort. He looked back to Grandma's documentation of his dad. Between the address on Diversy Avenue and his grandparents' ages, she'd added an additional note: "Shamus at 9:38 AM." He knew from somewhere that Shamus was Irish for James. Glancing back over both pages, he saw only his father's listing had the additional Irish moniker and what he assumed to be a time of birth. *That's strange!*

Leaning back in the chair, a feeling of obtuse neglect descended on him, weighing on his body and mind. Somehow, he'd never pictured Grandma in the role of mother. Even now it was hard to reconcile the short roundish figure, pinched-voiced, white-haired women of his youth with a mother raising ten kids. He shook his head at his lack of imagination, which had allowed him to never have asked a question about his grandfather, or any of his ancestors who'd lived only one or two rungs up from himself on his family tree. But what seemed strangest to him, especially as an only child, was why his parents hadn't spoke of the past, their parents and grandparents.

Eyes closed, he put his head back and tried to envision ten kids crammed into one house. *Just where was that?* The list revealed the ten births had occurred at seven different addresses. *Why would you be moving all those kids every year or two? Especially, as it appears, Grandma was always pregnant.* Even with the stereotype of prolific early twentieth century Irish Catholics, this seemed more than a bit daunting. *They must have been tripping over each other.* He really wanted to picture them all together, one big happy family, the Cullerton Clan, an Irish Catholic frolicking version of *Cheaper by the Dozen*. But it didn't ring true.

Kevin glanced at his watch. An hour had passed. Worn and frazzled from memory and input overload, and generally still feeling like crap, he laid the pages carefully on the side table. Running both hands over his face and through his grey hair, he leaned back again in the chair and let gravity close his eyes. He tried to recapitulate, but quickly began to drift. *Lots of past...more than he'd ever imagined. Lots of questions. Too many questions.*

But no answers or even speculations came before he dozed off. Evidently, blindly trolling around in the past could be exhausting. It was nap time.

February 16, 2016

Glancing over his right shoulder, Kevin squeezed into the middle lane. Traffic on the Kennedy Expressway was always crowded, but he'd actually expected worse. At ten in the morning the worst of rush hour was over. Nonetheless, he didn't miss dealing even with this amount of congestion. On the other hand, he still felt a kinship with the JFK dating back to his childhood when he witnessed part of it being excavated through his neighborhood. That seemed several lifetimes ago now. But, it still was the link that anchored his childhood and sense of home to the larger and inscrutable context called Chicago.

It was years since he'd last ventured into Chicago proper. Anticipation and anxiety crept into his chest as it always did when he headed into Oz, as he used to think of it when he was a kid. Growing up, the city with its unfamiliar multitudes of Oz-like inhabitants and strange neighborhoods seemed a quilt-like, fantastical place. He recalled being first swept into it, not by a tornado like Dorothy, but with Thomas in the boot of his uncle's station wagon, as they whirled backwards into and through the "Emerald City" and out the other side, not to Kansas, but to Indiana.

Over the years his sense of wonder and adventure had been replaced by simple street-smart commonsense. But now the wonder was back. He was energized and motivated by curiosity and his search for things buried a long time ago. Each minute carried him further into the heart and history of the city. He considered each mile not in terms of distance but in terms of time travel into the past. Kevin knew Chicago had – the same as he had – periodically invested in makeovers and reinventing itself. He also knew that for those who have known a place or a person for a long time, much of the past was usually visible just below the new surface, just as a parent often sees their child in the face of their grown son. *The past is there if you know where and how to look and listen.* And that was his intent.

Once past the Keeler - Irving Park junction, Kevin continued to maneuver towards the right lane. A few miles later he put on his signal and exited at Fullerton Avenue and turned east towards Lake Michigan. He used to drive this way to take dates to the Lincoln Park Zoo. It offered a bit of familiarity and nostalgia.

Several blocks later, as he crossed over the north branch of the Chicago River, he noted for the first time the architecture of the old iron bridge. His current quest had him viewing the city with new eyes, trying to see rather than just look. A few minutes more and he turned right on to Clark Street and continued south for several blocks. When he saw his destination coming up on the left, he was relieved to spot a large yellow vertical PARK HERE sign just a block further down on the right. He pulled into the facility, taking the ticket spit out by the machine. He found an open spot on the second level in the back. Kevin grabbed his portfolio and double checked the contents: yellow legal-size note pad, index cards, pencils and pen, a yellow and orange highlighter, along with a page of notes and questions he had brainstormed in hopes they might give direction to his search. *Definitely old school in an age of laptops and tablets.*

Heading down to the street, his steps echoed in the concrete stairwell. As he exited the garage and turned back north, Kevin noticed the park taking up the entire block on the other side of the street. Having been focused on parking, he'd somehow missed it. He spotted a plaque embedded in stone, so he jay-walked across Clark to read it: Washington Square Park, 1842 "Bughouse Square".

Wow! He had heard of Bughouse Square as a place for soap box rabble rousing in the late nineteenth and early twentieth centuries, but he had had no idea of its real name or where it was located. On this trip of discovery it was *an auspicious beginning*, he thought. He let his gaze and frozen breath wander into and over the entire square. Ironically, it contained a solemn silence even within all the surrounding traffic noises. He was taken in by the reaching, searching shapes and shadows of the leafless trees which lined the perimeter and pathways, like giant hands folding in and holding the square's history in place. Their dark relief stood in sharp contrast with the patches of scattered snow. He wondered about the history each had absorbed as it had taken root.

"The Hawk," Chicago's ever-present wind whipped frigid off the lake, across the open space, and caught him face on. He fumbled with raising the zipper of his coat and hurried towards the four-story pink granite facade.

The Newberry Library stands on West Walton Place between Clark and Dearborn, facing south onto Bughouse Square. Kevin took the steps one at a time, soaking up the winter sunlit Romanesque details. Opened in November of 1893 as the permanent location of a North Side free public library, it curiously owed its existence to the *non*-existence of Walter Newberry's grandchildren. A contingency provision in the successful businessman's last will and testament donated a considerable amount of money to fund the project – but only if his two daughters "died without issue." Fortunately for the city, if not for the Newberry family, the daughters had complied with the stipulation, and the library had been built.

As Kevin entered the impressive building, the consequences of existence and non-existence, of fate and history, felt pertinent. He stopped in the large entry hall space, a limbo between the sunlit exterior and the shadowy knowledge he hoped to uncover within. He had the feeling of entering the periphery of something, like the penumbra between darkness and light in an eclipse. He took a deep breath, considering how within minutes of leaving his car, the nineteenth century had already twice peeked out from the shadows; surrealistic, yet tangible. Bughouse Square and the Newberry building, in which he now stood, made him confident the ghosts of Chicago's Victorian era were here to be found.

He climbed the interior marble stairs, gratefully with no complaint from his knee. The hollow echo of his footfalls and the overall ambiance brought a slightly morbid notion to mind – was he, metaphorically speaking, entering the tomb of his ancestors? The last several minutes had captured the general tone and character he associated with that period. *How's that for Victorian melodrama?* To keep one foot in the here and now as a counter balance, he also thought: *This is really cool!*

He was already glad he'd come, and that he had given himself a few days to research and see what he could dig up. At the top of the stairs he entered through a large closed wooden door and approached the registration desk. He asked about the genealogy room and archives.

Kevin sat at a back table in a corner and let his eyes move over the space to acclimate himself. He took out a pencil and his legal pad with the names and questions. He had precious little to go on, only four names – three of which he'd never even heard before. When he'd first thought about coming to the Newberry, he had hoped to arrive with a detailed plan of how to proceed, but it never took shape. *Classic*, he thought. *Plan on planning, but in the end leave it to chance. Sometimes a good thing; other times, not so much.* So, he'd arrived in town with a motel reservation, a phone number, but nothing else beyond his primitive research kit. He figured he'd first find out what was available, and then ask for some guidance on how to proceed. Since finding the family names in his old file cabinet, he'd read enough to know the logical approach to genealogy was to start from the known – his grandmother – and then work backwards to his grandfather and then Patrick and Jane.

Once settled, he approached a librarian at the archive desk to inquire about resources. The fellow patiently explained how most of the library's books and documents were not shelved in the open for browsing. To limit handling, damage, and theft of old and rare materials, Kevin would need to request the materials he desired, and a staff member would retrieve them for him. He could request up to three sources at a time. After a brief discussion about Kevin's specific inquiry, the genial man handed him a search sheet and began to list potential pathways to follow. When he mentioned the library's collection of Chicago directories going back as far as 1839, Kevin's logical approach went out the window, and he took an intuitive leap. Based on some quick guesswork math, he requested three volumes – one from the mid-1850s, 1860s, and 1870s. His impetuous new hope was to jump backwards in time and find Patrick Cullerton. He returned to his corner to wait. His legs fell into a bouncing rhythm under the table while his eyes wandered the room, observing little as he worked to control his anticipation.

"Thanks," Kevin said to the to the archive assistant who carefully set before him three volumes of John G.W. Bailey's Chicago City Directory, each containing names beginning with the letter C. Picking up the books, Kevin was keenly aware of actually touching the past. It kindled a sense of awe tinged with reverence. The only other time he'd experienced anything like it was when he and some friends stood at Benjamin Franklin's grave in Philadelphia years ago. He had thought the side trip to the Christ Church Burial Ground silly, only to be completely surprised by the depth of the emotion and history he'd felt.

The fragile brittle feel and smell of the directories' thin pages made his current hunt for the past tactilely and viscerally real for the first time. The sensation was strong and heady. Setting two volumes aside on the work table, he carefully opened the 1875 directory. He randomly turned some pages. Something seemed odd. Then, he felt foolish. He realized he was expecting to see phone numbers. *Duh!* Without raising his head, he glanced side to side, hoping no one had guessed what had caused the puzzled look that had surely been on his face.

Savoring the moment and wanting to be as thorough as possible, he turned to the front of the book. Slowly turning one page at a time, he examined the information for possible historical context. Soon, however, his anticipation got the better of him. He flipped to the pages beginning with CU and moved his finger down over the small print: Culhan, Cullen, Cullert…Turning the page, the second name down began a listing of *Cullertons* – maybe a dozen of them. His finger crept further down the list: Benjamin, David, James, John, Mary – widow of Thomas …and then it stopped: *Cullerton, Patrick J., engineer. h. 141 29th St.* Kevin read it again. A sense of elation tried to rise, but something blocked it on the way to the surface. *Engineer? Train engineer, or engineer engineer?* It didn't feel right. His immigrant grandparents were probably not well educated or highly skilled. And 29th Street meant the South Side. He knew his dad had grown up on the North Side, around Irving and Kedzie and gone to Our Lady of Mercy School. A South Side address seemed wrong. *Close but no cigar.*

Patrick Cullerton must be a rather common name in a town that by the mid-twentieth century leaned towards Irish mayors and dyed the Chicago River green on St. Patrick's Day. He marked the page with an index card and picked up another directory: 1864-1865. He marveled at how such a small movement could take him from one decade to another, literally jumping backward into the last years of the Civil War. *Did I have relatives who fought in the war?* He'd never thought about it before, but the question tweaked his imagination. It would make sense. Chicago was a major railroad hub with troops and supplies coming through all the time. It had just never occurred to Kevin to connect his family with the war, or Fort Douglas – a notorious prisoner of war camp in Chicago, just a few miles south of the Loop – or with any of the many battles and generals he'd read about.

Refocusing, Kevin found the page where the mid-1860s' Cullertons resided. He quickly scanned down the column of given names. He was more than disappointed to find Patrick was not among them. He went through the list again… then he saw:

Cullerton, Jane …widow of Patrick h. 154 Townsend

Kevin stared at the words. He traced his finger back and forth under the listing as if to underscore it and etch it into his imagination. His mind floated in disbelief atop a flood of questions. He had just reached back through time, through one hundred and fifty-two years to be exact, through a century and a half of Chicago history and touched his great-grandparents, people whom he'd never heard of a month ago? Enveloped in the moment, he didn't want to think or move. He kept staring at the line to make sure it wouldn't somehow disappear back into the past. Then the flood-gates opened: *I'm too late; Patrick is dead. How did he die? Where was he buried? Where the hell is Townsend? What happened to Jane?*

He covered his face with both hands, trying to get his mind to slow down. It finally settled on an image of an Irish wake, with a corpse laid out in a rough wooden box in a darkened living room surrounded by women quietly weeping and hugging, and men drinking whiskey in the kitchen and on the front porch. He could not put a face on the man in the coffin or any of the gathered mourners.

Searching through older directories, Kevin found Patrick alive again at the Townsend address. 1856-57 was the earliest, and there his name was followed by the description: *"Ire. 5 yr."* This gave Kevin 1851-52 as probable dates for Patrick and Jane's arrival in the city. *Why Chicago? Were they married when they emigrated?* Another question popped into his head. He stood to return to the archive desk and his stiffness made him realize just how long he'd been sitting and how tense he'd been.

"Excuse me. When did Chicago actually become a city?" he asked a long-haired, pony-tailed man he'd not seen before. The young man, dressed in an open cardigan and loosened mismatched tie, tentatively replied, "Chicago was incorporated in 1837?" He glanced over at his older colleague who had first helped Kevin and received a nod. "1837," he repeated. *Only fourteen years prior to Patrick and Jane.* He really was falling through the looking glass and into the past. In just over an hour of digging, he had unearthed family roots solidly planted deep into Chicago's soil and history – deeper perhaps than those of the trees across the street in Washington Square.

Kevin returned to his table. He stared at the opened directories and the notes he'd begun, captivated by the detective work and lost in thoughts and questions. After having been declared a widow in the 1864-65 Directory, Jane Cullerton disappeared from the following year's directory and from the subsequent ones Kevin checked. *Had she died soon after Patrick? A broken heart? More likely poverty and/or disease.* Mid-nineteenth century Chicago was not a very healthful place to be, especially for the poor and burgeoning Irish immigrant population in the city, who died as frequently from disease as their brothers who were paid to enlist into the war effort.

Around noon Kevin changed tactics – a data flanking maneuver. Lunch never occurred to him. He reread the genealogy resource sheet he'd been given in the orientation and turned his attention to federal census documents which were still on microfilm. He liked the older technologies. They seemed more in tune with what he was doing. It felt appropriate to have had his initial success with actual old books. Now he'd try his hand with microfiche and then eventually, he figured, he'd have to work online. He headed to the far corner of the reading room where the microfilm was housed.

Damn, someone's ahead of me. He waited impatiently for the twenty-something girl at the desk to finish assisting a middle-aged woman. *Come on ladies, my time is short and I've got to find Jane.* In his mind he was tapping his foot loudly.

The twenty-something was named Louise. She gave him a professional and courteous five-minute tutorial on finding, handling, and using microfilm documents. She managed to give the impression that she wasn't bored to death and actually enjoyed helping people who wandered in looking for their past. Kevin appreciated that.

Her introduction taught him how to find the correct Cook County Census film, which was categorized by voting district and ward number. This would have been impossible without the Townsend address he'd already discovered. He thanked the research gods for having started there first. Kevin opted for the 1860 Census. He thanked Louise and retreated to the furthest cubicle and threaded the film onto the machine.

The initial blur and whirl on the viewing screen made him dizzy, but he soon learned to control the speed of the flashing text. As he began to focus and scan the pages, he was struck and at first momentarily amused by the information requested in column fourteen on the census form. It asked the recorder to indicate "Whether deaf and dumb, blind, insane, idiotic, pauper, or convict." He hoped there would not be any checks in column fourteen next to Patrick's and Jane's names. He found he was taking these crude questions personally. He did expect, however, that as mid-1800s Irish immigrants there may well be checks in column thirteen: "Persons over 20 years of age who cannot read and write."

It took time, surfing through the blurry pages and squiggles of 1860 handwritten script penned into cramped columns and rows, before he found what he was looking for on Townsend Street. But, all of a sudden there it was, accompanied by the same stunned feeling from this morning. Empty headed, chin cupped in folded fingers, he again stared in amazement.

House #154	Cullerton, Patrick	35	Laborer	Ireland
House #154	Cullerton, Jane	25		Ireland
House #154	Cullerton, James	4		Illinois
House #154	Cullerton, Mary A	2		Illinois

Based on his grandmother's list of children and her meticulous recording of their parents' ages at each birth, Kevin knew his grandfather wouldn't be born for another three years. However, he now knew about two older siblings. He printed the page. Picking up the copy, he checked his watch, realizing he needed to leave soon or get trapped in rush hour traffic. Feeling like he was on a roll, he decided to push his luck a bit more. He excitedly approached Louise at her desk.

"Hi, again," he said trying to affect his most charming voice. She looked up. He put on a smile. She looked at him quizzically and offered a grin. "I'm looking for Townsend Street, here in Chicago. Is there a map, or street guide I can check?"

Her grin became a smile. "You can check it online." Reflexively, Kevin's face must have shown his unease with digital searching. "Or you can check right over there," she said, extending her index finger towards the set of shelves along the near wall and under a sign that read "City Map References".

"Thanks," he said, hoping he wasn't blushing. "One of these days, I'm going to learn to read." He walked toward the sign, embarrassed by having his lack of research credibility so obviously displayed. He checked the street listings on a current map with no luck. He frowned. Feeling stymied and running out of time, he was trying to puzzle out an explanation for the missing city street.

"Did you find Townsend?"

He glanced over his shoulder at the girl. "No, I didn't. Not on this map anyhow."

"Hmm…What time-period were you interested in?' Kevin thought her "Hmm" sounded genuinely thoughtful and not euphemistic for "you stupid old sod."

"1860s."

"Ahh," she smiled a real smile this time. "Well then, there's a chance that Townsend had its named changed. Let's go check." She glanced to one of the public computers which was not in use but instead led him back to her work area where she removed a book from a drawer. "We don't keep this out for open use anymore, since…"

"Let me guess," Kevin interrupted, "it's online."

She smiled and continued. "It's a listing of the Chicago streets that have changed names over the years." She paged through the book until she found the entry and turned it so Kevin could see where she was pointing. Townsend was now Hudson Street. "Hmm," she hummed again. "Hudson is less than a mile west of here." Kevin was liking this girl more and more by the second. She added, "In 1909 Chicago also changed its address numbering system, because it was outgrowing the original system. We have a conversion book for that too," she said as she reached back into the same desk drawer and handed it to Kevin.

He smiled at her. "You mean it's not online?"

"Oh, it's there too," she said.

A half hour later, Kevin left the warmth of the Newberry, proudly bearing documentation showing that a century and a half ago, Patrick and Jane Cullerton, his great-grandparents, lived just blocks from where he was standing. He paused on the library stairs, zipping his parka against the cold and again surveying Washington Square. He wondered if any of the old trees were of Civil War vintage, and whether Jane and Patrick had strolled by to enjoy their summer shade and autumn colors. Or maybe, since column thirteen on the census had confirmed they had been illiterate, perhaps the Square, even back then, had been a place to hear and share news about the battles and local casualties during the war. *Surely they were aware and concerned about what was going on in the country?* 1860s Chicago would have been crammed full of illiterate recruits and the parents of soldiers eager to hear what was going on. Kevin wondered if Patrick's age and two young children kept him from the draft when Lincoln instituted it. *Perhaps not, maybe he'd actually died in a blue uniform. How would I find that out?*

He descended to the street. *How did they see themselves? Who were they? What did they think about the war, about Lincoln?* The directories and census had elevated Patrick and Jane from mere inked names on a piece of paper. They'd become tangible: Irish, immigrant, laborer, housewife and widow, father, mother, illiterate, and certainly poor. He tried to see their outlines among the lengthening shadows of the trees in the square. But try as he might they had no faces – only dates and descriptive nouns, which at least linked them to real history, so he could guess at their thoughts and attitudes. But it was sad to think he'd never hear their voices, or know them.

Cars in both directions lined up in front of him along Walton Place. Blinkers on, they impatiently waited to turn either south on Clark or north on Dearborn. He had missed his window of opportunity to beat rush hour. He didn't really care. As he again walked toward the garage, he had a lot to think about. He'd just added more than a hundred and fifty years to his family's life story, to his life story. He tried to picture Jane and Patrick walking, as they surely had, along this very street. Their images were vague, distant, their backs turned to him, backlit by the low sun. Yet they felt very real. He pictured baby Mary Ann riding in Patrick's sinewy laborer arms, while young James toddled along ahead, urging them on to their future. *Why did I never hear anything about these people? Would I be proud of them? Hell, would they be proud of me?*

As he reached the PARK HERE sign, he paused a moment before reentering his world. He glanced back across to the square and hoped Patrick and Jane were holding hands as they walked through theirs.

February 17, 2016

It took over an hour of stop-and-go traffic to get back out to the motel near O'Hare Field. Kevin's first stop was a beer in the lounge to unwind from the drive and look over his notes. Twenty minutes later, while sipping a second beer and waiting for the cheeseburger he'd ordered, he remembered he wanted to talk to his cousin Colleen. It was her name his mother had printed on the back of the sheet of previously nameless Cullerton ancestors, the names in his file cabinet which had started this expedition. His dinner arrived, so he decided to wait until he got back to his room and showered before he made the call.

Colleen was his dad's youngest brother's daughter. She was about eight years younger, and, as with all of his cousins, was Christmas card friendly, but not close. He could not remember seeing her since her mother's funeral. *When was that…early eighties? I know it was after Grandma died.* He was sure Colleen's mother, his aunt, was buried in the same cemetery as his grandmother and wondered if that implied some closeness which had allowed Colleen to pry the family names from her. Or was it just girls asked more questions about family than boys did?

Before leaving home, he got her number from his address list, adding it to his cell phone contacts. Going through the list, he had questioned why he felt compelled to send cards every year. Usually in early December he'd start thinking of family, and the cards were his only link to them and his own past. He'd write some simple message like, "Thinking of you. Merry Christmas." He'd sign it, "Cousin Kevin from Wisconsin." It was silly, probably inane. He knew he did it for himself, more than for them.

Back in his room he hit send and hoped the number was still good. If she was the original source for the four Cullerton names Kevin had walked into the Newberry Library with that morning, he thought it only right that he share his findings with her.

"Colleen Johnson?"

"Yes?"

"It's Cousin Kevin, from Wisconsin."

"Kevin! Really? How are you? My God, it's been some time. What are you up to?"

"Well actually, I'm here in Chicago, Rosemont really. I came down to…" Kevin filled her in on his mission.

Colleen confirmed that she had probably been the original source of the information. In high school she needed to hand in a family tree project to keep from flunking her social studies course. Grandma had been staying with them that winter for some forgotten reason, but she had been mysteriously peevish and tight-lipped, only saying, "I don't remember." Colleen had to literally beg, shedding real tears in fear of flunking, until Grandma finally capitulated and gave her the few names that had come down to Kevin by way of his mother's notes.

Kevin shared what he'd discovered, and Colleen was enthusiastic. He included his self induced apparition walking back to the parking lot. "Like, I was walking in the footsteps of great-grandparents who, up until I came across the names you pulled out of Grandma, I'd never had heard a damn thing about. I admit I was your typical head-up-my-ass, self-centered teenager, and I sure didn't ask many questions about my parents' life before I graced it, but still, isn't it weird no one ever mentioned these people? Were your parents like that?"

"My dad was, just like Grandma. Never said a word about family, let alone his father. It was like…" Colleen suddenly stopped.

Kevin's pulse increased with anticipation. "Like?" he urged.

"I just remembered! I have something you're going to want to see. If I'd known you were interested in this family stuff, I would have sent it to you."

"What is it?"

"Do you remember Mom is buried at Calvary Cemetery in Evanston?"

"Yeah, I do. Grandma is buried there too, right?" Kevin asked.

"They're side by side," his cousin replied. She paused again as if she was thinking. "Can you meet me out there, at Calvary, tomorrow morning, say about 11:30? I have a meeting in the morning, but I can get free by then."

It was hard not to press her about the "something", but he had already interrupted her evening and he was beginning to fade. He could wait. He'd already had enough secrets revealed for one day. He would sleep in and meet her late morning and still have a full day left at the Newberry before heading back home.

"Sure, it would be great to see you, and I admit you have me curious." He checked his memory with her. "Calvary is on Sheridan Road right, just north of the city limits?"

"Yep," she replied. "You can get in from Sheridan." Kevin could almost hear the smile in her voice. "See you in the morning then, and Kev? Be prepared to have your mind blown." She disconnected before Kevin could tell her to say hi to her husband Orv and the kids.

He was too keyed up to read himself to sleep. He decided a nightcap would help him go over his thoughts one more time. He went down to the lobby bar but brought the drink back to his room to ponder what he'd learned and Cousin Colleen's last comment. He sipped and swallowed the Jameson slowly like a breath in a meditation. The history, feelings and impressions lined up and washed over him without editing or rationalizing. *My God! 1860.* Kevin remembered Lincoln was nominated at the Republican National Convention in Chicago that year. Might his great-grand parents have passed him on the street? As a woman, Jane couldn't vote then, but *did Patrick cast a vote for Abraham Lincoln? Could he vote if he was illiterate?* No answers.

More questions queued up, sundry versions of the basic who,

what, where, when, why, and how. Most had to do with his grandfather, Grandma's apparently long-dead husband, the never mentioned Edward P. It was frustrating. So far, he'd learned nothing about him.

It dawned on Kevin he now knew more about his great-grandparents than he did about his own grandmother. And definitely more than he knew about his grandfather, who he'd begun to think of as "my rogue grandfather." *Ten kids, but not one mention of you anywhere? Why is that? Did you have too much or too little effect on them? Just what kind of a man were you? What kind of a father?* Kevin took a sip of his drink. He swirled the remaining brown liquid around his glass. *You may be AWOL for now, but I'll find you.*

He drained his drink, musing again how each found piece of the puzzle raised more and bigger questions. Patrick was dead by 1864, but how long had Jane survived? *Is it plausible Dad knew her? Did Grandma know her?* He wondered how Grandma would have gotten along with Jane, her mother-in-law. His own mother once mentioned she and Grandma had lived together during the war while Dad was overseas. He'd gotten the impression it wasn't always smooth sailing. *But why were Grandma and Dad, why were all the siblings so hush-hush about Edward? And... where the hell is that man?*

The next morning was again cold, sunny and crisp. Kevin left early to give himself time to meander and reminisce. He toured his old neighborhood. He saw Ted's Pharmacy was still there but under a new name. A minute later he was face to face with his old house. He drove around and down the alley. The blue spruce his dad had planted now dwarfed the garage, truly making it look like a shed. He took a slow lap around Holy Gospel, his old school. The playground area where so many knee scrapes had occurred was now buried under a new and modern church building. On the back side of the block, he pulled to the curb across from the corner classroom under the old church where as an eighth grader he'd spent the afternoon praying for JFK on that November afternoon over half a century ago. That day had been the beginning of the end of his childhood, the demarcation line between the concerns of a child and what would come next. His last shrine on this impromptu pilgrimage was Thomas' house. He drove by slowly but didn't stop.

He zigzagged northeast, taking lefts then rights as his fancy dictated. Eventually he reached Rogers Park. He'd always liked the area. It was named for Phillip Rogers, an Irish settler who purchased the land around 1836 for his cabin and farm from the government at $1.25 per acre. The village was annexed into Chicago in 1893, becoming Chicago's northernmost outpost along Lake Michigan. With Loyola's lakeshore campus near by and Northwestern University just a few miles farther up the lake; the area had the feel of an urban college environment. He and his college friends played English darts at the Bottleneck on Broadway and frequented a coffeehouse that played classical music records while they'd play chess on Fridays after classes.

Broadway merged into Sheridan. Kevin drove along the lakefront road named for the cavalry general of Civil War fame and Indian war infamy. His genealogy work had motivated him to begin reading about 19th century Chicago. Not long ago, he'd read that Sheridan had been in charge of quelling the looting and chaos in the aftermath of the 1871 Great Fire. That made him a Chicago contemporary of his great-grandmother and her children, including his rogue grandfather.

Checking his watch, he saw his timing was good. He crossed Howard Street, the border line with Evanston. The east gate of Calvary came up quickly. Kevin turned in between two six-foot stone obelisks that anchored the wrought-iron fencing. The cemetery's long central driveway ran straight across the flat acreage, connecting the east gate to the pointed arched main gate at a considerable distance on the west side of the property. He assumed that would be where he'd meet up with Colleen. In spite of the cold air, he lowered the car window and slowed to a crawl. Crypts and Gaelic crosses stretched in all directions, giving the cemetery a definitive Irish accent. Their style projected a bygone era where bulk and size advertised wealth and status. Some tombs lodged their occupants right up against the lane, insisting they not be overlooked or forgotten.

Tall trees were scattered about, reminding Kevin of those he'd been contemplating yesterday in Bughouse Square. This morning at the motel a quick online search had revealed Calvary's main driveway had once been lined with elms that dated to the cemetery's creation and consecration in the 1860s. They'd been lost in the 1960s to a scourge of Dutch elm disease, which had also killed the lone tree in front of his childhood home. His dad had loved and nurtured that tree, his tree, and had hated losing it when the city cut down all the elms. Eventually it had been replaced with a maple. *Funny the odd things one remembered.*

Kevin took special interest in checking out the names and dates. Most were Irish, including a couple of Cullertons. It was a common name, but he wondered if any were his relatives. Probably not. The size of the headstones and crypts spoke of money.

He reached the west end near the business office and spotted Colleen stepping from a red SUV, her breath visible in the chilly air. Although he'd not seen her for many years, her stylish dark coat, bright smile and long black hair with a few grey highlights made her easy to recognize and brought back memories of her irreverent playful personality. Seeing the Wisconsin plates, she waved as he approached. After a hug and some pleasantries they stood under the winter sun and quickly briefed each other about the state of their families and life in general. Their conversation turned to Kevin's current quest. He briefly again summarized yesterday's discoveries, emphasizing the coincidence of the Newberry being mere blocks from the family's original homestead on Townsend and his growing curiosity about their absent grandfather. Even to himself, Kevin sounded like an overly enthusiastic kid.

"Let's go inside the office," Colleen suggested. She seemed familiar with the place and sat at a small oval table along the far wall. No one seemed to be around, which was fine since Kevin's immediate questions were for his cousin and not cemetery staff.

"So, enough of me babbling on. What's this blow-my-socks-off mysterious 'something' that you have to share? I have to say, you've got my attention."

"Well," she smiled, "if you'd told me you were interested in family genealogy, I'd have gotten it to you a long time ago," she teasingly reprimanded.

He responded with, "We're Cullertons. We were bred never to ask or share anything about family."

"Here's the short version of the story," she began. You already know Mom and Grandma are buried here. Well, I came out here a year after Mom died to leave flowers and couldn't locate the grave. I thought I knew right where it was but couldn't find it, like it had disappeared. So, I stopped in here." She pointed at the office counter. "That's when I found out that a headstone had never been ordered for Mom or Grandma."

"What?" Kevin was incredulous. "How could they not have headstones? That's just not right. What kind of goofy is that? If that's how the family dealt with each other after they died, it's no wonder we never heard any family stories." He paused, not sure what he was feeling – sad, mad, confused. "Why would they do that?"

Colleen moved her purse from the floor at her feet to her lap. Kevin started in again, but without the outrage in his voice. "What was this about, do you think? Surely it wasn't money. It's like they took 'dead and gone' literally; like 'bury and forget' is the family motto."

"Well money wasn't an issue for our family," Colleen concurred. "When I asked my father about it back then, he refused to discuss or explain anything. Said it wasn't my business. I was irate, but he wouldn't budge." Then she reached into her purse, pulling out a single sheet of paper folded in half. "This doesn't explain any of that, but here's what they gave me when I came looking for Mom's plot that day. It's what I wanted to show you." She handed it to Kevin.

It was a xerographic copy of two overlapped 5x8 index cards. Each contained a typed list of names. Kevin's eyes locked on the top line.

Owner: Finnell, Richard.
Date of purchase: June 20, 1868
Size of lot: 10 x 16
Number of square feet: 160

Kevin looked at his cousin. "1868? And Finnell? That's grandma's maiden name."

Colleen stared back at him with the pleased look on her face of one who had just given the perfect gift. She nodded. They both briefly turned to look as sounds from the back office area indicated that someone had returned to duty.

"And Richard Finnell was?" Kevin inquired.

"Her father."

"Ho - ly shit," Kevin whispered.

"I thought you might say that," his cousin replied.

Kevin's eyes scrolled down the page, carefully reading each typed name and date. His head was slowly shaking back and forth in disbelief. He began counting. "One, two, three … ten, fifteen…twenty, twenty-one." He looked back up at Colleen and slowly mouthed the words "Twenty-one?"

"Actually, twenty-two," she corrected and pointed to the document "One of them has 'and child' after her name."

He looked down again. "Twenty-two bodies in a 10 x 16, 160 square-foot grave?"

"Yep," she confirmed. "And if you notice, Grandma, 1978, and then my Mom in 1981 were the last two. And by the way, she has a headstone now, and so does Grandma."

"But that leaves twenty others," Kevin said.

He scanned the sheet again, looking for something. "I only see two Cullertons on the list," he said. "Your mom and Grandma, and both were Cullerton by marriage. All the rest are either Finnells or … do you recognize any of these other names?" He turned the sheet so she could see and pointed at some of unfamiliar surnames.

Colleen shook her head, "Nope, can't say any of them ring a bell. Do you want to go see the grave? I'd like to say 'Hi' to Mom. We can talk on the way."

"Absolutely. I need to apologize to her for not making her graveside service. But, give me a moment. I want to check something first." Kevin took a few steps over to the office counter. He aimed a "Hello?" towards the back room. A balding middle aged man appeared still in his unzipped outside coat and apologized for having stepped out. The clinging smell of tobacco smoke explained his absence. Kevin introduced himself and made a request of the man who jotted the information on a sheet of Calvary Cemetery notepad.

The sun took the edge off the frigid air and there was no wind to speak of, so they walked the path. Colleen led him towards what her document referred to as Lot 22, Block 4, Section C – the crowded Finnell site. The grave was well off the main drive, toward the south boundary fence in what Kevin assumed must be the cheap seats.

They returned to the office thirty minutes later. Their conversation had been easy and comfortable, mostly about family and memories of the various aunts and uncles they knew growing up. Both agreed that Aunt Mary, who had died of cancer back in the mid-1960s, had been a favorite. "She's the one I wished I had thought to talk to back then. I bet she would have known the most and been the most open," Kevin said.

Colleen said, "I was just a kid when she died. I wonder where she was buried?"

"If I ever knew, I've forgotten," Kevin replied.

He'd just stood over more than one hundred years of his relatives' accumulated bones – only two of whom he had ever met. The family tree had suddenly sprouted from a single limb to an expansive tangled oak whose branches had only looked dead and whose buried roots could be unearthed and followed. His brain felt numb. There was a lot to process, feelings and information tumbled around inside.

The same man was behind the counter when they reentered. "I think I have something for you. Cullerton, you were looking for, right? Patrick, Jane, or Edward?"

The man held out a sheet towards them. Kevin and Colleen looked at each other for a moment before Kevin took it. It looked similar to the one she had given him only a half hour ago. Together they looked at the paper, then back at each other.

"Ho-ly shit!" Colleen stammered.

"Ho-ly shit, indeed," Kevin repeated. "I guess we found them."

The next afternoon, Kevin left the Newberry Library at 2:00 hoping to beat traffic this time. He planned to drive straight home. He wanted to sleep in his own bed, with Nelson, and to share what he'd found.

Traffic through Chicago and out the Edens to the toll road and Milwaukee had required his full attention. As the daylight and traffic dwindled between Milwaukee and Green Bay he began to think over the last three days and all the information he now possessed. The sheer quantity of names pushed him way beyond the questions he'd previously considered. He now had more family details and documentation than any living Cullerton. It made him feel good, part of something big, even though he didn't know what it meant – if anything.

He looked forward to organizing and following up on all the names, and then sharing what he learned with all the cousins. If he could get it together over the next ten months, he could send it out as a holiday letter and gift. That would add some pizzazz to his Christmas cards. Other than Cousin Colleen, he wasn't sure how interested all the others would be. But that was up to them. For Kevin, it would be his way of contributing something. He hadn't added to the future gene pool of the Cullerton family. In fact he'd actively made sure not to do so. Now he could contribute in another way. *Surely giving the family their past, their history, is a worthwhile thing, isn't it?* He imagined some niece or nephew, long after he was dead and gone, handing their kids a book with the family tree and saying, "Your great-great-great-cousin Kevin rescued the family from the Chicago Fire." Cullertons would never again raise a kid who had to struggle with a family tree assignment or grow up not knowing how they fit into a larger picture. They were a family with deep roots in the city landscape and history. The idea motivated him for the moment. Then over the next several miles, he wondered why it mattered so much to him.

He exited the highway when his stomach reminded him he hadn't eaten since a morning bagel and banana at the motel. He stopped at a drive-through and ate on the road so as not to delay getting home. Finishing his sandwich, he sipped lukewarm coffee as he drove through the darkness. His mind, as it often did lately, went to his rogue grandfather. A vague memory stirred; his mom once implied she had thought the never mentioned Grandpa Ed was already dead for some time when she and Dad married in 1937.

Well he now knew more than his mother had. Edward P. Cullerton was indeed very alive in 1937, albeit elderly. And he would remain alive for another seventeen years until 1954 when he was buried in Calvary Cemetery – along with seventeen others, including Aunt Mary – in a second unmarked 10' by 16' family plot. It had been purchased in 1869 by Jane Cullerton for her long dead husband Patrick. This last detail was in itself another mystery. The Calvary cemetery record clearly documented that Patrick – who Kevin knew to be dead by 1864 – had been "Removed from Old Cemetery with 2 others." *What the hell did that mean?*

So many thoughts flowed that Kevin began to wonder if his new knowledge was more curse than blessing. The euphoria of his discoveries submerged under a tidal wave of questions – most of which caused more confusion. *Did Dad know his father was alive? Why did Mom think the man was already dead? And, why were Grandma and Edward buried in different plots? Crazy weird, no matter how you dice it.*

This was getting way too confusing. Why hadn't he asked his Aunt Mary about family when he had a chance? He had found these people, his people, but he'd never really know them, or their stories, or hear their voices. Not unless he could go back in time. *I should get one of those DNA kits they advertise on TV.*

March 26, 2016

Saturday night cable television was, as usual, a disappointment. Even the Golf Channel rerun of the day's play in Texas failed to spark any interest. The Masters in a couple of weeks should change that, especially if a warm spell here in Wisconsin melted the remaining snow banks hiding in the shady spots around the house. The mail from yesterday and today was still on the countertop where Nelson had left it. Kevin leafed through the pile of charitable requests and catalogues while a single cube of ice chilled his Jameson. He pulled out the cable bill and an odd envelope hand addressed with his name on it. *No doubt, a new gimmick to entice me to open yet another request for money.* The rest of the pile went into the recycle. He took the mystery envelope and his drink to his reading chair where Robert Cromie's *The Great Chicago Fire* lay next to his computer atop his piles of genealogy notes, lists, and research.

The house was dark except for his reading lamp and the night-light in the bathroom down the hall. Nelson was already in bed. Their individual rhythms naturally divvied the quiet hours. She owned the early morning, he the late evening. He used his time to read and reflect; and since his visit to the Newberry Library last month, his family genealogy gave him plenty to consider.

He enjoyed the detective nature of the work. There was a tangible pleasure and sense of getting somewhere each time a new piece of information fell into place. His old compulsion for documents and files had returned with a functional vengeance. He purchased a couple of fire proof boxes, telling Nelson, "Now that I've found these folks, I don't want to lose them again." As he'd find hints or evidence from online sources or by rethinking already collected materials, he would mail off to the Cook County Clerk for documentation for this or that relative's birth, death, or marriage certificate. It was like assembling an endless jigsaw puzzle, having never seen the picture on the box cover. He accepted being animated and frustrated in turn as he tried to stitch the past together.

There were serendipitous pleasures in the work. As a kid sitting outside of his father's bedroom and listening to his radio at night and then later as a music student, he'd fallen in love with 19th and early-20th century composers. Discovering relatives who were alive when Beethoven and Brahms, Debussy, Stravinsky and Bartok were débuting their creations – not that he pictured his ancestors as classical music lovers – was emotionally attaching. The genealogy reconnected him to the music. It made him feel larger as it looped in his mind while he worked, etching neural pathways and adding to his sense of history and time.

He sat and reached for his book. For right now, the next hour or two were his to enjoy getting lost in Cromie's details of the chain of events that led to the destruction of much of 1871 Chicago, possibly including his own ancestral home. Kevin leaned back, raising the leg rest, and opened his book to where his Ex Libris bookmark, which Nelson had given him years ago, peeked at him from page thirty-one. He sampled his drink, decided it needed a few more minutes, and began to read. When he reread the same paragraph for the third time, he stopped.

Something was distracting him. His eyes drifted to the envelope next to his glass. He replaced Ex Libris and set the book down. He took up the letter, examining the front and back. *No return address. Postmarked three days ago in Chicago. OK, you got me, I'll open it.* He slid his finger under the stamp end of the flap and slit it open. He removed a single sheet wrapped around another sealed envelope, with his name typed in the center. The envelope had no address or stamp. It had been tri-folded to fit inside the original envelope which now lay on his lap. He unfolded the paper.

Dear Kevin Cullerton,

I'm sorry to tell you that my dearest friend Pat Kerneki (Patricia Thom) passed away of cancer last December. Toward the end she gave me the enclosed envelope and asked me to mail it to you at this address three months after she was gone. Of course I had lots of questions but she wouldn't tell me nothing other than what I already knew - you were her brother's closest friend a long time ago before he died in Vietnam. Her instructions were odd and like out of a movie, but she made me promise to do them. I loved her so I'm doing all this. But I must admit I am <u>very</u> curious. I'm sorry if you did not know about her passing. I hope she sent you something important and that it makes you happy. She always made me happy and I miss her.

Sincerely,

Mrs. Rita Naska

Kevin stared at an imaginary spot six inches above the piece of paper he held. His vision hung suspended in mid-air, not even penetrating beyond into the darkened hallway. His thoughts hovered, like a frozen digital TV image. He knew he was deliberately not processing the words he'd just read. He wanted to un-see and un-hear them, to hold them at bay like a young child might do by shutting his eyes and covering his ears in a useless attempt to avoid what his mother was telling him.

Eventually his mind segued and took off like a stone flung skipping over a watery abyss. He felt as if his life had suddenly been cut up, frame by frame, scattered on the floor, and now two individual frames from very different parts of his existence (each with its own attached theme music and mood) had randomly collided. The dissonance was jarring. He continued staring at a singular spot in space, feeling the mash-up of present and past – of sadness and fondness and gratitude – jumble together so there was no way he could tell one from the other. Only when he finally released the backed-up air from his lungs did he realize he'd been holding his breath. His exhalation signaled an unwanted reentry into the present time and space. He reread the note.

Kevin took a mouthful from his drink, swallowing it slowly, letting the whiskey burn focus his mind. He closed his eyes. *Do all moments exist side by side?* How else to explain the vivid re-living of such an old experience, the slow motion replay of two or three hours from another lifetime? The pleasures of a long ago night mingled with the sadness of the words on the page in his hand. The feelings, the images, lay side by side, simultaneously in both his heart and in his brain.

He leaned his head back against the cool leather of his chair. He tried to think of the last time he had seen Pat. The only two memories he could muster were the time they had run into each other and talked in the junior college cafeteria, and then, of course, the other was that unexpected night he so willingly lost his virginity with her. Like most people, the memory of his "first time" – the complex mixture of facts and myth – was preserved deep inside. He could still recreate those few hours in his mind's eye, every detail except *why* it had happened. Sitting here in the night, alone with the strange letter and the ice melting in his whiskey, he realized he had never known; nor would he ever know. Even at the time, he knew it wasn't love, for either of them. Real fondness, but not love. He remembered their urgent intensity, but also knew for certain it hadn't been just lust. *It was like we needed to share something.* For those few hours they'd floated together as if on top of water, but as soon as he had left her bed, they each, by necessity, had swum back into their individual separate lives and futures.

The memory of that night was still bittersweet, and tinged with guilt. He and Thomas had spent that December night – the night of the first Vietnam draft lottery – at a local tavern which didn't card too closely. All eyes had been fixed on the small TV mounted in the corner of the bar as July 12, Thomas' birthday, came up number fifteen. Thomas' response had been silence. Kevin's had been a loud "SHIT!" which, when explained to the barroom, brought a deluge of shots and beers upon his friend. Some were bought to commiserate, some to celebrate, each according to the personal political proclivities of the buyer.

Kevin only vaguely recalled helping Thomas to bed that night but very clearly could picture Pat blocking his exit in the dark hallway outside her bedroom. She knew Thomas' number had come up early, assuring he'd be drafted soon. He wondered now whether or not that night had also been bittersweet and tinged with guilt for her.

He had not thought these thoughts nor thought of Pat in many years now. He didn't even know where she and, *what was her ex's name – Tom, no Tim* – lived anymore. After Thomas' funeral, after Kevin had finished trying to learn and write music in the late 1970s, which thankfully had led to his teaching degree, he moved to Wisconsin. For awhile, he exchanged Christmas cards with Mrs. Thom, but he never knew what to write. He'd heard of Pat's divorce via one of her cards. In the mid-80s, Mrs. Thom's holiday greeting included the news she, now in her fifties, was going to be remarried. She invited Kevin. He was happy for her but declined. Too many old memories. After that, he'd lost track of both mother and daughter, and that long ago lifetime melted away, like the ice in his whiskey.

Kevin shook his head. *The point is…* but he found that he couldn't remember what the point was. He took a breath. *How long since my last one?* Another sip helped ease the emotions. He reread the strange letter a third time straight through. When he finished, he set it down, and wondered if he should thank or curse Mrs. Rita Naska for sending it.

He turned his attention to the other envelope. He turned it over and over, but there was nothing except his typed name. It held only a few sheets of paper. He hesitated like a person might before jumping off a height in a dream, wondering if the water below was deep enough or if it hid rocks below its surface. He took another deep breath and carefully opened it, feeling as if he was opening a casket. Three sheets of folded paper. He gingerly unfolded them.

The top one took Kevin by complete surprise. It was a drawing. It looked to be Thomas' work, pre-art academy, pre-Vietnam. He'd never seen it before. There were two young faces in the picture. One was Pat, looking over her bare shoulder at the other, his face. Their eyes captured something suggestive and sensual. The picture was in colored pencil, which was unusual for Thomas. He preferred pencil or charcoal. Nonetheless, the style was his.

Kevin studied the faces. They looked so very young, late high school, or early college. *But why would he have drawn us together?* He assumed the following pages would explain.

He set the drawing down and took up the other two sheets. Another letter. At the bottom he saw Pat's signature. He'd been expecting to see Thomas'. He guessed Pat must have sent the drawing along as a last memento of those many years he'd shared in their house. Kevin raised his glass to her, and drained his drink. *Thank you, sister of my only true friend.* His fondness for her made him feel young for a moment. He began to read and found out how devastatingly right his assumption was.

November 1, 2015

Dear Kevin,

It's been a long long time, hasn't it? Maybe too long but that can't be changed. You'll have to be the judge. I found your address on Mom's old Xmas list. I'm glad I kept that. I hope it is current and this gets to you. Otherwise I'll be very disappointed. When you read this, I'll already have been dead for awhile. How strange that is to say about yourself. Can you feel disappointment after you're dead? I've mostly come to grips with that and besides I'm very tired and always feel like crap and my cancer (ovarian) has spread all over. My body isn't what I hope you remember it to be, though it was pretty dark that night wasn't it?

It's hard dying, but the hardest part has been watching Tommi (she prefers Tomina, but I always call her Tommi, just like I did with Thomas). She is trying to put on a positive face. We've cried together and laughed and talked a lot. I told her stories from before she was born, about the early days and about Tommy and what was he like. I still have several of his drawings. Last month I was telling her that funny story about Tommy and you getting busted by a cop in sixth grade for smoking on the roof of the ice skating hut at Norwood Park (I was always thankful to you guys for not ratting me out and telling Mom that I was the one who gave you the cigarettes).

Anyhow Tomina's daughter, Samantha (Sam) -Yes, I'm a grandmother - noticed that whenever I told stories about my brother you were always in them. I was always jealous of the bond you two had – I didn't even have that with Tim – by the way we divorced when Tomina was seven. You should know that Tim was / is a good guy. We just weren't meant for each other. He was all work and I guess I wanted something else – something like you and Thomas had. Tim remarried a long time ago and moved to Texas. I'm very glad that Tommi and Sam have a relationship with him though they don't get to see each other much.

I'm going to lay down and rest for awhile. I'll finish this later.

Tuesday, November 4 (2015)

It was a tough few days. I better finish this but it's hard and I see I've been rambling. I guess I want you to know that everything is ok with Tommi and Sam and Tim, so when I tell you this you don't have to do anything. AND PLEASE DON"T BE TOO MAD AT ME!

That night (December 1, 1969, see I remember) when you brought Tommy home late and drunk, I had been out with Tim who was home on leave. We had sex and then he tells me he had re-enlisted for six months without even talking to me about it. I was furious and scared for him and maybe for me too. He tried to explain his stupid logic to me, but all I could think about was that he'd made this decision without asking me. Then when I got home, I found mom in tears. She had watched the Draft Lottery and seen that Tommy's B-day came up #15 and she was sure he would be drafted right away – which he was.

Anyhow I guess the two things were too much for me. I was confused and angry about everything. Later that night when you brought Tommy home and put him to bed, I suddenly had an overpowering desire to – well to do what I did. I am certainly not sorry because – and here's the hard part – I ended up with Tomina who has been the joy of my life plus you made me feel closer to my brother than I ever had before or since. Both were because of you – and for that I have always been grateful. (Did you know that 'Thomas' means twin. I always thought of you two like you were twins – is that sick or what?)

I'm sure you're wondering why I think Tomina is yours and not Tim's since we had sex that same night. He used a condom. Three months later when I told him I was pregnant, he just accepted that it had been defective. It had happened to another buddy of his. He was actually happy because he wanted kids and then because we had a small quick wedding and he didn't have to go through a big production. For the record, you were the only other man I was ever with until well after Tim and I were divorced.

Why didn't I tell you? Two reasons. First of all I was still going to marry Tim and did not want to hurt him or his relationship with the baby. Second, I knew you would want to "do the right thing" and that would not have been good. Remember you didn't want any kids. And it probably would not have been good for me either. If we got divorced, it would have been way too awkward for Thomas and Mom. Anyhow, I knew Tommi was yours from the start. A mother knows these things. Then as she grew up there was never a doubt in my head.

Why am I telling you now? It's because I think you deserved to know that the very best of you –and I always thought there was a very lot of "best" about you, will go on and on through Tommi and Sam.

Thank you for Tomina (and Samantha)

Thank you for being the best friend Thomas could have ever had

Good by and God Bless (yeah, it's silly, but I'm still Catholic)

Pat Thom

OXOXO

PPS. Tommi does not know.

PPPS. Just before he left for Vietnam, Tommy gave me this drawing of us. I think it was his way of telling me he wasn't completely passed out that night.

Nelson finished reading the letter and looked at Kevin over her reading glasses as they sat in bed with their second cup of strong coffee – hers with cream, his black. Between them on the quilt sat a metal bowl holding a few crumbs and the paper baking cups from their ritualistic Sunday muffins.

Kevin responded to her quizzical look. "I've been awake most of the night. I have no idea what to think, let alone believe."

"And…this woman is the sister of your buddy Thomas who was killed in Vietnam?" she asked. "The one you..."

Kevin interrupted, "Yes, that one."

Kevin had told Nelson about Thomas before they'd gotten married. However, in order to not rip open any scars, he had outlined him in minimalistic terms: best friend through school, excellent artist, draft number fifteen, died in Vietnam. After they'd been married awhile, one night after making love Nelson asked Kevin about his "first time." No details, just who and when. With Pat being from another state, and from literally decades before he and Nelson had met, Kevin figured it was safe to surrender her identity since she was safely tucked away in the long ago.

"Do you believe it's really her and it's true?" she asked, setting her coffee cup and glasses on the nightstand. "I don't get why she would be telling you this now. It seems like a pretty shitty thing to do."

"I don't know what to believe. But, yeah, it's her. No one else would know those details. It's weird, but thinking back now, I can remember sometimes feeling like she was studying me, or maybe her brother, or maybe both of us. Every once in awhile I'd catch her looking at the two of us, not like she was staring, but like she was thinking or curious about something. It was always very brief and not as weird as I'm making it sound. She'd just be there and then gone and then sometimes I wouldn't even see her for weeks at a time. She was older by a couple of years so when we were young I never paid much attention. At least until she started to get boobs. Then I did my own secret staring."

"Well, I still think she was a rather thoughtless bitch telling you now! Surely, she must have known it might have negative effects on you – on us. And what about her daughter and granddaughter?" Nelson looked back at the letter on her lap. "Tomina and Samantha? Tomina? Really?"

"It was her way of honoring her brother. So..." Kevin turned on his side to look at his wife, "Does it have a negative effect on you?"

"Maybe. I don't know yet. How about you?"

Kevin took the letter back and looked at it. "She said PLEASE DON'T BE TOO MAD AT ME."

"I think it was really thoughtless on her part. What's the point? Trying to tidy up loose ends before dying?" Nelson vented. She turned back to Kevin and asked, "And you really never had any idea at the time?"

"Not in the slightest. I bought the whole thing just like her fiancée did. It never crossed my mind."

Nelson turned completely to him. "So, are **you** mad at her?"

"I don't know yet."
"Do you know what you're going to do?"
"Nope."
"I do, but I'm not sure how I feel about it."
"What?"
"You'll have to decide for yourself."
"But you know already?"
"I do."
"How?"
"Because I know you. And obviously, so did she."

June 27, 2016
(AM...)

Nelson, dressed for work in her usual stylish but professional dark slacks and white blouse, stood on the porch watching him depart. *What must she be thinking*, Kevin wondered as he pulled out of the driveway. *What the hell am I thinking?* He gave a last wave out the window and a brief goodbye tap on the horn. He knew she was right; this was something he had to do on his own. But deciding exactly what that was and how to handle it proved elusive, and scary. His default option was the easiest and safest – if he didn't do anything, there'd be nothing to handle. After weeks of changing and re-changing his mind, over and over, the doing nothing option still held considerable appeal but only in his head, not his heart. *I'm too old for this. If I was thirty, or even forty, it might make sense to find out, but not mid-sixties. Why should I even want to know if she's my daughter? Doesn't curiosity supposedly kill the cat? Obligation? If Pat never saw fit to tell her, why should I get involved? What good can come from it at this stage? Like Nelson said, "What's the point...tidy up loose ends before dying?"*

Yet, here he was. He slowed at the corner stop sign, keenly and fearfully aware that this journey of an emotional thousand miles had already taken its first step when he contacted Tomina, but this next step could easily end in disaster. Right now, the only thing he knew for sure was he wanted some breakfast on his way out of town.

The posted speed increased to 65 mph. Kevin set the cruise at 70 mph and took a bite of his egg and cheese sandwich, followed by a sip of black coffee. Eating relaxed him a bit. He considered starting the audio book he'd gotten from the library for the trip. Oddly, for a music teacher, Kevin now preferred listening to books whenever he traveled any distance. From experience he knew the length of a Robert Parker story matched pretty well with the mileage to Chicago and back. He enjoyed the author's wise-cracking Bostonian private-eye who went by the single name of Spencer. As book heroes often do, Spencer always knew just what to say and how to say it. He was never at a loss for words. That was something Kevin rarely experienced and he hoped some of it might rub off, because as of right now he had no idea what he was going to say when he got there. The character was famous for his wit and charm and his code of honor, but not his emotional depth. That was perfect because Kevin was already way too deep in the emotional end of the pool. However, after another sip of coffee, he decided against hitting the PLAY button.

As he chewed another bite of his sandwich and tried for the hundredth time to conjure up a game plan for how this might unfold…if he didn't lose his nerve…if he didn't come to his senses and turn around before reaching Chicago. His brain swung wildly from thought to thought like a monkey being chased through a jungle of tangled branches. He was getting nowhere. Within two more miles, before even finishing his breakfast, he gave up and pushed the CD button and Spencer began his tale, hopefully giving Kevin's monkey brain something to grab onto.

It was just shy of two o'clock when Kevin pulled beneath the shade of a tree in the parking lot. He was at his preferred motel in Rosemont on River Road, which gave him easy access to the Kennedy Expressway. He also liked that from here, the drive into the city took him past his old neighborhood and under the Harlem Avenue overpass near which, as a kid, he had watched an army of bulldozers dig and plow westward toward where he now was parked.

He checked into the room he'd booked. Tossing his bag into the corner, he stiffly flopped onto the king-sized bed. He rubbed his achy knee and then folding his hands behind his head, he closed his eyes. Finally free from the concentration of negotiating highway traffic, he became aware that his heart rate was accelerated and his head was buzzing. It felt empty and vacuous from both the drive and the coming meeting. He glanced at the red digital numerals of the clock on the bedside stand. He had two and a half hours to pull it together.

It took a few minutes of slow breathing before his thoughts began to coalesce. The events of the spring flipped through his head like slowly fanned playing cards. He inspected each for some clue as to how to proceed. Back in late April, about a month after Pat's letter hit him like a tsunami, he announced to himself and to Nelson that he couldn't take it any more. He needed to try to find out something about his "maybe" daughter but wasn't sure how to find her.

Nelson said, "It's about time. Maybe then you – and more importantly, I – can get a night's sleep. I'm not retired like some people I know." Then she added, "I've got something for you." She left the table and went to the room she used for her office. When she returned she handed Kevin a note card. "I figured you couldn't leave this alone. So, I took the liberty to find her for you. I have to admit, I was curious for my own reasons. Anyhow, I found that woman's Facebook page still online."

"You mean Pat's?" Kevin asked.

Nelson answered as if the name had a bitter taste for her. "Yes, Pat. Anyhow, according to her page her daughter Tomina's married name is Larkin. She teaches at this school." Nelson pointed to the name she'd written on the card Kevin held. "The school's webpage has her school contact information, but the photo is tiny and taken at a distance in her classroom. Her features are hard to make out." Nelson added, "I don't know if Chicago schools are still in session, but even if not, she must check her school email over the summer."

"What would I do without you?" Kevin said and gave her a kiss.

Nelson said, "And don't ever forget that." After a pause she added, "But, Kevin…" she looked him in the eyes and took his hand, "make sure you've thought it all the way through. Contacting the daughter as an old friend of the family to express sympathies is one thing. Dropping the 'Daddy' bomb on her might ease your psyche and curiosity, but understand that she may not appreciate being told that much of her life has been a lie. Personally, I would not cope well with finding out I wasn't who I thought I was, or that my mother had kept something so important from me." She kissed him on the forehead. "I'm sure you'll keep her needs ahead of your own."

Another agonizing week stretched the calendar into May before he worked up the courage to contact Tommi – for Kevin had found himself thinking of her as Tommi. However, he couldn't and wouldn't let his mind go any further and refused to allow himself to think of her as his Tommi, or his daughter.

Finally, Kevin emailed the school. He had checked online and knew Chicago Public Schools were in their last few days of session, but that didn't mean she'd respond to his message. He typed "Friend of your Mom" in the Subject line. He apologized for contacting her at work. He wrote he had heard through a friend of a friend of a friend that Pat had passed away awhile ago. He offered his condolences. He hated the duplicity but couldn't think of any other explanation for tracking her down and contacting her. He spent a sleepless night, mostly on the couch so Nelson could sleep. The next afternoon a reply was in his inbox.

> Hello Kevin Cullerton,
> I do know who you are. Mom said her brother, Thomas, and you were very close. She spoke fondly of you.
> Mom passed away last December after a long fight with cancer.
> Thank you for your condolences.
> Tomina

Hoping to keep some contact going, Kevin replied, telling her how he and Thomas used to drop Pat at the junior college on their way to St. Brendan and how she'd ride along sometimes when they'd explore the suburbs. Tomina's reply suggested he email her at home, and gave him the address. He felt flattered. Then scolded himself for reading too much into it.

So as not to appear needy or intrusive, Kevin waited forty-eight hours before responding. He assumed her life, work, and her daughter – he was trying hard not to think of her as *his* grandchild – would limit her time and interest in correspondence with an old family friend from before she was born. He knew she might well want to hold him at arms' length. He tried to prepare for that. *Then why would she give me her home email?*

When he responded he simply wrote:

> Hi,
> I just want to check I have the address correct. Hope the end of the school year goes smoothly. I know they can be hectic.
> Kevin

Once school was out, she responded with a few questions. His reply and a few questions of his own led to a regular exchange. Her emails became the focus of his day. Kevin kept his messages brief and focused: additional condolences – originally for her mom and then, when she told him, for her husband and his parents who had been tragically broadsided by a drunk driver when Samantha was only three. She was a middle school teacher, so he asked about the school and her classes. He felt some irrational pride about her being a teacher, but for his own part, only mentioned he himself was a retired music teacher, not wanting to bore her with details. He asked Nelson to read his messages and also her responses. He wanted confirmation that he wasn't saying anything stupid or missing something between her lines.

Tomina asked a few general questions about her mother, grandmother, and Uncle Thomas. He was surprised she seemed to know so much about him. Their exchanges touched off some long ago memories for him which had not been visited since … *since when...* since what now was a lifetime ago – and seemed like someone else's history.

At first, Kevin fought with himself, trying to think of her simply as an artifact from his distant past – like his report cards he'd come across in his file cabinet, not as a part of his present, and certainly not of his future. But no matter what else she may or may not be, she quickly became a living link, a thread to his history, his youth, and his long dead friend. *Thread? Shit, considering how my emotions and thoughts bounce around, it's more like a bungee cord.* In spite of himself, her words, her electronic digital blips on the computer screen, turned her into a real person to him. Every few days her words magically fell out of cyberspace and into his inbox. And encrypted within the disembodied text, though she couldn't possibly know it, were his memories. They would plunge him into the past only to quickly jerk him back into the present, forcing him to again think about the future and how this all might play out. The only thing he knew for sure was he did not want to lose hold of that connecting cord or do anything to cause it to break.

In the last week of June, Tomina suggested that if he was ever coming down to Chicago, and wanted to stop by, she had some old pictures he might like to see. His heart raced. He edited his reply a dozen times to make it sound neutral. It shrank, with Nelson's help, from a long rambling paragraph down to, "I'd like that."

Keep her needs ahead of yours... With Nelson's words echoing around his head, he woke up suddenly on the motel bed. He hadn't realized he'd dozed off so deeply. He sat up too quickly. A sharp stab in his chest flickered across his consciousness like the flash of a strobe light, so quickly he wondered if he'd really felt it. He felt dizzy from the sudden move, but it passed in seconds. He glanced at the clock again. There was just time for a shower to clear his head before heading into the city. Hopefully, inbound traffic wouldn't be too heavy.

Kevin exited the Kennedy and headed east on Diversey. His dad had been born someplace down here. He couldn't remember the number. He thought about his grandmother's handwritten list of her children which he'd come across several months back buried in his old cabinet in the basement and noted the coincidental geographic brush of the past against the present.

Fifteen minutes later, having circled the block twice to find a spot to park, Kevin was standing at Tomina's door, trying to get his finger to ring the bell, when the inside door abruptly opened. Her photo from her school's website, which Kevin had repeatedly studied, had allowed him to harbor doubt about her being his daughter. But there are perceptual differences in the way the brain sees a picture versus a living face. Except in the hands of true artists, photographs, much like a corpse, reveal only a simulation, a recognizable surface image. But life animates from somewhere inside and shines through the surface images. Facing her now, even through the screen of the storm door, his doubts began to evaporate. The face wasn't so much either Pat's or Thomas', but rather that of their mother, Mrs. Thom. He took in a quick breath.

"Well, hello. You certainly are prompt. I heard your car door," she smiled as she unlocked the storm door.

Say something, you idiot. "Hi, I'm Kevin Cullerton."

"I know who you are." She held the door open so he could enter. "You really don't look all that much different from Mom's photos. Come in. Come in." She pushed back her shoulder-length brown hair – much the same color as Kevin's before the grey took over. Her smile never wavered.

"That's kind of you. Thanks for inviting me. It was generous of you." Kevin's face flushed as he stepped past her. He flashed back to a childhood memory of having the same reaction when greeted by Thomas' mother long long ago. He hoped his red face wasn't as obvious as it felt. *Don't break the cord, you dummy.*

He stepped aside to give her space to close and relock the door. When she turned back, her familiar blue eyes met his. *Were Mrs. Thom's eyes blue?* Tommi was taller than her grandmother had been, but her hair and build was strikingly similar. *What color were Pat's eyes?* He couldn't remember. Had he ever been aware of her eye color? Before that impossible night he'd always kept Pat in the opaque category of "best friend's sister".

"Come and sit down. I've got coffee on and lots of pictures." She smiled at him again. Kevin had often wished smiling came easier to him. He remembered Pat had a nice smile, but she decided when, and with whom, to use it. Tommi's seemed to just naturally appear without any conscious decision on her part. Could such a thing be an inherited trait? If so, did it mean Pat was wrong and she couldn't possibly be his. Either way, Pat's final words from her letter hummed in his brain like current in a wire. "*Tommi doesn't know.*"

Kevin followed her into the small dining area, which was separated by a half wall from the kitchen. Floor length green curtains hung open on the windows facing the street, allowing the late afternoon sun to light the room. A table and six chairs, suggesting a possible earlier optimism for a large family, took up most of the space. Two old shoe boxes, each marked with the words "Mom's Pictures", sat atop the maple surface. One was opened. A small stack of photographs lay next to it, as if she'd been looking at them while she waited. Kevin could make out the upside down old Polaroid of Thomas in uniform flanked by himself and Pat. He remembered Mrs. Thom taking the photo in front of their house. It had been two days before Thomas deployed. He and Thomas, and sometimes Pat, had spent those last two days talking and reminiscing. Then, for awhile, their lives and thoughts could only be glimpsed through the snail-mail letters they exchanged and the drawings that Thomas sent him. And then the case hardened forged link of their bond was snapped, and all that remained was a flag draped casket and the pain and tears.

"Have a seat, Kevin, please. Do you want some coffee?" she asked as she continued on into the kitchen area.

The warm aroma of strong coffee reminded Kevin of home. *Maybe she is…* "Absolutely. It smells great – just black please." Kevin chose a chair with his back to the windows, allowing him to study her while she poured the coffee.

"Did you find the place okay?" She set a couple of mugs between them, along with a small plate of Girl Scout thin-mint cookies, his favorites, and some napkins.

"I did. I have one of those plug-in GPS things. I'm directionally challenged so it's a huge help, especially as I've gotten older. I remember my way around Chicago pretty well, but it definitely cuts down on the stress and anxiety of trying to find unfamiliar places, especially in the dark. I call it Sacagawea."

Tomina added some sugar to her mug. "It takes an intelligent man to know the value of a Sacagawea." She looked at Kevin with an impish teasing smile. In turn he saluted her with his mug as he lifted it towards his lips. He couldn't help grinning at her wit and her recognition of the reference. S*mart and attractive...probably not mine...hmmm.*

"Pardon me?" she asked.

"Sorry," he realized that he'd *hmmmed* out loud. "Nothing. I was just thinking." Not knowing what to say, he took a sip of his coffee. "It's good," he added to cover his blunder. "Thanks."

She took a sip from her mug. Kevin took the opportunity to look a little closer. She wore no makeup, and didn't need to. She had a tiny blue post in each ear and still wore her wedding ring. When she set her coffee down she surprised him by saying, "You know, I remember seeing you once."

Kevin's brain skipped like a bumped needle on an old vinyl record. "Really?" Pat had been heavily pregnant with her at Thomas' funeral. But after that, he'd only seen her a few times, while she was still a baby. He'd only given her a smile and maybe a tickle, since; of course, it would never have crossed his mind she might be *his* baby. "How could that be? You were just an infant?"

"Actually, it was some years later, but before Dad and Mom had split. I remember I had just gotten into our car, so you wouldn't have seen me. It was in that small mall at Harlem and Foster. Mom had picked me up from Grandma's and taken me to Turnstyle for some groceries and a snack. Do you remember that place?"

Kevin did. Especially vivid was the memory of being startled awake in his bed one night in the middle of the summer. It wasn't long after he'd gotten his car. He woke to the sound of loud popping and was sure it was the sound of exploding paint cans from Frank's store just down the alley where he worked. He recalled the eerie glow in the night when he looked out his bedroom window. Luckily, at least for his boss, instead it was the Turnstyle building burning, which was a block further down the street.

Tomina continued, "I don't know why I remember. Anyhow, I had just gotten into the backseat when Mom said, "Wait here a minute. I just spotted an old friend." I saw her hug you and talk for awhile. When she came back, I asked her, 'Is that the man in the pictures with Uncle Thomas? Actually, that's probably why I remember. I recognized you, from a picture she kept on her nightstand."

Having his memory jogged, Kevin did recall the meeting, but way too much life had passed to recall any details. Besides, at the time there had not been a compelling reason to store the memory. He asked, "Picture?"

"Mom had family photos scattered about, and most of those of her brother had you in them. There were some old ones even going back to when you guys were at Holy Gospel with those cute little snap-on ties. The one with you two in your Cubs Little League uniforms is also in one of these boxes. Mom said you two were so proud to be on the Cubs, because that was your favorite team." She sipped some coffee and continued. "By the way, Samantha's a huge Cubs fan. She said they're doing real well this year." Tommi looked at the photos already out on the table. "I'm guessing this was the last one, though?" She reached over for the photo he'd already noticed and placed it in front of him. "This is the one Mom kept on her nightstand; I think it was her favorite."

Kevin studied it closely for several seconds – or maybe it was an hour – before looking back up. "It is… or, it was, I should say, the last picture we ever took together." They sat in silence for a bit.

Feeling a need to lighten the mood, Kevin said, "If you don't mind my asking, where's Samantha? Does she go by Samantha, Sam …or…?" Kevin opened his hands in the universal gesture meaning please fill in the blank. "I think you mentioned in your emails she's sixteen?"

"Sixteen, going on thirty-six. She should be home soon. She had a softball game. She's looking forward to meeting you. I've always called her Samantha," she explained. "She signs her name as Samantha, and her friends call her that, but of course, to Mom she was always Sam or Sammy… just like I was Tommi instead of Tomina. I used to correct her all the time… till I was blue in the face. I finally gave up. I guess it was because Mom hated being called Patricia. It made her feel like she was in trouble when she was called by her full name. She said she decided early on she was a Pat, not a Patricia. Even towards the end there, through all the medical problems and pain, she'd correct anyone who called her Patricia."

Tomina sipped her coffee again and looked over Kevin's shoulder and out the window. He sat quietly, not sure how deeply or painfully the conversation might be drilling down inside her. In the silence, he made a mental note of her preference for her given name. After a moment and a little more coffee, she gave Kevin a smile and continued.

"You knew, of course, Mom named me for Uncle Thomas. She'd said she was the only one who could call him Tommy without him getting mad."

Kevin confirmed, "That was definitely true."

Tomina went on, "I remember when I was young, lying on her bed one day staring at that photo," she indicated the one of Pat, Thomas, and himself that still lay in front of him. "I knew it was taken just before her brother left for Vietnam, but still Mom looks so happy in the picture, so I asked her why. She said because just a second before Grandma took the photo, it popped into her head that she was going to name me Tommi. Then we'd all be connected, like a family. The way she said it made me assume she included you when she said family. That's why I was thrilled to hear from you."

"I'm glad I hadn't spooked or scared you."

"No. Quite to the contrary; it was a very pleasant surprise."

Needing a break from the turn in the conversation, both Kevin and Tomina again sipped at their coffee in silence for a few moments. Neither had meant to wade into such deep water, at least so quickly. Each seemed to be "reading their own tea-leaves", so to speak, as they focused on the cup in their hands and the memories in their heads.

When their eyes drifted back to each other's face, Tomina gave a short laugh and confessed, "I hope you'll find this funny, but with all those photos of you and my uncle Thomas around, somewhere around eighth grade I remember asking Mom if you guys were gay." Glancing away in a bit of embarrassment, she didn't notice the look of amusement in Kevin's eyes. "After all, I think there was only one picture of you two with girls, before a prom, I think. All the others were just Thomas or you two together." She drained her coffee without looking up.

"And," Kevin asked, "What did your Mom say?"

She looked at him again and smiled. "Mom laughed, and emphatically said, 'I can assure you they weren't gay.' Then she gave me a Mona Lisa smile, like the one on your face now, and walked away."

Kevin thought he was caught. *Shit!* "I…I was just thinking Nelson, my wife, will be glad to hear that." They shared a genuine laugh.

"Years after Mom and Dad divorced, I found out Dad hadn't been so hot on my name. He thought it weird for Mom to name me after her brother. He said Tomina Kerneki sounded like I was adopted from East Europe or something. Mom thought his sense of spousal loyalty was threatened. Mom initially considered calling me the Spanish Thomasa, but after a big fight they compromised on Tomina, which she immediately shortened to Tommi. At first I didn't mind because I was quite a tom-boy – no pun intended. But by eighth grade, I wanted a girl's name, and declared from then on calling me Tommi could earn you a black eye."

"How feminine," Kevin teased.

"In Mom's case, she'd get a cold shoulder for a couple of days. Dad always called me Tomina." Kevin was becoming acutely aware that each time she used the word "Dad", he felt a bit of jealousy stir. *She obviously doesn't know.*

She continued on, enmeshed in her own memories and not Kevin's reaction. "Throughout my teen years Mom and I struggled over who I was going to be: Tomina or Tommi. I'm sure now, it was important to her because her brother died. But down deep I was struggling to be the person I wanted to be and not get tied to the past. Anyhow, eventually I realized it didn't matter. I could be both. Heck, don't you think, people see who they want to in each other anyway? So, what does all that say about Mom, or me for that matter?"

Kevin had the answer to this one. "It means you are definitely your uncle's niece. When Thomas and I were in elementary school, he'd just about get in fights with kids who called him anything but Thomas." Kevin hesitated, and then continued, "Yet, you know, sometimes, in private, I would call your uncle, Mr. Thomas. At the time, I thought it was clever, but I also knew it was my way of telling him how much I respected him, wanted to be like him. He seemed to understand. He even addressed one of his letters to me from Nam: To Mr. Kevin, and signed it, PFC Mr. Thomas."

Now it was Kevin who paused to contain his thoughts and feelings. "I haven't thought of him this much in quite awhile. Somewhere over the years, I guess, I finally let him go, let him die. I mean, how long can we keep a dead person alive?" He realized his coffee mug was in his hand so he set it down. He looked at Tomina and then back down at the table. A reflux of loss he'd thought was buried long ago rose inside. He touched the corner of one eye with the knuckle of his right hand, and then set his chin on his right thumb with the index finger extended up over his lips, as if he didn't want to say anymore. But he did.

"Your uncle and I were very close. We were like a closed loop. We'd talk and tell each other everything… well, almost everything. In all that time together, only once did I out and out lie to him. And that was just to cover up something I thought would hurt his feelings."

"Should I ask?" Tomina asked.

"It was just stupid, kid stuff. I got jealous, pure and simple. Jealous of his art talent. I wanted to be an artist too, to make pictures that people admired, something worth putting a frame around. But I didn't have it. Not even close. So, I got afraid he'd leave me behind, I guess. We were only ten or so. I got so scared and upset one night I cursed him in some stupid prayer, then immediately tried to take it back. Still, I always felt like a Judas. Somehow, I've never lost the guilt. When he was killed, it took me a long time and later some therapy to stop believing he died because of my prayer all those years earlier."

Tomina simply said, "That's sad… and sweet. But you guys stayed friends, close friends if the pictures don't lie."

Kevin continued, "We did, very close. And we came of age together in an interesting time with a great folk music and, of course, a rock'n roll soundtrack, right up to when he went off and his helicopter was shot down. Eventually, I drifted into studying music. At first it was like art all over again – high interest, limited talent. But I found I had enough ability, if not talent. I didn't quit this time and I worked hard and made it through. In some weird way I felt it honored Thomas' memory – and my dad's." After a pause he added, "Just after graduation my dad had a heart attack."

Kevin stopped, suddenly realizing that mentioning his dad's death might make Tomina think about her own losses. "I'm sorry. I didn't mean to go there."

She smiled, but sadly. "That's okay."

"Still, I'm sorry. I guess my point is that I had no idea who I was, or even what I wanted to be. And with the two most influential people in my life gone, I didn't have a clue as to how to figure it out. Luckily, graduation had come with a teaching degree, so I could at least make a living. I needed to escape Chicago, and my childhood, and, I thought, the ghosts of my dad and your uncle. So I jumped at a teaching job up in Door County when it came up."

Kevin forced himself to stop, realizing he had hijacked the conversation and gotten way too personal, way too fast. The poor girl had somehow innocently turned the key to a crammed-packed closet in Kevin's head and out it tumbled. He sheepishly grinned at her and shook his head. "Wow, again I am sorry. You didn't invite me here to bore you with my life story." He needed to put her back in the lead of the conversation – give her control so he wouldn't go off like he just had. *Get her end of the cord back in her hand or she falls out of your life. Ask her a question.*

"I assume you went into education on purpose and not as a fall back position like I did?"

Tomina leaned forward on her elbows. "Kevin, there is no need to apologize. I know enough from the photos and pictures here and from Mom's stories to realize that you were part of the family long before I was born. Mom kept that picture of her and you guys in her room. You were all together in the photo, side by side, arm around each other's shoulder. So how about we just recognize we are long lost family in a way, and not worry about saying or not saying the right thing."

She looked at the Polaroid of him and Pat flanking Thomas before he left to go and die. She placed it back in front of him. "If you have any doubt, here's the proof." She pointed to her mother in the picture. "Notice Mom's belly? It's really a picture of all four of us."

Her smile washed over him. The cord was safe and stronger than he could have ever hoped, with her on one end and him on the other. His face broke into a smile, wider and more easily than he could remember a smile doing in a very, very long time.

"Mom? Is he here?" A girl's voice exploded from the entry hall.

Tomina took a napkin and blew her nose. "We're in here, honey. Come on in and say hi."

From behind Kevin's line of view, Samantha inserted herself into the room. Kevin began to stand. A stiff neck and cranky lower back and knee, exacerbated by the long drive and internal tension of the conversation, made him move in slow motion and kept him from swiveling his head.

Tomina continued the introduction. "Honey, this is Kevin Cullerton, Nana's friend from…"

Kevin continued to rise and pivot as the girl hijacked the introduction. "I know who he is, Mom. Hi, I'm Sammy. Mom's been excited to meet you."

Surprised by the girl's use of "Sammy" instead of Samantha, Kevin looked to Tomina. Her face showed even more surprise than he felt.

He finally was on his feet and turned to take in a stocky frame and grass-stained uniform. "Glad to meet you, Sam…my?" The hesitation coincided with his eyes reaching her nose stud and the orange ponytail that contrasted with her ash blond hair. *Oh shit!* Kevin absolutely despised piercings – always had. For him they were so "in your face", like somebody picking their nose while they talked to you. He'd been completely in support of his school's policy to try banning piercings a few years before he had retired. He'd even changed restaurant tables a couple of times – much to Nelson's embarrassment – because the waitress or waiter had metal in her or his face. "Please. Call me Kevin."

He was aware his tone sounded less warm than he'd tried for.

"Great! Did you guys look at the pictures yet?" she asked as she reached for a cookie. Not waiting for an answer, she continued, "I'll join you, okay? Let me get some milk first." She stepped into the kitchen and opened the refrigerator.

Tomina shrugged her shoulders at Kevin with a confused grin. She raised her eyebrows and gave her head a slight shake, while mouthing, "That's odd." Then she asked Samantha over her shoulder, "How was the game?"

"Fine, I had two hits, not too sucky. We won. Kevin, Mom, you want some more coffee?" she asked back across the half wall divide.

They both declined and Samantha joined them, taking another cookie and the seat at the head of the table between them. She looked at the photo in front of Kevin. "Mom, isn't that the picture Nana had in her bedroom?"

"It was, yes. I was just telling Kevin that since Nana was pregnant with me, it's actually a picture of all four of us."

Samantha said, "That's awesome. You two are linked more than you ever thought, huh?"

The girl's comment ricocheted around Kevin's brain like a stray shot. He couldn't see any reaction on Tomina's face to indicate she'd picked up on the similarity to her own comments a few moments ago. He glanced down at the photo. He saw his younger self looking naively back up at him from a long ago place, from a time that had faded into the shadows along with his long-dead best friend and his recently dead sister – who was possibly carrying *his* child. In the unblinking eyes of the photo, he tried to see reminders of the past, or glimmers of their individual destinies. Because he was looking down, he failed to see Samantha watching him or her slightly bemused grin.

Sammy took charge and insisted they go through the previously unopened box of pictures first. "We've got to start at the beginning." She explained how after her nana got through her first round of chemo, but before she had gotten too sick, the three generations of girls had spent hours together sorting through and organizing the family photos. Box one held the Thom family pictures, pre-Tomina. Sammy pulled pictures from various bundles as if she knew exactly the photos she wanted him to see. Kevin tried to focus on the faces. Once upon a time he'd met many of these folks but had little recollection, except for Thomas' Uncle Bob. He was impressed, however, by how many of them Sammy knew. She seemed to have familiarity with just about all of them. Family obviously was important to her.

After twenty-five minutes, Kevin excused himself to use the bathroom. Washing his hands, he tried to focus on the girl's genuine interest in her family and wash away his snide unkind thoughts about her build and nose stud. *I can live with the orange hair, but that stud...and extra pounds?* When he returned, he found his coffee had been refilled.

"Ready for this box?" Samantha eagerly asked.

Kevin glanced down at the Polaroid that still lay on the table like a gnawing, unanswered question. "Well, let's find out." He nodded to Sammy to start up again, trying hard not to look at her nose.

"These are the ones Mom thought you'd be most interested in," she announced as she again took charge. Slowly and dramatically, like a magician inviting the audience into the illusion, she reached into the second box. Through the window behind him, the late afternoon sun was now low enough that Kevin saw his own shadow on the table in front of him. Into it, Samantha began to lay out photos one by one like a Taro dealer. Picture by picture, Kevin's past stepped into the present, passing from one type of shadow into another. Samantha chose photos randomly. Kevin felt like a marionette on a string, jerked forward, then backward through his life and friendship with Thomas and the family. There were dozens of pictures. They ranged from old instamatic Polaroids to SLR color film. Kevin was surprised by how many of them he was in. The box contained more of his childhood and teenage self than his own memory.

Sometimes Tomina or Samantha asked about a particular picture. When prodded, Kevin found his sixty-six year old brain still carried the invisible context of those years. Each image was like knapping off shards, producing flakes of details and memories. Each was a random page of his life mixed and scattered by time and now reshuffled and dealt out before him. His mind frequently felt overloaded with images and bits of long-ago conversations.

He answered their questions as succinctly as possible so as not to bore them. They seemed genuinely interested and eager to gain a glimpse into their own past – their prehistory. He kept his explanations focused on the event or on the other people in the shot, especially Thomas. But, sometimes one or the other would ask about his personal memories or feelings about someone. At one point, Sammy even asked him, "What did you think of Nana back then; did you think she was hot?"

Tomina interrupted with, "Samantha, that's not polite."

Kevin simply said she was his best friend's sister and besides, she was older and engaged. He couldn't bring himself to add, "to Tim" or "to your grandfather."

The girls encouraged him to reminisce, and for more than an hour they talked together about dozens of moments frozen in a time that, Kevin mostly assumed, only held meaning for him. Along the journey and the telling, Kevin avoided long narratives but a few photos propelled him on. A picture of him and Thomas facing from the rear seating well of a green station wagon had him reliving the thrill of that backwards flight down the Kennedy and Dan Ryan, his first car trip downtown and across a state line. The girls were incredulous that he'd grown up without a family car.

Another photo was identifiable because Mrs. Thom had written on the back 1963 SCHOOL PICNIC, Cedar Lake. The pictured showed a young Thomas and a skinny version of Kevin in swimsuits at a beach. Pat was behind them, making finger horns above their heads. Kevin explained the annual junior high picnic trip, but, of course, skipped what had happened that day under the diving raft. However, he couldn't help smiling at the memory. When Tomina smiled at his smile, he found himself wondering. *Did that day lead to all this, to her?*

June 27, 2016
(...PM)

"I'd like to take you two out for dinner," Kevin said. He was exhausted from the emotional journey he'd just been on but didn't want the visit to end.

Samantha quickly chimed in. "How about Senarighi's?" she suggested.

Tomina seconded the idea as she returned the pictures to the box. "They make a good pizza and their pasta is handmade."

"Sounds good by me. I haven't eaten since this morning," he replied.

"Let me go shower and change," said Samantha. "I'll be quick." She disappeared up the stairs just off the kitchen. *She moves deftly*, Kevin thought, but couldn't help himself from adding, *considering the extra pounds*. He immediately felt small and petty.

He tried to process the afternoon and what it meant, if anything. He still had no idea what to believe or think. He wasn't even sure what he was feeling at the moment. So many memories and emotions had tumbled out on their dining table. Still, for some reason, he felt calmer now than at any time since he'd gotten Pat's letter. He reminded himself to just enjoy their company and keep their needs first. He could think about all the rest of it back at the motel. He'd call Nelson, and she would help him process some of it. He'd have to sleep on the rest. Sometimes sleep helped him filter out the real from the unreal. Other times, his subconscious dreams floated images or thoughts that made him question just what was real.

"Kevin, I'm glad you came," Tomina quietly interrupted his thoughts. She smiled that great warm smile at him.

"So am I," he said across the table. "Thank you. This has been a real gift."

"I have one last thing I'd like to show you before Samantha comes back down." She reached over and produced a legal-sized manila envelope from the seat of the chair to her left. It had been hidden by the table. "Samantha has seen these, of course, but I thought you might want to look at them by yourself." She handed it to him and said, "I'll go freshen up too," and left him sitting there holding the envelope as she headed upstairs.

Kevin slowly unwound the string clasp. He pulled out a stack of drawings about an inch thick. Even before they were completely free of the envelope, Kevin recognized them as Thomas'. The third one down was of a 1957 Thunderbird. He remembered witnessing that picture coming to life on Thomas' desk in his room a long time ago, the day his childish thoughts of being a great artist died, the day he lied to – and later cursed – his friend.

The collection documented Thomas' maturation in subject material and technique. The last drawings were from his art school, pre-Vietnam portraits followed by scenes and faces from "over there". Kevin had a few similar drawings entombed in his safety deposit box. They'd come along with Thomas' letters. Anyone could see how the war had focused his friend's eye, his skills, and his compassion. You could see and almost smell the fear, terror, and weariness he had captured. Every face told a story, was a study in humanity. Kevin locked them away after Thomas died. It was an attempt to ease his own pain and disgust with himself for still envying Thomas' ability to capture raw emotion and reality with so few pencil lines. He hadn't looked at them since.

Unlike the jerky randomness of the photographs Samantha had laid before him, Tomina had arranged Thomas' drawings in chronological order. So it made sense that the last several pictures, the Vietnam phase, were the most mature in spite of being the most spare. However, when Kevin reached the last drawing, his marionette string snapped him upright again, causing his mind to stumble and crash. It was a pre-Vietnam rendering, out of sequence. One that, until last March, he'd never seen before. It was a black and white charcoal portrait of Pat looking over her shoulder at him. It was almost, but not quite, identical to the colored pencil version that had arrived like a grenade with Pat's letter and which had blown up his world and retirement, possibly forever.

From the upstairs landing Kevin heard Samantha telling her mom she was ready and was heading back downstairs. But the drawing in his hand held his full attention. It was more skilled than his version, and it was dated in Thomas' writing in the lower right corner *Dec '69*. His colored version was, he was quite sure, not dated at all. Back in March when it had arrived out of the blue, he had never thought to question its authenticity. It had been close enough to Thomas' style to match his distant memories. But now, having just gone through a chronological sampling of Thomas' work, it seemed probable the one in his hand was the original. Why was it on the bottom of the stack, at least a year out of proper sequence? He decided one of the girls must have been looking at it and simply put it at the back of the stack instead of its proper chronological spot. *Why is there a colored version? When was that done?*

He was still staring at the picture when Sammy entered through the kitchen. "I'm all ready. I hope you're hungry because they have great ...." She stopped when she saw the picture in Kevin's hand. Hesitantly she asked, "What's that?"

Kevin showed her. "It's a drawing of your nana and me. I've never seen it before." This wasn't a lie since the one at home was, he now assumed, a copy, or perhaps an earlier draft. He was confused but didn't want to lie to the girl if he didn't have to. "It surprised me. As far as I knew, Thomas never drew us together."

Samantha said. "I guess Uncle Thomas had some secrets, even from his best friend, huh?"

Senarighi's was a small storefront restaurant run by two retired teachers with a passion for cooking Italian. It sat in the middle of the block with apartments above. From the handwritten menu on the wall, Tomina had ordered linguini, and Kevin agreed to share Sammy's favorite specialty pizza with her. Dinner conversation started out in safe territory. Tomina and Kevin talked teaching, the ridiculous political controversy over Common Core educational standards, and the general state of education. She told him about her students and school. She loved her kids and took her teaching and professional skills and growth seriously. Samantha wasn't shy about offering her perspective and experience with good and not-so-good teachers. She thought she'd be a great teacher, but could never put up with the general behavior of kids.

Kevin told them about Nelson. They were surprised that he'd been over fifty when they'd met and married, he for the first time. He kept his end of the conversation short so he could focus on Tomina. He wanted to learn all he could, however, he couldn't help adding, "And, no, it wasn't because I was gay, just cowardly."

"WHAT?" Samantha sputtered, almost loosing a mushroom from her mouth. Kevin explained what her mother had said to him earlier.

"But you'd have made an awesome dad," Sammy said.

Over the years, Kevin had heard versions of this from time to time, and it always made him cringe. While he could freely admit to having been too selfish to marry, he preferred not to admit to the bigger issue – that marriage and kids presented too many unknowns and challenges. Turning his fate and happiness over to a wife and kids had always scared the hell out of him. He'd felt inadequate to the task and sure he'd have screwed it up. So he gave his standby remark to parry the compliment: "Teaching gave me more than enough kids in my life." The remark was always accepted at face value. It even made him think his avoidance of the whole thing had been a rational decision. But now, sitting here, with Tomina and Samantha across from him in the booth, he wondered if fate had circumvented his decision, making him a dupe in his own life.

Tomina briefed Kevin on her mom's life. After their divorce, her parents had remained on speaking terms. But by early high school, her dad Tim had remarried and moved to the Dallas area. "We talked by phone, but the next time I saw him was at my wedding. He always paid child support, but I wanted a father, not a check." She looked at her daughter and added, "But it's not as bad as losing your father like Samantha did." She put her hand on her daughter's shoulder and caressed her neck.

"I was pretty young," Samantha said. "I really don't actually remember much, mostly from the pictures and Mom." Kevin thought of how Thomas and Pat also had grown up with no dad. He didn't mention it, not wanting to interrupt Tomina's story.

"In the meantime, as you maybe remember, Mom could be stubborn, and a bit…'impetuous', to say the least. After their divorce, I craved stability and consistency but, sometimes I felt like Mom was the teenager, and I was the adult. We'd clash pretty hard, but I guess that's just the nature of mother-daughter relationships. Right, Samantha?"

Samantha glanced up from her phone, which she had just begun to check for something or other. The light sparkled off her nose stud. Kevin hoped his tiny wince didn't show. "No comment," the girl replied, taking another bite of pizza perhaps to stifle further commentary.

"Mom dated occasionally." Tomina took a sip of her chardonnay and continued, "And even had one guy she considered marrying, but it didn't work out in the end. By then, I think she was too independent. She had a good job as a secretary for a VP at a publishing house – coincidentally, of educational materials."

Tomina took a bite of her food. Kevin said, "I had a favorite aunt when I was a kid who had a similar job, a secretary high up in some kind of publishing. She never married either. I'm sure she would have had the opportunity, so I guess she liked her independence too. Maybe it says something about successful, strong women."

Sammy set down her phone and jumped back into the conversation. "Did you come from a big family?" she asked.

"No, I was an only child, but my dad came from a family of ten kids. I've been working on our family's genealogy this winter and found out a lot of things I'd never heard of growing up."

"Ten kids?" Sammy said. "That must have kept your grandparents busy."

"Well, actually one of the things I've discovered was that my grandmother raised them pretty much alone. It seems my grandfather was rather mysteriously not around a lot."

"Well he was there at least ten times," Sammy quipped.

"I'm sorry, Kevin. Samantha, like her nana, can sometimes be a bit impetuous, not to mention, inappropriate." Tomina gave Samantha a gentle elbow to her ribs.

Kevin raised his glass, "Here's to grandparents. Good or bad, we wouldn't be here without them." Tomina and Kevin sipped their wine and Samantha her root beer.

He continued, "You were saying your mom worked at a publisher?"

Tomina picked up her story. "Yeah, she really liked it. She'd bring samples home for me to critique sometimes. Anyhow, she was planning on retiring when she got sick."

"Where's the fairness in that?" Sammy added.

Tomina again rubbed her daughter's neck. "As things got worse, we sold her house and she moved in with us. Samantha was a great help and comfort for her. With teaching, doctors, medicines, insurance, I couldn't have done it without her. She and Mom were two peas in a pod. They'd spend hours talking. Mom loved sharing her pictures and stories with her. They'd talk on and on like two conspirators or something. Mom said Samantha had her sense of mischief and her brother's artistic ability. She was right. Samantha really is quite a good artist."

As Kevin listened, the pizza began to form a knot in his stomach. The thought of the girls dealing with Pat's death and its accoutrements was more than sad. He somehow should have known, somehow should have been there to help, somehow... changed history? But obviously from her letter it was clear that Pat hadn't wanted him to know anything. *She'd protected me? Knew I couldn't handle a baby, be a good father...or?*

A sudden thought flooded out everything else in his mind. It so startled him that he looked stricken, or like he was choking. He had no idea where it had come from. Tomina reached across the table and placed her hand on top of his. "Are you okay?" She leaned forward and with the ball of her thumb gently wiped Kevin's cheek. He hadn't been aware of the tear. "That's enough about Mom for now," Tomina said, apparently thinking the tear was for her mom.

Kevin wanted to believe it was for Pat, or maybe Thomas, or for these two women with whom he already felt a bond, or even for himself. But he knew and he feared it was for the unthinkable thing that was peaking at him from the shadows of the past. Tomina added, "You are a good man, Kevin Cullerton. I agree with Samantha. You would have been a great father."

He found himself reaching for another piece of pizza to stick in his mouth and hoping he wouldn't choke on it.

July 13, 2016

After the visit to Chicago, Kevin tried to convince himself now that he had met Tomina and Sammy, that the thing to do was just let sleeping dogs lie. There was no need to pursue this any further. An occasional email and Christmas card would allow him to keep in touch, to monitor their situation. If they were ever in need, he'd be happy to help, even financially. Tim Kerneki – the man who was "Dad" in Tomina's world – was alive in Texas, so Sammy had a grandfather. They didn't need him in their lives to complicate things.

But that course of non-action never would sit comfortable in his gut. He found himself replaying their meeting in his head, trying to assess and reconcile new thoughts and feelings with the old. Tomina had called him "family in a way." *What does that mean? There would be obligations that came with being family in a way? Do I owe it to the Thom family to pursue this? Surely, a casual relationship would be sufficient?*

Kevin's doubts, frustrations and fears were a jumbled constant. The feelings were sharpened because he could not decide what he wanted to happen. He found it difficult to work on his genealogy because he'd see himself in his rogue grandfather. He wondered how much contact the man had kept with his ten kids after he'd split. Did he help them out with money, or send Christmas cards?

Damn it, Pat. Why didn't you say something before you died, when I could have talked to you about this and found out what the hell you were thinking– what the hell the truth is?

Nelson listened and offered comfort but not advice. Kevin was pretty sure her opinion was that Pat was a crazy bitch, so he left it at that. He appreciated that since the first time he'd showed her Pat's letter, she never raised the point again. She was constant in her belief that he had to make up his mind about what to do. He wasn't so appreciative of that. Three weeks after he had met his "maybe" daughter and granddaughter, he was no more settled on a plan forward than when he had first got the letter last March.

Two fundamental anxieties took turns, like two monkeys, racing around in his brain. Each chased the other's tail round and round. Here we go 'round the mulberry bush. The chatter they produced was deafening at times. At times they grew from monkey to gorilla-sized. When this occurred during the day, he'd start another household project just to focus on something else. When they intruded on his evening, he'd try working on his genealogy until Grandpa Edward P. inevitably raised himself from the dead and tormented him. Then he'd find himself aimlessly flipping channels on cable TV. Because Tomina, and later Sammy, had mentioned the Cubs were doing well this year, he'd look for their games. If they were winning, he'd watch and relax a bit. If they were behind, he'd change channels to avoid the added stress, and not jinx a possible comeback. That they were winning at over a .600 pace, boggled Kevin's mind. He wished he believed in a heaven so he could talk to Thomas or his dad about what was going on in Wrigley Field.

But often there was just no hiding. Both monkeys scared him. Each was dangerous in its own way. Both sprang to life at dinner that night with Tomina and Sammy. Each was circumstantial, but taken together they were driving him crazy.

The first had burst like an aneurysm in his head. It had so startled him that Tomina had taken his hand and asked what was wrong. The thought was as bizarre as it was unbidden; he had no idea where it had come from. However, little by little, he was afraid he was seeing clues in his tangled facts and memories. *Was I a proxy for Thomas? Had her fear for her brother allowed her to act out some subconscious fantasy beyond the realm of brotherly love?* Kevin remembered how Pat had mounted him after he'd confessed his own exotic dream. *Does that explain the unusual name? Even if Tomina is Tim's, wouldn't deciding I was the father better fit her sublimation?*

Pat had told Tomina that Tim harbored some jealousy about her relationship with her brother. Kevin wondered if Tim was on to something that he had missed all those years. *Was I too close, unable to observe other than what I expected to see?* Kevin didn't want to believe any of this. But if it were true, he might have missed it. He was wrapped up in his own close friendship with Thomas, with no reason to look beyond the nose on his own face. His genealogy was proving how myopic he had been with his own parents' lives. And, of course, none of this would have occurred to him when Pat was suddenly pregnant, because he and everyone else naturally believed Tim was Tomina's father.

Kevin spent lots of energy trying not to consider, let alone accept any of this. To whisper the questions out loud, or write them down, would make it feel too real. Even if he could send off for a document or look up the answer on the internet, he knew he probably wouldn't. Ignorance, however, was not bliss. The whole idea hurt him, though he wasn't quite sure why. Maybe he was afraid it might reflect badly on him, though again he wasn't sure how. Nonetheless, for now suppression was better than knowing. He never brought these thoughts up with Nelson, though not doing so felt a bit like cheating on her, like he was somehow putting Pat ahead of her. He didn't want Nelson to think Pat could be that crazy, because he didn't want to think it.

The second stress, the other monkey, chasing him was his growing concern about the extent of the pain he would unleash on Tomina and Sammy if he handled this father/daughter situation poorly. It joined monkey number one when Tomina had agreed with Sammy that he "would have made an awesome dad." Somehow it made him feel more guilty about this whole crazy mess. He was sure if he brought up the question of her paternity, she'd think he was the crazy one. Without confessing all the details to Tomina and making Pat the bad-guy, there was no reason for her not to reach that conclusion. It would be infinitely more emotionally logical for Tomina not to believe him, than to believe her mother had deceived her and everyone else. Even if he showed her the letter, he couldn't conceive she wouldn't hate him for exposing the lie. He was trapped, and he had never been the courageous type who could gnaw off his own limb to escape.

In an effort to distract Kevin from his futzing and mumbling, Nelson suggested the lawn needed cutting. He knew he was driving her nuts, so he readily agreed. He cranked up the gas engine and again – for the millionth time – tried to picture himself telling Tomina and Sammy the truth. He'd show them the letters. They'd see Pat's words, they'd see he hadn't known, hadn't run away – like his grandfather had.

But how would that help now? Surely, it would snap the tenuous bungee cord that bound them together. He wasn't sure he wanted to get any closer, but he didn't want to lose them either. And, what if he was Tomina's dad? What kind of a father or grandfather would he be if he caused them pain and the loss of their identity, or equally bad, walked away from them? Before he even finished this thought, Kevin questions brought him full circle again. He thought of the ten kids with the name Cullerton written after each one. He pictured a shadowy, featureless Edward P. Cullerton walking off to wherever he ended up. But he had known the children were his. His age was listed with each one of them. *Surely, that's a lot different than finding out you're a father when you're already in your sixties and retired ... Isn't it?*

Kevin stuck orange foam plugs in his ears against the roar of gas push mower. The color of the plugs reminded him of Sammy's orange ponytail – and her pierced nose. He'd mentioned these details to Nelson when he'd first got home. When he'd expressed his dismay, she laughed for a full minute before finally adding, "Beautiful, you deserved that." He'd added that though he liked the girl, Sammy was rather pushy and a bit loud, attributes he'd never liked in his students. But now, as he found himself wishing her a little thinner, he was struck with shame. *What kind of a grandfather gets worked up about a nose stud or orange hair...or weight? What would Sammy or*

Tomina think if they knew me as well as Nelson does? Would they laugh, or would they hate me for being so damn petty?

Two laps around the side yard with the mower and the monkeys were still pinballing around his skull. He needed more distraction. He left the mower running while he went in and found the small music device Nelson had given him on his birthday. She'd showed him how to download music and since then, whenever he was exercising on his elliptical or doing mindless work around the house, he was able to enjoy the randomized downloaded songs of his past: Simon and Garfunkel, Gordon Lightfoot, The Beatles, and of course, some Beethoven.

He broke a sweat as he mowed from the shade of the side yard into the sunny back. Familiar sforzando orchestral chords, each followed by the flash of piano scales and arpeggios, made him stop and increase the volume. On his second sweep around the perimeter, he was humming along with the strings as they played the opening theme. The *Emperor Concerto*, as always, chased away every thought, emotion, and memory – except one.

It had been the summer of 1975, a year after his father's retirement. Kevin's piano teacher had mentioned Vladimir Ashkenazy was performing the piece at Ravinia Park – the outdoor summer home of the Chicago Symphony. She considered Ashkenazy the best of the young pianists. Kevin knew and loved the music, officially named Piano Concerto Number 5, in E flat Major, Opus 73. Premiered in 1811, Beethoven's publisher referred to it as an "Emperor of a concerto", and the pseudonym was coined. Kevin called and reserved two tickets that afternoon and invited his dad who seemed genuinely touched. Kevin was delighted. This would be the first time he could take his father someplace special.

Kevin taste and love for classical music had been acquired by osmosis. The process had been subliminal and binary. In the cartoons and commercials of his youth, famous themes often served to set the mood or sell a product for everything from Bugs Bunny to Quaker Oats. Every household had a TV, so every kid recognized "ba-ba-ba-BUM" or the *Lone Ranger's theme* "da-da-dunt, da da dunt, da da dunt dunt dunt" long before they'd heard of Beethoven or Rossini.

The second influence had been his dad's walnut-grained Zenith radio. In Chicago, WFMT played classical music at night, and Mr. Cullerton listened in bed before falling asleep. He went to bed early because he was up before dawn to get downtown. At first, Kevin began to notice the music when he'd go in to kiss his dad goodnight. One night, he asked about a piece that caught his fancy. After that, his father always left his door opened a crack. Kevin took to sitting on the kitchen floor and listening. They never talked about the music, but both father and son cherished the connection. Kevin felt the music flowing from the old Zenith was a direct link to his father's world.

Eventually he told Thomas about the little ritual. At first, he was wary to say anything because he didn't want to make Thomas feel sad since he didn't have a father to share such things with. He brought it up one night while staying over, starting the conversation with their agreed upon signal for serious talks, "I hope this isn't going to feel like I'm pissing on your shoes, but..." Not only wasn't Thomas hurt, he flipped on his radio and they searched for WFMT. It became part of their routine when they stayed at each other's house. They'd climb into bed and on came WFMT, soft and in the background while they talked or read, until they fell asleep. Over the years, Thomas became part of the secret ritual.

During the ride to the concert, he and his dad finally talked music – though it had been more a soliloquy on Kevin's part. They parked the car and began walking the few hundred yards to the main gate. Kevin kept the pace slow. His dad still walked around the neighborhood, but he was not quick. He smoked plus a few years ago he had missed the bottom rung of a ladder and twisted his knee so badly it still gave him trouble. Being old school, he never went to a doctor to get it checked. Kevin carried a thermos of coffee and a small cooler with Brown's chicken, along with two folding lawn chairs. Sitting on a blanket would not have been comfortable for his father, and he didn't want anything to distract from their evening together.

The music wouldn't start for another thirty minutes so they

had time to eat and talk. When they got situated and settled, Kevin asked, "Would you like some wine?" Surprisingly, his dad said yes. Mr. Cullerton enjoyed a highball on the rare occasions his parents hosted a get-together, or visited with friends. Once in a great while, he'd have a beer in the evening, usually a Special Export. A birthday gift of six bottles could last him half a year. Kevin returned with two plastic glasses of Chardonnay, and they each took a piece of chicken.

They dined in silence for awhile, enjoying the atmosphere and doing a little people watching. Shorts and tee shirts mingled with full formal attire, and everything in between. When Kevin reached for a second piece of chicken, he said, "Dad, I talked your ear off about Ashkenazy but I never asked if you know the *Emperor Concerto*. It's one of my favorites."

His dad wiped a bit of grease from his lips with his paper napkin. Inspecting what was left of the chicken leg he held he deposited the bone back into the container and took a sip of his wine. He sat back in his chair and said, "Let me see." He closed his eyes, hesitated a moment, and then began, with small hand movements, to conduct and hum the beginning of the opening theme.

Kevin sat wide eyed as his father divulged a part of himself that his son would never have guessed at – a closet conductor and hummer. Kevin sometimes conducted while driving if a favorite piece popped up on the radio. But he'd never seen his dad do it, nor had he ever heard him hum music before. "Dad! Where did you learn that? That was really cool."

"The radio tends to play the famous composers a lot. I must have heard *The Emperor* dozens of times. And...," he hesitated as if to grab a memory out of the past, "I remember seeing it conducted in England during the war."

"Really?" This was the kind of stuff Kevin was hoping to hear about. "Ashkenazy recorded this last spring in England with the London Philharmonic. Helen Regelin, my piano teacher, said he did a brilliant job."

"I was in Birmingham, not London, at the military post office there. On week-ends, I'd visit ruined castles, see some of the famous cathedrals. Your mother has some old postcards hid away somewhere. Anyhow, one Sunday I went to a concert at the local music hall and they played it. I was pretty impressed."

"You know," Kevin confessed, "my interest in classical music came from you and your radio."

Mr. Cullerton was moved by his son's comment, a verbal acknowledgement of an unspoken bond. He looked into the early evening sky beyond the pavilion roof and stage where the musicians were now seated and warming up. A cacophony of instrumental timbres filled the air. Kevin was about to ask his dad a question when they went silent, and an oboe beckoned to its brethren with a long vibrato-less note. Kevin knew it was an "A", not because he had a good sense of pitch, but because orchestras always tuned to an "A." He wondered if his dad knew that. He wasn't going to ask and sound like a know-it-all. The rest of the orchestra grabbed onto the note as their touch-stone and began to tune. First the woodwinds, then the brass, followed by the strings.

The tuning sounds faded, replaced by the silence of collective anticipation. It was in that few moments of silence, while a couple thousand people settled awaiting the conductor's entry, Kevin stood. He bent and put his arms awkwardly around his dad's shoulders. "Dad, I am so glad you came. And, I'm sorry it took me so damn long to ask. I love you." Then he leaned in and kissed him on the forehead.

The moment exploded into applause as Maestro Carlo Maria Giulini walked briskly on stage. Kevin sat down and turned his chair to face the pavilion. But instead of joining the applause he reached over, placing his hand on his father's. If he had turned to look, he would have seen proud contentment on his dad's face but not recognized the sadness behind the old man's eyes. Even if Kevin had seen it, he'd not have been able to name it, for it belonged to his father alone. It was rooted in the type of melancholy which only happens when something frayed and broken in the past comes in contact with a joyful moment in the present. When buried ghosts escape and drift into a specific moment in the here and now. A moment like when your grown son takes you to a concert, kisses you, and says he loves you.

Jim Cullerton knew the ghostly shadows. He'd carried them all his life. One was a ten-year-old Jimmy Cullerton, wishing for such a moment with his own father. The other was *that man*, shriveled, old, and dying in a corner bed of a nursing home. Both memories were so sad in so many ways.

Two hours later, the crowd flowed back out the gates toward their cars and the commuter train station. Kevin waited outside a men's room for his father, replaying parts of the concert in his head.

"Hello, Kevin." He turned to see his piano teacher. With her tall, thin, erect posture and reddish-brown hair drawn tight in a bun, Helen Regelin presented both a formal and formidable presence. She looked classic, and in her day could have taken Ingrid Bergman's place in one of the old timeless movies like *Casablanca*. Most undergrad piano students were intimidated by her demeanor and bearing. But she and Kevin, who was older than most undergrads, had immediately liked each other. They had a close, but professional student/teacher relationship. He had a mountain of respect for her. She had taken him seriously in spite of his lack of technical facility at the keyboard, and had gone out of her way to encourage his interest in theory and composition. Through her, Kevin learned how to really listen and to transcend the mere facility of a performer to play fast and clean. She taught him to hear and think like a composer, not just a music teacher.

"Did you like Ashkenazy?" She reached into her purse, extracting one of her trademark long, thin, black cigarettes. Kevin knew she was checking to see if he'd noted the pianist's nuanced performance and interpretation.

"I didn't hear a phrase that wasn't perfectly shaped. All the way here, my poor dad had to listen to me go on and on about what you'd explained to me, and it was all there. Thanks for telling me about the concert. I loved it, and I'm sure my dad did too."

"He did," Mr. Cullerton said as stepped close beside his son to allow others to pass. Kevin turned. "I'm glad I didn't oversell it. Dad, this is the poor lady who listens to me bang away at the piano every week. Helen, this is my father." They each extended a hand. Kevin took pleasure at the linking of two such important parts of his life.

Helen noticed Mr. Cullerton's cigarette and raised hers. He struck his lighter, and she leaned into the flame like a noir Bogart and Bergman scene come to life. In that instant, standing next to his father in the warmth of the night and the magical afterglow of the perfect performance, that small flame in the dark held to a cigarette imprinted an image onto the threads of Kevin's mind where the unasked questions about his father's life would hang forever like undeveloped photos in a dark room.

Kevin and his father sat in the Ford and waited for the parking lot traffic to thin. After awhile, Kevin slipped the car into gear and pulled behind the last cars waiting to exit. His dad said, "She seems very nice."

Kevin glanced over to him. "Helen? My piano teacher?"

"I'm glad I met her."

Kevin wanted to ask why, but was being waved forward by the policeman on traffic control. Heading home, the darkened car lit only by the dim illumination from the dashboard, provided Kevin and his father a quiet space to be with their own thoughts about the evening. Both were comfortable in the silence. About half way, a question occurred to Kevin. "Dad, were you stationed any place else overseas besides England; you know, during the war?"

"I spent a few months in Paris."

"Did you get to see much of the city?"

"A bit." For the first time on this special night, his dad sounded reluctant.

"Did you see the Eiffel Tower and Notre Dame? Did you get to The Louvre?"

Mr. Cullerton reclined his seat several inches, moving his face out of the soft luminescence. "Just once." He folded his hands on his stomach and closed his eyes. "Thanks, Kevin. Let's do this again."

August 1, 2016

Kevin hit the power button on his PC and headed to the kitchen for coffee. He took his first sips standing at the screened back door, enjoying the warm morning air on his skin. At the porch feeder the birds took turns intimidating each other. A feisty goldfinch relegated a pair of chickadees to ground feeding for dropped sunflower seeds on the lawn. Its tenure was short lived as a female cardinal swooped in, chasing him off to a nearby birch. *Thus is life.* Kevin headed back to his computer. Before checking the latest election chaos on the national news sites, he opened his email.

> Samantha wants to know... July 23, 2016
> Hello Kevin. We're both enjoying the summer. I'm planting flowers around the house and catching up on my reading. Samantha and her friends are at the beach or playing ball when she's not working at a local art store. She's working 20 hours a week and getting some money saved. She asked me to see if you wanted to go with her to her softball team's Father –Daughter outing at a Cubs game on August 1st. I'm not much of a baseball fan unless she is playing, and of course her Grandpa Tim lives in Texas. She said to tell you it's a night game. I told her I'd ask, but not to get her hopes up. She'll understand if you can't. But do stop again when you're back in the city. We'd both like to see you again.
> Tomina

Kevin's gut twitched whenever Tomina referenced Tim as either "Dad" or "Grandpa." He walked back to the kitchen to check the calendar hanging on the fridge. He and Nelson penciled events here in order to avoid conflicting engagements. Then he stuck his head into the bathroom and hollered over the exhaust fan to Nelson in the shower. "Honey, do we have anything happening on August 1st?"

"Really! Can't this wait until I'm out of the shower? Did you check the calendar?"

"I did, nothing marked there. I just got an email from Tomina."

Nelson stuck her head out from behind the curtain. "Oh? What did she say?"

"Sammy asked if I'd go to her father–daughter outing at a Cubs game. You know, since her real grandpa lives in Texas. She thought I might like to see a night game at Wrigley."

Nelson cocked her head slightly and said, "Her *real* grandpa?"

"You know what I mean," Kevin said. "As far as she knows, he's her grandpa, and I sure can't say I know, or want to know, any different."

Nelson smiled at him, "Have at it." She gave him a quick flash of her wet breasts and disappeared back behind the shower curtain. He hesitated a second wondering it that had been an invitation, but headed back to his office.

He took a sip of his now cool coffee and hit REPLY.

Tomina,

Glad you're relaxing and catching up on your reading. Thanks for the invite. I'd love to take in a night game with Sammy, as long as you're OK with that. The lights at Wrigley were put in after I'd moved to Wisconsin so it would be new experience. Send me the details and tell Sammy we have a date.

Kevin

The group took their seats in the grandstands along the first base line. The girls wore their team jerseys. Sammy augmented her outfit by wearing a Cubs cap and dying her ponytail Cubby blue. She was seated next to one of her teammates and Kevin had the aisle seat next to her. The weather was perfect, not too cool even here in the shadow under the upper deck. The lights, which had been added in 1988, were on, but it would be awhile before they overtook the sun setting far out to the west beyond Clark Street on the third base side. Kevin looked around, feeling a lump of emotion grow in his throat. He wasn't sure if it was nostalgia, or the invitation from Sammy.

The crowd swelled, filling every corner of the ballpark. Even the rooftops across Waveland Avenue, on which private bleachers had been erected, were filled. This was crazy. Never in all the years he'd followed the Cubs on WGN was the park ever this full. He breathed in the energy.

"Thanks for the scorecard, Kevin. I'll keep it as a souvenir." Samantha was penciling-in what she called the "for sure starters". Kevin watched as the last name appeared in the number nine spot.

"Kyle Hendricks? He's been pitching pretty well, hasn't he?" Ever since the Cubs started to pull away in the National League East, they'd been getting more and more coverage on national cable and Kevin now had a passing familiarity with the starters. He still, however, was keeping his excitement under wraps. After all, he'd lived through '69, '84 and '03.

"They've all been doing great this year," Sammy replied. "This is going to be the year. Look at this place. I can feel it, can't you?"

Kevin remembered saying these exact words to his dad many times; until he'd grown old enough to learn the universe didn't work that way. "Well Sam, it's my sad duty as a well-trampled Cubs fan to remind you that they haven't won it all since the year my dad was born. Hope is important, but it is a double-edged sword."

Sammy asked, "When was your father born?"

"1908. Actually, not too far from where you live."

"1908! That's crazy."

"It is," Kevin agreed. "But you think that's crazy? I recently found out his father, my grandfather, was born in 1863; we're talking during the Civil War. But that means he was alive when the Cubs won two World Series." Kevin added, "Sadly, by my time, they were known as the doormats of the National League. But who knows, maybe these things jump generations." He felt safe knowing Sammy couldn't guess at the veiled implication behind his words. "Have you heard of the Curse of the Billy Goat?" he asked her.

Sammy said, "Yeah, Coach told us about that. But this year they're going to turn the goat into goat burgers." Just then, the massive crowd rose and roared their approval as the Cubs took the field, all obviously more than quite willing to throw themselves on that double-edged sword called hope.

As the first pitch was delivered, Kevin again marveled at the 40,000+ fans crammed into every corner of the park. It seemed unreal: night baseball at Wrigley, August and the Cubs in first place, not to mention sitting next to a teenage girl that might be his granddaughter and who he hadn't known existed until eight weeks ago. He wanted a beer, even a $10 one, but had promised himself he'd not drink while Sammy was in his charge. Instead he signaled to a vendor working his way up the aisle and bought them both a pop.

Hendricks, the Cubs' starter, got through the first inning unscathed. As the teams switched positions Sammy asked with the soda straw still between her lips, "When was the last time you were here?"

Kevin searched his memory. "I don't remember exactly. My dad brought me a couple of times when I was a kid, and then he let me come and vend with him a couple more times when I'd turned sixteen. Once after that with your nana's brother. So it's been a long time."

"I'm sixteen," she said.

The succinct comparison made Kevin a little uncomfortable so he changed the subject. "You know, the night lights give this place a ghostly surrealistic look, but it still feels like the Friendly Confines."

Sammy slurped her soda and said, "I know about surrealistic paintings. I like the way they mix all kinds of weird stuff together." The comment impressed Kevin; the loud slurp didn't.

In the bottom of the first, the Cubs put two runners on base. With two outs, Kevin assumed they'd be abandoned there, like in the old days. Instead, the shortstop, Addison Russell, lined a ball down the right field line, scoring both runs. Standing with the crowd to applaud, he said, "Well, young lady, maybe this *is* the year."

Sammy chatted with her friends but always filled Kevin in on their conversations. He realized he hadn't noticed her nose stud and felt a little pride in the fact he hadn't. Maybe there was hope for him yet. Still, he did check the next time she turned his way. No stud. He wanted not to be glad about that, but failed.

A few innings later, Sammy circled the conversation back and asked, "Were your father and grandfather Cub fans?" The question put a grin on Kevin's face.

"Dad was. Growing up, his whole family was. Even his mom and sisters, and that was long before girls played most sports. Dad never mentioned his father, but somehow I got the impression the old man wasn't much of a fan of anything." He left off what he was thinking: *Except maybe carousing or gambling.*

In the bottom of the sixth, Hendricks helped his own cause and singled in a run, and then went on to pitch a complete game - Cubbies 5, Marlins 0. Sammy was ecstatic and Kevin found himself thrilled. A rush of nostalgic emotion swelled when Chicagoan Steve Goodman's iconic 1984 song "Go Cubs Go" poured though the speakers. He still played a CD mix of Goodman songs on occasion. Like Kevin and his friends, the Chicago singer-songwriter had been a long-suffering fan. Ironically, he'd earlier written a song called "A Dying Cubs Fan's Last Request." As fate would have it, just weeks after Goodman's death, the Cubs made the divisional pennant playoffs against the San Diego Padres. They had easily won the first two games and then proceeded to lose the next three in a row and be eliminated – again.

As he and Sammy and the rest of their group headed for the exit, Kevin told Sammy, "I'm pretty sure this was the first time they've won while I was in the park."

She said, "Maybe now you're a good luck charm." She linked her arm through Kevin's. He tried not to freeze up. But as they left the ballpark, he quietly sang along: *Go Cubs Go. Go Cubs Go. Hey Chicago, what do you say, the Cubs are going to win today. Go Cubs Go...*

When they got close to the house, he could just make out Tomina sitting on the front steps. Sammy enthusiastically waved the white W flag Kevin bought her as a parting souvenir. Over the course of the year as the victories mounted, the crowds had taken to waving the W flag to Goodman's anthem to celebrate each win. Now, literally thousands waved at each home game. In spite of the late hour, Sammy let out a whoop for her mother's benefit from half way down the block. It startled Kevin, but he refrained from hushing her. He also was still feeling thc flush of victory. He just waved.

They approached the steps, and Sammy hollered. "Another W, Mom. We need to order Series tickets now."

"Samantha, hold it down. It's almost eleven o'clock." She looked at Kevin. "You had a good time?"

Before Kevin could respond, Sammy jumped in, "It was GREAT! 5-0. We creamed 'em. Kevin is a good luck charm. No way they don't win the pennant and World Series now."

Kevin hastened to add, "I wouldn't buy tickets just yet. Besides, remember that's the first time they've ever won while I was there. Maybe you're the charm?"

"Mom, did you know the last time the Cubs won the World Series was the year Kevin's father was born?" Sammy looked at Kevin, "What year was that again?"

"1908."

"Yeah, 1908. And you know what else?" Her words rushed on. "His grandfather was born in the Civil War, and he saw the Cubs win two World Series."

Kevin was tickled that she had paid attention when he'd mentioned his dad and grandfather but jumped in to straighten out her facts. "I said he was alive at the time, not that he saw the games, or even paid attention to baseball."

"Wow, can you imagine Mom? That's like when Abraham Lincoln was president."

The teacher and amateur historian in Kevin kicked in. "Did you know the bed Lincoln died in after being shot is here in Chicago, at the Historical Society? Matter of fact, I'm stopping there tomorrow."

Sammy had been calming down, but her excitement peaked again. "Mom, can I go with him? Please? I've never been there and it would be educational and all. I don't have to work tomorrow."

Tomina tried to give Kevin some room to maneuver. "Whoa, young lady. It's rather rude to invite yourself. Kevin may want some quiet time without you pestering him with a thousand questions." Both looked to Kevin. Samantha with a "please" look on her face, and Tomina with an expression that said, "I'm sorry."

"It would be fun to have you along. Actually, both of you are welcome if you're interested. I'm only going for a couple of hours because I'm driving straight home afterward. I just want to do a little follow-up on the research I've been working on. I'm trying to find out if my great-grandparents' house was burnt in the Chicago Fire." To Samantha he added, "That was where the grandfather I mentioned was born. He would have been only eight years old at the time of the fire."

Samantha turned to her mother. "Can we go Mom? PLEASE?"

August 2, 2016

Kevin still called it the Historical Society rather than by its current official title of Chicago History Museum. Before heading to Chicago to accompany Samantha to the father-daughter outing, he'd browsed their website. Founded in 1856, The Society originally stood at the corner of Dearborn and Ontario a few blocks away from its current location. He was sure his great-grandparents would have passed the building many times. By 1856, Patrick and Jane Cullerton were settled in the young city, and their oldest son James, the family's first native Chicagoan, would have been about one. These small historic details and links gave Kevin pleasure. His own Chicago roots were growing deeper and stronger. Unearthing facts and connections provided a sense of familial belonging and connection, an anchor of sorts. It stood in direct contrast to the sense of confusion, and of having been set adrift, which he struggled with since learning of Tomina and Samantha and all they represented.

His pre-trip browsing also had uncovered the original Historical Society and most of its collection was burned in the Great Chicago Fire of 1871 which, ironically, was exactly what he wanted to investigate. For some time he'd been wondering about his family's fate in the fire. The decision to visit was on his to-do list even before Sammy's invite to Wrigley Field.

He picked up Tomina and Sammy at 9:00 the next morning, a slightly overcast and muggy day. On the way, he'd told the story of how the heat and drought in the Midwest that October of 1871 had been so intense and widespread that on the very same night his family was fleeing the fire in Chicago, the town of Peshtigo, Wisconsin – just across Green Bay from where he now lived – had burned with greater loss of life than in Chicago. Simultaneously, fire storms had attacked southern Door County, killing several and stopping just a few miles short of his home in Sturgeon Bay. "It's a tragic but interesting link. When I was in grammar school, all I remember was a cartoon-like picture of O'Leary's cow kicking over a lamp in our history book and Thomas drawing some pictures of the fire that our teacher hung up in the classroom. Thomas knew more about Chicago geography and history than I did."

Sammy asked, "Did Nana Pat like history?"

Kevin answered over his shoulder, "Pat wasn't a history buff. She was more of a 'seize the day' person, at least when I knew her."

"Carpe diem," Sammy said, as if it were her life mantra.

"Exactly." Kevin tilted his head toward the girl in the back seat, and asked Tomina, "How'd she get so smart?"

The parking lot adjacent to the Museum was closed for construction. They circled awhile until Kevin found an open spot on Clark Street a couple of blocks north. He fed the parking meter, and they trekked back along the edge of Lincoln Park. Hoping he wasn't boring the girls, he explained what he'd learned about the park's early history as the Old Catholic Cemetery. It had been his great-grandfather's first final resting place, until the city wanted the water front for a new park. Bones were exhumed and moved, including Patrick. He told them last February he'd gotten the burial record showing Patrick "& 2 others" had been reinterred in a plot Jane had purchased up in Calvary Cemetery. Sammy was intrigued by Kevin's theory of the extra bones which had been shipped and reburied with his great-grandfather. Tomina was more taken by his story of the flames and smoke chasing refugees, possibly including Kevin's young grandfather, into the unfinished Lincoln Park to take refuge in the recently opened graves.

The trio entered the museum off Clark. As the uniformed lady processed his credit card for tickets, Kevin asked, "Are they adding more parking? The lot was closed."

She explained, "They were supposed to be done two weeks ago. But every times they digs out there, they keeps coming on more bones and the whole shebang grinds to a halt while they figures out if they is old bones or new bones." Sammy began to retell Kevin's story to the woman, but with others waiting in line, Tomina prodded her along.

They headed toward their first stop: Lincoln's death bed. When they came around a corner and spotted the posted sign, Kevin and Sammy simultaneously exclaimed, "Shit!"

Exhibit Closed
On loan to the Springfield Lincoln Exhibit
July 15 – August 15

"Samantha, language please," Tomina said it more out of habit than reprimand.

"God, I'm sorry girls. I didn't see this on their website," Kevin said. "I shouldn't have opened my big mouth about the bed."

"No problem," Tomina consoled. "We can just come another time. It will give you a reason to come back this fall."

Sammy interjected, "He's got to come back for the World Series anyhow. But I really did want to see the bed. Did it have blood stains? Wouldn't that really be awesome, like we were really there when Lincoln died?"

Kevin said, "I don't recall if the stained pillow case was part of the exhibit when I saw it years ago. I do, however, remember an uncle at my dad's wake telling me a story he'd heard when he was a kid. He didn't know if it was true. But he said he'd heard my great- grandma had seen Lincoln's casket while it was in Chicago on its way down to Springfield for burial. It's one of the only family stories I ever heard, so I'm sticking to it."

He looked back at the CLOSED sign. "Damn. This history and genealogy stuff can drive you crazy. You can't get or see what you want, and when you do, it raises more questions than answers. It's like chasing moving shadows."

"Tomina smiled her smile at him. "Let's go find the Chicago Fire exhibit you wanted to see."

They retraced their steps and followed the signage. Sammy casually said, "You know, Mom, we should look into our family tree." Kevin's heart missed a beat and a shiver raced up his spine.

They were seated in a small darkened theater, several minutes into the narrated film before his initial panic subsided. The thought of Tomina and Sammy taking up family genealogy had thrown him off kilter. When a semblance of rational thinking returned, Kevin realized that, of course, Tomina's birth certificate would show her parents to be exactly who she thought them to be: Patricia Thom and Timothy Kerneki. That would be a good thing, right? From there, further documents would simply follow those family trees. *There's no reason to panic, so why do I feel so uneasy? Luckily, Tomina gave no indication she was interested. She seems perfectly content with their boxes of photos.* He let out a slow controlled breath and focused on the show.

The screen showed a sequence of still images, drawings and photos, of the fire and its aftermath. Some he recognized from books and online sites he'd already seen. The narrator's tale tracked the events of that parched hot October, starting with the rash of city fires which had been erupting since late September, including the big Saturday night fire in the lower West Side on the evening before the Great Fire. That burn took much of the fire department's men and equipment until 3:30 Sunday morning to get under control. By then four blocks had been destroyed. More ominously, men, horses and equipment were exhausted.

The main event began a bit after 8:30 PM on that same windy Sunday evening. It started on the South Side, in a milking barn along the alley behind a tiny shingled cottage at 137 DeKoven Street. The house was owned and occupied by Patrick and Kate O'Leary and their children; he was a laborer and she ran a neighborhood milk route. Although the barn did hold five cows, a calf and a horse, there was never any specific evidence behind the legend that a cow kicked over a lamp. Nonetheless, newspaper accounts and contemporaneous drawings cemented the tale into Chicago's mythology. The nearest fire companies were on the scene fairly rapidly for the times, but the conflagration had an unstoppable foothold.

In the dimness of the museum theater light, Kevin glanced at the girls. They seemed entranced as the sound effects and the narrator's vocal urgency rose to match the inferno's speed as it rushed north and east. The track of the blaze was dictated by rising winds from the south, Lake Michigan on the east, and the south branch of the Chicago River on the west. It spread rapidly, inflaming infectious panic in all in its path. The screen filled with new illustrations and the sound track rose in volume. They combined to capture the dense and panicked throngs of wagons, horses, carts, families of terrified men, women, and children crammed together in fear of their lives as they fled northwards across the Randolf Street Bridge, hoping the main branch of the river as it turned to empty into the lake would stop the flames. The images of children being carried and dragged along struck home with Kevin. The next sketch depicted a scene which must have sent renewed surges of dismay and despair through all who had thought they'd escaped over the bridge. Dozens of docked wooden sailing ships in the river were engulfed in flames. The fire jumped the water as easily as a child jumps a puddle.

The images followed the catastrophe northward. Kevin knew his great-grandmother Jane Cullerton and her children, including his young grandfather, were just blocks downwind on Townsend Street, along with other relatives he'd discovered living there and on nearby Wesson Street. The knowledge kindled belated concerns for their safety but also agitation about all the family and stories that never got passed up the family tree far enough to reach him.

On the screen, the flames were hurdling their way towards his family. *Were they sleeping, were they watching its approach? Did they have time to save anything other than themselves?* When he'd earlier seen some of these illustrations in his research, they had produced curiosity but no personal reaction. Now, however, watching this simple still-image video and the inexorable progression of the fire produced a visceral emotional reality he'd not appreciated before. He wondered if his own dad had known about his father's traumatic first-hand encounter with one of Chicago's most tragic events. Perhaps his father had been as oblivious about his own dad's early life as Kevin himself had been?

Kevin's sensibility was floating in the darkness somewhere between the unfolding drama on screen and his own personal thoughts when the narrator's words broke through to him:

"No one ever knew how many died. 120 bodies were recovered after the fire, but official guesses of the number of dead ranged from 200 - 300. Many were found near the river, in the narrow bewildering maze of dead-end alleys leading from Townsend and Wesson Streets. When the Chicago Avenue Bridge burnt, vehicles and pedestrians turned north toward Division Street and were trapped."

The credits ran, the screen went dark and the lights came up.

"Kevin?" Tomina shook his arm.

He looked at her and said, "I want to show you something. Come on."

He led them to a large city map display on which the swath burned by the Great Fire was shaded in brown. "Remember at the end there, when it said many of the dead were found around the Chicago Avenue Bridge?" He pointed to the map where the Chicago Avenue Bridge crossed over the river. "And many were trapped in the mazes off of Townsend and Wesson streets?" Tomina and Samantha looked at each other and then nodded. Kevin slid his finger a fraction to the east, to Townsend and Wesson streets. "Well, guess where my eight-year-old grandfather's family was living on October 8, 1871?" He tapped his finger on the wall map to emphasize each numeral as he said them. "1, 5, 4, Townsend Street. I can't believe I never heard a peep about it growing up."

Tomina said, "Oh my God, do you suppose any of them were killed in the fire?"

"Not as far as I know. But I sure don't know much. I have to assume they would have known all those alleys and streets. But for the life of me, I'm baffled; if my grandfather and family were caught up in that kind of history, wouldn't you think those stories would have been passed on? I wonder if my grandfather ever told them about it, or did my dad and aunts and uncles let it die?"

Sammy asked, "Was your grandmother alive then too?"

"No, she wasn't born for another ten years. So I can understand why she never talked about the fire. My grandfather was eighteen years older than her, which seems a bit weird in itself, but it makes me wonder if she even knew about his fire experiences. It seems the entire family was big on keeping secrets." As they were leaving the museum Kevin considered the ironic connection to his own situation.

Back at their house, Kevin thanked them for coming with him. To Samantha he added, "Thank you for inviting me to the game. I really enjoyed it a lot and was proud to be your honorary grandpa for a night."

He congratulated himself on how smoothly he's slipped that in without actually giving anything away. Sammy replied, "Well, like Mom said, you're at least a Thom Family Grandpa, aren't you? I mean, you were so close with Thomas and Nana."

Not feeling so clever anymore, Kevin clarified, "Well, I was your uncle's best friend for sure. I think your nana just put up with me."

He walked around to the driver's side. As he opened the door, Sammy lobbed another grenade. "Oh, I forgot. I was going to ask you before. Did you and Nana ever date?"

"Samantha," Tomina again intervened. "Now is not the time for more questions or invasions of Kevin's privacy."

Sammy smiled and said, "You can tell me next time, okay?" She turned and quickly disappeared up the front stairs.

Tomina shook her head, "I have got to work on that girl's manners." She shyly smiled at him. "Have a safe trip. Thank you for coming and taking good care of Samantha." She followed after her daughter.

Kevin started the engine and buckled himself in. He looked up toward their front door. "Dang that girl," he muttered. *That's the second time today she scared the hell out of me.* He pulled away from the curb and headed for home. *And damn you, Nana Pat. What have you done? What did we do?*

September 20, 2016

The sound of the garage door slowly humming itself open almost lulled Kevin to sleep. *How can golf in a cart make me so tired?* A shower and nap were calling. He crawled out of the car and grabbed the mail from the box at the street. Nelson would be home soon so he left the garage opened.

He tossed the mail in the usual spot and headed for the shower. Afterwards, he donned black sweatpants and a red tee shirt bearing the logo of his old school. Feeling refreshed, he took his mail from the stack to sort while he lay out on the screened porch. Comfortably propped against several pillows, he tossed an AARP magazine and some solicitations to the side, leaving him with the official-looking envelope from the Clerk of Cook County, Illinois he'd been waiting for.

Finally!

Kevin's dive into family genealogy last winter had quickly grown from curiosity to near obsession, consuming his time, energy, and imagination. In the beginning, after he'd found the list of names in his old file cabinet, information and remembrances had come from living family members, especially his sole remaining aunt – by marriage – now in her nineties. He liked that his hunt prodded him to reconnect with family he hadn't seen in years. Then he began to find peripheral background information in books and online. It was there he had learned about the Newberry Library.

The Calvary burial records he'd gotten when he and Cousin Colleen visited the cemetery last February were his roadmap. It was a scavenger hunt. Deducing relationships began even before he got back home that day, each name and internment date hinting at connections to the others buried along side. Then he began accumulating more documented facts about their lives from various sources. No detail was too small to capture his imagination.

Tracking and obtaining family certificates brought pleasure, often frustration, and invariably always new questions. Evidence of births and deaths, baptisms and marriages, along with prized census data covered his desk. Nothing was as satisfying as holding a paper copy of documented evidence in hand. It all made its way into his files but only after hours of examining each, analyzing and pondering them line by line, sometimes even letter by letter with a magnifying glass when needed.

He'd gotten and spit into the little vial for a DNA kit. Six weeks later he had in hand the charts and graphs outlining his predominately Irish lineage. He could feel his roots reaching across the Atlantic. This motivated him to find the manifest for the ship Washington, which had likely brought his great-grandparents Patrick and Jane to America.

Gradually the details spun a story, and a family mythology took shape. Each bit of information encouraged the narrative along a trajectory, or sometimes shoved it in a new more complex direction and the original story began to modulate.

At first, naturally enough, he'd seen his grandmother as the main theme, the main character. After all, she had been the center of the family for his father and his siblings and he'd actually known and spent some time with her. Now, however, Kevin began to see it differently. His grandfather, his dad's absent father, had taken over center stage. The very man who despite seemingly never having been around; appeared to have infected the development of all the other characters and story lines. So now, nine months after he'd begun his search, the main theme of the Cullerton past had shifted. He was getting somewhere, though he didn't really know exactly where "somewhere" was or why he was working so hard to get there. The work gave him a sense of accomplishment. But there was something else driving him on. Something, or someone, had begun whispering in his inner ear: *no better than me* and *you better hurry up*. It had started very softly, more felt than heard. Lately it was becoming more frequent and more clearly audible. Kevin decided the voice belonged to his grandfather. He kept this to himself and never mentioned it to Nelson.

He sat up straight on the daybed and removed the contents of the envelope. He'd requested his grandparents' marriage certificate, and he hoped that's what he had in hand and not the all too frequent NO RECORDS FOUND message. He dreaded another dead-end.

The license was issued by Peter B. Olsen, "*Clerk of the County Court of said Cook County, and the seal thereof, at my office in Chicago, this 30th day of March A.D. 1903.*"

Below the clerk's signature was an affidavit: "*I, James J Hurley, a Catholic Priest, hereby certify that Mr. Edward Cullerton and Miss Mary Finnell were united in Marriage by me at Chicago in the County of Cook and State of Illinois, on the 30th day of March, 1903.*"

"YES!" No longer sleepy, Kevin went to his office. He sat at his desk looking at the license on which **"Genealogy Purposes Only"** was stamped in red ink. Rereading for anything he might have missed, his eyes stopped on the year 1903. *A hundred and thirteen years ago. Wow! ... Wait.* ***1903?***

He pulled a file and seconds later was looking at Grandma's list. One name and date jumped off the page at him. In fountain pen, in her own handwriting, was Uncle Ed, his father's oldest brother. The one he'd never met.

Edward Cullerton: born April 21, **1902**

1902? Kevin leaned back in his chair. *Well, that starts to explain a few things.* Evidently, his tight-lipped grandma, the devout old woman who lived on her own out in Round Lake throughout the 1970s, and who lived until age ninety-six because once her daughter Mary had said she'd live that long, gave birth to Uncle Edward exactly eleven months and nine days before the Rev. Hurley pronounced her as wife to a man who no one ever mentioned. *Did Edward Patrick then kiss the bride? Would she let him kiss her? They had nine more babies.*

Kevin considered his feelings. Then as now, lots of babies were born to unmarried parents. He felt no sense of shame or embarrassment for his grandparents. Instead, he felt exhilaration at having found the information. *I wonder if Uncle Ed ever knew. Did Dad?*

Kevin tried to imagine Grandma's pregnancy. Why wait eleven months to get married? Why not minimize the scandal, and back then it would have surely been considered a scandal. It would have been more convenient and socially adept to marry as soon as possible. *Why the long delay? What was Grandma thinking? She would have been twenty-one, but he was eighteen years older. Was this consensual passion, seduction…or…or something more forceful? That could be why she was hesitant to marry the guy.*

He didn't like picturing any of this, especially the latter scenario. It was hard enough to reconcile a young pregnant, scared, and unmarried girl with the woman he had known as Grandma. *What would she have been like back then? Was she naïve? Was she in love with Edward, or just an easy mark for an older man, a friend of the family?* Kevin knew they had lived within a couple of blocks of each other. He didn't want to contemplate the fear and difficult conversations, or lack of them, during those many months between finding herself pregnant and marrying that man. He wondered if the bride and groom's mothers were in attendance, and what they must have been feeling?

He recalled how distraught and panicked he had been the one time he believed his girlfriend might be pregnant. A few moments later that was replaced by the confusion, anxiety and anger he'd been feeling toward Pat for sending Tomina and Sammy into his life. He found himself considering his grandfather's side of this story and decided he needed another shower to sort out his emotions before explaining it all to Nelson when she got home.

1977-1978
Grandma

September 22, 1977

The Village of Round Lake, Illinois, sits north of Chicago in Lake County, not far from the Wisconsin border. Its existence is owed to Mr. Amarias White, who around the turn of the twentieth century donated free land to one of the several incarnations of the Milwaukee Road Railroad in exchange for building a station near the lake.

Although not owing his existence to Mr. White, Kevin Cullerton was born in his village in 1950. After his father returned from WWII, his parents lived there with Kevin's grandmother in the small house she owned. Mr. White's station served as the beginning and end of Mr. Cullerton's long commute each day between the outlying hamlet and Chicago's main post office downtown.

A year later his parents relocated into the city, something, of course, Kevin had no memory of. However, a few trips to visit Grandma by train over the following years left a permanent, though hazy memory of the place. Memories of those trips, along with today's date, September 22, was why Kevin was asking for directions to Catalpa Street as he paid for his gas across from the Round Lake Railroad Station.

He headed east until he saw the Piggly Wiggly grocery store. Kevin recalled laughing out loud at the silly sounding name each time he saw the place on those childhood visits. He signaled and turned right. Even without seeing the address, he recognized the place and pulled up out front. He sat and stared at the structure, and the memories, and at the past in general.

As an adult, returning to a long-ago place often presents a dissonance between recollection and reality. Kevin tried to reconcile the juxtaposition. Places are almost invariably smaller than one remembers. But Grandma's seemed especially tiny. Also, it was hard to assign a shape to the construction. It never moved in one direction very long before a new angle or direction was introduced. The original cottage couldn't have been more than 700 square feet. An addition provided maybe another 200 square feet, introducing more geometric shapes to the roofline. Had his dad built the extra space back while they were living there?

A false facade extended beyond the corner of the building, giving the illusion of additional length. Its octagonal window offered not a view into the interior, but rather of the brown exterior faux-brick shingled siding. An illusion. A false promise of insight. Surely it had not been his dad's idea to include the useless window.

Thoughts of his father came easily as he sat there, this being the six month anniversary of his heart attack. He imagined the four of them – more than a quarter century ago – living in this tiny odd house. He hoped he had been a contented baby. If he had been colicky he must have driven them all nuts in such a confined space. Dad and Grandma had lived in a house overstuffed with kids, so maybe they'd learned to ignore all but the most desperate cries. However, he wondered how Mom had handled living in her mother-in-law's tiny house with a new baby. *That couldn't have been easy.*

He felt a little guilty at not having asked his mother to come with him. He conjured memories of their walking into Kolbin's Funeral Home just a year ago. They had arrived ahead of time to share some private minutes before relatives and friends started inquiries into how they were holding up and what exactly had happened. When they first entered from the parking lot, through which Kevin had ridden his bike hundreds of times as a kid, he had approached the casket with trepidation. His mom had come home and found her husband on the floor. His body was already at the hospital morgue before Kevin got home from giving music lessons that day. This would be the first time seeing his dad as a dead person.

He and Mom stood looking down at the familiar face of the man who was now gone. Kevin was waiting for emotions to swell again, but what rose instead was a confused question. "Did Dad really part his hair on the right?" His mother reached into her purse and showed him a picture. Sure enough, the part was on the right. Appalled that he couldn't recall such a basic fact, he wondered what other obvious things about his father he'd missed. His arm went around his mother's shoulder, as much to console himself as her.

Throughout the two-night ritual, he took the opportunity to have conversations with his Dad's remaining siblings, all of whom were between three and eleven years younger than his father. He learned his dad, who never owned a car in Kevin's lifetime, was once part owner of a 1930 Chevy and had been quite a good mechanic, often fixing his buddies' cars before the war. Uncle Joe, the youngest of the troupe, reminisced about how Jim would spend his time reading and studying, but come summer was singularly devoted to baseball. He regaled Kevin and the others with how Dad's favorite comic strip included a fictional pitcher named Howie, whose impossible roundhouse curveball would start behind the hitter before breaking over the plate. He'd spent hours trying to emulate the pitch and in so doing became a successful Little League pitcher. He got picked up by the ward Alderman's team and had matched up quite well against the top teams from across the city.

"Of course," Uncle Joe added, "your dad picked up the nickname Howie." Kevin wondered how his dad might have felt about that. He didn't mention his own personal distain for nicknames from his own grammar school experience.

Throughout the waking and burying of his father, Kevin was surrounded by relatives and he gradually began to sense something missing, something darker within the family. It was covert, mostly in what was not said, who was not mentioned in the stories. The closest he got to it was an overheard cryptic remark by Aunt Kitty that seemed to reference their "old man". But with the loss of his own father, and his mother's grief, he let the vague sense of family secrets slip away.

Sitting in his car outside Grandma's house, Kevin decided the overall look of the place, half hid as it was behind waist-high near-leafless bushes resembled a prehistoric over-sized mollusk composed of angles instead of curves and an unseeing octagonal eye. When he finally disembarked and approached the house, he saw the snail-like structure precariously levitated on blocks two feet above the ground, leaving a tight crawl space beneath. An incongruous disconnected concrete slab with three steps and a rusted iron railing rose from the dormant grass and weeds. Kevin filled his lungs with the cool spring air as if he were about to dive into Round Lake itself.

As he reached the stoop, his grandma pulled open the door. Apparently, she'd been watching for him. "Hello, hello, come on in." Kevin followed her into the snail's shell. The small seating area of the front room held some familiarity. A few paces further through a doorframe lay a small kitchen area. Her hunched back, white hair and sweater continued in that direction. To his left was her bedroom. The bed, dresser, and straight back chair with a folded blanket draped over its back took up most of the space. A crucifix hung above the bed on faded flowery wallpaper. Three more steps and they were in the kitchen. Through the back window, he could see the yard was overgrown and tangled with the brown debris of the last couple falls and winters. "Sit, Kevin. I've got some tea on."

He watched her add milk and two spoons of sugar to each cup, bringing them to the small kitchen table in red patterned china cups which Kevin thought must be older than she was. Growing up, he'd rarely drink tea. His parents were instant coffee drinkers. But sometimes, when he was sick, his mother would make him a cup of tea. She also made it with milk and two spoons of sugar. He wondered if Mom had gotten the recipe from Grandma. He'd try to remember to ask her.

When Grandma sat, Kevin could finally look her full in the face. Bare round lenses held together by a minimal wire frame added to her roundness. Slightly obscured behind the shine of clean lenses, were eyes which surely once upon a time had been keen and bright blue. Brushed snow white hair and ample bosom completed the stereotypical early twentieth century grandmotherly figure. Her voice wasn't high pitched but came from high in her chest, squeezed through tightly stretched ninety-five year old vocal cords. "It's a long drive all the way out here to visit," she said.

"It wasn't bad," Kevin replied sipping his tea, enjoying its sweet warmth. "I wanted to come today. I hope you don't mind. I didn't really get to talk to you at Dad's… well, since the funeral, and … Anyway, I was hoping to talk to you after the cemetery at the luncheon, you know, about Dad. But Uncle Tom had already taken you home straight from the church. I should have gotten out here long before this."

"That's okay. Young folks are always so busy."

"I guess time…I guess I got caught up in my own stuff. Anyhow, I was pretty selfish about the whole thing. I mean, sure, I lost my father, but Mom lost her husband and you lost a son. Both of those must be even harder than losing a father. I loved him, but I didn't really know him, not like you two did." Something came to mind, something he had been curious about ever since Aunt Kitty's comment at the wake. "What's harder, Grandma, losing your husband or your children?"

As if to lock them closed, the old woman pinched her lips between a gnarled thumb and index finger. The washed out blueness of her eyes hinted at a storm. Kevin sheepishly looked down into his tea cup. When no reply came he tried to undo the question. "I guess kids, even adult kids, aren't supposed to die before…" He trailed off, not wanting to insinuate anything, but finished by adding, "I mean, don't parents usually figure they'll go before their children? It must be hard." Finally, he looked back up at his Grandma.

Her eyes had settled back into their gray-blueness. "Kevin, when you're as old as I am…" She started again. "My Jimmy – your dad – is in heaven now, with the others. I expect I'll be seeing them again pretty soon now." She blew on her tea, took a sip, and looked out the back window.

"How did you keep track of all of them, especially," he risked another gambit, "after Grandpa died? That must have been before I was born?"

His grandmother again gazed into the yard. Her brow furrowed as if she were squinting, trying to see something in particular. When she finally answered, it was to neither of Kevin's questions. "When your dad was young I called him Shamus. He was the only one of my children I called by his Irish name. Your dad always had his nose in a book, even when he was little. He read everything: stories, history, even poetry. He was a serious and good boy and, even more than the others, he loved school and church. He was an altar boy at Our Lady of Mercy, and he never missed a mass. Then he went on to the Quigley Seminary high school to study and begin becoming a priest. I was so proud of him. I prayed for him every night. But he got worn out and sick after two years and never went back. It broke my heart. I never told him that, but he knew. He told me he just wasn't sure anymore and didn't want to do something he couldn't do right by. That's the way he was you know, always wanting to do the right thing."

Kevin watched Grandma again looking out her window. He wished he knew what she was thinking and what he should say. He wished he could know all the things she knew about his father and about their family. He resigned himself; he never would, or could know.

"I have something you might like," she said suddenly as if the idea had just occurred to her. Slowly getting up, Grandma went to her bedroom and returned with a decorated container, slightly smaller than a shoe box. She set it on the table and eased herself back down onto her seat. Without looking up, she opened the lid and fingered through the contents before extracting a worn black and white photo and setting it in front of Kevin. "That's Jimmy in the yard on Kimball where we were at the time."

It was of a young boy. Kevin picked it up carefully, almost reverently, so as not to harm the surface of the old photograph. In the lower left corner she had written *"Jimmy 1917."* He moved his eyes around the slightly blurry background. Wooden rails and posts held up a chicken-wire fence. Shrubbery hid most of what looked like a neighbor's garage, and the ground appeared to be dormant grass and leaves. It was obviously a special occasion for the slight lad wore a too large six-button double-breasted overcoat that hung to his knees.

His hands didn't reach the end of the sleeves so only his fingers showed. A collared white shirt contrasted with the dark coat and neck tie he wore slightly askew. On his head was a small brimmed woolen cap with a muted plaid pattern. The brim was peaked in the middle as if he frequently grabbed and pulled it down tightly upon his head. Kevin wondered what side the hair was parted on back then. The boy's face did not shy away. He looked straight into the camera with nothing to hide.

Kevin peered into the face of the nine-year-old who happened to be his dead father. He hoped to see, to find, something in the image of the person they had just buried one year ago. But the face had faded after six decades of looking into the camera, and no message was forth coming. Kevin knew his dad wasn't looking far into the future as he got his picture taken wearing the oversized coat which was undoubtedly a hand-me-down from his older brothers. "Did you take the picture, Grandma? He's all dressed up."

"It was his ninth birthday. His brother took the picture. Eddie had a camera he'd bought second-hand. He liked to take pictures, mostly when people weren't looking. It made his sisters so mad." It didn't occur to Kevin to ask if she had any of those pictures.

Looking back to the photo, Kevin said, "You know, Grandma, I can almost hear you telling Dad, 'Now, Shamus, look at the camera and stand still'." His grandmother smiled at that. It was a real smile; the only one Kevin could ever remember seeing on her face.

The young face in the picture looked innocent and trusting. Kevin saw the boy's slender nose and that his ears stuck out a bit from under his cap. He recognized the traits from his own childhood pictures. The connection brought to mind enigmatic lyrics from a Beatle's song: "*I am he, as you are he, as you are me, and we are all together.*"

"What's that?" Grandma asked. Kevin realized he'd muttered the lyrics out loud.

"Oh, nothing, Grandma. They're just some nonsense words from a song. Do you have any other pictures in the there?" He pointed to the closed box as he handed her back the photo.

She said, "You keep that one, honey."

Kevin was touched. He was surprised by how much. She was passing his father to him, or at least a piece of him, a piece of Dad's history that wasn't buried, that he could hold on to. For a long moment, he was connected to his father, like when they'd gone to Ravinia and listened to Beethoven together. *When was that…two years ago? How could that be?*

He made himself ask, "Are you sure, Grandma?"

"You should have it now," she said.

She looked into the box, keeping the opened lid between him and the contents. "Wait a minute," she said. She again stood. She closed the lid and placed the container of pictures on her chair. She shuffled down the hall and returned with a framed photo in her hand. Setting the box back on the table, she looked at the photo she'd brought from her bedroom. Kevin wondered who it might be and what she was thinking and feeling. When she stood it on the table, he immediately recognized Aunt Mary.

"All of us cousins loved Mary," he said. "Sometimes she'd come upstairs for Christmas dinner with us kids at Uncle Bud's. She'd talk to us and listened like we weren't just kids. We thought she was so cool. We couldn't understand why she wasn't married."

He'd forgotten how striking his aunt had been. The black and white picture was a three-quarter head and shoulder profile. Mary looked to be in her late thirties, maybe early forties, and in her prime, wearing a short pearl necklace and tasteful clip-on earrings. Her poise and beauty were obvious. So was her confidence. Her hair was neatly coiffed in the style of the day. It was a professional shot; the background blank and the lighting strong from her right and slightly above. It put her left cheek, jaw and hair in shadow while highlighting her symmetrical face and elegance. The contrast of strong light and dark shadow hinted at a strong but complex nature. It also gave the picture the quality of a pencil or charcoal drawing, reminiscent of how his friend Thomas used to manipulate light and dark to bring his drawings to life. *Too many ghosts.* To clear his thoughts, he said, "She was a beauty, Grandma."

"Oh my heaven's sake, yes she was. Mary was a top editor for a big publishing house downtown, right in there with all the guys."

The added comment again raised for Kevin the question as to why his favorite aunt hadn't ever married. He recalled that Grandma lived with Mary off and on for years before moving out here. He himself was living at home until Mom could sell the house, so he knew first hand how that could cramp one's love life.

"Were Mary and Dad close when they were young?"

"Like peas in a pod those two. They were the two quiet ones. The others were always off-and-on mad at each other, but I don't think any of them were ever mad at Mary or Jimmy. They were the ones all the others talked to. Mary knew more than me everything that went on in that house."

They talked for awhile longer, but Grandma had abruptly put the past away and avoided going back there any more. Kevin changed a couple of light bulbs for her, rehung a picture, and got the toilet to stop running. He went to the Piggly Wiggly and got her stocked up before kissing her goodbye. He knew she was lonely, but had no idea what to say. Instead, he promised to visit again now that he knew the way.

Back in his car Kevin stared at the house again before making a u-turn and heading back up Catalpa. At the corner, a sign pointed the way to Round Lake Beach. With so many thoughts and feelings fresh in his mind, and in no hurry, he followed the arrow further east.

He parked in the open, next to the public beach area. He turned off the engine and rolled the window half way down in order to taste and smell the spring air. *Mom must have brought me here in the summer while Dad was working… if for no other reason, so she and Grandma could get a break from each other.* He wondered again how the two strong women had managed to get along. He wondered how his father had negotiated that minefield.

His glance slid down the shoreline. Too cool for the village populous or early season cottage dwellers to swim or sun-bathe, the only living creatures in view were some ducks at the water's edge. *How many generations of ducks have come and gone since I was here last*? He imagined himself as a toddler, sitting and getting sand in his diapers and mouth, mounding, with his mother's help, wet sand into hills and castles and watching as they got washed away. He considered how many of Grandma's hills and castles had been washed away in her long life. The thought didn't depress him. It was just recognition of the passing of time, of change… and of loss.

He looked down at the picture staring up at him from the passenger seat. He asked his nine-year-old dad, what he thought of his life and choices, and in retrospect, what he had thought about fatherhood. He thought of things he would have liked to ask his dad about, and he wondered what his dad might have told him if he had known he didn't have much time left.

Twenty minutes later he headed home. Again passing Catalpa Street, he thought of the tangled brown of Grandma's backyard. He hoped it would soon produce a few flowers for her to look at. Surely everyone deserved that much when their children died. He promised himself next time he'd clean it up some, maybe bring some colorful perennials to plant.

At the train station he turned south and felt himself being pulled back toward the city. He accelerated and looked in his mirror, thinking about his dad coming and going through those station doors. He turned on the radio.

… are he, as you are me
and we are all together.

Memory and reality scrambled in Kevin's head as John Lennon's gravelly voice went on…

I am the walrus
Goo goo g'joob…
…I'm crying

Kevin again glanced in the mirror, back at the receding station… and saw so was he.

I'm cryyyy---inggg

Individual tears independently moved down his cheek. He was sure the lyrics were nonsense... Lewis Carroll, Through the Looking Glass, nonsense. He was just as sure the feelings were not.

If the sun don't come
You get a tan from standing in the English rain

Kevin's eyes moved back and forth from the mirror to the road ahead, like a coin flipping through the air, the head side trying to get a glimpse of its tail side.

Goo goo g'joob

The station, then the village, dwindled and became invisible to the mirror. He drove on. Knowing life and traffic demanded that of him.

Goo goo g'joob

February 9, 1978

At the mass Kevin sat next to his mother trying to remember what he wanted to ask her. It stemmed from his visit to his grandmother's just five months ago. Then it surfaced. He wanted to know how Mom and Grandma had gotten on when they lived together, especially in Round Lake after he'd been born. Considering that, and the fact they had lived together during the war, the relationship seemed a little distant, but not abnormally so, not in his family. He had no childhood memory of the two women having a private conversation, not even on the phone. As he got older there hadn't been all that many opportunities to observe the two of them together – that was if it had ever crossed Kevin's mind to pay attention to such a thing… which it didn't. On the rare occasion when Grandma was at an uncle's house for a holiday get-together, there was usually a crowd, and he and his cousins were always off playing, or talking, or sneaking cigarettes. But now the thought was on his mind again. However, sitting here in a church at Grandma's funeral mass didn't seem like the right time.

Center front was the casket beneath the spotless linen. Altar rails were a thing of the past, so the coffin hovered on its gurney abandoned where the pallbearers – Kevin, three uncles, and two other cousins – had left it at the instruction of the funeral director. It gathered onto itself the serendipitous pallid strands of winter sunshine which tumbled through the church's skylight. Similarly, it also commanded the eyes and private thoughts of Grandma's remaining grown children, as well as, dozens of grand and great-grand children. Kevin wondered what his mother and his uncles and aunts might be remembering. Each would have a perspective shaped by personal recollection, memories and perceived realities. There'd be no use in asking. He knew from his dad's wake less than two years ago, their generation wasn't much for sharing personal thoughts or events beyond minor short anecdotes.

He thought of Grandma, relegated to a rectangular box under the white pall with her beloved cross embroidered in gold thread. Once upon a time, he had been aware of only three real dead people. The images came back to him one by one: the small collapsed body of his mother's aunt in her casket surrounded by the smell of flowers; the face of Thomas' dead father, which he only knew from photos around Thomas' house where he'd spent so much time; and Jesus, who he had tried so hard to draw hanging on his cross, only to fail time and time again. But now, at age twenty-seven, he knew, or knew of, so many many more. So many, that he'd given serious consideration to the idea that the dead just might hold more sway than the living.

The gathered family knelt, stood, responded, and sang their way through the first part of the mass. Kevin found himself thinking about the small casket-shaped box in which Grandma had stored her pictures; the one in which *"Jimmy 1917"* had laid at rest until she, so surprisingly, had exhumed her son and shared him with his son.

The celebrant priest escorted an elderly priest, also in vestments, into the pulpit. Kevin looked to his mother, confused by this breech in the regular protocol. She whispered, "Monsignor Cahill used to be pastor at Our Lady of Mercy. He's got to be older than your grandma."

The ancient cleric propped himself up. The congregation, virtually all of whom had been raised Catholic, took the signal and sat. Kevin's eyes fixed on the Holy Card he'd placed on the pew next to him. The front was, of course, a picture of the Virgin being assumed into heaven amid a cloud of angels. Grandma would be pleased, he thought. He flipped to the backside.

Mary Celia (Finnell) Cullerton
April 9, 1881 — February 6, 1978

He stared at the dash between the dates. *Such a small line, for such a long life: technically, just an elongated hyphen used to link related ideas.* In Grandma's case it literally linked centuries. And contained in that dash, hiding in that symbolic span between Grandma's birth and death, was her life, which included his father's and mother's lives, and even his own so far. It contained the mingled and complicated history of several families. He hoped it held more joy than heartbreak. But he didn't think so. The thought made Kevin sad.

The old priest had begun speaking the stock generic words of a Catholic eulogy. Kevin's thoughts began to drift back to the mystery and meaning of that dash between birth and death when Father Cahill's inflection changed and he transitioned from scriptural references. "Let's not dwell on the brevity of life, but rather on the fullness of Mary's time on this earth. Can you even imagine when Mary – your mother, your grandmother, your great-grandmother – was born, there were only thirty-eight states in the union? Five years earlier, headlines in the papers – because radio, let alone television, had not yet been invented – were about General Custer and the Little Big Horn. Mary Finnell and her sister and brothers played in Chicago's dirt streets years before horseless carriages appeared in the city."

"Grandma had siblings?" Kevin whispered the words out loud. He looked to his mother for confirmation he'd heard that correctly and for some elaboration. But she put a finger to her lips and nodded towards the priest, directing Kevin's attention back to the eulogy.

"Mary's mortal remains lie here, but Jesus has already welcomed her home. Her life journey literally took her from horses and wagons to landings on the moon. She saw much and bore much, but her life was always strengthened by her love for her children and for God. Now she truly deserves eternal rest with her Lord and Savior."

Kevin was awed by the span of history. He looked again at the Holy Card and that dash, which held so much life, separating her birth from death. During the remainder of the mass, he glanced around at all the gathered relatives and at his grandmother's casket. He thought about his dad and wished it could be true that he and his other deceased siblings were there to greet Grandma. Only once, near the end of the mass, did he briefly wonder whether his missing grandfather was there. But with Grandma gone, Kevin dismissed any thoughts of the man – at least for a very long time.

2016

October 10, 2016

Last year, 2015, in mid-October the Chicago Cubs and the better part of the North Side of the city entered the National League Championship Series with high hopes. But as 107 years of history and the Legend of the Billy Goat would predict, hope was all they had going for them. The New York Mets swept them in four games straight. However, this was 2016, and hope, as they say, springs eternal – especially for Cubs fans. On Friday and Saturday, October 7-8, the Cubbies took the first two games of their five-game Divisional Series from the San Francisco Giants. Yesterday, Sunday, October 9, was a travel day and the teams headed to the West Coast for tonight's game three. The Cubs' ace, Jake Arrieta, was pitching. What could go wrong?

Today was also the official Columbus Day holiday and Chicago Public Schools were closed. Samantha Larkin had spent last night at a slumber party to celebrate and speculate on the Cubs' path to the World Series, discuss boys, and generally have a good time with her friends. She had promised her mom she'd be home after lunch to do her homework and help with chores.

With her daughter safely gone, Tomina Kerneki Larkin had enjoyed the quiet solitude and was currently delivering a basket of laundry to her daughter's room. Samantha ironed her own shirts and pants – she owned only three skirts for special occasions – and put her own stuff away. For a sixteen-year-old girl she was quite organized and mature in her habits and opinions, if not her approach to life. For the most part, Tomina appreciated this.

Tomina laid out her daughter's sorted clothes on her bed. The room was a good size. Her husband Bill grew up in this very room and it had been plenty big for him and his brother. When Tomina and Bill first got married, they had rented a small apartment over on Wolfram near Sheffield Avenue. They loved the neighborhood, the apartment, their friends, and each other. They tried for kids, but nothing happened except a lot of enjoyable sex. They decided to just forgo birth control and accept whatever happened. Then Bill's parents, James and Michelle Larkin, decided to move to the suburbs and offered Bill and Tomina a great deal for this place. It was only a mile from their apartment which made it all the more appealing. Both of them were working, she teaching and he a lawyer in a firm that focused on Workman's Comp cases, but it was his parent's additional financial help that allowed them to afford the house. A year after moving in, Samantha had been born.

Tomina sat next to the clothes on the bed. It had been her mother's and came with her when she moved in after getting sick and selling her house. Afterwards, Samantha had begged for it. Tomina feared nightmares, but Samantha's logic and persistence won out. The bed was queen sized with head and foot boards of red, slatted wood. It stood taller than most, the top of the thick pillowed mattress almost three feet off the ground. The height had been helpful in caring for her mother at the end. Tomina smiled as she remembered Samantha as a child struggling to climb up on the thing to play or to snuggle in with her nana when she'd stay over. In the end, she decided no one, including herself, had a better claim to the bed after her mother passed away on it last December, in this very room – Samantha's room – in which her daughter had insisted Nana stay. Tomina was very proud of her daughter for that.

For awhile, Tomina sat, as she sometimes did, and took inventory of all the things that spoke of her daughter. On the wall opposite was a poster of Serena Williams caught in mid-stride of her powerful backhand. Next to it was another poster, an assortment of various shots of Wrigley Field. Hanging from it were the souvenir white W flag and score card Kevin had bought Samantha back in August.

Another wall held a couple of prints: one was a Van Gogh self-portrait in muted colors of the artist staring defiantly, as if demanding something of the viewer. Tomina remembered buying it for Samantha at the gift shop during a visit to the Art Institute a few years ago. They both had loved the Van Gogh exhibit and paintings they'd admired in the upstairs gallery. Tomina expected her daughter to pick one of the artist's bright sunflower paintings, but instead she picked out this slightly disturbing portrait.

The other print was by Salvador Dali. Tomina couldn't bring herself to buy her daughter one of the bizarre surrealistic images that had made the artist famous. They compromised on an earlier work called *Girl Standing at the Window*, a realistic image of exactly what the title implied. Every time Tomina saw the print, she wondered what the girl was thinking, which always made her ponder what occupied her daughter's reflective moments. Both prints were odd choices for a teenage girl. Tomina decided Samantha's taste in art had matured faster than in other areas of her life.

Against the far wall were two desks side by side. One was for homework and currently held her daughter's school backpack and an old blue and grey electric typewriter that Nana had used back in high school. Above it was a small poster Tomina had given her daughter for her thirteenth birthday: *Don't Believe Everything You Think*. She some times wondered if she'd bought it for herself. She wished both of them might heed those words a bit more often.

The other surface, a well used drawing table, was a gift from Nana. It had been Thomas', and had originally come from a second-hand store. Its adjustable incline plane was at about a thirty degree angle. Clipped to it was a sheet with the beginnings of three sketches of heads in different positions. No details had yet appeared to give a clue to an identity. The desk had a few drawers, into which it had never occurred to Tomina to look, and side gutters, currently containing pieces of colored chalks, charcoal, and clips. On top was a coffee can with dozens of colored pencils sticking out.

Her eyes moved to Samantha's drawings hanging around the room. Like many girls, she liked horses, and there were a few of them, along with one dog and two cats. Tomina was taken with how well her daughter captured both anatomy and motion. However, it was obvious; Samantha preferred people and portraits. There was a collection of her friends and teammates. Some were faces, some full body – often in throwing or batting postures. There was one of Tomina herself. In it she was smiling, and she was pleased to see, more attractive than she thought realistic. There was a double picture of Nana Pat. One captured her, irreverent "twinkle-in-her-eye; I've got a secret" look. The other was of her in repose. Eyes closed and a face completely at peace.

As Tomina stood she noticed the framed photograph on Samantha's homework desk. She walked over and picked it up. She'd seen it a million times. Each time still hurt. Her husband Bill and his parents stood arms around each other and smiling broadly at Tomina behind the camera. It had been taken in James and Michelle Larkin's backyard of their Glenview home not long after they'd moved in. Unlike her parents, Bill and his folks were always laughing and joking. Tomina still pictured the three of them talking and smiling together in the car moments before the drunk raced his pick-up through the red light and killed them all. The picture and memory didn't produce tears any more, just emptiness and ache.

She set the photo down next to Samantha's heavy book bag sitting on her laptop. The laptop, too, had come with Nana. She had used the machine mainly for email. When her mom got to the point she was no longer able to hit the proper keys, she sometimes dictated messages to Samantha, who would type and send them for her. Weeks after the funeral and not feeling up to it herself, Tomina asked her daughter to check Nana's laptop for any messages that needed answering. When her daughter asked about using the machine, she said she could keep it for homework so she wouldn't have to carry her school laptop back and forth.

Tomina lifted the backpack off of the computer and set it to the side. As was her habit at school with student devices, she lifted the top to make sure it was turned off. The blue power light was illuminated, and a moment later a list of files appeared. There were folders for Samantha's classes, one for her softball team, one labeled "Misc." and a few others with friends' names. Tomina's finger was pushing the cursor towards the X to close the file page before hitting the power button when she spotted a folder labeled "Rita Naska." Rita had been her mother's best friend for many years. She had died the year before her mom. She remembered how devastating the loss was for her mother. While Pat was herself dying, she more than once had said she was grateful Rita had gone first so she wouldn't have to go through the hell of losing her best friend.

Tomina assumed the folder was left over from her mother, and so it wouldn't be snooping to take a look. She opened it and the hairs on the back of her neck stood straight up. The file held one document, labeled "Kevin C." She could not think of a plausible connection between Uncle Thomas' friend and Rita Naska. The file made no sense. Her curiosity spiked, but so did a loud whispering in her head which suggested she should just back out and power down the laptop. But the file was here on the computer her daughter used, that she herself had given to her, so there was really no choice. Primordial concern for her child's well-being had been stirred, so forward was the only possible direction. She read.

Dear Kevin Cullerton,
I'm sorry to tell you that my dearest friend Pat Kerneki (Patricia Thom) passed away of cancer last December. Towards the end she gave me the enclosed envelope and asked me to mail it to you at this address three months after she was gone. Of course I had lots of questions but she wouldn't tell me nothing other than you had been her brother's closest friend a long time ago before he died in Vietnam. Her instructions were odd and like out of a movie, but she made me promise to do them. I loved her so I'm doing all this. But I must admit I am <u>very</u> curious. I'm sorry if you did not know about her passing. I hope she sent you something important and that it makes you happy. She always made me happy and I miss her.
Sincerely,
Mrs. Rita Naska

Tomina sat down at her daughter's desk, staring at the text on the screen. She was unable to rationally or emotionally make sense of what she was seeing. *Rita died before Mom. How… Why would she be sending a letter to Kevin so it would be delivered after Mom died? This makes no fucking sense! Is this how Kevin heard about Mom, and why he all of a sudden contacted me?*

"Mom, are you up there?" Samantha's hollered.

Tomina jumped.

"I'm home. I've got left over pizza for dinner. The game starts at 7:00. Arrieta is pitching, so no worries." What could go wrong?

October 11, 2016

Nelson stood behind Kevin's chair reading the message on the screen. Her expression showed nothing, but her eyes said everything.

"What do you think?" he asked.

"Honestly, I have no idea. Other than Tomina's mother was fucking nuts, and should have kept her damn suspicions and letter to herself. What are you thinking?" she asked.

He stared back at the monitor, his head slowly shaking back and forth.

Help - Can we talk? October 11, 2016 (1:07AM)

Dear Kevin,
It's 1:00 AM. I haven't been able to sleep. I found this (see below) on Mom's computer and I assume Samantha has read it. I can't make sense of it. It's got me confused, and upset – though I don't know why I'm upset. I don't know who to talk about this with, except for you. It's crazy! Rita died a year before Mom did, so she couldn't send it. Did you get a letter from Mom? I'd like to talk to you before I ask Samantha about it.
I feel a little better now that I wrote this. I've got to go. I need a few hours sleep before school tomorrow / today. Maybe it will make more sense then.
Tomina

Kevin reread the message that Tomina had copied, even though he had it all but memorized from the first time it had appeared out of nowhere last March. He began to ramble, trying to let his anxiety out. "I'm not capable of thinking right now. Tomina must be exhausted and I'm as confused as she is. How could this Rita Naska have sent Pat's letter when she's already dead? How do I tell her what was in the damn letter? I can't deny I got it now. She's going to hate me."

Nelson put her arms around his neck to calm him. "I don't think she's going to hate you. It seems she didn't have any idea what her mother was up to. She's just looking for help and answers, and hopes you have some. This might be an opportunity, don't you think? To get everything on the table. She must know her mother was loony."

Kevin swiveled his desk chair around. Deep seated and long buried loyalty to Thomas made him not want to hear Pat criticized, not even by Nelson. He chose his words carefully. "You know, that's not the impression I got when I was down there. Tomina didn't always get along with her mother, but she did not think she was delusional. And Samantha sure thinks the world of her grandmother."

"Okay." Nelson replied. "All I'm saying is that women caused you a lot of anxiety and lost sleep and now her daughter seems at wit's end because of it."

Kevin turned back to the message and slumped in his chair. Nelson rubbed his shoulders as reconciliation and kissed the top of his head. "You've done nothing wrong, and you have nothing to apologize for. This whole thing has been bizarre from the beginning." She kissed him again. "Do you want me to stay home today?"

"No. But thanks. I'd just drive us both crazy. You go ahead and get ready for work. I'll be okay."

Nelson headed for the shower, adding, "I'm guessing you'll be driving down to Chicago again."

Kevin remained slumped. He didn't know if he was scared, anxious, or just plain nauseous. Up until now, his worry was for Tomina and himself. Now he worried about Nelson's anger and concerns. She'd been a saint and unbelievably supportive up to now. He knew if the shoe was on the other foot, he would not have been as unquestioning. Did she still believe he had done nothing wrong? He wasn't sure anymore.

This was leading nowhere. Kevin forced himself to straighten his back and sit up. To distract himself, he checked the score from yesterday's playoff game, which had been his original objective when he sat at his computer. Last night he had watched for nine innings. When the game required extra innings, the tension got to be too much and he went to bed, only to lie in the dark, staring at the invisible ceiling for an hour before falling asleep.

Giants top Cubs on walk-off homerun in 13th

The damn Billy Goat had raised its bleating head again.

October 14, 2016
(AM...)

Kevin Cullerton did not see himself as a chronic pessimist though he did concede Nelson was probably right when she'd say he worried too much. But he admitted it reluctantly because it pissed him off. He preferred to think of himself as realistic, with good coping skills. He was comfortably retired with friends, had hobbies like golf and genealogy to keep him busy, and the future looked fairly predictable. What could go wrong?

However, he was not coping very well at the moment. Declining health and aging – and more recently, the narcissist the Republicans had nominated for President, and oh yeah, now the Cubs' probable collapse – regularly crept into his conscious mind. He tried to remain stoic. After all, health and age were predictable, and the latter two concerns were only possibilities. Predictability and mere possibility did help some to mitigate the amount of time he dwelled on each. Pat's letter was another story, in a class by itself. It, and the mess it had dragged him into, had not been predictable, and it had moved beyond possibility into the realm of probability, and whatever that would mean.

Lately, he felt betrayed by his past. Shouldn't personal consequences be more closely linked in time and place to an event; not fall out of the sky a half-century later. He'd never really considered the potential for the past to crash out of the shadows into the present.

Sure, he knew it at the abstract macro level, in the hypothetical, but not in his own all too real life. It didn't seem right or fair. Hadn't he tried his best to avoid, or when needed, cautiously manage situations with long-term consequences? Hadn't he started saving early and for the most part taken a prudent and practical approach to major decisions like his career and life choices? Hadn't he put off marriage at least until he was secure enough in life and in himself to commit to the relationship? And hadn't he made it abundantly clear he did not want kids?

Kevin passed through downtown Milwaukee with these thoughts stuck in his mind like an itch he couldn't find a way to scratch. He found himself asking God – on the off chance divine intervention was a real thing – to PLEASE help, or at least PLEASE don't let this end up really bad or ugly. Maybe, he thought, he should have worked harder to hang on to his childhood Catholic faith.

He picked up Interstate 94 toward the Illinois border, and began thinking again about how bad this would make him look in Tomina's eyes. The fact that he'd done nothing wrong and had only wanted to protect her from Pat's revelations was not defusing his concerns. If he had only followed the initial inclination of his head instead of his heart, and ignored the letter, and not made contact, he wouldn't be driving to Chicago again and into God knows what. If he hadn't responded, then even if Tomina had contacted him about the Naska message, he could have denied having received any correspondence … though, he immediately knew he wouldn't have done that. But at least he could have said he thought it was a hoax or mistake and he'd simply ignored the entire thing. They were half-truths, but sins of omission were more doable than an outright lie.

When he'd gotten Tomina's 1:00 AM email, Kevin hadn't phoned her because he didn't trust what might come out of his mouth. Instead, he replied via email, saying he'd drive down tomorrow. He'd told her it wasn't a problem; he had some other things he needed to do in the city anyway. She said she'd get a sub for her afternoon classes, so she could meet Kevin before Samantha got home from school. She'd thanked him three times. He wondered if she'd be thanking or cursing him when he left.

He pulled into the CASH lanes to pay the toll. Before merging back into traffic, he again reached inside his jacket pocket to assure himself Pat's letter hadn't somehow disappeared. He also checked the address he had scribbled on the envelop that held the two photos he'd brought. Further along, he took the Edens Expressway and in surprisingly good time was on the Kennedy. He exited at Diversey, glancing at his watch. He had, as he'd hoped, arrived early. He had something he needed to do, though he didn't know if it would help him or not. He drove past Tomina's street, continuing east for another four blocks. When he got to the address, he pulled to the curb.

Kevin studied the façade of the old building. It stood closer to the street than the adjacent homes as if wanting to make sure Kevin spotted it through the constant traffic. Two front doors indicated it was a duplex, with two living spaces, but he couldn't tell if it was divided into two floors or back and front facing apartments. He had no idea which door or dwelling was the one. Another uncertainty. Nothing seemed for sure anymore. A stream of cars intervened, disrupting his view and thoughts. Another frustration.

He took the photos from his pocket. Two versions of his dad stared at him: *Jimmy 1917* and a 1972 picture from his parents' thirty-fifth anniversary party. It struck him that his father was dressed up in both. Festive occasions and dressed up was not the way Kevin remembered his dad. He'd usually envision him at home in a white tee shirt, working around the house: helping him fix his bike, cutting the lawn or painting the siding, and usually with a cigarette hanging from his lips.

Looking at the building through the passing traffic, made Kevin recall how often the Cullerton family had moved. There had been seven addresses on Grandma's list. The 1900 Census listed his grandfather as a foreman at a wholesale grocery. There was no reason to believe he still held that job in 1908 when Kevin's father was born across the street from where he sat. Were the frequent moves caused by hard times, his grandfather's menial skills, or because the rent money had been gambled away? In light of knowing what he did, it was hard for Kevin to give the old man the benefit of the doubt.

Why did I think seeing the house might hold some meaning for me? Maybe, he thought, because years earlier he had recognized the symbolic sway of the deceivingly simple dash between obituary dates, and this house had been where his Dad's dash began. Kevin looked at the 1972 picture of his father, taken just four years before his dash ended. How does a person's entire life and essence get packed into such a tiny symbol, a mere punctuation mark? He wondered perhaps along with the dash, a + or a – sign should be used to at least represent the person's contribution and effect on life in general. It would be placed after the date of death. He visualized his father's dates 1908-1977+. But who would get to decide?

Kevin pictured his grandma as a twenty-nine year old woman again pregnant by her forty-seven year old husband walking down the street with four other small kids in tow. He hoped she was relatively happy back then. He hoped she had something to smile about. He found it hard to imagine a woman smiling on the verge of giving birth to her fifth child in six years.

Where, exactly, in all this was his grandfather? *Did he come home and smile at his kids, the children he'd fathered and should have been more responsible for? What did he think as he walked up the street toward the building where his latest child was about to be born? Was he there when it happened?* Kevin realized, though the thought hurt, that if he'd been in his grandfather's shoes, he'd probably not have been happy about the whole situation. *Would I have deserted like he did?* He didn't want to contemplate an answer to that question.

He found it impossible to physically imagine his grandfather into the scene. He'd never seen a photo or heard a description of the man. How do you visualize such a figure? He closed his eyes, but his subconscious refused to provide a real person. Instead it proposed a hovering, transparent figure. As he opened his eyes, a large U-Haul box truck flashed within inches of his window startling him and splashing its yellow hue onto the ghostly image, which vanished by the time the truck passed. Not long ago he'd discovered how and when his grandfather had actually first vanished into the world of shadows. It was on the 1930 Census when Mary C. Cullerton had declared her status as WIDOW and listed her oldest son Edward as Head of Household. Kevin felt sure Grandma and her son Edward would have placed a negative sign after his dates if he'd actually been dead and she'd put up a headstone. 1863-1954^{-}.

Would Dad have agreed? Why do I care? He had an answer even before he finished his question… *because what if I'm not so different from your father. What if I can't…*

A CTA bus rumbled by. The vibration shook his car, severing the thought in mid sentence. Kevin felt he'd wandered into the past and had just been violently yanked back into the present. *Can't I be in both at the same time? Surely, there's some give and take between them.* He considered all he didn't know about both his grandfather and his father, their lives, their dashes. *Can what you don't know about the past hurt you? Or, is it just better all around that there are things a person will never know?*

He checked the time. When he replaced the photos into their envelope and back into his pocket, he removed Pat's letter. He didn't open it, but absent-mindedly transferred it to his pants' pocket. Then he circled the block and headed back to Tomina's, hoping he would handle today more like his dad than his grandfather.

Tomina had the door opened before Kevin reached it. "Thanks for coming." She nervously started talking, "I'm sure there is some obvious explanation I'm missing. I, just for the life of me, can't make sense of it, and can't let it go. But I couldn't sleep and … anyway, after I emailed you, I was afraid you'd think I was nuts and we'd never hear from you again.

"At school I told Teri, my best friend, and she said I was right to let you know, since your name was in it and all. Anyway, now I feel a little silly. You just drove almost three hundred miles, and I'm babbling." Her eyes looked tired and worried. She looked a bit sheepish and her smile seemed apologetic. Kevin realized how much he loved her smile and never wanted to hurt her in any way.

They went inside. Kevin said, "I was going to visit some college friends out in Northbrook anyhow." In fact, he had arranged the visit after deciding he had to – wanted to – come.

She led him into the living room and urged him to relax while she got some coffee. Kevin sat on the sofa. His hand went to his jacket pocket and he panicked when all he felt were the photos. Then he remembered and checked his pants to reassure himself. He began to second guess himself about bringing the letter with him.

To distract himself, he looked around. He'd not taken real notice of this room before. They'd always sat around the dining table, *almost family-like*. He forced that thought from his mind. The space was neatly kept with just enough clutter to show it was lived in. Kevin stood to look more closely at a grouping of photographs on the opposite wall. There was an artistically skewed symmetry to the arrangement. He assumed Sammy had a hand in that. At its center, Tomina's husband Bill lovingly held a laughing toddler version of Sammy high in the air. Spiraling out from this core were pictures of Tomina or her mother, always with Sammy, who aged in each picture. Looking closer at the most recent of those with Samantha and her nana, Kevin tried to see the girl he'd known so long ago, in the face of the woman in the photos. He decided they might, or might not recognize one another if they'd passed on the street.

Feeling some jealousy at not being a part of any photo, he cussed himself and walked over to see other pictures on the side tables and shelves. Most were of Tomina and Bill, Samantha, or all three. He lifted one of a very young looking Tomina and Bill with Samantha as a toddler between them. The love in Bill's eyes was evident as he looked at his wife and child. Kevin's heart filled to bursting with an overwhelming sadness for Tomina and the agony she must have endured losing Bill so suddenly and tragically. How could she have survived that? How does one continue after such intimate loss? Long ago he'd anticipated this vulnerability, and avoided it. He knew it would have crushed him, like Thomas' death had. He still considered himself a coward.

He put the picture down with hands made unsteady from the flush of emotions and his anxiety about what might be coming. The photo toppled face down. He tried again as Tomina returned. "I couldn't have made it through losing Bill, losing all three of them that way, if it hadn't been for Samantha. Thank God for kids, huh?"

Kevin straightened up but didn't turn around. He didn't want her to see the shame on his face. He said, "It must have been awful for you, and for Sammy. You're much stronger than I could have been." He returned to the couch. Not trusting his shaky hands, he let her place his coffee on the table.

Tomina settled on the other end of the couch. Wanting to delay her question about Pat's letter, he preemptively started. "Thanks for the coffee. So, tell me about Rita Naska."

Tomina curled her legs beneath her. Her natural smile seemed weak and Kevin's heart hurt again. "Well," she began. "Rita was Mom's best friend, but in some ways, her polar opposite. She was irreverent and single-minded like Mom. But while Mom wasn't one to explain or share what was going on in her head, you always knew what was happening in Rita's life and what she was thinking and feeling about it all. She once told me, 'You know I love your mom, honey, more than anyone, but she sometimes makes me crazy. She's like a Sphinx. It drives me nuts'.

"I knew exactly what she meant. I loved Rita. She was so funny and brash. And she was truly Mom's closest friend." It was obvious Tomina did love her mother's friend. She took a breath before continuing. "Anyhow, she had a stroke about a year before Mom got diagnosed. Mom found her. She'd gone over for coffee and Rita was lying in her kitchen. Mom called 911, but she died in her arms before they got there."

Tomina stopped. The smell of the coffee penetrated Kevin's consciousness and he lifted his cup, grateful his hands had quieted. They looked at each other. She smiled. He wanted to but couldn't. Instead he soaked up hers, like a thirsty man handed a glass of water.

"Kevin?"

His heart sank, then rose, then settled, all in the moment it took for her to ask.

"Rita's email said she was sending you a sealed letter from Mom. I don't get how that could have happened since she had already passed. It doesn't make any sense. But, can I ask, as friends, did she?"

"Send me a letter?"

She just smiled at him.

"Yes...she did." His heart rose into his throat. "And it came with Rita's email as a cover letter."

Tomina's smile disappeared, and with it, went something in Kevin.

"When was that?" She paused for a second then added, "If I may ask."

"Of course you can. I got it late March."

"Before you contacted me... at school the first time." she softly stated.

"Yes." He felt like a kid wanting to confess, more fearful of what she would think than of any penance. "The whole thing threw me for a loop, and I didn't know what to believe or do for the longest time."

"Well," Tomina said moving her legs from beneath her and putting her feet on the ground. "I'm glad you decided... to contact me, I mean. At first your email seemed too bizarre to be coincidental, like Mom was pulling strings in heaven. I remember Samantha saying 'she probably is, so don't over think it'. She reminded me of the old pictures and how Mom used to say you were virtually part of the family, like her second brother, back before Thomas died. And Samantha was right. It has meant a lot to both of us. Though I can't tell you how uncanny it was that she told you to call her Sammy, like Nana did."

"Uncanny?" Kevin asked.

Tomina's smile seemed more relaxed. "Well, maybe just unexpected."

She stood and walked over to the shelving unit where the television sat. From the shelf, she picked up a framed photo behind non-glare glass and handed it to him.

It was the picture they'd bonded over: Thomas in uniform, himself, and Pat pregnant with Tomina. "After your first visit Samantha said we needed to frame it so it wouldn't get lost, or just buried in the picture box." She took the photo back and smiled at it, and then at him. Kevin felt a tear, and he knew if he tried to say anything there'd be more. She wiped his cheek with her thumb.

"I'll be right back." She replaced the picture and disappeared around the corner. He knew she was just giving them both time to collect themselves. He finally took his jacket off. Taking his photos from the pocket, he placed them facedown on the couch.

He declined more coffee when Tomina returned. She sat. "What are these?"

Kevin nodded toward them. "More family photos." She carefully flipped them over.

"The one dated 1917 was my dad on his ninth birthday. The other is his and Mom's, anniversary in 1972, when he was sixty-four. I think I told you Dad was born not far from here. I stopped there before coming here. I thought these might help me connect and get a feel for the place, maybe spot a family ghost or two."

"Did it?" she asked.

"No, I can't say it did. It was all too long ago. But I had to try."

"Do you believe in family ghosts? Sometimes, I feel like Mom is still here, giving the pot a stir every now and again." Tomina studied the pictures. "You looked like him as a kid. I'll bet if I got out some of those early pictures of you and Uncle Thomas, you'd be hard to tell apart."

The thought made Kevin feel good. "I'd like to think I have some of him in me."

"I see you in this other picture too," Tomina said. "Around the eyes, and nose, the full head of hair."

"I'm most grateful for the hair." Kevin paused. "I thought you might like to see them. I'm not sure why." Then, suddenly, he was. He wanted her to see his father – and his mother. He hadn't known he wanted it until she pointed out the similarities between him and his dad. Then he very much wanted his parents, and their maybe granddaughter, all together at the same time, in the same room with him.

She held out the photos to Kevin. "Are you much alike?"

"I hope so." Kevin put the pictures back into his coat pocket.

"Anyway, I didn't mean to change the conversation about your Mom's letter." That wasn't true, but he let it go.

She asked, "Would it be rude of me to ask what Mom wrote in her letter? Not the details, I know that's private. But was it from long ago? Like I said, she wasn't exactly an open book about a lot of things."

"Actually, it was from close to ... when she died. Although, as Rita's note said, it wasn't mailed for awhile. She told me she was dying, and she told me about you and Samantha and how much she loved you and how much you both meant to her. She reminisced some about Thomas… and me a bit… you know, back in the day. I guess as our futures get shorter, we tend to look backwards, try to figure out how we fit into some kind of a bigger picture."

He'd told the truth and had avoided bringing up the second half of the letter. Then he had a moment of ex-Catholic déjà vu – and those damn lies of omission.

Tomina smiled at him. Maybe all his PLEASES on the drive down had helped after all.

"Well, her letter at least makes sense. And I'm glad she wrote to you, because that led you to contact us. When I see Mom in heaven, I'll thank her for that."

Kevin hoped that much would stay true. "Funny, your mom wrote about seeing Thomas in heaven."

Tomina stood. "Speaking of Thomas, would you like to see some of Sammy's – hell, now you and Mom have me calling her that – I mean, Samantha's drawings, since she seems to have inherited her talent from him?"

Having avoided his greatest fear about this afternoon, Kevin was relaxed and genuinely interested in seeing Sammy's art. "I'd love to," he said.

"She keeps them upstairs in her room. She's actually quite shy about showing them."

Upon entering Samantha's room, Kevin was immediately attracted to her drawing table. "Was this Thomas'?" he asked.

"It was. Mom gave it to Samantha for her eighth grade graduation."

The heads Tomina had seen outlined and clipped to the desk had been worked on. Kevin noticed the multiple erasure marks showing Sam had tinkered with changing angles and features. Tomina said, "I saw these when I brought up her laundry the other day. Then you couldn't tell who they were."

Kevin replied, "Well, now it's clear. Who's the other guy? He looks familiar."

"Her grandpa, Tim. Samantha hasn't seen him in at least a couple of years." Kevin was aware she had not referred to the other sketch as her father. "I wonder what made her sketch you two together?" So did Kevin.

He looked up to the collection of drawings on the wall. "She is good. Maybe as good as Thomas was at her age. It's a little hard to remember since Thomas didn't do a lot of portraits until he got older... not that he got to get much older, but you know what I mean. Does Sammy ever talk seriously about studying art, or doing something with her talent?"

"She has an independent study with one of the high school art teachers, instead of the standard class, which she could have taught. But in reality, right now, she's focused on getting through Algebra alive. Oh, and getting the Cubs to the World Series."

"Amen to both causes! But I hope she stays with this, even if it's as an amateur. I'd have died to have this much talent." He pointed to the portrait of Tomina amidst the others on the wall. "See how she angled your head, like you're looking over your shoulder. That's not easy." Kevin studied the picture a little closer. "It reminds me of something, probably something about the way Thomas did that. Anyway, she's better than I ever anticipated. You know how parents tend to exaggerate their kid's talents. But if anything, you didn't do justice to her work. You must be very proud."

For a few moments they both quietly studied the other pictures hanging there. Finally, Tomina said, "Well, as long as we're here, let me show you the Rita File I found on her laptop." She stepped over to the desk and hit the power button.

Kevin asked, "Are you sure? I don't want to be prying into her personal space."

"Kevin, she's sixteen. Besides, I'm sure the file was just left over from Mom, though I thought Samantha had deleted all of that stuff when I asked her to shut down Mom's email account. She must have been as baffled as I was when she stumbled on Rita's note. The poor kid! I just didn't want to bring it up with her until I'd talked with you. I hoped I'd have an explanation to give her."

The laptop signaled it was ready. Tomina leaned over and clicked on the document. "Samantha came home while I was reading it and startled me so bad, I panicked. I didn't even turn off the computer. I just closed the top and put her backpack on top of it again the way she had it. I don't know what I was afraid of. Just upset and confused by the message, I guess. I'll delete it after I talk with her. I don't want her getting the wrong message, like I think she was doing something wrong." Tomina closed the file.

"Look," she said and moved the cursor over another file. "I forgot about this "Misc" folder. Maybe this is Mom's too." She clicked on it. The screen blinked open. It contained seven more folders. All were clearly labeled: car, church, house, letters, passwords, work, and Xmas. "Mmmm, I'll have to go through these," Tomina said. "I think I can finally do that now without melting down." Seemingly at random, she chose the "letters" file and clicked. Again the screen blinked and displayed more files folders. Most were labeled with names. Tomina said, "They're all relatives or Mom's friends."

She pointed to a file labeled Tim. "There's Dad. I'm not sure if I want to read those. I'll have to think about that. What's this one?" She floated the curser over a file marked in all capital letters DO NOT SEND and double-clicked.

October 14, 2016
(...PM)

November 1, 2015

Dear Kevin,
It's been a long long time…

Tomina sat as if her legs had gone weak. She glanced up. Kevin experienced pure and sudden fear, as if caught committing a vulgar act.

"It's to you?" she asked in surprise, questioning what she was looking at. "November! Mom was living here by then. This was just weeks before she died."

The blood drained from Kevin's head, and faintness deepened across his consciousness like a shadow. He looked for someplace to sit, took a few steps to the bed and sat on the edge. His elbows were on his knees and his head lowered into his hands.

Not having noticed his reaction and retreat, Tomina continued to read the opening lines.

… It's been a long long time, hasn't it? Maybe too long but that can't be changed. You'll have to be the judge. I got your address from Mom's old Christmas list. I hope it is current and this gets to you. Otherwise I'll be very disappointed. When you read this, I'll already have been dead…

"Oh my God, Kevin! I'm so sorry. Is this the letter Mom sent to you?" When she didn't get a response, she turned around, seeing Kevin sitting in obvious distress on the bed. She stood and went to him. "Are you all right?" She sat next to him, putting her hand on his shoulder. "Are you okay? It's the letter, isn't it? I won't read anymore. I'll just close it up. I'll delete it. It was between you and Mom. I shouldn't have been so nosey and slow."

Kevin shook his head and sat up. He looked at Tomina. Her eyes were wet with genuine concern. He wanted to memorize her face and that look, because he wasn't at all sure he'd ever see it again.

She asked, "Are you better? I'll delete it." She started to get up.

He grabbed her arm and said, "NO," more forcibly than he meant to. "Just…just sit a minute and let me think." His grey head went back into his hand and his elbow back on his knees. The flush of fear was fading but not gone. He felt nauseous, realizing he needed to finally decide right now. He took a deep breath, trying to clear his head.

"I'm sorry, I didn't mean to holler. It's just… it's just…" But he couldn't create a coherent thought. He sat up again and looked at her, afraid he had scared her. Her face was empathy and encouragement, so natural and easy he was sure she wasn't even aware of it. He could imagine her comforting students, encouraging them when things got confusing. It would be enough to keep them trying, to let them know she was on their side, just as he felt now.

"Okay, I think you should read the letter. Just up to where she says she needs to take a break. Don't go any further, okay, promise? When you get there, just stop and close it."

"Kevin, I don't need to read any of it. I'm okay with that."

"No, I think you should. It just startled me when it popped up like that. It was like the night when I first got it out of nowhere and opened the envelope. Go ahead, read the first part, then close it, okay?"

"If you're sure you want me to." She ran her fingers along his back as she rose. It gave him courage and helped him believe he was doing the right thing. Tomina moved back to the desk and sat facing the screen.

Kevin pictured each word leaving the screen and entering her eyes. He watched for any movement or twitch that might reveal a reaction as the words lodged and arranged themselves in her consciousness. He thought he saw slight stiffening in her back. He imagined she was reading the line about his "remembering her body, and that dark night". He heard the soft click as she closed the file. It came quicker than he'd anticipated. The seconds before Tomina turned around were an eternity of hell. *Did she read beyond the first section?* He braced himself so as not to overreact. She turned around and faced him, hands on her knees and her back straight. She leaned toward him. Then her eyebrows arched and her smile appeared.

"Well, it looks like once upon a time you and Mom shared a moment which she remembered quite fondly."

Kevin interjected quickly, "It was before your parents... before she and Tim were married. I never planned..."

"Kevin, it doesn't matter. I'm not judging. I assure you, I know Mom was no saint. Remember, I grew up in the same house with her, and Grandma Thom hinted more than once that some of Mom's exploits had led her to despair." Tomina stared down at her own hands for a moment before continuing.

"It doesn't take a genius to guess what happened that night. And whatever it was, I'd bet Mom instigated it. But it doesn't matter to me." She looked back up at Kevin. "Look, we both know Mom was complicated. Patience and restraint were not her strongest virtues, especially if she felt pushed or confused. She'd take action, any action, and then deal with the consequences – until she couldn't anymore. It took me a long time to understand that about her. I was so different. I'm sure that's partly why my parents split.

"After Bill was killed, I thought about Mom losing her dad when she was only in first grade. So I told her how angry I was about Bill dying and asked how she had coped. She told me she hadn't had time to be angry about her dad; she had a little brother to look after. I think that's how she managed. But her repressed feelings had to affect her, made her who she was."

Kevin quietly added, "When Thomas was killed, your mom spent as much time comforting me as she did her mother."

Tomina asked, "Didn't someone say that adversity doesn't make character, it reveals it?" She took a tissue from her slacks and wiped her eyes and nose. "In Mom's case, it may have been both."

Kevin stood, not knowing quite what to do. Tomina rose and put her arms around him, with her head on his heart. As if forging a link or perhaps reconnecting a broken chain, they stood together, silently acknowledging the messy and confusing past that had brought them together.

Tomina rose on her toes and kissed his cheek. She lowered herself, and he gently kissed the top of her head. Both wished Pat could rise again from her bed and unravel the truth. Each worried what that truth might do to the other's life.

Tomina broke their silence. "Kevin, just remember it was always obvious you held a special place in Mom's heart. That was why when you contacted me, I invited you to visit and go through the old photos. I hoped to hear your stories about Mom. Like I always tell my students, stories bind people to each other. It was why I was happy when Samantha asked you to the ballgame. As I keep telling you…" she smiled at Kevin and finished… "we're family. And, Mr. Cullerton, I have the photograph to prove it. So like it or not, we're tight."

Kevin squeezed her hand. "I like it very much… But it scares me too. I feel like a kid taking a test on a book I haven't read."

"When Mom moved in and I knew we didn't have much time, I tried, for the first time, to understand what her life was like. I'm so grateful we had that time together. But I also came to realize what I thought I knew about my parents' lives was mostly fiction – more novel than biography. Maybe, that's why the old pictures are so precious. They show bits of reality, but they also prod the imagination, for good and bad. I think that's why we hang on to them and why families pass them on. Maybe it's what made you bring your dad's photos when you went to see where he was born. Maybe you were trying to imagine new chapters to his story?"

Kevin grinned and said, "Mrs. Larkin, how'd you get to be so smart? Unfortunately, in my family, there were no stories and damn few anecdotes or even pictures. So in my case, any story I tell is going to have to be fiction."

They shared a few more quiet moments before Tomina nodded her head in the direction of the laptop, and asked, "Were you worried I'd be upset you and Mom had something once? I'm no prude, though Samantha sometimes tries to make me feel like one. So please don't worry. In fact, I like the thought that... well, let's just say, that you and Mom were that close."

Kevin actually smiled and though it ventured too close to his secret, he said, "You are everything a parent could hope for in a daughter. But, no. That's not the part that worried me."

With most of the tension in the room eased, Kevin needed to move. He walked to the window. The street was lined with cars. His was across the street and half a block down. He let his attention focus on a maple tree, still with most of its leaves hanging on in full color twirling in the breeze and bright October sun. But suddenly a cloud dulled the light as a gust of wind snatched a handful of leaves from their tenuous moorings. He watched them twist and tumble and disappear down the street.

A decision suddenly broke into his consciousness and with no segue he abruptly said, "But, I think you're right." He went to the laptop, moved the cursor to the closed file and hit DELETE. Surprised but not upset by his non sequitur and sudden action, Tomina watched him.

Kevin kept his back to Tomina. His eyes went to the sketched faces clipped to the drawing table. "The rest of the letter was mostly the same," he lied, and then added a bit of truth, "mostly just personal details. It's probably best all around if it's deleted. I know it's your computer, and so I don't have the right, but..."

"It's all right, Kevin." She sensed his conflict and uncertainty return. "It was Mom's letter to you, not me. If it's upsetting, then deleting it was the right thing."

Kevin hated the feeling of hiding something so important from her. Even more he hated the idea of hurting her, or of her hating him. He couldn't live with himself if he destroyed what she and Pat had forged in those last days. Worst of all, he had no rebuttal to his grandfather's voice again whispering in the back of his head. *You're no better than I was. No better, not one bit.*

Tomina said, "Let's go downstairs and I'll make a little lunch if you want. Samantha will be home about 4:00. She took a deep breath and hesitantly added, "And, Kevin, I have something else to tell you before she gets here." Before Kevin could ask, she stepped around him to shut down and close the laptop but stopped when she saw a message on the screen.

Are you sure you want to remove this file to the Recycle Bin?
File: DO NOT SEND
Date Created: 11/01/2015 11:40 PM

"It's asking if you're sure you want to delete the file." Tomina said, and then added, "Look. Mom wrote this late at night. She was on some pretty strong pills to help her sleep by that time. It must have been really weighing on her mind if she couldn't sleep. …and that's kind of weird, don't you think?"

Kevin reached to complete the deletion. "What's weird?"

"Why would she call the file 'DO NOT SEND' – and in all caps? She must have written it and changed her mind and wanted to make sure she didn't inadvertently send it to you."

Kevin bent closer. "But it did get sent to me; so she must have changed her mind again."

"Are you sure it's the same letter you got?"

"The first part looked the same. I didn't read the whole thing before I freaked out on you."

Tomina said, "Maybe you should, just to be sure before you delete it." She clicked on the NO box and the file reappeared on the screen. "Take a look, and then delete it. I'll wait in the kitchen."

After she left, Kevin sat and skimmed. He knew most lines by heart. Rereading Pat's letter, Kevin decided he no longer thought it a confession. Because of what had just happened between him and his maybe daughter, the words no longer sent his heart and stomach into a panic. Being here in this room, steps from the bed in which Pat had died and with her daughter just downstairs, felt like an out-of-body experience, like picturing a character in a short story; one he still wasn't convinced was going to turn out well.

He quickly read the rest of the letter. At the very end of the text his brain stomped on the brake pedal, and his thoughts skidded to an abrupt stop.

Pat Thom
OXOXO
PS Don't worry, Kevin. You'll never see this letter. I just needed to write it so I could sleep.

Before he was aware that he'd ordered his hand to move, Kevin was unfolding his copy of the letter. He looked at the bottom of the printout. On a hunch, he reopened the Rita Naska message and checked the file date: March 22, 2016. It had been written, or at least modified, just days before he received it in the mail. He hadn't noticed that before. March 22 was the anniversary of his dad's death, and he remembered the letters had arrived a few days later. Tomina had said Mrs. Rita Naska obviously couldn't have sent it. *But if not her... who?*

Kevin had no lack of questions racing through his head. He now decided against deleting the file. Saving the original DO NOT SEND version with the original PS, now seemed important to unraveling this whole thing. He closed all the files and powered off the laptop before heading downstairs. He was aware of his anger rising. He needed some answers.

Tomina was at the dining table. A fresh cup of coffee was at Kevin's place, "*my place?*" He sat, keeping his eyes on the cup. He wanted – no, he needed – to ask the first question calmly and without anger or accusation in his voice. "Tommi," he said, unaware he'd just used Pat's diminutive, "the postscript in the laptop file is different, very different, from what I got in my letter. Since you pointed out that Rita Naska could not have mailed it..." He let the pause hang in the air between them.

Tomina looked as if she might choke on her coffee. "Are you sure?" she asked.

Kevin continued, struggling to sound calm. "And my letter was altered in a way that raises a lot of questions." Before asking he consulted his gut. No warning came. "Did you send them?"

Tomina looked directly into Kevin's eyes. No smile, but also nothing that indicated hurt or avoidance. She took a sip from her cup and said, "I've been sitting here thinking, trying to make sense of this. But let me answer you first, and I hope you'll believe and trust me: No. I didn't mail it. And I've never seen that letter or Rita's message before now."

Kevin's gut response was *Thank God she's not angry.* "I want to believe you… no, I do trust you and I do believe you. But, if you didn't, and Rita didn't…"

Tomina held up a hand to stop him. "I hope you'll keep on trusting me. I said upstairs I have something to tell you before Samantha gets home, but I need to start at the beginning."

"When I was six or seven, I overheard Mom and Dad arguing. They'd do that from time to time, like most couples, I guess, but this somehow seemed more intense, more important, so I listened from my room. I could only make out parts of what was said, and I sure didn't understand much, but it really scared and confused me. Dad kept asking about me and getting upset by what Mom was telling him. Not long after that they got divorced.

"But I kept thinking about the argument. It was stuck inside my head and, well, you know how children invariably blame themselves when they don't know what's happening to their world. People who claim 'what you don't know, can't hurt you' are awfully naive. I'm quite sure 'what I didn't know' was a big part of why Mom and I butted heads so often."

Tomina lifted her cup but didn't take a sip. She set it back down and continued. "When Mom got sick and moved in, we finally were able to talk in a way we'd never done before. I came to understand how much she loved, respected, and wanted to protect me, and she came to understand how I felt. One day while Samantha was out, I brought up the argument I'd overheard between her and Dad, and how it had haunted me.

"I'll never forget how Mom sat in her chair and stared at the ceiling for the longest time before she said anything. Then she starts off by saying she had every intention of dying without telling me this. She said it was absolutely unfair to a lot of people and she'd fully expected to spend a long time in purgatory for it, but the truth wouldn't have done anybody any real good. Needless to say, I was scared to death by then. She added that since I was a mother she hoped I'd be able to understand this from her perspective."

Tomina looked at Kevin, gathering her courage to go on, but Kevin interrupted her story. "I hope to hell I'm not making a terrible mistake here, but this might help if you read this first." He slid the paper from his pocket across the table.

"Is this ... this is your letter?"

He nodded. "I'm guessing this is the real reason you invited me to visit. And now, I have to hope you'll trust me, and in case this is a huge mistake, trust that I never want to do anything to hurt you or Sammy."

"Now, I'm scared again," Tomina said. "That sounds too much like Mom." She took the offered pages and read.

"Mom never said anything about..." Tomina stopped, and then restarted. "You mean we've been trying to protect each other from something we both knew about from the beginning?"

Kevin relief was visible. "Why didn't you say something? This must have been much harder on you than on me."

Tomina said, "Because it just wouldn't have been fair to you. How could I just pop out of the past with something like that? What would I say, Oh, hi Kevin, I'm Pat's daughter. Would you mind taking a paternity test?"

"I admit," Kevin said, "I've been a basket case since the letter showed up. At first it made me crazy and angry. Then it scared me to death. I didn't want to believe it. But once I met you and Samantha, that all changed and then I was worried if I ever told you, you'd hate me."

"You poor guy! I told you that first visit that you'd make a good father, and the fact that you've been trying to protect us from our past proves I was right."

Tomina glanced back down at the letter she still held. Her lips pursed and twisted before she asked, "The letter is dated the first of November. By then she'd already told me about this. That's when we started going through all the old photos. So why would she say I didn't know when she'd already told me?"

She looked back to Kevin. "She must have drafted the letter before she told me and then forgot to change it. Does that make sense? What was the picture she refers to here?"

Kevin took a long breath, letting it out slowly. "What doesn't make sense is the PS on the letter on the laptop. It says she had no intention of me ever seeing this. That's why the file was called DO NOT SEND. It was just her way of getting it off her chest. And the picture I got was a copy of one of Thomas' drawings you showed me on my first visit; the one with your mom and me looking over our shoulders at each other." He paused in thought. "Much like that sketch of Tim and me, Samantha has on her desk."

Kevin and Tomina looked at each other for a long moment, each hoping the other would state the most obvious solution to the riddle. Tomina stood and took his hand. She led him back to the living room couch where they'd started. This time they sat next to each other.

"I need to finish my story," Tomina said, "and I want to tell it surrounded by the family photos, and without a table between us." Kevin reached over with his thumb and wiped her cheek. When she returned the favor, he was surprised that her thumb came away wet too.

"Mom's story was basically the same as in your letter, except of course, without the graphic details. That night must have been one emotional ride for you guys between Uncle Thomas' draft lottery number, and then Mom... well, you know.

"Anyhow, while Mom was dropping her little bombshell on me,

I finally asked what she and Dad were arguing about that night I overheard them. She said Dad kept asking her if I was his daughter, and she'd reply she didn't know, until finally in the heat of the moment she told him she doubted it. Obviously, he was crushed by this, and very angry. Then it got really weird. She said Dad thought Uncle Thomas was the father. I had no idea why he would say that or even why Mom would tell me that detail. But of course, I asked what she told Dad."

"What?" Kevin felt like he'd been kicked between the legs. He was barely able to get the question out, "What did she say to that?"

"She told him, she didn't know. I remember screaming at her. She told me to calm down… she'd just been angry because Dad – I mean Tim – this is God damn confusing isn't it? Mom said he had always been jealous about how close Mom and Thomas were especially when she wanted to name me after him.

"As you can imagine, I was really upset and confused and mad. Surprisingly, Mom stayed calm and actually did a really good job of talking me down. Of course, she had the advantage. She was already on meds for her cancer.

"I asked her several times if Dad really could have thought Uncle Thomas and her, uh…well... I also asked, if not one of them, who?"

The fear still tingled throughout Kevin's entire body. "What did she say?"

"She was prepared for the question. She handed me Thomas' drawing of you and her staring at each other over your shoulders. The one you saw in with his other pictures."

Kevin said, "I'm guessing that's the original of the copy I got with your mom's letter?"

"I'd say so," Tomina nodded.

Kevin let his breath out. "The one Sam's drawing of you looking over your shoulder reminded me of?"

Tomina just gave one nod. Then they both slowly shook their heads side to side.

October 14, 2016
(... PM)

After Kevin had left for his friends, Tomina found herself back on the couch, legs tucked up underneath. She had tried so hard to keep this from Samantha, at least until she came to terms with the possibility herself. Now she felt foolish. She mulled over what she needed to talk about with her daughter. She had no idea how to start the conversation or how it would go. She wanted to believe their bond was strong and they'd work it out eventually.

Her emotions for both her mother and daughter started flipping between anger and compassion. Her mother had explained that she'd kept her suspicion to herself – *after all, wasn't it only an unproven suspicion on Mom's part? There was no proof* – because she didn't think it was fair to everyone involved, not at the time and certainly not toward the end. Hadn't she herself just used that same excuse with Kevin? Wasn't that really why she hadn't talked to her daughter, telling herself she'd wait until Samantha was older? But when would be the right time?

Tomina's hips and mood shifted. *Why didn't Samantha come to me when she found Mom's letter? How long ago was that?* She'd asked Samantha to check Mom's email back in early February. Had she found it then or later after she'd started using the laptop? *How long has she known?* Tomina couldn't tell what hurt more: the thought of her daughter dealing with this on her own or that Samantha had not trusted her enough to come to her.

She wasn't sure why Samantha did what she did, but she absolutely believed her daughter's motives would be honest, albeit, naive. Maybe she assumed if she could get Kevin to contact them, things would work themselves out. But, Samantha should have known better. Hadn't all the losses they'd already gone through taught her life is not a movie or a loosely plotted feel-good novel? With Bill and his parents gone, and Nana Pat, and with her genetic link to Grandpa Tim being questioned, how could Samantha not know this? How could she not know life isn't about happy endings?

Tomina closed her eyes and after several breaths the answer came. *Because she's a sixteen-year-old optimist who loves life and her nana and needs to believe life is fair and balanced… and isn't that exactly the way it should be at sixteen? And isn't it my job to help her weather the bumps and crashes and somehow teach her how to keep going while learning that life is one long slow letting go. How the hell does one do that?*

Not having an answer to the last questions caused Tomina to hold her breath while her eyes filled with tears. She didn't let her breath out until the she was sure she wouldn't cry. She wiped her eyes and let her mind proceed.

She felt sure Samantha could not have thought through all the ramifications of contacting Kevin, or the difficult position she'd put both Kevin and her in. Tomina also knew her daughter didn't know that she already knew about Nana's secret. They'd always made sure those conversations happened while Samantha was out of the house. There was going to be a lot of tangled motives and feelings to unravel.

She considered the absurdity of the situation, of all three of them, Samantha, Kevin, and herself, each hiding Nana's secret from each other. *Actually, that's not quite accurate. Samantha wanted Kevin and me to find out. She wanted us to come together and stumble into the truth. What did she think or hope would happen then?*

Before she could reach out to Samantha, she had a lot of things to work out for herself. *Where to begin?* She thought about a glass of wine, but wanted her head clear so as to not do or say anything stupid and get off on the wrong foot when Samantha got home. Instead, she leaned back, closed her eyes again, and framed question one. *When did this start… with Mom and Dad's argument when I was a kid … when Mom told me last fall … according to Kevin's letter it started on December 1, 1969, in Mom's bedroom.*

Tomina smiled at the thought. She remembered what it was like to be in her early twenties. She'd have preferred Mom wasn't engaged at the time. But what was done is done, and right or wrong, she – and now Samantha – had their own choices to make. Actually, since Samantha had already made her first one, it was her turn.

Tomina went over the conversations with her mother. Did it really matter who her dad was, after all these years? Wasn't she the person she had chosen to be: Mrs. Tomina Larkin? Why should she let what happened so long ago matter?

Kevin was simply a character in her mother's stories, an image in the family photos. And now she knew he was also a caring and nice old man – as was Tim. But both were distant, though in different ways. Tim became distant emotionally after the divorce and then geographically when he remarried and moved to Texas. Kevin was closer emotionally but distant in his seeming ambivalence about their status. True, he had mentioned DNA as the only positive proof one way or the other. But he'd said it as a fact, not as a suggestion. He was saying it was her decision. He sure hadn't seemed anxious to find out. *Do I want to know? After all these years, do I want a dad in my life; beyond…beyond what… a nice old man in Texas and another in Wisconsin?* Won't *finding out hurt one of them…or both? … Maybe they'd both be relieved to find out they were off the hook. Considering the circumstances, I couldn't blame them.*

Trying to find perspective, Tomina's thoughts went to of all the students she'd taught who had missing fathers. Close to half her current classes lived with single parents or split time between two households. Growing up with a single divorced mom made her empathetic but also keen on letting the kids know that while a missing or absent parent dug a big hole in your life, it didn't define them and it wasn't an excuse for not trying their best and doing the work. She could hardly not follow her own admonishment.

But, this wasn't something she could bury or plow her way through on her own like her mother had. She had to decide how to handle this with Kevin and with her daughter. *Why didn't Samantha come to me when she found Mom's letter*? Samantha's decision to deal with this on her own made Tomina sad, proud, and she had to admit, a bit miffed. *I'll have to get rid of the annoyed part before we talk.*

"Mom, I'm home," Samantha's voice broke through her thoughts. "I didn't see Kevin's car. Isn't he here yet?

Tomina wiped her eyes and cheeks and took a very deep breath. "I'm in here, honey."

October 16, 2016
(AM ...)

"Good morning," Nelson said from the kitchen table. "What time did you get home last night?"

"About 1:00. I stayed for part of the Cubs game. I finally left Northbrook in the middle of the fifth inning and listened to the rest on the way home. I thought they were going to blow it, but they came back."

Nelson sensed Kevin didn't want to jump right into his conversation with Tomina, so she gave him some space. "There are pancakes under the cover you can heat up. The coffee may need reheating too."

Kevin put the stack in the microwave and poured a coffee. After the machine's three beeps, he put his coffee in while he buttered the pancakes. He carried his breakfast to the table.

Nelson said, "I saw the first two innings. The crowd was going nuts. She paused briefly before adding, "So how are Lee and Kathy and the kids?"

"Everyone's fine. Even after all this time, we always find something to laugh about. Of course, a few beers probably help."

"Did you tell them about Tomina?"

"I'm not able to laugh about that yet. Besides, this is all from way before I met them. They know I had a good friend killed in Vietnam but we've never talked much about that."

Nelson finished her coffee and stacked her dishes. She

felt tension but wasn't sure if it emanated from herself or Kevin. She looked around the kitchen before asking. "And…Tomina and Samantha? You're text Friday night just said 'went well…have stuff to share, home Saturday night'."

"I'm sorry I was so mysterious and curt. I needed to do some thinking before trying to explain it all. And actually, I didn't see Sam. I left before she got home from school. We thought it best Tomina talk to her alone."

"Oh?"

Kevin swallowed a fork full of pancakes. "Do you remember the O. Henry short story 'Gift of the Magi'? I think Tomina and I just played out our own version of it."

While he ate, Kevin narrated his way through the visit and conversations. It took all of Nelson's will power not to keep interrupting with questions. She felt her agitation and impatience rising. The second he finished, she said, "This isn't O'Henry. This is some sort of soap opera. I don't even know where to start. Did you talk about a DNA test to clear this up?"

Kevin said, "Well, no, not really, not other than to put it on the table as the only definitive answer."

"But neither of you said, let's do it; let's find out for sure?" There was a moment of silence, but it carried the repressed weight of the last seven months. Nelson continued. "So she told you all along she was trying to protect you?"

"Well, she didn't just come out and day that. We kind of stumbled on that realization. You can guess what a relief it was, for both of us."

"And you believe her?"

"Why wouldn't I believe her?" Kevin was surprised by the tone of the questions. He hadn't anticipated this reaction.

"Well, based on her mother's sudden deathbed revelation, don't you think there's good reason to be skeptical of everything?"

Kevin took a slow breath. He felt squeezed between Nelson's questions and his desire to believe and protect his maybe daughter and his own youthful memories of her mother. "Pat only told Tomina about this when she pressed her mom about their divorce."

He hoped he hadn't sounded too defensive or like he was taking sides.

Nelson continued as if she hadn't heard. "And you said Tomina just accidentally clicks open a file she supposedly has never seen before, and lo and behold, there's Pat's letter?"

Kevin reached for Nelson's hand, but she drew it away. He felt as hurt as she looked. "What's going on, babe?" He touched his face which stung as if he'd just been slapped.

"I'll tell you what's going on." Nelson stood and put her dishes loudly into the sink. Kevin was about to go after her when she returned and sat again. "Do you know how much time and worry you've put into this? How many days and miles driving back and forth? You may not have noticed, but this hasn't been easy on me either. I admit at first I didn't know what to think or how to react. I thought maybe it was a prank, maybe from one of your old buddies. Later I figured even if it was legit, it was from so long ago it didn't matter to me, to us. But it does, a lot. The more stressed you became, the more angry I felt. But I wasn't going to dump that on you and it wasn't something I could bring up at lunch at the office, could I? 'Oh guys, a funny thing happened. Kevin just found out he's a father'."

Nelson put her face in her hands for a moment. Kevin's heart almost broke. When she looked up, her face was wet. "I know you never wanted kids. Teaching was more than enough for you. But I did."

Kevin said as tenderly as he could, "You never told me that before."

"There wasn't any reason to. By the time we met, we were both too old for kids even if you had wanted some. My ex never wanted children either. And after a few years, I knew we weren't going to make it and I didn't want to chance having kids with him. Do you have any idea what that feels like for a woman? You're whole being is longing for children while you are actively making sure you don't have any?"

Kevin again reached for Nelson's hand. This time she let him take it.

Nelson took a napkin from the holder and wiped her eyes. "I'm sorry. This isn't about me. I know that. But it hurts to think either you're being jerked around, or you might all of a sudden have a daughter and granddaughter. I know it's got nothing to do with fairness, but..." Nelson stopped talking. She put her other hand on top of her husband's.

Kevin knew he'd been so consumed with his own fears and concern that he'd failed to seriously consider hers. Guilt showed on his face. Nelson squeezed his hand. "Kevin, I promise you, I'm okay now. I just needed to get that out. I truly am happy things turned out as they did with Tomina."

Kevin reached across and brushed Nelson's cheek. "I've been a selfish bastard about this. That's why I didn't want kids in the first place. I barely have the capacity to let one person into my life at a time. And I swear that person is you. But you were able to see every one's needs from the beginning. You even warned me to consider their needs above mine. And you were right. But I couldn't leave well enough alone, I had to contact them. And even though I tried to keep their needs first, I forgot about you, and how this might be affecting you." Tears sat at the edge of his eyes. "I'm the one who needs to apologize, not you. I'm so sorry."

Nelson felt the tension leave her body as if the window had been opened and clean air swept through the room. She took Kevin's hand and said, "Obviously, I'm not ready to laugh about this yet either. But, someday I will. I promise. Now tell me again how you and Tomina figured out this was Samantha's doing."

Kevin settled into his reading chair and studied the brown envelope from his cousin Colleen that had come while he was in Chicago. He'd updated her once by email but hadn't talked with her since February when they'd met at Calvary Cemetery and his family tree had bloomed from a stump to a massive live oak. So much family had come to life that day, he'd never again think of a grave as the end of someone, or as a final resting place. He was still trying to identify some of the people buried in the two plots – one bought by his great- grandmother, Jane Cullerton, and the other by his grandmother's father. Each held the bones, or at least the dust, of twenty-plus people. Most were relatives, but not all. He had used census data, birth and death certificates, and obituaries to link together many of his immediate relatives back through his great-grandparents. Others with the Cullerton or Finnell name, he assumed would be relatives, but he could only guess at their connections. Others, he speculated were either neighbors or friends and their children. Back before metal coffins and concrete burial vaults, back when his relatives and their neighbors had all been poor immigrants, it was possible to share and reuse the plots. That spoke of poverty but also of family and a sensibility that must have gotten derailed along the way. Kevin slid his finger under the sealed flap. He wasn't expecting anything from Colleen, but considering the last time they'd met, his excitement rose.

Inside were a yellowing folded sheet of paper and two photographs paper clipped to a note. He looked at the photos. Each figure was dressed in a dated fashion from long before Kevin's time. The young woman, in her high neck black dress and double strand bead necklace, looked vaguely familiar. The black and white image made her eyes look soft and sad. The other, a young man in buttoned jacket, starched collar and tie, was not familiar. Kevin read the note.

In it, Colleen explained that she'd recently gone through her dad's stuff to see if there was anything that her own kids might want to keep. She'd come across a folder from when Grandma had stayed with them a long time ago. He read the rest of Colleen's note:

> Since you're working on the family history, I thought you might like these.
> The paper is some kind of insurance application.
> The old photos are pretty neat. One is Grandma as a girl. I think my dad said she was about eighteen. A bit of a looker, huh? Who'd have guessed?
> I made copies for my kids so you keep this one.
> I don't know who the guy is.

Get in touch when you solve the mysteries or get down this way.
Love, Colleen

Kevin was drawn to the photo of his young grandmother. The boys of her day would definitely have given her a second look. It was strange trying to reconcile this young woman with his stooped, old, grandmother. He turned to the other photo. His first thought was that the picture was his father's brother Richard who had died as a boy. But the face staring back was not that of a fourteen year old. It was a man's face. Then it struck him. *Of course! Who else could it be? But why would she keep his picture, the man who'd left her and their ten kids to gamble and carouse?*

Just a few days ago, he'd sat in front of the house where his dad had been born and couldn't picture his grandfather in the scene because he had no picture or description. He stared at the image of the man. Except for a cleft chin, the general makeup of his facial features and his full head of hair were Cullerton traits. The eyes and gaze, however, seemed to challenge him. They seemed cold, self-indulgent, or maybe he was projecting that.

"Are you the voice?" he asked the face in the picture. He listened, but heard nothing. He looked carefully at the image, trying to see into the man. "Are you the one telling me I'm no better than you just because I'm scared to admit to a daughter? That's not fair, old man. I wasn't there when Tomina was born, when she grew up. I didn't walk away from a wife and child, let alone a house full of them. It's not fair. It's not the same. So leave me the hell alone."

The face staring back at him wasn't buying it; the eyes still mocked his request. Kevin suddenly felt self conscious talking to a picture.

He held the two photos side by side. Both were studio settings, posed shots wearing their Sunday best. They may have been taken to celebrate their engagement or wedding. But if it was a wedding picture shouldn't Grandma have been in white? Was her black dress significant, or simply her best dress? Maybe the picture of his grandfather was from before they were married. Maybe she'd kept it to remind her of the man she'd loved rather than the man she married or that left her children.

Thinking of their wedding, Kevin retrieved the copy of their 1903 marriage certificate from his files. The dress and suit could be from then. Were these commemorative photos? But why wouldn't they have a picture taken together? *It would be too sad to think they didn't. But I can see Grandma burning it after they'd split.* He considered what it meant that she had kept these separate pictures until the end of her life. It made him very sad for her.

Kevin set them aside and looked to the other folded paper, an application for hospital insurance entitlement to the Social Security Administration. Included in the information, Grandma had listed her current (1964) address as 1231 W. Granville, Chicago, ILL. It was the fourth address listed over the last five years – *a lot of moving for a woman in her eighties.*

She'd also recorded her late husband's name, Edward Patrick Cullerton and his date of birth, April 5, 1863. At last he had a precise date. Both name and date were duly and accurately noted in the appropriate boxes.

The adjoining box requested "Date for Marriage." And here his grandma had printed March 31, 1901, two years prior the actual marriage and therefore making her first son legitimate.

Grandma, you son-of-a-gun, you! Was 1901 a memory lapse, or were you rewriting this little bit of your history?

Kevin leaned back in his chair. He wished he could go back in time and tell her that by 1964, nobody cared and to go ahead write in 1903. However, he felt sure she cared. He felt sad that she had probably carried the shame of an out-of wedlock baby around with her as her worst sin in a life that lasted ninety-six years. A small corner of his secretive Grandma's shadow, hidden in that long dash between her birth and death, had finally become real and was visible, like a bit of slip peeking below her dress hem. He liked that very much. It made him want to root for her in a way he'd never had before.

October 19, 2016

Kevin knew it was a ridiculous waste of time and energy. Still as much as he tried to shake it off, the Cubs losing games two and three to Los Angeles was a drag on his energy and mood. He tried to muster some of Sammy's confidence. But he'd seen this before. 1969, 1984, and 2003 were the most painful examples. The Cubs had just scored exactly zero runs for two games in a row and now trailed in the series 2-1. Young fans wondered how that could happen. This was going to be THE YEAR. Older Cub fans knew – it was the damn goat. He'd have to muster the courage to watch game four tonight.

Even as concern about the Cubs, not to mention Tomina, Sammy, and Nelson, mounted and kept him mentally on edge, Kevin was physically bored. The weather was damp and cool, hard on his bad knee, and he didn't want to work in the yard or golf, even though the season for both was dwindling. He found himself in the basement folding clothes from the dryer. Heading back up the stairs, the old file cabinet peeked out from beneath the steps. He hadn't revisited it since back in January when he'd first discovered the old shirt box and fallen down the genealogy rabbit hole.

He set the laundry basket down and flipped on the lights. The cover sheet was still turned back from his last visit, reminding him of his unfinished excavation. He opened the bottom drawer. Taking out the cardboard box, he sat again in the same chair in which he'd fallen asleep the last time.

The letters he'd discovered that day were filed away upstairs, but the old school records were still in the box. He set them aside and examined a plastic bag which held an old Timex wrist watch. The black leather band was dried out, the hands frozen at 9:22 on the 22nd. The watch model did not display the month, so there were twelve possibilities. His father had died on the 22nd of March, but Kevin couldn't believe the battery had given out at the same moment as his dad's heart. It had to be coincidence. The bag also contained his father's Chicago Public Library card. It was stamped to expire December 1, 1977, nine months after his heart attack. Because of Pat's letter, Kevin knew the date was exactly eight years, to the day, after Tomina had been conceived – either by him or Tim.

The usual question came to mind. *Do I really want to know?* He recalled a friend, a Chicago cop. He and his partner had been assailed by a drugged-up gunman when they'd stopped to use the bathroom at Henrotin Hospital. Shots were exchanged and the gunman died. Later, his friend told Kevin that both he and his partner had requested not to know whose bullet had killed the guy. Kevin had renewed empathy for their request. He pushed the thought away.

Below the plastic bag Kevin found a flat paper bag, the size a store would use for a birthday card. Inside were several items, starting with an envelope on which his mother had written *"Cards from Dad."* The printing was surprising until he saw that the contents were from the war, years before his mother's eyes had gotten so bad she could only print in block letters. He opened each item, treating them as historical artifacts offering a rare glimpse into his parents' world before he was born.

The first was a small envelope from Pvt. J.A.Cullerton, 1st Base Post Office, UK. It was stamped NOV 17, 1944 Army Postal Service and "PASSED BY" an Army examiner named Lt. Morton. It was addressed to:

Mrs. Julia Cullerton
3124 Montrose Av.
Chicago, 18, ILL.

The address must be where his mother and Grandma lived while his dad was overseas. The paper card inside was embossed with a silvery swan design and pre-printed message: *Greetings on the Anniversary of Our Wedding*, and a short corny verse in rhyme. *Not very romantic or personal.* It was signed simply: Jim, 22 Nov 1944 – their seventh anniversary date. *Really, Dad, you couldn't come up with anything more then your name and date?* This seemed sad even by his father's standards. Then he thought of the watch, *again, the 22nd.*

Next came an old photo. It was his father in uniform posing with eight others in front of Queens Pub. Three of the other four men were in uniform and all four were paired with women. All except his father. He wondered about his dad on his own overseas, without Mom. He would have been about thirty-seven. Kevin found his mind dancing around the possibility of his father having ever having been with another woman. He thought of his night with Pat. She had been engaged to Tim and yet he hadn't let that stop him. On the back of the picture he read:

For Jimmy Cullerton
Love
Dolly & Walter

Kevin assumed Dolly and Walter was the older civilian couple in the photo and probably the pub owners. Moving on, he found black and white postcards of Kenilworth Castle ruins and Litchfield Cathedral and a third with colored scenes from Warwick Castle. All had been passed by the censor and mailed from England. Setting them aside, Kevin found his attention and imagination hijacked by the next few items.

The first was a September 1944 concert ticket to the National Symphony concert at Birmingham Town Hall. He stared at the print for several moments as the ticket pulled on a deep memory. He sat quietly like a fisherman trying to entice a fish. Then it was there, past and present converged. He and Dad …Ravinia… a summer picnic and Chicago Symphony concert. He remembered his father telling him he had first heard the Beethoven piano concerto in

Birmingham England during the war. *This was the concert! This was the exact ticket!* Holding it in his hand, over seven decades after his dad had purchased it, was like finally finding and reading the end of a favorite short story that had gotten misplaced in life's clutter. It was a tangible link, an unexpected closing of a circle. Kevin sat back for a few minutes conjuring in his head Beethoven's themes and orchestration while holding the ticket, just as he had held his dad's hand that perfect summer evening so long ago.

When the memory and reverie finally let him go, Kevin examined two wallet-sized Base Post Office ration cards with Cullerton, James A, Pfc. typed on both. Beige was England, and green was France. Kevin recalled at thc concert, his dad had mentioned he'd spent his last few months in Paris. Here was proof. He enjoyed thinking about his dad exploring the famous museums and galleries. He knew his father enjoyed art; he'd even done some oil painting after he'd retired. Kevin found himself wondering why his dad had never taken him to any of Chicago's world class venues. It had been through Thomas that he'd been introduced to the Chicago Art Institute. Together they'd spend hours exploring and discussing the art. Thomas would point out and explain famous examples of the techniques he was learning about in his classes. It was his friend's way of sharing and keeping Kevin attached to his own journey. Kevin reciprocated by bringing Thomas to university concerts and to Orchestra Hall for the Chicago Symphony's Friday afternoon concerts, where their student IDs could get them in cheap. *How long ago was that?*

The final piece of evidence from his father's soldiering life was a small folded scrap of fragile newspaper from the Chicago Daily Times, dated October 22, 1945.

Chicago News Briefs
101 Chicago GIs dock in N.Y.
Aboard the **Brandon Victory**
which docked at New York
yesterday, were:

He found his dad. CULLERTON, J. Pfc. He hyper focused on the name trying to see his father disembarking among the thousands of troops. He conjured up his young face based on the pub photo he'd just seen. He tried to imagine his father as a soldier in the context of the returning troops, the ship, the ocean, England, Paris, a world war.

The concert ticket had revived a wonderful personal memory, but seeing the actual troop ship and date on which his dad returned from the war connected world history and his family. He wished he knew what his father had been thinking out there on the ocean on his way back to his wife, mother, siblings and civilian life. Would it have been the practical concerns: getting his job back at the post office, figuring out where they'd live now, catching up on how his brothers and sisters had been fairing? Kevin wondered if having survived World War II, the Great Depression, and the 1918 lethal flu pandemic (which had taken his brother Richard), his father's world view and sense of self and purpose had changed much. As he approached New York, might he have been thinking about legacy and having his own kids… becoming Kevin's dad?

He began to put everything back into the box when he saw another smaller envelope. It had one word on it: Grandma. The writing seemed to be his father's. *Maybe I should take up graphology as a new career?* Inside was another small newspaper clipping.

O'Rourke – Mrs. Jane, January 24, 1919, beloved mother of James and Edward Cullerton, Mrs. John Carroll, Mrs. Michael Smith, and Mrs. Adam Franenholtz, and the late Mrs. John F. Owens, at residence 1612 Indiana to St. John's Church where a requiem high mass will be celebrated, then by carriage to Calvary.

He recognized his grandfather Edward and his brother James. From the Calvary Cemetery records he'd learned O'Rourke was his great-grandmother Jane's second husband's name. The other women he'd have to match up later with his census data, but they were obviously his grandfather's siblings. The family tree was again sprouting leaves.

Kevin was touched that his dad had saved his own grandmother's obituary. He wondered, in light of the strained family relationship, how well his dad knew Jane Cullerton-O'Rourke. Was he as much in the dark about her life as he himself was with his grandmother?

He wasn't familiar with St. John's Church but thought maybe he'd drive by and take a look some time. A genealogical tour to all these old places appealed to him, just to get a feel for the family's geography. There were several lifetimes of untold family stories buried around the city. He knew he'd never unearth them. But, maybe visiting the settings might be fun, even insightful. Maybe he'd ask Tomina, maybe even Sammy to ride along. Then again, maybe that would be pushing things too far, too fast, or in a direction he wasn't sure he wanted to go.

Kevin put everything back into the file cabinet. He'd reached the bottom of the bottom drawer, so this time he pulled the sheet down over the drawers, covering his small pieces of history, leaving his family behind, at least temporarily. He picked up the laundry basket and went upstairs. With his foot, he closed the basement door on his past and turned his thoughts back to the Cubs game tonight. As he headed to the bedroom to put the clothes away he mumbled to himself: *I can't be a coward and hide from whatever the baseball gods have in store. What kind of a "maybe" grandfather would I be if I didn't watch; I can't let Sammy face the Billy Goat alone?*

October 22, 2016

The Chicago Cubs are going to the World Series! No joke, no curse, just the Cubs' first National League pennant since 1945.

Even after watching the game on television, Kevin read several headlines and reports online before convincing himself it was indeed real. He'd shared texts with Sammy during and after the game. Nelson had watched the game with him, but was now in bed asleep.

He was standing alone on his back porch in the chilled Wisconsin night, thanking the baseball gods he'd lived to see this actually happen, when he realized he was melancholy because he really wanted to share it with Thomas and his dad. How many hours – must be hundreds – had he and Thomas spent talking about Cubs' players and games or pretending to be Ernie Banks hitting heroic home runs to win a World Series. He pictured himself back at Wrigley with his father sitting high up in the third base grandstands learning how to fill in the scorecard and then some years later working side by side selling hotdogs, pop and Cracker Jack popcorn from a trailer beneath the stands while they judged the game's progress by the cheers or groans coming from above.

Like an improvised coda, another thought followed as Kevin

stared into the chilly night sky. He wondered if back in 1945, while the Cubs last World Series appearance was in progress and the troops, including his father, were beginning to ship home from Europe, if his dad had ever talked to his own father about those games – or anything else, ever.

The cold finally sent him back to his room. He checked to confirm the World Series would begin on Tuesday, in Cleveland. Then he just sat at his computer, staring at the headlines and grinning like an idiot – it was really happening. He told himself that getting into the series was all he needed. Pigs do fly! The actual World Series would just be superfluous icing on the cake, winning too much to ask.

He immediately knew it was a lie. They HAD to win! They couldn't get this far and not win it all… could they? His grin faded, so he read the articles again.

October 25 – November 1, 2016

Game 1

Kevin was at his desk early Tuesday staring at the Wieboldt's shirt box next to him. He'd awoken three times last night, and each time the box was on his mind. At 6:00 AM he finally went down and retrieved it from the file cabinet. Now, he shifted through the same items he'd found last week, picking each up, one by one, as if holding it might help him better understand its significance in his father's life. For lack of any actual plan, he started his PC, created a file labeled "James A. Cullerton," and began a list.

Grandparents:	Patrick and Jane Cullerton
Parents:	Edward Patrick Cullerton & Mary Celia Finnell
Born:	November 23, 1908 at 1054 Diversey; Chicago
Siblings...	

He worked diligently adding items for three hours, frequently consulting his file notes and the mementos in the box for names, locations and dates and any additional scraps of information he might include. He scoured his dad's birth and death certificate, the sacramental records he'd obtained from Our Lady of Mercy Parish, his parents' marriage certificate and all of the war correspondence and artifacts in the box. No detail seemed too small. From the Mass card at Dad's funeral he even recorded the plot and section site at Maryhill Cemetery where his parents lay side by side.

When he completed the project, he sat back and stared at what he had – an incomplete sampler of the events of his father's life. At best they were only headings or chapter titles of the life subsumed by the dash on his father's headstone. Maybe what Tomina had said to him was right. He was trying to add chapters to his dad's life, to lengthen his dash. At first when she had suggested the idea, Kevin thought it just a clever metaphor for his interest in genealogy. Now, he knew it was more, a belated attempt to understand the man he'd loved, but felt he hardly knew.

His list, the dates and events, was only a skeleton, with no living flesh attached. It offered scarce more insight into the man who'd fathered him than he'd gained by parking outside the house and staring at the door behind which his dad had been born. No list can explain a man, or his life. How could it? It was little more than a collection of Wheres and Whens and told almost nothing about the Who, How, and most importantly, the Whys. It reminded him of how history was taught back when he was in school. Names, dates, wars, winners, test. Next chapter, more names, dates, wars, etc. What was always lacking was the story, the human narrative that gave life to any context.

It was frustrating. He'd never know the "Why" to the questions he most wanted answers to – the answers that would help him understand his father and grandfather. He thought about Tomina and his own paralyzed inability to actively move her from a "maybe" to a "definite" Yes or No. He could have asked her to take a DNA test and then they'd all know where things stood. But he had done no more than weakly hint at the idea, feeling it was a threat. What was the Why behind that?

After his last trip to Chicago, Nelson asked him about his hesitation. He couldn't explain it to her, or himself. He couldn't put it into words. He couldn't tell her about his grandfather's shadow and words. He hated that a big part of him didn't want to step up and become a father, a grandfather. What would that even look like at this point?

But why should he feel threatened just because his grandfather had failed as a father? *"You're the same as me."* His grandfather's voice had become a constant buzz in his head ever since Cousin Colleen's photo gave a face to the voice. Kevin knew he was letting this get too big in his mind. He was creating a self-fulfilling prophecy. He hadn't wanted children when he was young. So, was all this angst simply his resentment at fate subverting and tricking him, making him the fool? He felt a coward. The best he could do was to leave the decision in Tomina's hands.

In spite of his grandfather's despicable abdication and although he tried, Kevin couldn't build a serious animosity toward the man. He was just too far removed, and his own dad had created an effective invisible barrier of silence between Kevin and his father's callousness. *Dad never lied about his father. He'd simply omitted the man, just like grandma did on the 1930 Census,* even though the man didn't die for another twenty-four years. *Can one so easily dispense with the consequences of their past? Is that even possible?*

Staring out his window, Kevin wondered if he might have been better prepared to fight off his grandfather's admonition, if only he had been the least bit curious or persistent growing up, if he had probed and insisted on hearing the stories. He'd like to know if Edward Patrick Cullerton, his grandfather, had ever lain eyes on him as a baby, had ever held him, or laid a curse on him. The old man would have been eighty-seven when Kevin was born, but it would have been possible. *Did he even know I had been born? Did Dad ever tell him?*

Kevin pulled his mind back to the present. He looked at the list he'd made. Compared to his own life, it was amazing how much his dad had dealt with. Was it because of that, or in spite of it, he had been a good father? Was there something there, some hint, of how Dad had successfully managed that feat, an accomplishment both his own father and now his son had run from?

He saved the document. He had leaves to rake.

Just before midnight, Kevin sat back at his PC to email Sammy. He knew the message was as much to ease his own disappointment as Sam's. He cc'd Tomina.

> SUBJECT: OUCH!
> The ghosts of the last 108 seasons must weigh
> a ton. Hopefully the loss will focus them.
> Kevin
>
> PS... THANK YOU again for the phone call and apology last week. I'm guessing the conversation with your mom was difficult for both of you. The whole situation is crazy and it's difficult for all of us to sort out feelings. Your nana was a good woman. You know that a lot better than I do. Your mom has told me several times how close you two were. Losing her must have been hard. I know how much family means to you. I could see that the first time I visited and you walked me through all those photographs.

Game 2

When Nelson left for work the next morning, Kevin was still in bed. "Tough night, huh? The headlines said 6-0. I'm sure they'll do better tonight." She squeezed his hand and kissed him goodbye.

An hour later, after a long shower and some breakfast, Kevin carried his coffee to his room. He couldn't face scrolling the news of the game, so instead he pulled up the list he'd started yesterday. He looked it over again as he sipped and tried to sort out his feelings. Each line begged more questions without yielding any understanding. The problem was each event was both a beginning and an ending for his dad. Each episode was the result of other events, unseen and unknown, and frustratingly unexplained. *How do I reconcile all this with the man I knew, let alone with the man I didn't know?*

He wanted answers. It was a puzzle, and puzzles always frustrated Kevin. He considered whether or not it was solvable. *Are there just too many missing pieces to bother? After all, you can never really know another person, even your father. God knows there are parts of me I'd prefer no one ever know. Why can't I be satisfied with what I have and know already? Still...*

He decided he needed another list – this time of his own memories. He closed his eyes and the first image to drift into his mind's eye was Dad, cigarette dangling from his lips, helping him fix a jammed bicycle chain in the backyard. He typed that, hit ENTER and again closed his eyes and repeated the process of remembering, allowing himself to fall back through time and letting his father come back to life.

As he plumbed deeper and deeper, the list slowly grew. When he went dry, he began a third list with three columns: Felt | Knew | Heard. Other pieces and images tumbled out. He went back and forth, like a slalom skier speeding down hill, leaning into each bend and curve, moving back and forth between the past and the present, between forgotten memories and the keyboard. One moment he was having tea with Grandma at her house in Round Lake and the next he was in the basement with Dad cutting his hair, the tickling buzz of the electric trimmer on his ears and neck. Each intangible memory was painstakingly converted into slightly more tangible words and added to one of the columns on the lists.

An hour later, he printed them out: the dates, memories, feelings, and seeds of stories. Kevin laid them side by side, moving his eyes back and forth, looking for a pattern of colors or edges to help frame the random puzzle pieces into some kind of a whole.

Game two started at 7:00 PM. Kevin sipped his second Jameson as the first pitch was thrown. More out of loyalty than interest, Nelson sat with him on the couch with a glass of wine. The Cubs scored three runs in the top of the fifth to go ahead by five. Kevin finally started to relax and breathe again. Nelson kissed him and said, "You take it from here. I'm going to bed."

With relief help in the last few innings the Cubs notched the win: 5-1. The series was tied, one game apiece and would now move to Chicago and the Friendly Confines. It would be historic, the first-ever night World Series game at Wrigley Field. The future was looking brighter again.

Game 3

The next night, just before midnight, Kevin hit SEND then went to bed only to lay awake for an hour.

No runs again! I'm not going to panic. All they
have to do is win 3 of the next 4. Haven't they
done that several times this season?
No problem right?
Kevin

Game 4

CUBS FALL 7-2
Does anyone smell an old Billy Goat?

SUBJECT: No Worry
Ignore the headlines. Look what Mom found. Cleveland has lost 3 games in a row 7 times this season. AND GET THIS! The

Cubs have won 3 in a row, TWENTY TIMES! Almost 3 to 1 (see my math is getting better). LOL Sammy

PS Can you came here for game 7…Mom said it was fine. My hair is already Cubby blue. Let me know and I won't wear my nose ring….Mom told me you don't like it.

Game 5

SUBJECT: 1 down and 2 more to go
My heart can't take 3-2 wins. Do you know who Ernie Banks was? He's buried at Graceland Cemetery just a few blocks north of Wrigley Field. Thomas and I use to imitate his unique batting stance, with our right elbows held high. I saw Ernie's ghost hovering just above the lights at the game last night cheering along with everyone else.
I guess your mom busted me on the face jewelry. Did she tell you I tried to get it banned at our school when I was still a teacher? If it's any conciliation, Nelson always gets on me about being an old fart when I mention it. Anyhow ignore my lack of modern fashion and WEAR the nose ring. Maybe if the Cubs win, I'll wear one too. For now, it's back to Cleveland on Tuesday.
Kevin
PS I meant WHEN they win. I might be able to make it down for game 7. Isn't it a school night?

Game 6

SUBJECT: Why the Cubs will win
I know Mr. Cub played in the Negro League and was one of the first black men in the majors. What a goofed up world that was. I also know Ernie used to always say "Let's play two"? Well that's all we need - 2 more games.
Do you know why I'm sure the Cubs will win? This is so cool! It's been 108 years since they won a world series, right? Well do you know how many stitches are used to sew the cover on a baseball? 108 !!! AWESOME huh?
Mom wants you to come and stay here for game 7 on Wednesday. She even dug out that old pic of you and Thomas in your Little League Cubs uniforms.
PLEASE! We'll get some Senarighi pizza and you can even have a beer. Mom put some in the fridge. Text Mom after tonight's game. LOL
Sammy

Late that night, Kevin packed his overnight bag and texted Tomina: See you at 6:00 for pizza.

November 2, 2016

Game 7

After Nelson left for work, Kevin went to the ATM for some cash. He then stopped at the library for an audio book. He rooted around looking for something different. He checked out *Listen to the Whitethroats*, a collection of short recollections about trout fishing in the Arrowhead of Minnesota. He had no real connection to northern Minnesota other than a long ago canoe trip to the Boundary Waters with Lee, his college buddy. It was the coincidence of the author's name, Senarighi, which had caught Kevin's attention. Thinking of Tomina's and Sammy's favorite restaurant he couldn't resist. It seemed an omen, like Sammy's 108 stitches on a baseball. Not taking the book might be a slap in the face of the fickle baseball gods. And while Kevin didn't believe in such nonsense, he wasn't willing to take any chances.

He stopped back home to pick up his overnight bag and grab a bite to eat. As he headed south, he thought about the note Nelson had left him. "Have fun Grandpa. Why don't you invite them for Thanksgiving? It's time for me to meet them."

He got to the house at 6:20, only twenty minutes late. Not bad considering the traffic. Samantha opened the door wearing an old Cubs tee shirt. When Kevin's eyes opened wide, she said, "I kept this when we gave away Mom's clothes. I had to wear it tonight. I think it was Thomas'. Do you recognize it?"

The last time he'd seen the shirt was the night Tomina was conceived – either by Tim or himself – and Pat had pulled it off over her own head and tossed it into a corner of her room.

"I believe I do," Kevin said breaking into a big grin.

Not sure how to interpret Kevin's gesture, Sammy said, "If the nose is too much, I'll get rid of it. You never actually answered whether it would bother you."

"It's perfect, you're perfect," he replied. "It's gotten the Cubs this far, so don't you dare remove it. Besides, what would blue hair be without a nose stud?" He hugged her, aware his spontaneous comments and gesture felt like the truth.

"I'm sorry I'm late," he said when Tomina came into the room with her purse.

"You get settled in," she smiled at him. "I'll go get the pizza."

The TV was on but muted. As soon as Kevin got situated on the couch, Samantha asked if he wanted a beer or some pop. "Thanks, but I'll wait for the food. I can't believe this. Game seven! Thomas and I used to dream about this happening. But I never thought I'd see it."

Samantha released the foot rest on her chair and said, "I asked Mom to get the pizza instead of sending me so I can apologize again in person about… you know, this whole thing."

"There's really no need, Sammy. I can understand your reasoning. Maybe some day… well …" Kevin paused, not sure what he wanted to add.

Sammy plowed on. "Toward the end, Nana asked me to reply to emails, you know, stuff for her friends. One time she dozed off while we were together and I started clicking around on her laptop and came across the letter marked DO NOT SEND and, well, I shouldn't have, but I got nosy and read it. I must have said something out loud because she woke and could tell something was wrong. I can sometimes fool Mom, but never Nana. She asked what I was looking at and I told her. She got that deer in the headlights look, but she wasn't mad at me. She never got mad at me, but I could see she was worried.

"I asked her if it was true and she said she wouldn't lie to me. She never did, I mean, never lied to me. Sometimes she'd say it's none of my business, or she wasn't going to talk about something, but she never lied to me."

Samantha looked to the TV screen, before continuing. "It was clear from the letter that you didn't know anything about this. I asked if Mom knew and she said yes, but only recently. She said, "Honey, sometimes we do things in life, and we just don't know why, or don't even want to know why. Sometimes it's the wrong thing; sometimes it's the right thing. Sometimes, we don't know which one it is until a long time later. Either way, there's always a price to be paid some time or another. What I do know for sure is I ended up with your mom and you in my life, and that makes it the rightest thing I ever did."

Kevin said, "That must have been a very hard conversation for you…and her."

"I really don't know Grandpa Tim that much since he's lived in Texas all my life, and so I was more concerned about Mom. Nana said Mom was getting used to the idea, but she was going to go absolutely ape-shit about me finding out before she was ready to talk to me about it. She said Mom would probably kill her before the damn cancer did and she couldn't blame her.

"I knew Mom had enough on her mind, so I told Nana not to worry and promised I wouldn't say anything until Mom brought it up herself. Nana asked me to delete the letter and I pretend to, but didn't. I'm not sure why. Maybe it was like Nana had just said: one of those things you do and only find out later if it was dumb or not."

Kevin gently said, "And you kept your promise to Nana, you never told your mother you'd found out."

"Yeah. But when Mom still hadn't brought it up months later, I started thinking she might be like Nana and would never say anything. That's when I started thinking that if you found out… maybe you'd call her. I didn't want to go the rest of my life not able to talk to Mom about it, but I also didn't want Mom to hate Nana after she was gone because I'd been nosey and found the letter." She took a breath and thought for a few moments. Kevin let the silence be until she continued.

"I'm not sorry it's all in the open now, but I am real sorry for causing you and Mom so much stress. I was being selfish."

Kevin wasn't sure if he should go hug her, so he just leaned in and said, "I'm glad it's in the open too, and I'm very glad I've met you and your mom. But I'm curious. It's obvious you had to change the ending saying I'd never see the letter, but why add the other stuff about you guys not knowing and why did you include the extra note from Mrs. Naska and send the drawing?"

"It would have all blown up if you just called up, because Mom didn't know about Nana's letter. That's why I added that she didn't know. After I sent it to you I realized I'd goofed up. I added the PPS and PPPS stuff before I deleted her actual PS, but hoped you wouldn't notice. I made up Rita's note to explain the gap in time between Nana passing and you getting the letter. And the picture, well I guess that was because Nana's letter mentioned she still had some of Thomas' drawings. I remembered the one of you and Nana when you were young, and well… I think I wanted to show off a bit. Nana always said I had Thomas' talent and so I copied it and sent it, hoping it was good enough to fool you. I hoped it would make you want to contact Mom."

"You did fool me, until I saw the original." Kevin ran his hand through his hair then added, "Sammy, I want to thank you for making me think about Thomas again. Over the years, I guess I had gotten to a point where I wanted to forget, and leave the past behind. But you made me realize I had also forgotten all the good times… and how much of myself I lost by forgetting him."

Kevin and his "maybe" granddaughter looked at each other across the living room and across two generations. Neither spoke for several seconds, but both nodded before a smile broke out on their faces.

Samantha asked," Can I ask you a question?"

"Sure."

"What happens now, I mean as far as what Nana said about you being Mom's dad and my real grandpa?"

"I don't know, Sam. What did your mom say? I think it's her call, and I'm sure she'll talk with you about it."

"I don't want to always be wondering."

"I get that, but would it really make any difference in your life? It's not like you'd be a different person if it was me instead of Tim."

"That's what Mom said. But maybe it's not about being a different person, but being the person you already are." She paused and suddenly looked confused. "I don't know... But not knowing sucks."

Kevin saw the Cubs were taking the field on the TV. He nodded his head towards the screen. "Thank you for inviting me to watch the game."

Sammy picked up the remote. "I was hoping you'd come, just in case… if they actually…well, didn't win. You'll understand. Mom will just say it's sad, but it's only a game. She only cares because I do. I still don't think she even knows the rules."

"That makes you a very lucky girl then."

"I know, but I'm talking about 108 years of 'wait until next year.' This would be front page news all over the world. It would be like when Obama was elected. I was only a kid, but we all knew what a big deal that was."

"Well, I'm not sure they are exactly equivalent, but I get the picture and I have to admit, I feel the same way. But if we end up with broken hearts, we'll be there for each other."

I'm home,"Tomina's voice rang out. "Did I miss anything?"

Samantha looked at Kevin. They smiled. Then she said, "No, Mom. You're just in time as usual." She pointed the remote and pushed the un-mute button, and they settled in for a long night.

When the Cubs' centerfielder Dexter Fowler put the fourth pitch over the center field wall for a home run, Sammy was up dancing and high-fiving Kevin and her mom, almost upending their pizza and drinks. Kevin was a bit embarrassed by the volume of his 'YES!', as the ball cleared the fence. Tomina was enthused by the mutual elation of her daughter and Kevin.

Cleveland tied the game in their half of the third inning tamping down the excitement, until the Cubs came back in the top of the fourth. Kris Bryant tagged up and barely beat a throw home from short center field. Then rookie catcher Wilson Contreras – who had only one hit in seventeen at bats coming into game seven – drove a curveball over the outfielder's head to score another run. The Cubs, as well as, Kevin and Sammy, had some breathing room.

What came next played out like a sugar high. First, emotions soared when the Cubs added two more runs. But then came the ugly crash. After getting two Indians out, Cubs' pitcher Kyle Hendricks walked a batter and was replaced by Jon Lester. Because of Lester's quirky style, veteran David Ross, who was retiring after this historic game, was brought in to catch. Though it wasn't visible on the TV screen, the Curse of the Billy Goat entered the game with him. Kevin and the girls watched in horror.

Lester got the next batter to hit a soft tap in front of the plate for an easy third out. But having just entered the game after sitting for five innings, Ross threw the ball far out of the reach of Anthony Rizzo at first base for an error. Cleveland had two runners on the bases. Then Lester bounced a wild pitch in the dirt, which slammed into Ross' mask before getting past him. The Indian runners sprinted around the bases as Ross literally stumbled after the ball. By the time he'd retrieved it, both runs had scored. Before millions of viewers who had tuned in to see history, the Cubs were suddenly the bumbling loveable losers of years past. Sammy held her hand over her open mouth in disbelief. Her eyes met Kevin's. Neither was able to hide the terror. Tomina tried to help. "Come on, guys! They're still winning 5–3. It will be okay."

For awhile, her words seemed prophetic when in the very next inning, one of those I-can't-believe-that-just-happened moments unfolded. David Ross made up for his comedy of errors by hitting a homerun and stretching the Cubs lead to 6-3. It put much needed oxygen back into the lungs of the living room trio. Kevin took a bite of cold pizza for the first time since the fourth inning and got a second beer to wash it down.

Cleveland failed to score in the bottom of the sixth. The Cubs were nine outs away from breaking the 108 year curse and winning their first World Series since October 14, 1908.

Neither team scored in the seventh inning. Six outs to go. Tomina and Kevin joined Sammy in a round of Go Cubs Go.

In the top of the eighth, after two outs, the Cubs' ace reliever, Aroldis Chapman came in to close out the game as he'd done so many times this year. Twenty-one pitches and three runs later, Cleveland had tied the contest: 6-6. The only words spoken during the debacle were from Tomina. "This is a frick'en nightmare!" she hollered more than once. Kevin knew there wasn't a Cubs fan over the age of fifty who in their heart of hearts didn't know this was coming. Then, befitting the mood in the living room, and of Cubs fans everywhere, it began to rain in Cleveland.

As it continued to fall, the Cubs failed to score in their half of the next inning providing the Indians the opportunity for their dramatic come-from-behind win in front of their screaming fans at home in the bottom of the ninth of game seven of the World Series. A shaken Chapman returned to the mound for the Cubs, and in an inning where it seemed none of them breathed even once, he gave up no more runs. There would be extra innings in game seven for only the fourth time in World Series history. And as if that wasn't enough tension, the rain became a downpour.

The umpires called for the tarp and a delay of the game, sending both teams to their lockers to await the outcome – Cleveland buoyed by a last-minute comeback to tie the game, Chicago devastated after losing a three-run lead. All they had needed was four more outs. Kevin felt it would take 108 stitches to hold his heart and nerves in place. He couldn't imagine what the team must be feeling.

Kevin looked at Sammy and then to her mom. Both exhibited the same tension he felt. The silence and pressure hung in the air until Sammy muted the TV and declared, "It's in the bag. What are you guys so worried about? Do you want another beer, Kevin? Mom, a little wine?" Tomina looked at the clock and realized it was only minutes before midnight and a new day.

Her emotional involvement in the game was evident with her response "Sure, why not, but just a half glass."

Tomina said she'd help Samantha get the drinks from the kitchen. Out of nervousness, Kevin pulled the edge of the curtain back and glanced up and down the street. No traffic went by. The neighbors' curtains and blinds were closed to the night, but around the edge of at least one window in every house there was a light, a telltale sign that at least one occupant in each residence was watching and suffering the tension with them. The girls returned and they all sat in their same spots. No one sat back and relaxed. Samantha unmuted the television as key events were being replayed. After about thirty seconds she suddenly muted it again and said, "While we're waiting for the Cubs' comeback, I have two questions. Mom, can I stay home from school tomorrow? We don't have anything important going on, and two, what are you guys going to do about Nana's letter?"

Tomina and Kevin looked to each other. "That's a pretty untimely question Samantha, not to mention rude to put Kevin on the spot like that," Tomina sputtered. She put her wine glass down. "Really, you ask that now, and expect me to say yes to staying home from school. I told you I have a lot of thinking to do about all this, and Kevin and I haven't talked it through yet, so you're going to have to be patient."

"But, Mom, don't I get a say in this too? It does affect me, you know."

"You know I know that, and we've talked about it already. I know you're anxious to find out, but it's not that simple for us." Tomina swallowed the entire half glass of wine.

Kevin was wondering if this had been on the girl's mind throughout the entire game, when he heard his name.

"Kevin said it's up to you to decide," Samantha said.

Tomina looked to Kevin who was wishing he'd gone to the bathroom. He wasn't prepared to have this come at him like a hundred mile per hour fastball, and certainly not during a rain delay in the tenth inning of the World Series – game seven. He knew he and Tomina had to talk this through. He'd expected they'd do so slowly over time so they could gauge what each was thinking and feeling. He should have been expecting that Samantha might pull the pin on another grenade to force the issue. It struck him that this was exactly the type of emotional confrontation that had made him not want to get married or have kids in the first place.

He felt Tomina staring at him. "While you went for the pizza, Samantha apologized and explained about sending your mom's letter, and she asked me for my opinion. I told her I thought you had the most invested here and said I'd probably go along with whatever you thought was best for you guys." His words sounded lame and distant, even to him.

Tomina set the empty wine glass down as if in slow motion. She looked to be collecting herself before speaking. "You really don't have an opinion or even a thought about this? Whether or not you want to 'invest', she used air quotes to emphasize Kevin's choice of words back to him, "in a daughter or 'invest' in being a grandfather. Would knowing the truth make any difference to you?"

Kevin was very aware that his face was blanching making him feel like a ghost. He also knew he had no control of it and he had no idea what meaning it might be reflecting back to Tomina. His blood, and maybe his life, was pooling somewhere in his gut. Her words came in and out of focus. He wanted to disappear but forced his eyes to hold Tomina's stare and absorb her anger and hurt. The hurt he'd tried so hard to avoid inflicting, yet caused so easily by his careless words.

"You're so interested in your family's past, but…"Tomina stopped and stood as if she was about to leave the room, but immediately sat back down. "But only if they're dead." She touched her empty glass and asked, "What would be best for you, Kevin? Did you consider maybe knowing *that* would be important to me? Or that maybe it would be important for me to know whether you're just a nice man who used to know my mom or if I'm obligated to send you a Father's Day card too?" Tears glistened in her eyes. She wiped at them then suddenly stood and went to the shelves where she grabbed that last photo of her pregnant mom, Thomas and Kevin. She looked at it for a moment and then held it out toward him. Kevin didn't know if the gesture was meant to give him his past back or to offer proof of their connection.

Without explanation, Tomina replaced the picture on the shelf and said, "I need to just go to bed. It's midnight already."

Sammy went to her mother and but her arms around her. "I'm sorry, Mom. I shouldn't have brought it up. My timing always sucks. You know that. Please don't be mad at Kevin. It wasn't his fault."

Tomina sniffled and spoke over Sammy's shoulder to Kevin. "I'm sorry. I'm not mad at you. I'm just tired and wound up from the stupid game." She hugged her daughter and said, "I don't know what's best, for any of us. I'm not over Mom's dying, or her damn secret, or losing Bill and his parents, or even Tim moving away. All of my life I've felt abandoned and now I feel threatened and scared about another person coming into my life, our lives, and..."

She didn't finish the sentence. Instead she squeezed Samantha and kissed her blue hair. "Look." She pointed to the television. "The rain stopped." Tomina picked up her wineglass and said, "I need to go to bed. You two finish watching the game and make sure they win. Samantha, you can stay home tomorrow, and maybe you two can do something special before Kevin leaves. Kevin, the spare room is made up for you."

Kevin stood and said, "Tomina, I…"

She came over and gave him a light hug. "You don't have to say anything." Her tired face managed a smile. "I'm sorry for getting all emotional. It just came out, and it was unfair to throw it at you out of nowhere. Please, watch the end with Samantha. We can talk later. There's no hurry to decide anything."

"Before you go to bed," Kevin said, knowing the timing was awful but he might not get another chance, "in case I miss you in the morning, Nelson wanted me to invite you two to our place for Thanksgiving. If you don't have plans already. She wants to meet you…and I really want you to come, if you can."

Tomina brushed his cheek with her lips and then kissed her daughter goodnight. "Go Cubs Go", she said. "I expect to hear good news in the morning." She headed toward the steps upstairs. Over her shoulder she said, "I'll let you know about Thanksgiving later."

Kevin sat down. Once again, his ability to know and say what he wanted had failed him, blocked by his fear of again saying or doing the wrong thing, his fear of acting and failing. Sammy returned to her chair, and they looked at each other. Neither knew what to say. Kevin could see Sam felt miserable about upsetting her mom. He knew it wasn't her poorly-timed question, but his own words and indecision that had really hurt Tomina.

He put his hand to his forehead just as Sam pointed to the television. Kevin looked. The game had resumed, and the Cubs designated hitter, gimpy Kyle Schwarber, stood on first base. Sammy undid the mute button, releasing the roar of the Cubs fans who seemed to fill half the seats around Cleveland's Progressive Field stadium.

Tomina stuck her head back around the corner. "What happened?"

"Mom, the Cubs have a man on first and nobody out."

"Really?" Tomina said. Then she smiled her real smile and both Kevin and Samantha felt the tension that had built up in the room evaporate. "Well," she said, "maybe one more inning." She came back to the couch and sat.

Samantha came over and hugged her. "Thanks, Mom." She sat next to her mother. Kevin wasn't exactly sure what she was thanking her mother for, but he too was thankful to have her back with them, all together on the couch.

A deep fly ball, an intentional walk and a double down the third-base line put the Cubs back in the lead. Hoping for an inning- ending double play, Cleveland issued another intentional walk. Instead, Miguel Montero rifled a single to left, driving in the Cubs' eighth run of the night, increasing their lead to two. Sadly, ominously, the inning ended with runners stranded on all the bases.

Their collective nervousness and apprehension quickly returned as the Indians rallied again, scoring a run which left them only one behind. At this point, Kevin was standing, unable to sit still. Samantha and Tomina sat on the edge of the cushion, holding hands and leaning into the screen. Anxiety spiked as manager Joe Madden walked to the mound and signaled for his left-hander.

While Montgomery took his warm-ups, not a single word was exchanged among the trio. They watched and listened as if any loss of attention would result in disaster.

What happened next, unfolded in the slowest of slow motion for Kevin. With the tying run on first, Cleveland's batter hit a soft groundball. Cubs' third baseman Kris Bryant cut in front of Biaz the shortstop. A lifetime of frustration caused Kevin to see the ball being booted and then thrown over the head of Rizzo at first. But this time, was different. Bryant cleanly gloved the ball, set his feet and as the "maybe" family held their collective breath, the white sphere traveled across the infield until all of its 108 stitches settled into Rizzo's glove... and the curse of the Billy Goat died.

They jumped, they hollered, they danced. They hugged, beaming at each other with mile-wide smiles. All the evening's tensions, anxieties, and heartache magically turned into a skyrocket of bursting pure joy and relief. It felt right they'd gotten to share this. Kevin thought of his dad and Thomas, wishing they had lived to see this. Looking into the girls' faces, he thought maybe they had.

November 3, 2016

The three empty wine glasses, which they'd used to toast the World Series Champion Cubs, sat on the kitchen counter. Kevin and Samantha had watched replays and analysis until 1:00 AM. Tomina had gone online and requested a substitute teacher before going to bed. Her outburst at Kevin was the primary reason she took the day off. She needed time to think and maybe explain.

Kevin was frying bacon for their breakfast, but the smells barely dented Tomina's focus. She had questions whirling around in her head even before her eyes opened this morning: *Did I mean what I said last night? Where did it come from? How can I expect him to make some sort of commitment before we know if it's true? What would that even look like...and why would he after all these years? I don't even know if I want to know; so why did I blow up at him last night. And why has Samantha so readily accepted all this?*

When they had talked that day after discovering Samantha had instigated Kevin into their lives, her daughter had made it all seem so simple. "Remember the photo, Mom. You even said we're family already." It felt like a circus of elephants parading round and round in Tomina's mind. Each idea held onto the tail of the previous, so she couldn't tell where the line began.

Samantha bounded down the stairs and into the kitchen. "Smells GREAT!" What a GREAT DAY to be a Cubs fan." She hugged her mother out of her trance.

Kevin asked, "How do you ladies like your eggs?"

Sammy said, "I remember Dad asking us that same question."

"Well, let's see if Kevin breaks the yolks, and we end up with scrambled like Dad always used to."

Minutes later, Kevin set their requests in front of them. Both were impressed. As they ate, Samantha said, "You know where we should go today?"

They spent an hour back at the Chicago History Museum visiting the Lincoln exhibition. The bed he died on was back from its sojourn to Springfield. Standing only feet from the Victorian walnut bed, all three were awed by the palpable sense of history and reverence they felt. The dark wood head and foot boards, the spooled legs and feet, grounded them and made them feel connected to the mortal man, who had to be laid angled across the bed to accommodate his height. Samantha was fascinated with all the 19th century artifacts from the room especially the blood-stained cape Mrs. Lincoln wore that night.

Heading back to the car Samantha thanked Kevin for taking them back to see the exhibit. "It felt like time traveling, like I was really there. Mom, you should bring your kids here on a fieldtrip. It would make Lincoln more than just the guy on the five dollar bill."

When they reached the car, Tomina asked, "Where to now?"

Twenty minutes later Kevin pulled to the curb and inched along until he came to 1612 Indiana. "Where are we?" Sammy asked.

"My dad's grandmother lived here," Kevin said as his eyes tracked over every inch of the classic brick Chicago-style two-flat. Each floor was its own apartment unit with a bay window facing onto the street. It looked well cared for. Kevin assumed it had been renovated and cleaned up more than once since his great-grandmother's time.

"Her name was Jane Cullerton. She and Patrick Cullerton came from County Wexford in Ireland. She lived here either with or after her second husband Nicholas O'Rourke died. So many questions still need lots of research." Compared to the house where his dad was born, seeing this building felt more *...more what... relevant? Historic? Maybe because we were just at the History Museum. Or maybe* *because Tomina and Sammy are sitting here with me?*

The girls asked questions. Some he couldn't answer, others he could. "If you remember when we were at the Chicago Fire exhibit back in early August, I showed you their original neighborhood on that fire map. That's where my grandfather was born and later where the infamous Cabrini-Green projects were built until they were torn down in the '90s. I guess neighborhoods, like people, change. That area went from a 19th century Irish ghetto to a 20th century ghetto for blacks. Now, I think it's partially surrounded by million dollar condos." Kevin added, "Some day if you're really bored, we can drive up to Evanston and I can show you the two Calvary plots where over forty of mostly unknown relatives and their histories are buried."

Sammy quietly ventured, "What if they're our relatives too?"

Kevin and Tomina turned and looked at her, but neither said anything.

"How about one more stop, then lunch is on me," Kevin offered. As he drove, both he and Tomina wondered what the other was thinking about Sam's question and trying to determine if they wanted the answer.

Kevin parked across from a small house on west Berteau Avenue, the home where his dad and nine siblings lived with Grandma, where his brother Richard died and where his oldest brother Ed became the head-of-household after their father left.

"I wish this place could talk," Kevin said. He turned to Sammy and said, "An uncle once told me when they were kids living here, they had a chicken coop in the yard for eggs."

"Is that even legal in the city?" she asked.

"I guess it was probably pretty common then. After all, horses were still being used for deliveries like for milk. Even when I was still a kid, you could have milk delivered to your door, but by truck. They even took the empties to use again."

"For recycling?" Sammy asked.

"No one thought of it that way back then, but yeah. Eventually, the horses became a problem to traffic, not to mention the horse droppings in the street."

Sammy said, "I've got an idea. Why don't you write some stories about those old days? You know, about your dad living here, and the big family with no dad and the chicken coop in the back…even the milk wagons. I bet you could make up some awesome short stories. I could help you if you wanted."

"Sammy, I can't even tell a joke without screwing it up, let alone write stories."

Tomina chimed in. "She's right. You have all that genealogy and history you've been working on and obviously you're curious about your dad's past. It might be a good way to pull it all together." She smiled her smile and said, "You know, add some chapters to their lives." Kevin smiled back.

Samantha couldn't help herself and added, "Maybe it might be for us too, right? I mean if it turns out…" Both her mother and Kevin turned and again looked at her, this time quite sternly. "Okay, okay, I'm just saying it might."

Kevin looked back at the house. "I have no idea how my grandmother got the money to buy this place." He looked back to the girls and said, "My grandma once told me she called my dad Shamus when he was young."

"That's an awesome name. I like it," Samantha said.

"It's Irish for Jimmy," Kevin explained.

"Well, there you go," Sammy urged. "That's your first story right there. Can't you hear your grandma yelling out the back door: 'Hey Shamus, ya'll fetch me some eggs from that there chicken coop'."

Kevin laughed, "Girl, you better work on your dialects. They were Chicago Irish, not South Carolinians."

They opted for lunch at a corner restaurant rather than a fast food chain. Over club sandwiches they talked: Cubs, Lincoln, history, and eventually landed on the old neighborhood where he and the Thom family had grown up. The girls wanted to see the house where he'd been raised.

Thirty minutes later, as Kevin exited from the JFK at Harlem Avenue, he told them of watching this very stretch of expressway being bulldozed and how he and Thomas would bike here to watch the concrete lanes get poured.

In a few blocks he turned onto his old street. Trees that had been skinny gangly things were now tall and impressive even with much of their colorful foliage scattered on the street and lawns. Top branches hung over the street, creating shadowy patterns moving in the cool early November breeze. When Kevin pulled up in front of his old house Sammy remarked, "It looks awfully small."

"Dad remodeled or refinished every inch of the inside. The man was amazing, he could figure out how to do almost everything. He finished the basement, and I had that to myself when I was a teenager. That's where I practiced piano and other instruments. Mom and Dad were either deaf or awfully patient."

He told them about the small garage in back, too small to hold his 1959 Ford. Down the gangway, Kevin saw the blue spruce his dad had planted was gone since his last visit. It made him a bit sad. Sammy wanted to stretch her legs and asked if she could walk around back to look. Kevin directed her around through the alley that he'd walked and biked countless times.

Tomina sat quietly as she watched her daughter start off down the block. She wanted to give Kevin time to pay his respects and summon his memories. In the quiet, she again considered this thing her mother, and daughter, had started. What if it was actually true, not just some intuitive impression or fantasy of her mother's? What if this small white house actually was the place where her real father grew up, where her real grandparents had lived and raised their son, her father? Her thoughts must have shown on her face, because Kevin started to say something, but she quickly interrupted him.

"Kevin," she turned to him. "I want to apologize again for last night. I shouldn't have blown up on you, but I've just got too many thoughts and feelings whirling around and I can't even get them clear in my head, let alone come up with answers, or make decisions. I'm forty-six years old, and I'd of thought I would be pretty solid by now in knowing who I am. But I'm not. I thought I was, but then everything changed, everyone died. And right now, Samantha and teaching are the only stable realities I have left. If I stray too far from them, I feel like I'm going to get lost or swallowed up and disappear."

When she finished talking she found her hands in Kevin's. She didn't feel like she wanted to cry. Rather she was a little amazed by the glimmers of truth entangled in all the unplanned words she'd just spoken. She squeezed Kevin's hands.

"Tommi, ever since I was Samantha's age and started dating, I began a list of reasons and rationales why I shouldn't get married, and why I'd never want kids. While my friends were looking for the right woman, I was looking for reasons why every girl friend was not the right one. It wasn't until I was in my fifties and met Nelson, that I finally accepted my list was constructed to avoid mistakes, to avoid conflict and uncertainty – to keep me safe.

"What I'm trying to say is that when you and Sammy fell out of the sky, my first reaction was – maybe still is – to find a reason not to let this be true. And, I found a perfect one in my long lost grandfather who was able to walk off and leave a wife and ten kids. How could I be sure I didn't carry that gene myself? Or... what if I let you in and screwed it all up, made you hate me, or I came to resent you. My grandfather did it, and I've done it before. So I let his shadow keep me from facing the fear of having a daughter and granddaughter and not being able to live up to all that might mean, including the possibility of being rejected or losing you."

Tomina squeezed his hands again, and said, "I once heard someone say that life and parenthood is one long letting go. Then it would make sense to avoid grabbing on in the first place. Or maybe the trick is to just enjoy the holding on as long as it lasts."

"It doesn't sound easy."

"It's not," Tomina said. She leaned over and kissed his cheek.

When Sammy returned from circumnavigating the block, their reflective mood went out the door as she got into the back seat. "How far did Nana and Thomas live from here?"

"Only a few minutes by car. I was able to bike it in ten minutes. But I tended to meander. I liked checking out the houses, old and new. New construction attracted us kids back then like flies. I'll show you."

He headed east, explaining this was his usual bike route over to

Thomas'. Seeing the shadow cast by the car out ahead of them he reminisced, "I used to try to catch my shadow when I biked along here. I'd weave back and forth and watch it move side to side, always one step ahead of me." He looked at Tomina who smiled at him and in the mirror at Samantha in the back seat. *But who knows, maybe I'm getting closer to catching it.*

Kevin took the girls on a quick trip around Holy Gospel School. He told them about the playground and Red Rover and how it often ended up in ripped pants and skinned knees and elbows. He told them of his one pugilistic moment of glory when he'd clobbered Peter Biggert and ended up grounded for the weekend. He paused for a moment to point out the corner classroom where he, Thomas, and the class prayed for Kennedy the day he was shot.

Then they drove slowly and silently past the old Thom's house. Tomina and Samantha had seen it more than once. And, of course, so had Kevin. All three chose to keep their thoughts to themselves.

2020

May 8, 2020

Nelson opened the door before the girls were out of their car. They waved and exited, masks in place. Over the last several days she'd been lost in her own world, trying to forget about the coronavirus pandemic, even though at every turn it affected and frustrated what she needed to get done. She been avoiding television or reading the news. She had no interest or energy to give to the outside world right now.

Tomina and Samantha approached, uncertain exactly how to handle this. It only took a few seconds before they worked it out. There on the front steps, in the warm spring air with the red maples lining the quiet street barely showing their newborn foliage, three generations of women embraced as only those who have shared a loss know how. Once inside, they hugged again and put their arms around each other to form a huddle into which Nelson said, "Thanks for coming. I love you gals." She helped carry their bags up to the guest room. "Why don't you settle in and then come out to the screen porch. Would you like something to drink?"

Ten minutes later, Tomina and Samantha found Nelson staring out the window. A pitcher of iced tea and glasses was on the table. Tomina sat across from Nelson while Samantha perched cross-legged on the Victorian style daybed and said, "All the way here we kept waiting to get pulled over because of our Illinois plates, and sent back home because of the stay at home orders."

"This would be so much harder without you. I know we could have just talked, but..." Nelson's voice trailed off.

Tomina said, "We really wanted to be here with you. Besides, we've all been following the guidelines and staying safe. We just couldn't bear to think of you here on your own." She and Nelson reached for each other's hand at the same time.

"Well as long as you're here," Nelson indicated the masks covering their mouths and noses. "We've already broken the rules and hugged." Samantha and Tomina folded their masks into their pockets.

Nelson pointed out the window. "Did you know Kevin built the pergola after he retired? He planted the ivy too; said it reminded him of Wrigley Field. Then little by little he added the bird feeders. In warm weather, I'd find him out here watching the birds or napping when I got home from work. At least once a week he'd ask, 'When are you going to retire and watch the birds with me?' And I'd tell him I didn't want to interrupt his naps. Now I'm going to have to keep the feeders full, or he'll haunt me about it."

Tomina asked gently, "Do you want to talk?"

"I thought he was napping out here as usual." She pointed to the daybed where Samantha sat. "An hour later, when he still hadn't come in, I checked on him. The paramedics said he'd been gone for awhile."

Samantha went to Nelson and hugged her. Their brimming eyes began to spill over. Tomina took a tissue from the almost empty box on the table and wiped her eyes. She tucked a tissue into both Nelson's and her daughter's hand. When Samantha sat again, Nelson said, "I really thought, like I guess everyone does, that we'd have a lot more years. Even with Kevin being six years older, I thought…" She wiped her eyes again.

"That's how his father died. His mom came home from shopping one day and found him dead. I'm glad Kevin wasn't sick or suffering like so many are with this damn virus, but I hate not having been with him. At least I got to see him and he didn't die quarantined in some hospital ICU." Tomina reached over and held her hand.

Nelson looked up with a smile made weak by the red wetness of her eyes. "I'm so glad for you two, but how ironic. You know, when he first got the letter and showed it to me, I hated your mother for-writing it."

Samantha broke into silent tears. Over the last four years she'd graduated from high school and was working on her bachelor degree in graphic design at Northeastern, the same university that Kevin had attended. Along the way, she'd decided constantly changing the color of her hair to match her whims wasn't such a good idea and now embraced her natural ash blond, still usually in a ponytail. She still sporadically wore her favorite nose stud, a classy diamond that Kevin had given her at graduation amid much laughter and teasing. "I'm so sorry, Nelson," she cried. "I was so stupid and selfish. I only wanted…" She stopped, buried her face in her hands. Nelson and Tomina moved to the daybed and put their arms around her.

"Samantha," Nelson leaned her head aside the girl's. "Don't be upset. Look at all the happiness that you've brought us. We've had most holidays together since then. We've celebrated your birthday every year and you got Kevin to more Cubs games than he had in his entire life."

Tomina added, "Think of how much time I'm on the phone with these guys."

"You both have brought Kevin and me so much joy. I can't tell you how many times Kevin said you made us a family. He was thankful and proud of you… both of you. And you know how much he loved your art. He said you were as good as your Uncle Thomas, and it was like his life had come full circle."

Nelson poured iced tea for everyone. They talked about school – Tomina's challenges of teaching and motivating students online while all schools were closed because of the virus which was particularly bad in Chicago and Cook County, and Samantha's frustrations: having to finish the trimester from home, not being able to make money at her job at the art store which was closed, and not being able to spend time with the boy she'd met in her art history class.

The mention of a new boyfriend allowed Samantha to, as she often did, change the topic. Nodding her head in her mother's direction, indicating what was coming was meant for her, she asked, "Nelson, I assume you'd recommend second marriages, seeing you and Kevin worked out so well."

Tomina shook her head and looked out at a nuthatch working its way down the truck of a birch tree in search of insects.

Nelson said, "I remember when Kevin first proposed. I'd been divorced three years and not sure I wanted to get involved so soon. Then when we started dating I wondered why he'd never been married before."

"When Kevin first visited us," Tomina recalled, "I told him I'd once asked Mom if he and Thomas were gay. Now that I think back, Mom's burst of laughter and unequivocal assurance he wasn't should have been a clue maybe she had first hand knowledge." Suddenly, Tomina blushed and hurriedly added, "Oh, Nelson! I'm sorry that was insensitive of me to bring up."

"Tomina, don't please. Neither of you should be worried about mentioning Pat and Kevin together. He and I weren't kids when we got married. We'd talked about and knew about each other's histories and previous lives."

Samantha said, "But you didn't know about Mom and me."

"No. That's a fact. We didn't know about you. But then you ended up as the best surprise either of us ever had."

Nelson reached for Tomina's hand again and continued. "Anyhow, I was curious why he'd never married, so I asked him."

"What did he say?" Samantha asked.

"Well, it was complicated for the poor guy." Nelson looked at Tomina and said, "I believe he told you some of this at one time." Turning back to Samantha, she went on. "Kevin was convinced he would have screwed up fathering."

"He'd have been a great father," Samantha interrupted.

"Maybe, but he didn't think so. He feared all the unknowns that come with falling in love and having kids. Then, early in his career when he was teaching elementary general music, a favorite beautiful little second grade girl died. He said he cried for days, that he wouldn't have been able to bear the hurt her parents went through. That fear stayed with him. Not long before your nana's letter, as you know, he started researching his family and confirmed that his grandfather had abandoned the family. That seemed to shake him, and he thought he might be capable of doing the same thing to you. He was worried about how long a shadow the old guy might have cast."

Nelson stopped and took a drink of her tea before concluding. "The bottom line seemed to be, he feared he was more like his grandfather, than his own father. My theory was that the thought of becoming the bad guy in his own life story was too much to chance."

"I know he was a good grandpa." She looked at her mother and Nelson and then blurted out: "Penumbra! That's what it was."

The women looked quizzically at each other then back to Samantha.

"Back before this whole pandemic-thing, I was painting a backdrop for the drama department and was struggling to get a shadow just right. One of my teachers showed me how shadows have something called a penumbra, a lighter outer space between the complete dark and the light. I think Kevin was, you know, caught in a kind of penumbra between his grandfather and us. You know like between the past and the future?"

"You've got one smart daughter here," Nelson said to Tomina as she poured more ice tea for the girl.

"Sometimes too smart," Tomina said.

Samantha playfully stuck her tongue out at her mother, and for the moment the mood was lightened.

The trio sat in silence, cushioned by the comfort of each other's presence and keeping their thoughts to themselves. Yet each knew what the other was thinking and feeling. They watched a parade of birds squabble over the sunflower seeds and two squirrels chase each other up and down tree trucks and through the branches. Eventually, Nelson said, "Before I forget, I hope you two know how grateful Kevin was for your suggestion about using his genealogy to write some short stories. It was a great outlet for him. He said it cleared up a frustration he'd had since childhood."

"I didn't know," Tomina looked to her daughter who shook her head in the negative. "We didn't know he was writing stories."

"Really?" Nelson said. "Then again, I guess it doesn't surprise me. He was a Cullerton." They smiled and nodded in agreement. "For all his complaining about his parents' and grandmother's secrecy, the apple didn't fall far from the tree." Tomina wouldn't allow herself to say it out loud, but she was thinking of her mother and how close she had come to taking her secret to her grave. And if she had, then Tomina wouldn't be sitting on this porch, at this time, with another broken heart and with the two people she loved most.

Nelson continued, "He just dabbled with writing at first and never said much about it to me. Then last fall, after his blood clot problems, he started working on them seriously." She appeared to think for a moment, "You know, I didn't relate the two things because his medication seemed to have solved the problem."

"The stories were Samantha's idea," Tomina said, "from a long time ago."

Samantha became animated. "I thought of it when he showed us where his dad grew up. He knew so many details about the family and the times it made sense to me. Can we read some of them?"

Nelson said, "I can look for them on his computer. I'd ask him about reading them, and he'd say when they were finished and after he'd done some revising and polished them up. But he never did offer, so I never pushed it. But I'm sure he wouldn't mind sharing them with you, especially since it was your idea. All I know about them is he spent a lot of time on them, so it was filling some need for him, and he enjoyed it, which was all I cared about. I also think he worried if I didn't like them he'd know and be hurt." Nelson gave a knowing look to the other two. "You know how easily men get their feelings hurt."

"Tell me about it!" Samantha agreed.

The women laughed, sharing another brief respite from their grief.

After a light lunch of salads, Nelson excused herself. "I'll see if I can find those stories." She sat at Kevin's desk listening to the computer fan hum as the old machine struggled to boot up. She'd spent much of the night after Kevin died here in his chair, thinking how he'd never sit here again, nor stare out this window trying to untangle his family roots and mysteries or trying to find the right words for what he wanted to show in his stories. A single tear eased down her cheek. As it slowly tracked its course, she thought about how quickly a person gets whittled down to a name on a bough of the family tree and survives only in the memories and stories of those left behind. She thought of Tomina and Samantha and smiled, knowing that when she herself was gone, Kevin would live a while longer through them. The tear came to a standstill at her jaw line. She didn't wipe it away.

As she searched the files, she pictured Kevin coming home from Chicago after watching the World Series game with the girls– *almost four years ago now.* He had been so excited by the creative possibility of trying his hand at fiction, trying to recreate a life for his father and family – at least, as he pointed out, as he filtered them through his own feelings, memories, and research. He had said, "Of course they won't be as they really were. But Thomas never drew what was really there; he drew what the thing or person became in his imagination." She looked up from the screen as her imagination replayed the sadness in Kevin's eyes when he added, "God, how I wanted to be able to do that."

The monitor finally came to life bringing with it the scanned photo Kevin chose for the background of his desktop. She studied the man's face. *I wonder what Kevin saw each time he looked at the image… the past... or something of himself.* Multiple icons popped up on the screen, bringing Nelson back to her task. She heard the girls leaving the kitchen and called to them. "Tomina, Samantha, come here and look at this."

The girls stood around Nelson. She pointed to the image. "Do you know who this is?"

They exchanged glances before replying together, "No."

"Well, ladies," Nelson said thinking she sounded a bit like her husband, "You are gazing at Kevin's very own 'maybe' grandfather."

"What?" Samantha leaned in to look more closely.

Tomina, whose face was already near to the screen, turned her head. She was face to face with Nelson. She smiled. "Really?"

Nelson felt the warmth in Tomina's smile that had captured Kevin's heart when he'd first met her. She smiled back. "He got it from one of his cousins who found it stashed away in their grandmother's belongings after she'd died. Kevin was sure it must be his rogue grandfather, but he never found any real proof."

Samantha quietly said, almost to herself, "There sure seems to be a lot of 'maybes' in this family." She put her hand on Nelson's right shoulder.

Nelson placed her hand on top of Samantha's. "Well, 'maybe', or not, you two gave Kevin a family. Between you and his genealogy, he finally found what he was looking for."

When Tomina sniffled, Nelson and Samantha turned to her. Her hand covered her mouth. She sat in the only other chair in the small room, the chair where Kevin opened the letter that changed his life and merged his past and present. Her eyes filled with tears. "I wish he had told me that. That's what I wanted to hear from him all these years." She held a tissue to her eyes. "Even in the beginning, I would have been okay with the DNA test if I knew that… that he actually wanted…," she wiped her eyes again and then her nose. "I always thought he was leaving it up to me to decide because he wasn't sure he wanted to commit, or deal with the results. Back then, neither was I. But if I'd known he… what it might mean to him."

She looked to her daughter. "You were the one brave enough to want to know the truth no matter what."

"That's okay, Mom." They fell silent, but continued to look into each other's face, until Samantha knelt besides her.

Tomina blew her nose and then turned to Nelson. "I'm sorry. Were you able to find the stories?"

Nelson said, "Kevin told me along time ago that you were the one who said there was no need to apologize, we're family of a sort."

She turned back to the monitor and said, "Well let's see here." She used Kevin's mouse and clicked on the short-cut document file, then on Genealogy, then on Family Stories. "Well that was easy enough." Several documents appeared, each with its own title. The girls stood again and the mood shifted in the anticipation. Nelson randomly clicked on the first story: *November 23, 1918 – Shamus.*

As soon as it opened, Samantha exclaimed, "Mom, look! That was my sentence from that day. When we were sitting in Kevin's car." She read out loud, "Shamus, hurry now, son… Remember, I suggested he start the story that way?" She read on. "…Eddie is ready to go."

"Who's Eddie?" Samantha asked Nelson, adding, "Can we print these?"

"Kevin's oldest uncle," Nelson explained. "He was named after the old man. Kevin figured he must have despised his father after he'd took off. Yet somehow, I always got the feeling Kevin wanted to give the old bastard the benefit of the doubt. He wanted to believe there was a reason, in spite of all evidence to the contrary."

"He'd be your great-grandfather?" Samantha looked to her mother. Tomina let the question hang in the air unanswered.

Later back on the porch Tomina asked, "Are you sure you want to use these?" as she pulled some pictures from her bag and set them on the table.

"No one here knew Kevin back then. His friends will enjoy seeing these as much as I did. After all, Thomas was as much a part of his life as I was, maybe more in some ways. So was your mom."

Nelson turned to look out to the yard, her head nodding as if to affirm what she had just said. She turned back to Tomina. "Look what I had printed up." She rolled out a laminated chart on top of the table. "I was going to give it to Kevin for our anniversary on Memorial Day. He had handwritten this on butcher paper so I had to sneak it out of his room and hope I got it back before he noticed. I actually had it in the car when I came home that day and... " She stopped, trying not to cry.

Tomina put her arm around Nelson's shoulder and leaned her head against hers for a moment. Then she unrolled the document as Nelson held her end down. Samantha stood to take in all the names. Nelson brushed at her eyes and said, "It goes from Kevin and his cousins back five generations to Ireland and has all the family Kevin found buried in Calvary, as well as many others not buried there."

Tomina let Samantha step in and hold the edge down so she could see better. "This is awesome, Mom, did you know about all of these people?" She looked at her mother, who was staring at one name on the bottom line of the family tree and didn't seem to hear. "Mom?"

The family chart did not contain spouses for Kevin's generation. Tomina wasn't surprised that Nelson had not added her own name next to Kevin's. She felt tremendous respect and growing love for this woman who over the last few years had become such a dear friend. Her gaze and focus was locked on the name, imagining it connected to another.

Kevin Joseph Cullerton ---------- *Patricia 'Pat' Thom*
1950 – ? *1948 – 2015*

Her mind's eye traced an imaginary vertical line leading to her own name, coupled to her beloved Bill's, and culminating in another connecting Samantha to the grouping.

"Mom?"

Tomina pried her eyes from the chart. "Oh, sorry. What were you asking, honey?"

"I asked if Kevin ever told you about all of these people." Concerned by the look on her mother's face she asked, "Are you okay, Mom?"

"I'm fine." Tomina smiled, not actually at all sure if she was or not and wondering if she was ready to be uprooted and transplanted from one family tree to another. However, she was sure of one thing. It was time that Samantha had her say in the matter.

"I'm fine," she repeated reassuringly to her daughter and to Nelson who had turned to her. "I was just thinking. This was a lot of work. I didn't realize how extensive Kevin's research had gotten."

"It was good he was retired," Nelson said, "and had the time. He'd get excited – not that excitement is easy to spot in a Cullerton – when he'd get some new piece of information or when he discovered some memorabilia from his dad's time in England and Paris during the war. It seemed like the war stuff was a big inspiration to his writing. He said it was like his history just started tumbling out of the past."

"Kind of like we did," Tomina said.

Nelson took both of them by the hand and squeezed. "I think you two were his main reason for writing and trying to pull the past into the present." She rolled up the Cullerton family tree and said, "Sit. Let's go over the pictures you brought."

After another hug, Tomina laid out a dozen old photos. Nelson looked for a few moments and said, "Each time I see these, I think of Kevin and Thomas like they were an old pair of comfortable shoes." She laughed and asked, "Did Kevin ever tell you about what he and Thomas..."

Tomina chimed in and together they intoned, "I gotta piss on your shoes." They broke into a peal of laughter. Feeling left out, Samantha kept asking, "WHAT? What did they say?" It was a full minute before they stopped long enough to fill her in, and then they all started off on another binge of laughing.

The spontaneous release that came with the outburst felt miraculous after days of emotions rubbed raw. Eventually they got back to the photos. They ordered them sequentially. "These are great. I love this one," Nelson said picking up the picture of the boys in their Little League uniforms. She stared at it, trying to see the grown men in the boys' faces." The last photo was one she'd noticed at Tomina's house. "Was this taken just before Thomas left?"

Nelson held the photo closer. "Your mother was a pretty girl. I see where you girls got your looks."

"Mom's in that one too, but you've got to look real hard."

"Samantha!"

"That's alright," Nelson said. "What do you mean?"

"Nana's pregnant with Mom in that picture."

Nelson again squeezed Tomina's hand while she looked to Samantha and said, "That makes your nana a very lucky woman."

The 2020 COVID-19 pandemic meant group gatherings, even wakes and services, were not being held. After some discussion and with some phone coaching, Nelson had setup an online group gathering with some of their closest friends that evening at 7:00. The plan was that everyone should have their own favorite beverage at hand, but also a shot of Jameson Irish whiskey for a toast – each household kept a bottle for when Kevin visited – and be ready to share a favorite story or two.

After the women posted the chosen photos online so that all could view, they took a break to rest and arrange themselves for the trip they'd been dreading. At 5:00, Nelson and the girls drove the few blocks to collect Kevin's urn from the local funeral home. They found courage and comfort in doing it together. They managed the transport without a tear being shed until they got back to the house.

The digital gathering seemed awkward at first, even though most of them were used to visiting their children and grandchildren, and even working and attending meetings, online from home for the last two month. But once the toast had been made and the stories began, everyone loosened up and Nelson's spirits buoyed. Some of the anecdotes were spurred by how Kevin's lack of technology skills and aptitude, not to mention patience, would have made attending his own sendoff, impossible. The uploaded photos also produced lots of joking and laughter. For Samantha, the stories gave glimpses into the life of the man who had stepped out of Nana's old photos.

But for Tomina they were like missing middle chapters in a novel. They were the selected short stories that filled in the huge gap between when she'd seen him hugging her mother in a parking lot in the old neighborhood a million years ago while she waited in the car, and the man her mother resurrected as she was dying, and then who appeared via her daughter's audacity. The man, who unlike herself was now free from the limbo of uncertain identity in which they'd ensnared themselves.

She found herself thinking back to the call from Nelson. She remembered sitting in her darkened living room with her arm around her grieving daughter. She told Samantha about a childhood memory Kevin had uncharacteristically once shared. How one afternoon his father had found him flustered and upset in the yard with his bike upside down and the chain snagged in the sprocket. At the time, her take away was the sweet image of a loving, patient father making things okay for his son. Now, however, what she remembered was Kevin's explanation of how inadequate and stuck he'd felt, because his dad had taught him before how to fix and adjust a bike chain, but it was too jammed and he was afraid he'd break it if he forced it too hard. She now knew that was exactly how Kevin had felt about her.

The evening ended with Nelson inviting everyone to block off Memorial Day, 2021 for a real in person get together and celebration of Kevin's life. She'd already made sure the date was on Kevin's cousins' calendars. Afterward, she thanked Tomina for sharing a few of her mother's stories about Kevin and Thomas. She hugged Samantha for tactfully talking about how Kevin had become "like a Grandpa" when he'd come all the way down to Chicago to go with her to Wrigley Field on father-daughter night, and then again when she needed a kindred spirit to help her get through "The Game Seven." When she added, "in spite of my blue hair and nose stud," there was genuine laughter throughout the group.

The women reconvened on the back porch in the twilight. Each sipped a glass of wine, tired, but sustained by their bond, closely linked in the metaphoric chain that had propelled Kevin through life. The shock was over. Now was the time for the missing and personal mourning, for finding a place to keep their loss while taking the first steps forward. It was also the time to carefully file away the memories and stories they would use when needed to fill the shadow that always comes after a death.

Nelson said, "There's another little ritual I'd like you to share with me."

They both looked to Nelson's tired and sad face. "Sure, anything you'd like," Tomina answered.

"I'll be right back." She left the room. The girls could hear her go down into the basement. When she returned, she placed an old shirt box on the table. Next to it she placed a storage envelope.

"This box is what started it all. Kevin found it buried in his old file cabinet. It had things his mother had saved for him from his childhood. It's where he found the names that started him on his family tree quest. It seems to be the natural place to keep some of the things that were so important to him."

She pointed to the envelope. "I have your nana's letter and the drawing you sent in here," she said to Samantha, "It was what brought you into his life – our lives. It also has a copy of his stories we printed." She set one of the "In Loving Memory" cards she had printed for the service on top of the envelope. One side was a picture of Kevin from long ago: longish scruffy hair and mustache and a pipe in his mouth. It had been taken at his friends' cabin at a small lake in Michigan just at the moment he'd finished a piece of music he'd composed. On the back of the card was a version of a short parable Kevin loved and kept on his office wall:

An old Cherokee recognized his grandson
had a struggle going on inside him. The old
man said, "My son, the battle is between two
wolves. One is fear and self-doubt, and in its
heart is anger, envy, and desire.

The other's heart is full of joy, hope, and truth."
The grandson thought for a minute.
"Which one wins, Grandfather?"
The old man replied,
"The one you feed."

Nelson asked Tomina to untie the twine that held the box shut. She asked Samantha to put the card into the envelope and then into the box and retie it. "That's as close to burying Kevin as I can handle. He'd be happy everything is safely documented and that we did it together. Now, just a little more wine while we take care of one last thing before I need to go to bed."

She refilled their glasses and handed Tomina a small package. "This is what you asked me to get for you."

"What's that, Mom?" Samantha asked.

Tomina looked to Nelson who nodded and said, "It will be okay.

You know he'd approve. After all, he left it up to you."

Tomina handed the box to Samantha, who again asked, "What is it?"

"Open it, honey."

Samantha did. She stared at her mother through tears that reflected the soft porch lighting. "Is this what I think it is?" she asked.

Tomina said, "It's a DNA kit."

Nelson explained. "Some years back Kevin sent his DNA in but just for the ethnicity analysis. He wanted to see just how Irish he really was. At the time he saw no reason for the family-match part of the test."

Tomina took over. "Honey, it's time you handle this the way you want. I'm fine with whatever you choose. While this won't match you up with Kevin, who knows, maybe you'll find out we're related to Abraham Lincoln."

Nelson had retired to her room and memories. After tears and many thank you hugs, Samantha fell asleep. Tomina, however, still sat up in her bed. Tomorrow, they'd go back home to Chicago. She had video lessons to prepare for her students, as the schools stumbled through the rest of the school year. Samantha was putting her portfolio together for a summer class at the Art Institute, which she hoped wouldn't get canceled. They'd already agreed that until the virus was controlled, she'd use the car, rather than risk riding the El to her class and to the internship she 'd gotten with a downtown designer.

Reruns of the last four years continued to play through Tomina's head. Knowing sleep wasn't going to come soon, she turned on the night light and quietly got their copy of Kevin's short stories from her luggage. She got back into bed, angling herself so the print caught the light with the least amount of shadow. On top of the stack was Kevin's last story, *St. Joseph's Home – 1954*. It was where Kevin ended, so it was where Tomina began.

Saint Joseph's Home

1954, November 23

With Chicago's rush hour, it took a full hour to get from work at the post office straddling Congress Parkway to the 5100 block of South Prairie Avenue. After a full day on his feet, traveling south rather than northward toward Julia and his four-year-old son was hard on both his mood and patience. Fatigue kept his mixed emotions bouncing between his head and stomach. Ever since the phone call last week from Mary, his sister, he'd been trying to sort out general anxiety from the other feelings that were bubbling up. He refused to let any of them reach the surface. Keeping them repressed meant he could just think of this as a duty, a favor to his sisters, a task to do and check off the list of family obligations. *Family obligation, talk about irony!*

To keep his mind from running to places he'd prefer it didn't; Jimmy Cullerton worked his *Daily News* crossword, just as he did every evening on the homeward commute. He always made sure not to finish it. Then after dinner he'd sit with Kevin on his lap. His son loved to call out each letter as Jimmy added them into the blanks. If he forgot a letter, unashamed he'd ask, "What's that one, Dad?" Jim always left a few words unsolved so Kevin could later sit at the kitchen table and fill them in with random letters, sounding out whatever word might pop into his head. Already, at age four, he showed some perfectionist tendencies and would get frustrated when he had trouble neatly fitting letters into the tiny boxes. Sometimes he'd use his beloved crayons to add color to black and white photos or draw his own pictures all over the newsprint before presenting the newspaper back to his father, and saying, "I done for you, Dad."

But tonight as Jim clacked along, he was having trouble focusing on words and clues. Images kept appearing into his head. He gave into them and folded the paper on his lap and closed his eyes. Mental pictures arrived fuzzy and distorted like a watercolor in the rain. Speech bubbles of repressed emotions hung over some like a garbled cartoon dialogue, resembling the random letters his son put in the puzzle boxes. He knew exactly what had prompted the unbidden images. He'd traveled this route a lifetime ago.

As Jim walked the few blocks from the station, the damp cold and the November darkness pressed him deeper inside both his coat and his thoughts. Mary's call had been followed up on Saturday, his and Julia's anniversary, by one from his oldest sister Kitty. He had assumed she was calling to wish him an early happy birthday which was coming up in a few days. She did, but she had other news too.

Later that evening, he and Julia had celebrated in their usual low key and low budget fashion. They'd asked their landlord and downstairs neighbors, the Levines, to baby-sit Kevin while they went to dinner at their favorite corner restaurant. They exchanged cards and said "I love you," which was about as close to romance as they tended. After finishing their meals, and figuring there wasn't going to be a good time to bring this up, Jim told Julia about Kitty's news. He lit Julia's and his cigarettes with his Zippo, clicked the top a few times as he often did when something was on his mind, then set it on the table between them and dove in. "Kitty told me the old man's dying… any day now. He's in a nursing home on the South Side."

"Old man?" she asked with some concern and confusion. She set her coffee down and rested her lipstick-stained L&M in the ashtray. "What old man?"

Jim looked out the window at the evening traffic going by. "Mine…" He paused. Julia didn't respond. Into the silence he added, "I should have told you a long time ago that he was still alive. But it…well, he was something I wanted to keep buried. I was afraid you'd want me to make up things with him. I couldn't explain it then, and I don't think I can even now. Somehow I thought the problems with my father were my fault. Maybe all my brothers and sisters felt they were the problem. The old man left home for good back around 1920, right after my brother Richard died."

Jim took a drag on his cigarette and faced Julia's silence. "At first, when we – you and me – started getting serious, telling you felt like a betrayal of Ma. Then after we got married it started to feel like I'd betrayed you by not saying anything. I'm sorry now I didn't just tell you. I'm pretty good at just burying that stuff."

Julia picked up her cigarette, took a drag and took her turn looking out the window as she exhaled. She turned and locked her eyes, brown on blue, with her husband's. "Jim Cullerton, we've been married seventeen years today, and I lived with your mother for how may years during and after the war? And neither of you ever saw fit to say a word about him? You knew what my father and step mom were like, and yet you didn't think I'd understand how messy families are? You couldn't share your feelings with your own wife?"

"I'm sorry," he apologized again. "It's just the way I was brought up, I guess. That man was out of our lives and I didn't want him to matter anymore. He sure didn't know or care about me, about any of us. I don't know how to share those things. But I admit you have a right to be mad."

Julia took a sip of her coffee. "I'm not mad, but it did make me sad, Jim, that you'd keep that inside. I've always loved you because you're a good man, not a perfect one. God knows, I'm not so easy to live with, yet you love me. Besides…" she turned her eyes down, took another sip of coffee and set the cup back down. She took a last drag from her cigarette and crushed it out slowly in the ashtray while a small grin moved from her eyes to her lips.

"When we got married, I just assumed your father had been dead for a long time. While you were overseas, I asked your mother about him once. It was almost a week before she'd talk to me again. And believe me, that wasn't easy in that small apartment. I was glad I was gone all day to work, and I learned quick not to bring him up again – at least to her. Later, I asked your sister Mary about Ma's harsh reaction and she told me about your father. She also told me not to expect you'd ever say a word about him."

Julia's grin widened. "Anyhow, I've made my peace with that part of you long ago. Now buy me a sundae for dessert. I don't think I've had one since our last anniversary."

Jim looked at his wife and smiled his uneasy smile. "I should have known. Between you and Mary a guy didn't have a chance."

"Always remember that Mr. Jimmy Cullerton."

"So, what should I do?" he asked.

"You'll do what you always do… the thing that needs doing."

He'd prayed on it at Sunday mass, but no divine escape revealed itself. He couldn't afford to take a day off; the mail volume flowing through the fourth floor at the post office was already increasing for the holidays. Besides, now that they had Kevin, he preferred to save sick days in case of emergency, not that he ever took one anyhow. But by the time he got home from work on Monday, he knew he had to go…if only to get it over. He told Julia over meatloaf at dinner. He'd go from work tomorrow, even though it was his birthday - number forty-six already. "Okay. Your cake will be here when you get home." It was Julia's way of saying she approved and understood the need to go face his past.

It was only now, as he quickly covered the last block to the St. Joseph's Home, that he allowed the links between past and present to be joined. It had been on another birthday, his tenth, and another cake waiting at home, decades ago… *Thirty six years, a Second World War ago, a wife and child ago. Was that the last time I'd seen him? Back then, the old man wasn't even sure who I was.* Jim tried tossing that memory into the gutter with the butt of his cigarette. Both sent sparks upon hitting the pavement.

Surely, I must have gone back there a few more times with Ed? He searched his memory as he hurried along, but no actual intervening meetings appeared. What did come into focus, however, was the old lady, his Granny, and how he had stood there in the kitchen transfixed by her sudden appearance and words. Chain-linked to that image, another recollection followed. A cold day, soon after that first visit when he'd sneaked back; compelled by a need to make sure she was real – and really his grandmother. He'd learned so much that day, about his secret family and his old man. Jim updated the math in his head as he walked on, letting another part of his city brain monitor and guide him through the pedestrian and street traffic.

1954 minus 1863 made the old man ninety-one. A big chunk of time. He reached the corner and waited for the traffic light to stop traffic and allow him to continue. Across the street was his destination, a squat hulking giant. He felt very alone standing there about as far as he could get from Julia and Kevin and still be in the city. Still, wanting to enter on a positive note, he tried to appreciate, if not the man, at least what the old man had lived through. He was literally from a different era, from a Civil war, from horse-manured streets and a wooden city on fire, destroying his house and whatever his life had been prior to that October night. Jim pictured his father digging ditches, hauling bricks and debris as the city rebuilt itself, leaving people like him in the ashes. *Was that why the old man couldn't cope, couldn't...*

Jim Cullerton didn't let himself finish the thought. *I'm here to fulfill an obligation, not to remember, and certainly not to make excuses for the man.* Standing there with his hands in his coat pockets, the past seemed close and inescapable. His long passion for reading history had certainly implied this, but this was visceral, and so much more personal. Here among a half dozen other bundled people, he stood alone bidden by a phone call to again come face to face with that man after all this time. Here he was in spite of having told himself dozens of times over the years that this part of his past was long over and gone and good riddance.

Only when the crowd of homeward bound pedestrians moved to cross the street was he aware that the light had changed. He hesitated considering a last smoke before... *before what?* He truly didn't know. His eyes took in the sporadic dim lights in scattered windows along the front of the old building. He rocked on the balls of his shoes once, and then crossed.

Saint Joseph's Home was the third such institution for the aged run by the Little Sisters of the Poor. Dated from 1891, it looked its age. Jim assumed his father, and probably most of the patients, would look even worse. A nun of indeterminate age in black habit and white head-cover checked a list through thick glasses and directed him to the third floor. He climbed the weakly lit stairs, trying to think of something to say and not sure what he would be walking into. The halls looked and smelled of limited maintenance and old people. He came out on the third floor and after checking a couple of room numbers to get his bearing, turned right. He couldn't avoid thinking that each room he passed held the ghosts, living and dead, of long ago Chicago. A time when the man he was about to see was young, before he started fathering and ignoring his children, before breaking whatever marriage vows he and Ma had made. A new thought came to him. *When were they married?* He had never wondered that before. All he had to gauge from was his oldest brother Ed's age, and he couldn't remember what that was for sure. Julia would, even with Ed gone west since before they were married and their contact down to only a Christmas card each year: "All is well. Happy New Year!" Jim knew it was Cullerton shorthand for "I remember, and I love you."

The room held six beds, three along each wall, with one dirty window on the outside wall, which was opened an inch at the bottom. Only two beds were occupied at the moment. The prone occupant in the back corner had two women sitting along side. He hadn't called anyone about coming today so he was surprised, and grateful, to see Mary and Kitty. They rose and gave him a hug, but no words were exchanged. They continued to stand. Jim looked at his father lying with a cover to his chin, mouth slightly open, eyes shut. The old man's breathing had a rattle in it. Seeing him, Jim didn't feel much one way or the other. He wished he could.

Mary broke the silence. "He mostly sleeps. Thanks for coming."

"How long has he been here?" Jim asked, realizing he hadn't asked when they'd called.

Kitty answered as she sat back down, "Four months. He was in Elmhurst with me before that. You knew that, didn't you?"

Jim nodded, "I'd heard. Margaret or Isabelle mentioned it at the time. I should have called."

Kitty continued, "When he got in bad shape he wanted to come here. I never figured he'd last this long... considering."

"Why here?" Jim asked. "It's not very convenient for you. Not that he'd ever consider your convenience." The uneven steam heat was cranked up so he finally took off his coat and hat, laying them on the adjacent unoccupied bed. Mary sat, but he remained standing looking down at his father.

"That was an interesting story. Only time I remember him hinting at having any remorse. He told us," Kitty explained, "the Little Sisters ran St. Augustine's home back in the old neighborhood just blocks from the house on Townsend where he grew up. He said when he was in his teens, he and his buddies used to make wisecracks at the old men sitting outside playing checkers in their robes, or parts of old union blue uniforms. Later, when he lived with his ma and Uncle James on Indiana Street, he found the same nuns had built this place not too far away. Said it was as good as any place to come and die."

Jim asked something he was wondering. "Did you always know about his brother and Granny Cullerton? For years, I thought Ed, Richard and I were the only ones who knew. Ma never let you girls go for her money, did she?"

Kitty looked over to Mary and they laughed. "She didn't have to. Her mom, Grandma Isabella, went down there all the time. Lots of her friends had moved to the South Side from the old Goose Island area after the fire. Before her stroke, Issy used to go by streetcar every week or two. Sometimes she'd bring me along...though I couldn't let Ma know. She'd of disowned us."

Mary took over the story. "When Kitty got older, Grandma Issy asked me to go with her. I always enjoyed listening to them go on about the old days. That's how I learned the family lost their house in the fire."

"Secrets and more secrets," Jim muttered more to himself than to his sisters. He turned back to Kitty. "You said he asked specifically to call me. Did he say why?"

A thin wheezy voice rose from the bed, "'Cause I got something to ask you." They all turned their attention to the old man looking up at them. Mary took a damp cloth from the bedside basin and wiped his brow and a bit of spittle from the corner of his mouth. Hearing his father's voice, Jim could imagine the sunken eyes and white-stubbled face as the man he'd met in that dimly lit front room so long ago. He tried to grab onto what he was feeling, but it wouldn't stand still.

"You girls go take a walk or something; Jimmy and me gotta talk." Hearing his name come off his father's lips now only made Jim's feeling swirl faster, harder to pin down.

The girls exchanged a look and then rose. "We'll get some coffee and be back in five minutes." Kitty admonished her father before leaving. "You shouldn't be talking too much now." The girls looked at each other again, Mary nodded, and they headed out the door.

Jim wondered if there had been a double meaning in Kitty's words, something beyond expressing concern for the old man's comfort. He sat in Mary's empty chair, wondering if he should talk first, not knowing what to say and scared of what he might say if he did speak. With a visible effort, the old man rolled his stiff neck to see his seated son. "I saw you there that day?" Jim had no idea what he was talking about, and it showed on his face.

"That day, outside St. John's, when we was burying my ma. I saw you, I did, hiding in the back there of the church after Communion. That's why I was looking for you when we come out. I spotted you over by the store where you was hiding. At first I figure it was your Ma you was hiding from. She'd of been fit to be tied to find you snuck there. I almost told her, just to get her goat."

The sudden rush of so much talk exhausted his father's air. He coughed a thin nonproductive cough. His breath, rapid and shallow rattled in and out of his mouth. It required the old man to close his eyes and wait to catch his breath again. He finally calmed some and continued, though his eyes remained aimed at the high ceiling. "Then it come to me, maybe you was hiding from me as much as your ma, so I didn't call out to you. But now I gotta ask. Why'd you come? I was no da to you and the others."

To his surprise, Jim's response readily poured out of him. "Your ma knew who I was that time I came with Ed. But you didn't even know if I was Tom or Jimmy, but she knew me."

His father answered with some agitation. "I know'd who you was straight off. I was just having a go-on with Ed. God help me, but I always had a need to rile that boy. He had your Ma's scorn in his tone when he'd come. It got my dander up. I know you was Jimmy, same like I did now. An sure I'm selfish, and I'll pay for that soon enough, but I know my sons." He paused to catch his breath again, "So," the old man repeated in a near whisper now, "what made you come?"

"Because Gram-ma knew me, and I wanted to know why, how… because I needed to understand something, I don't know what… maybe what happened between you and Ma, why you left all us and never came around. I never even knew about your ma, Jane, or that I had your brother's name. I wanted to know where I came from... why we weren't a family."

Jim let some of the tension that had crept into his voice fall away before continuing. "If you saw me in the church and by the store why didn't you wave or make some sign, anything to show you knew who I was, that I existed." He wiped a single tear from his eyelid. In resignation he said, "Hell, Dad, even telling Ma would have at least showed something, like maybe you cared some."

If his sisters had witnessed the scene, they'd have been amazed by the sheer volume of words coming out of their brother, let alone the emotion. For sure they would have noticed the word "Dad." Jim took a deep breath, and as he let it out, it carried his last words to his father. "I thought you didn't see me that day. I was glad about that then, but later it made me angry. How does a man ignore and leave his own kids?"

His father barely whispered, "I know that part. I could never give love or even take it, from Ma or you kids. That ate at me. But it just wasn't there and I can't be sorry for something I ain't never had in me."

The old man blinked twice as if to punctuate his last words. Then his eyes closed. Jimmy leaned in close to see if any breath remained. When he was close enough that he could feel the wisp of warmth still coming from his father, the old man barely whispered, "That's what I needed to say." Then he went silent.

Jim was buttoning up his coat when Mary and Kitty returned with a cup of coffee for him. He looked back at his father. The old man's eyes remained closed. Jim could see a slight flutter going on behind them. "Thanks girls, but I've a long ways home. Thanks for calling." He kissed each on the cheek. He turned to leave before they could begin asking questions about what was said. After a couple of steps he hesitated and considered going back and kissing his dad's forehead. He didn't.

Almost to the door, he heard his father's voice. He turned back only to see his sisters talking softly over the old man who was asleep, or perhaps already dead. Still, he was sure he'd heard it, clear as day. "Lá Breithe Shona dhuit, Shamus."

August 7, 2020

Nelson got up, set her book down and went looking for her cell phone. She'd been on the back porch where the ceiling fan balanced the warmth of the evening. The phone was on the kitchen table ringing. She saw who was calling, sat and happily answered. "Hello, Samantha. How are you? How's the internship going?"

"It's fun, though I only go in twice a week. The rest is still working online. They like my work and have hinted at a job when I graduate."

"How could anybody not like your art?" Nelson asked. "You sound excited. What's up?"

"Nelson?" There was a pause before Samantha launched into her news. "Do you remember when I told you that my DNA came back and showed I had a fair amount of Irish, but that it didn't really mean anything because we know Dad was part Irish and the last name Larkin is English and Irish?" She paused.

"I do remember." Nelson responded. "Did you find out something more?"

"Well, last night... on my ancestry page... I got a leaf."

"A leaf? What does that mean?"

"A leaf shows up when a possible connection is made with someone else who did the DNA test and allowed the information to be matched and shared."

Nelson felt her pulse quicken. "Yes. What did the leaf say?"

Samantha needed a few seconds before she could ask her question. "Do you know anything about a Colleen Johnson? The leaf note said we might be distantly related, something like fourth cousins removed or something like that."

More silence.

"Nelson? Are you still there?"

After a very long breath, Nelson said, "Samantha, you might want to sit while I tell you about Kevin's Cousin Colleen and their little adventure at Calvary Cemetery."

THE END

Acknowledgements

My Mother, Helen – for leaving me a Wiebolt's box

Cousin Maureen – This book could not have been written without our trip to Calvary

Scott Powers – for caring, reading and early and constant encouragement

Terie Johnson – for reading and encouragement when I started and needed it most

Jim Black – for reading and unfailing support throughout this long process

Dale Johnston – for expressing interest in the old man and changing the focus of the story

Ernest Anderson – for reading chapters and long enjoyable conversations over lunch

Paul Leline – for reading chapters, beer, burgers and golf

Lee Kivi – for taking me on my first wilderness canoe trip and his photography skills

Alan Kopischke – for proofing early chapters

William Kennedy – for insightful and thoughtful commentary

Cousins Pat, Nancy and John – for reading and being encouraging

AND...

Sally Collins – for chapter by chapter commentary and encouragement

Kurt Haberl – for a novelist's eye, comments, and advice on structure

Linda Thompson – for her invaluable editing skills which made this effort so much better

CPSIA information can be obtained
at www.ICGtesting.com
Printed in the USA
BVHW071217090522
636528BV00002B/9

9 781977 228895